Oddly ★ Normal

WRITTEN & ILLUSTRATED
by OTIS FRAMPTON

IMAGE COMICS, INC.
Robert Kirkman – Chief Operating Officer
Erik Larsen – Chief Financial Officer
Todd McFarlane – President
Marc Silvestri – Chief Executive Officer
Jim Valentino – Vice-President

Eric Stephenson – Publisher
Corey Murphy – Director of Sales
Jeremy Sullivan – Director of Digital Sales
Kat Salazar – Director of PR & Marketing
Emily Miller – Director of Operations
Branwyn Bigglestone – Senior Accounts Manager
Sarah Mello – Accounts Manager
Drew Gill – Art Director
Jonathan Chan – Production Manager
Meredith Wallace – Print Manager
Randy Okamura – Marketing Production Designer
David Brothers – Content Manager
Addison Duke – Production Artist
Vincent Kukua – Production Artist
Sasha Head – Production Artist
Tricia Ramos – Production Artist
Emilio Bautista – Sales Assistant
Jessica Ambriz – Administrative Assistant
IMAGECOMICS.COM

 ISBN: 978-1-63215-226-8

Chapter 1
Be Careful What You Wish For

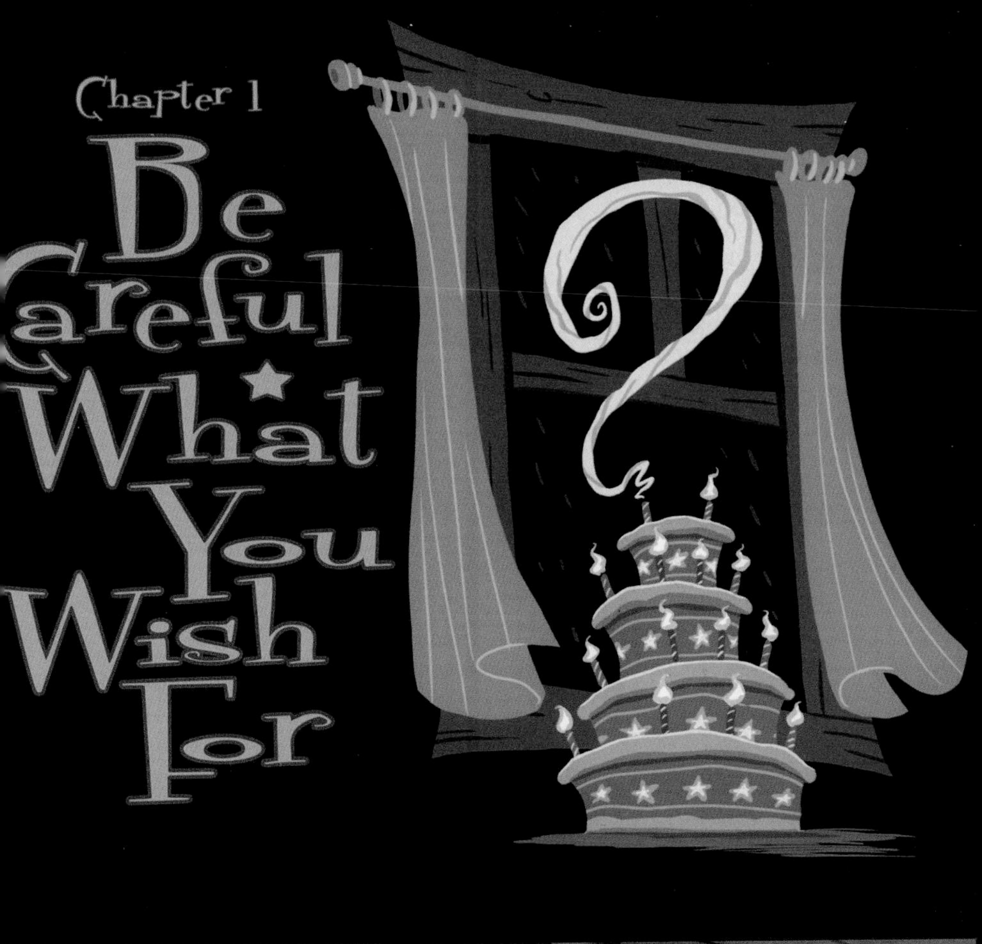

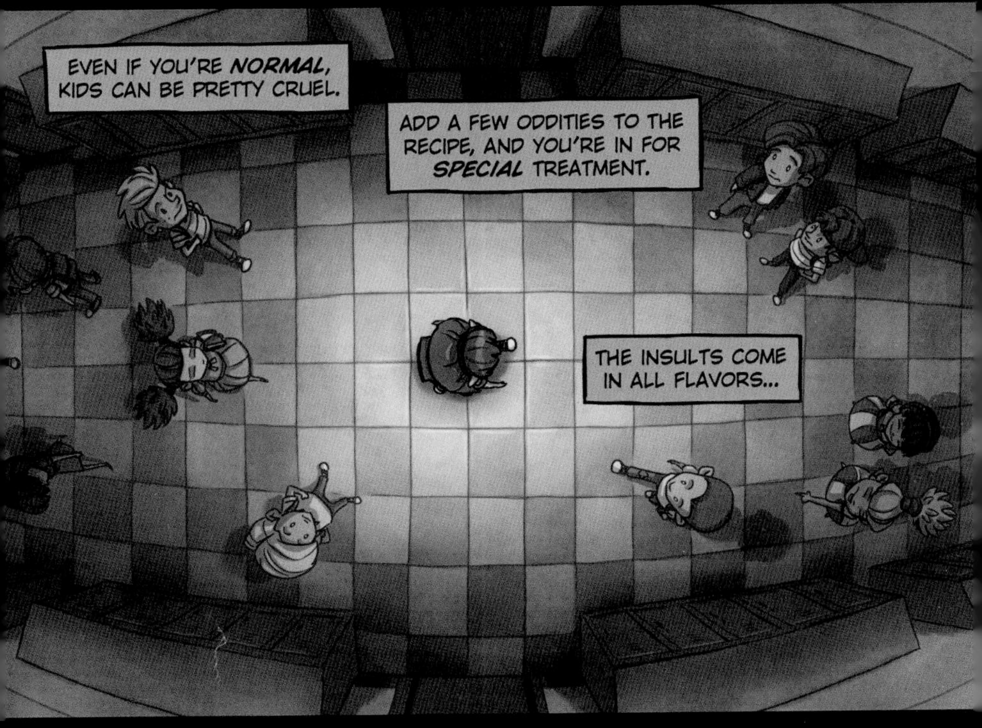
EVEN IF YOU'RE ***NORMAL***, KIDS CAN BE PRETTY CRUEL.
ADD A FEW ODDITIES TO THE RECIPE, AND YOU'RE IN FOR ***SPECIAL*** TREATMENT.
THE INSULTS COME IN ALL FLAVORS...

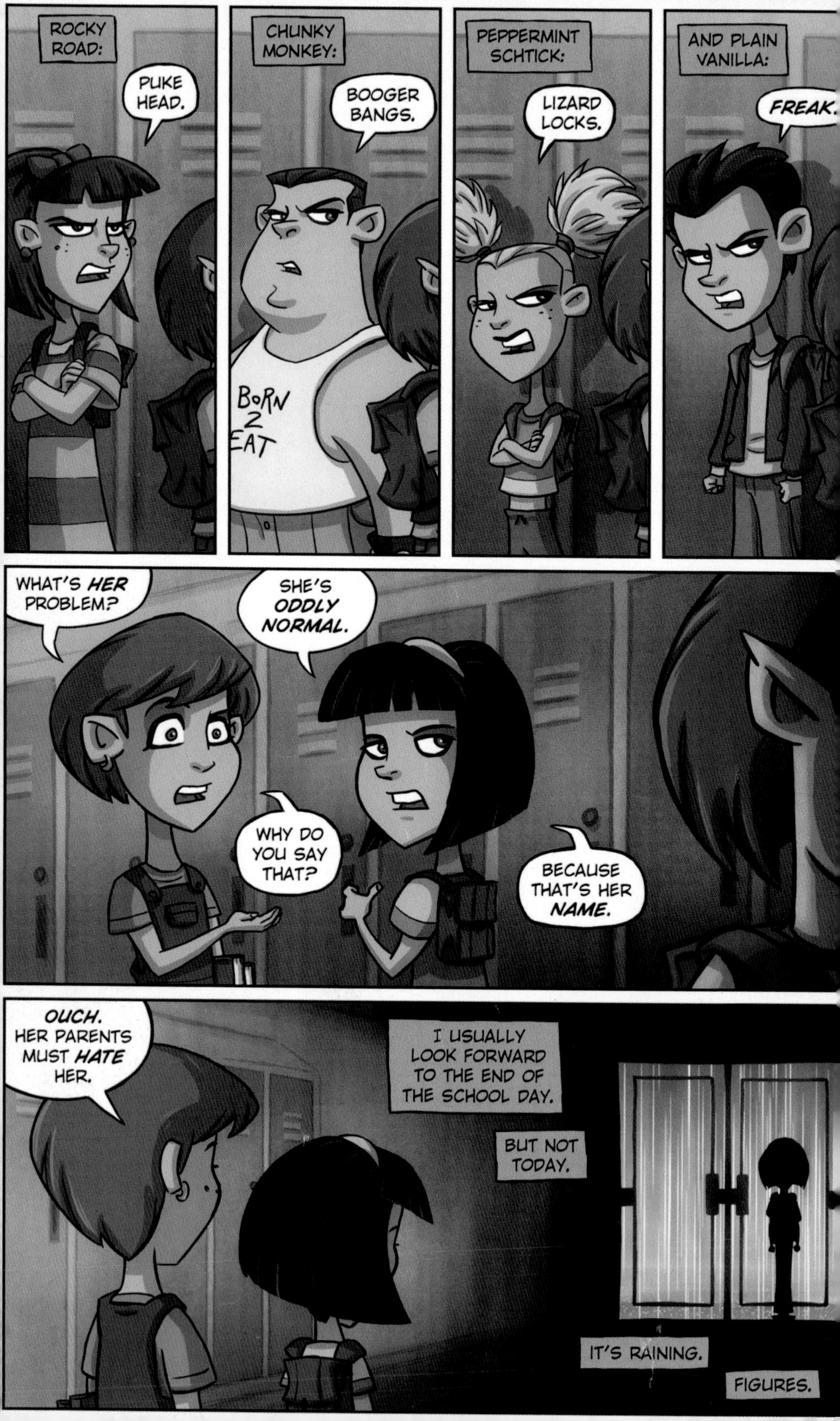
ROCKY ROAD:
PUKE HEAD.
CHUNKY MONKEY:
BOOGER BANGS.
BORN 2 EAT
PEPPERMINT SCHTICK:
LIZARD LOCKS.
AND PLAIN VANILLA:
FREAK.
WHAT'S HER PROBLEM?
SHE'S ODDLY NORMAL.
WHY DO YOU SAY THAT?
BECAUSE THAT'S HER NAME.
OUCH. HER PARENTS MUST HATE HER.
I USUALLY LOOK FORWARD TO THE END OF THE SCHOOL DAY.
BUT NOT TODAY.
IT'S RAINING.
FIGURES.

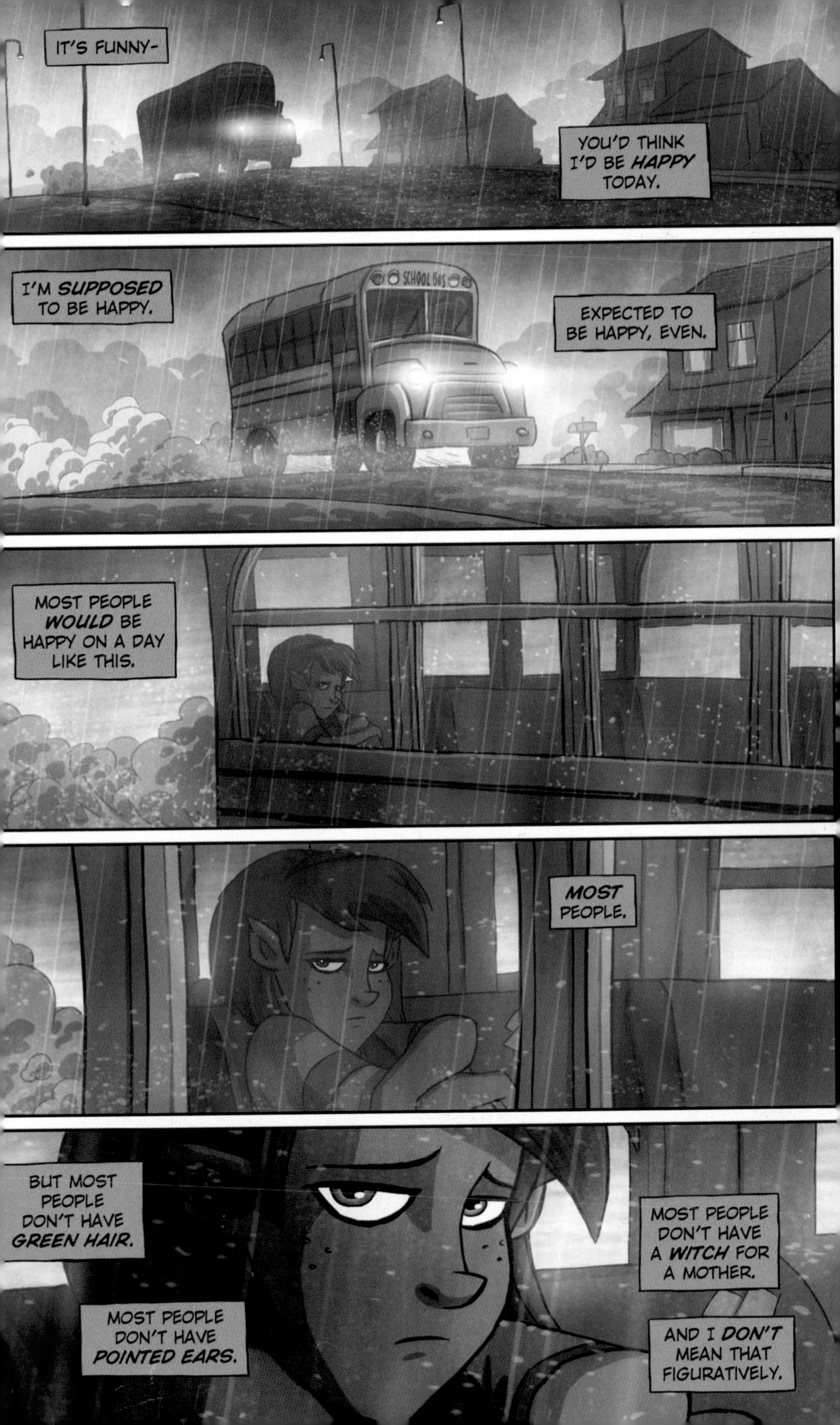
IT'S FUNNY-
YOU'D THINK I'D BE HAPPY TODAY.
I'M SUPPOSED TO BE HAPPY.
SCHOOL BUS
EXPECTED TO BE HAPPY, EVEN.
MOST PEOPLE WOULD BE HAPPY ON A DAY LIKE THIS.
MOST PEOPLE.
BUT MOST PEOPLE DON'T HAVE GREEN HAIR.
MOST PEOPLE DON'T HAVE POINTED EARS.
MOST PEOPLE DON'T HAVE A WITCH FOR A MOTHER.
AND I DON'T MEAN THAT FIGURATIVELY.

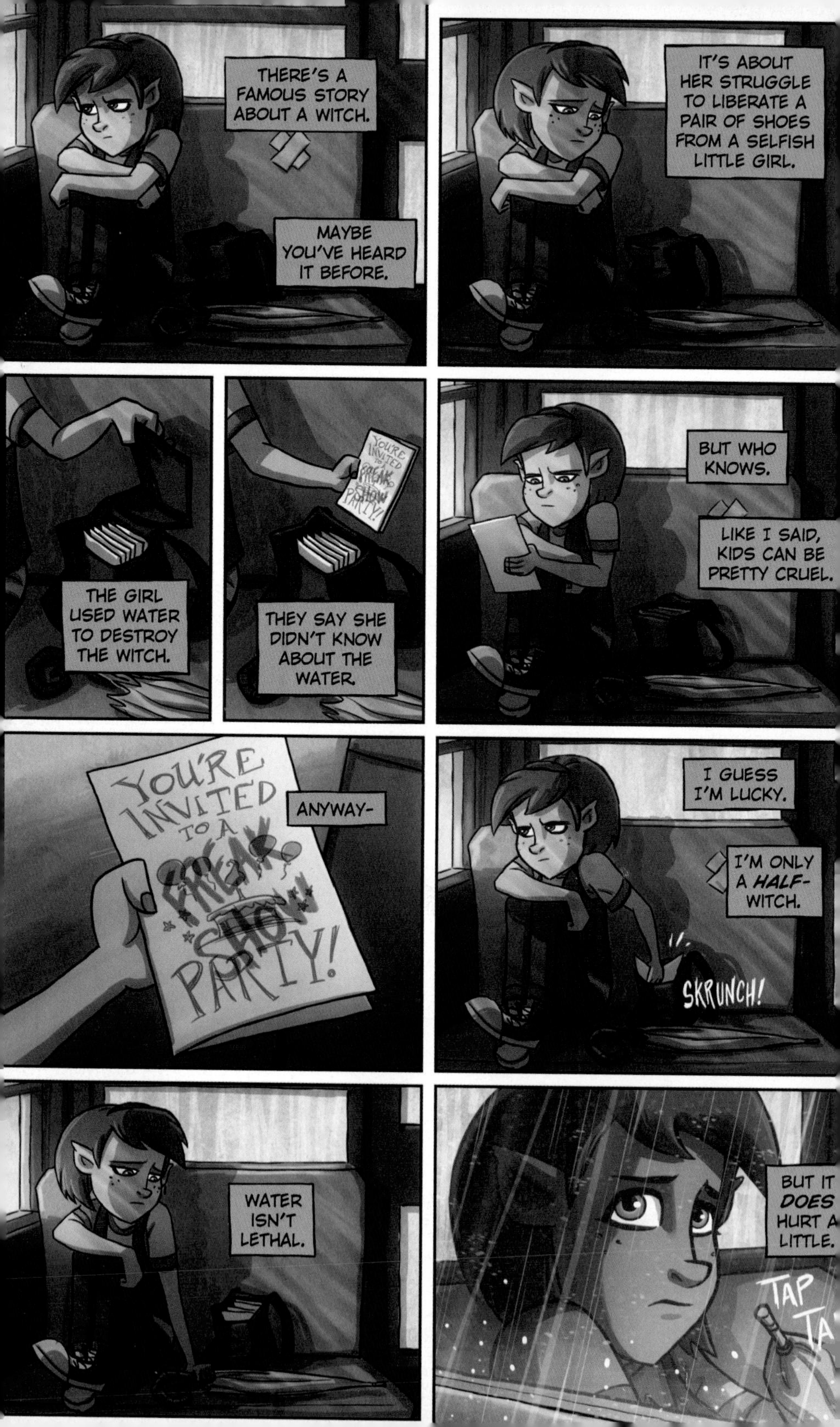
THERE'S A FAMOUS STORY ABOUT A WITCH.
MAYBE YOU'VE HEARD IT BEFORE.
IT'S ABOUT HER STRUGGLE TO LIBERATE A PAIR OF SHOES FROM A SELFISH LITTLE GIRL.
THE GIRL USED WATER TO DESTROY THE WITCH.
YOU'RE INVITED TO A FREAK SHOW PARTY!
THEY SAY SHE DIDN'T KNOW ABOUT THE WATER.
BUT WHO KNOWS.
LIKE I SAID, KIDS CAN BE PRETTY CRUEL.
YOU'RE INVITED TO A FREAK SHOW PARTY!
ANYWAY-
I GUESS I'M LUCKY.
I'M ONLY A *HALF*-WITCH.
SKRUNCH!
WATER ISN'T LETHAL.
BUT IT *DOES* HURT A LITTLE.
TAP TA

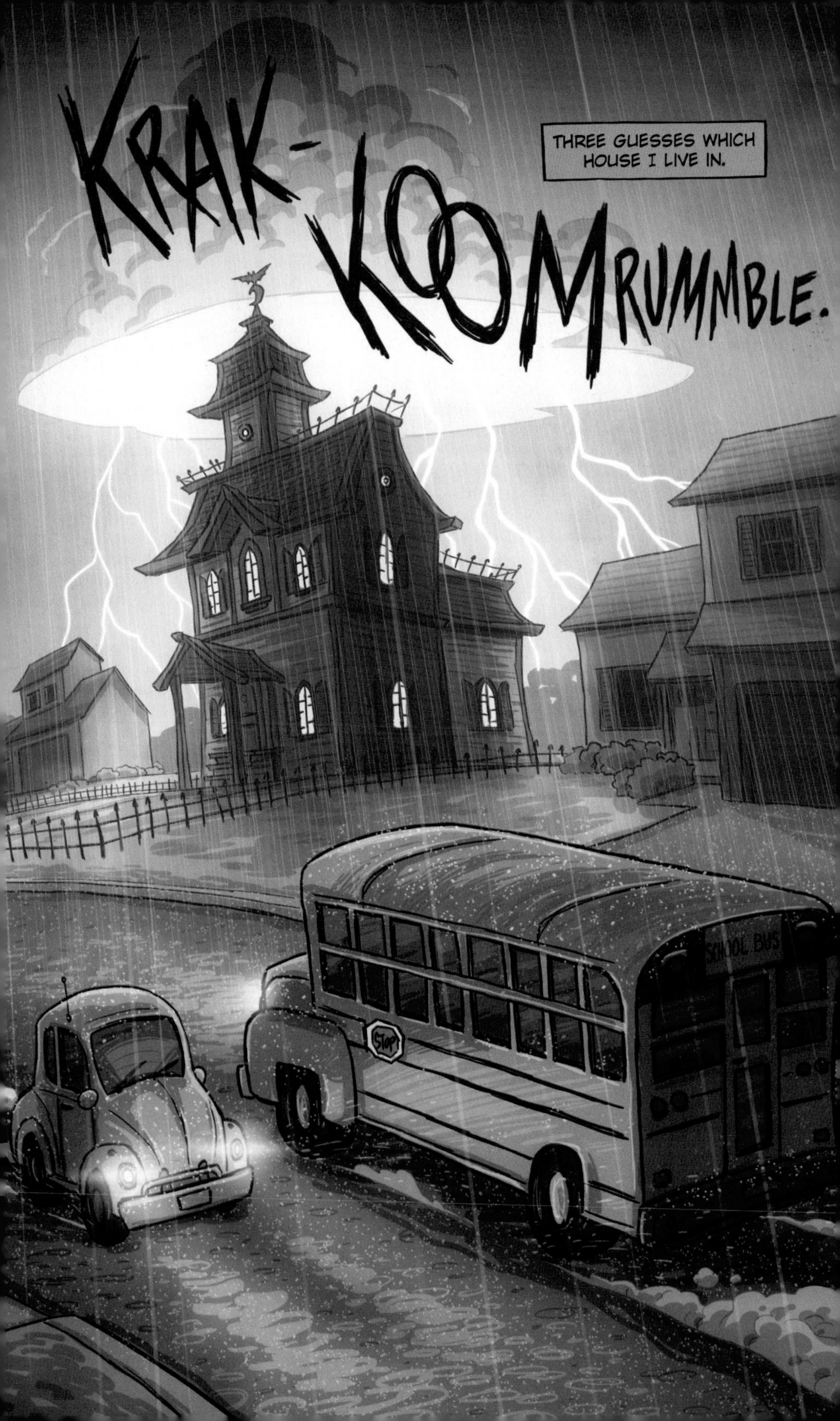
KRAK-
KOOMRUMMBLE.
THREE GUESSES WHICH HOUSE I LIVE IN.
SCHOOL BUS
STOP

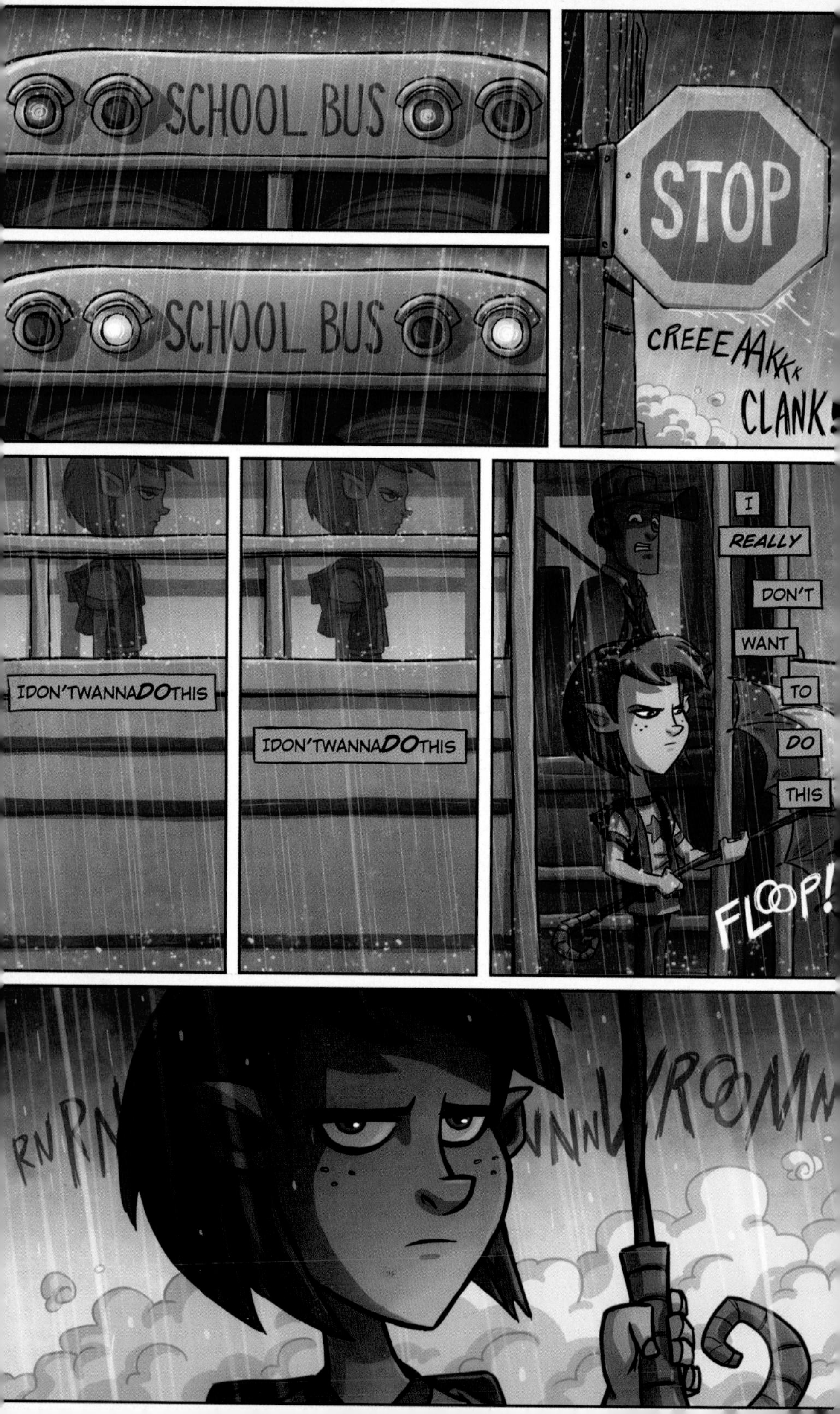
SCHOOL BUS
STOP
SCHOOL BUS
CREEEAAKKK
CLANK!
IDON'TWANNADOTHIS
IDON'TWANNADOTHIS
I REALLY DON'T WANT TO DO THIS
FLOOP!
RNRNNNNNVROOMM

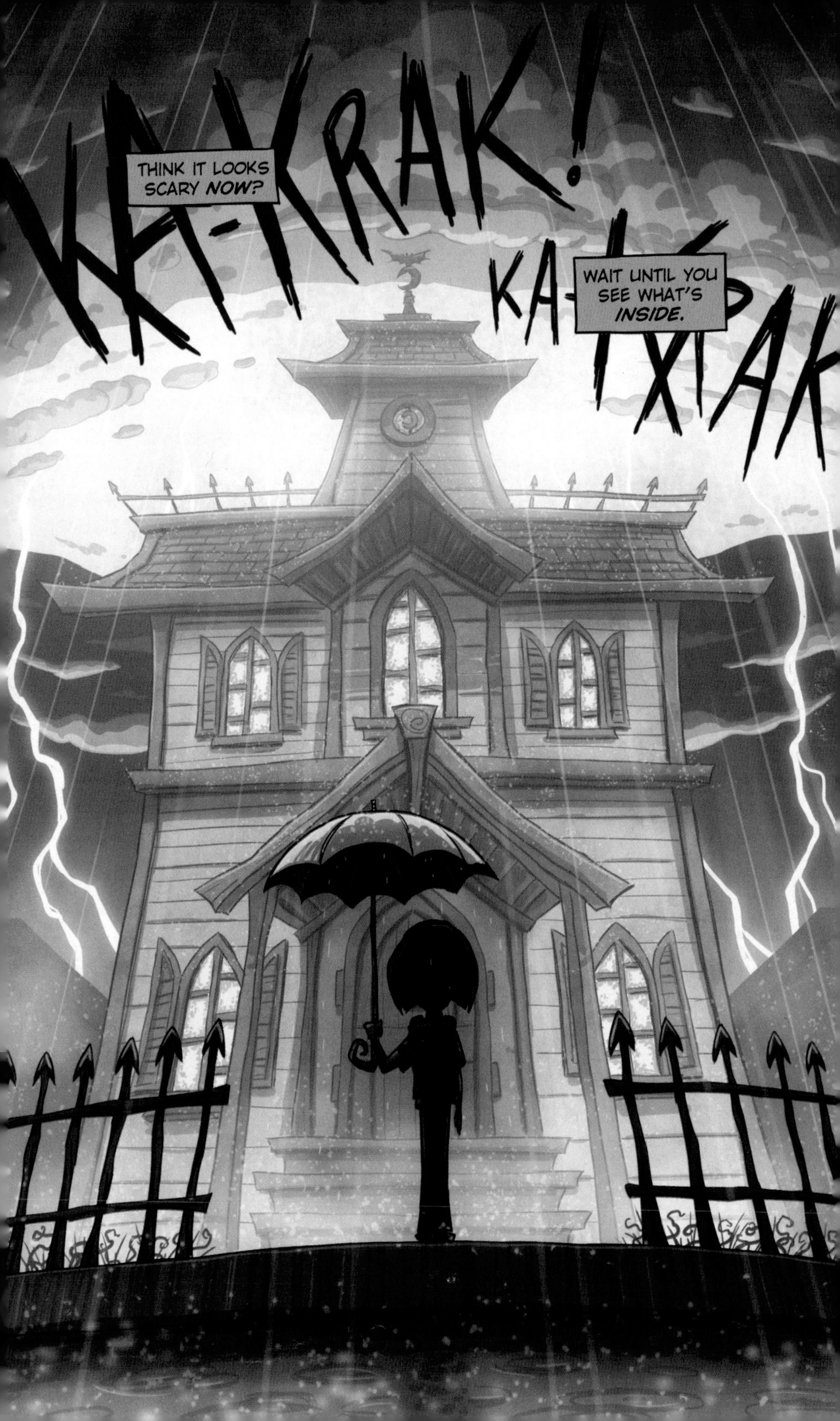
KA-KRAK!
THINK IT LOOKS SCARY NOW?
KA-KRAK
WAIT UNTIL YOU SEE WHAT'S INSIDE.

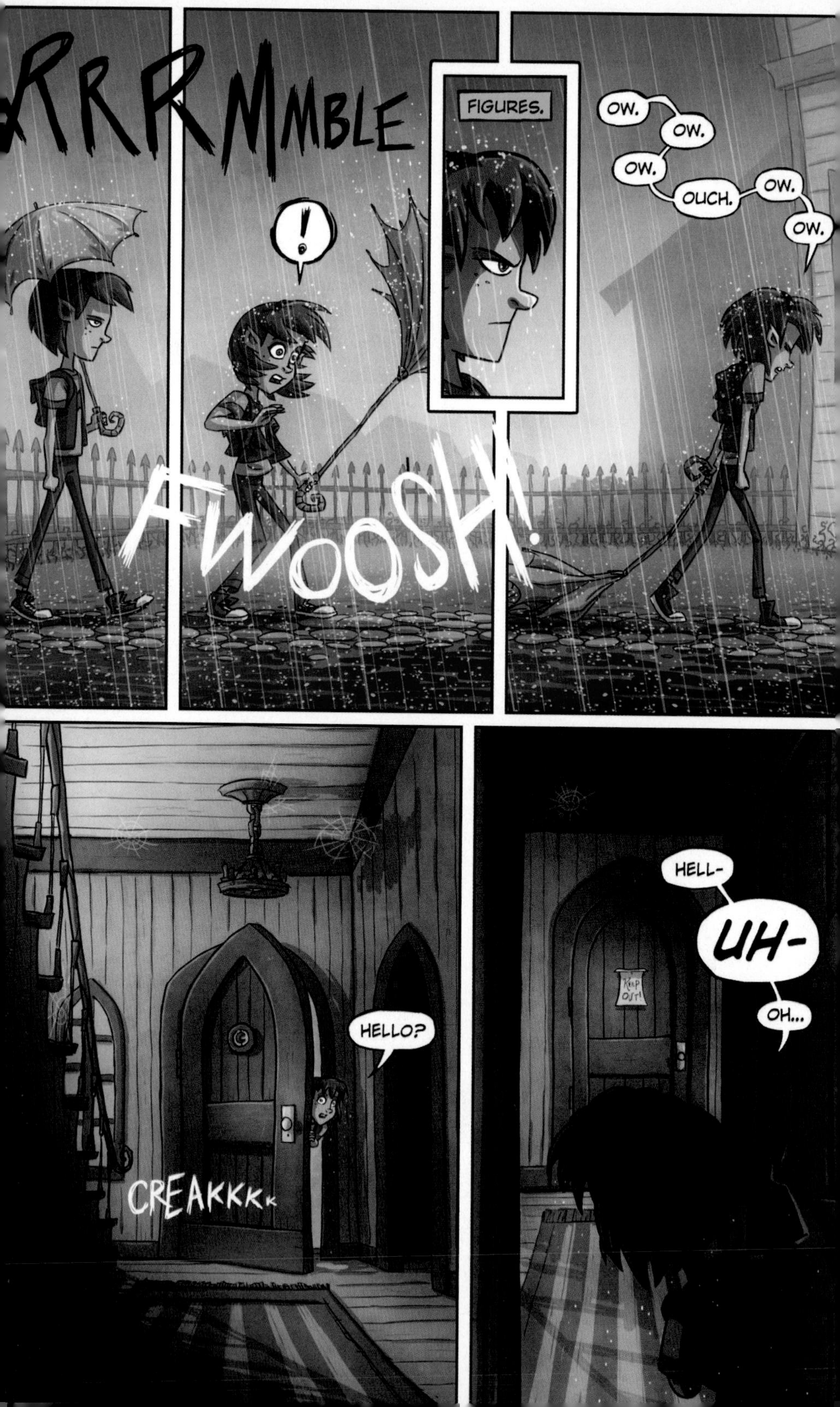
RRRMMBLE
!
FWOOSH!
FIGURES.
OW.
OW.
OW.
OUCH.
OW.
OW.
HELLO?
CREAKKKK
HELL-
UH-
OH...

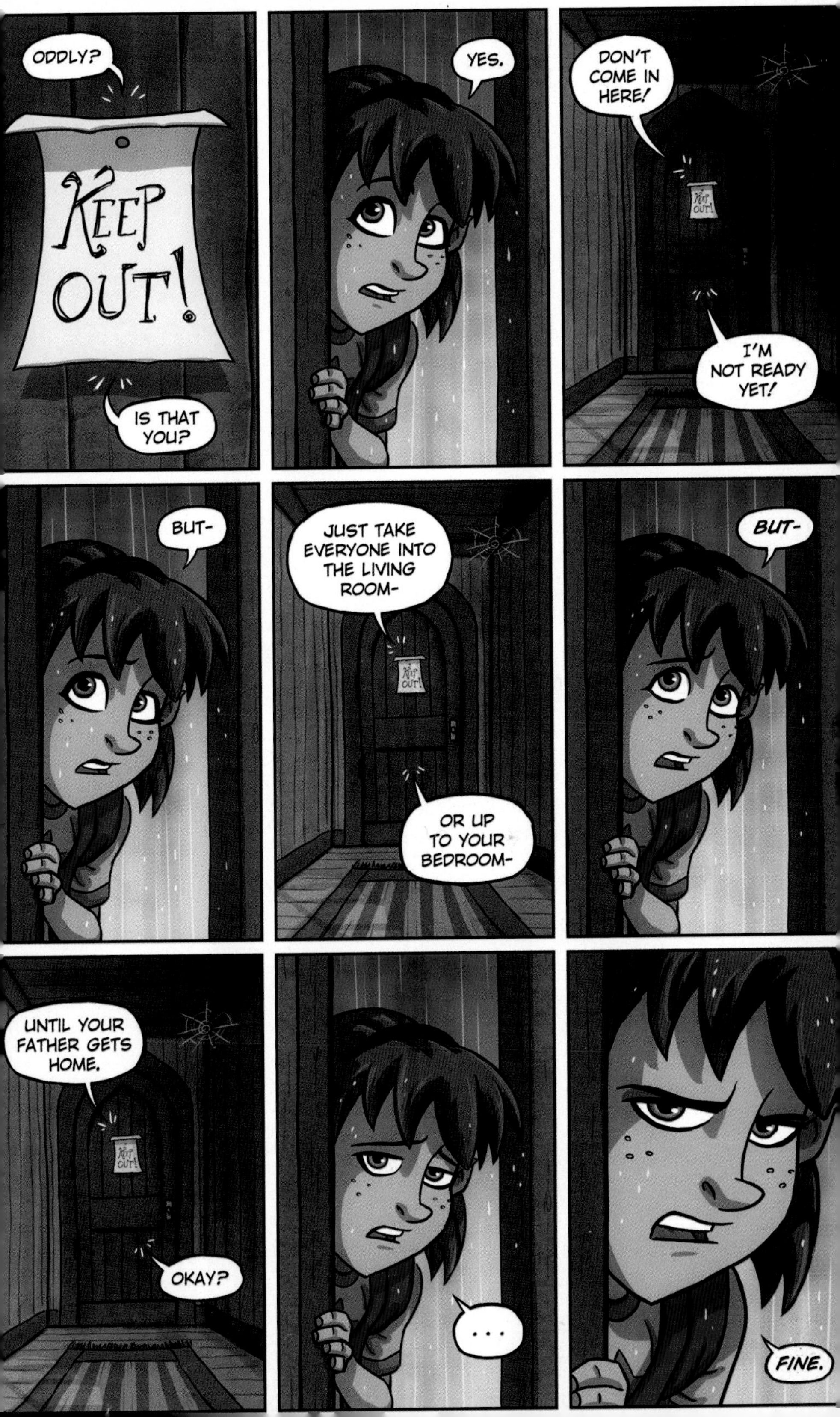
ODDLY?
KEEP OUT!
IS THAT YOU?
YES.
DON'T COME IN HERE!
KEEP OUT!
I'M NOT READY YET!
BUT-
JUST TAKE EVERYONE INTO THE LIVING ROOM-
KEEP OUT!
OR UP TO YOUR BEDROOM-
BUT-
UNTIL YOUR FATHER GETS HOME.
KEEP OUT!
OKAY?
...
FINE.

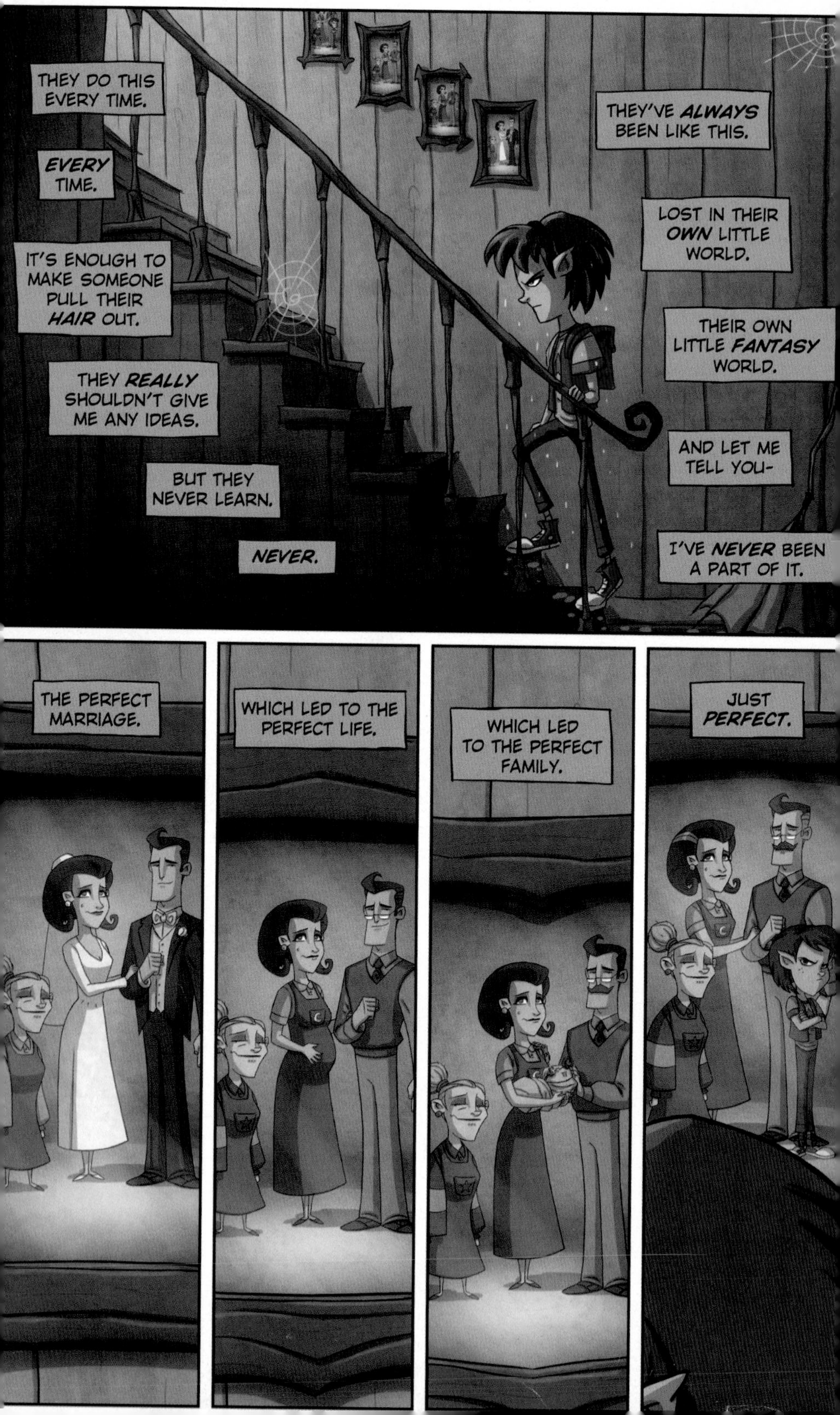
THEY DO THIS EVERY TIME.
EVERY TIME.
IT'S ENOUGH TO MAKE SOMEONE PULL THEIR *HAIR* OUT.
THEY *REALLY* SHOULDN'T GIVE ME ANY IDEAS.
BUT THEY NEVER LEARN.
NEVER.
THEY'VE *ALWAYS* BEEN LIKE THIS.
LOST IN THEIR *OWN* LITTLE WORLD.
THEIR OWN LITTLE *FANTASY* WORLD.
AND LET ME TELL YOU-
I'VE *NEVER* BEEN A PART OF IT.
THE PERFECT MARRIAGE.
WHICH LED TO THE PERFECT LIFE.
WHICH LED TO THE PERFECT FAMILY.
JUST *PERFECT.*

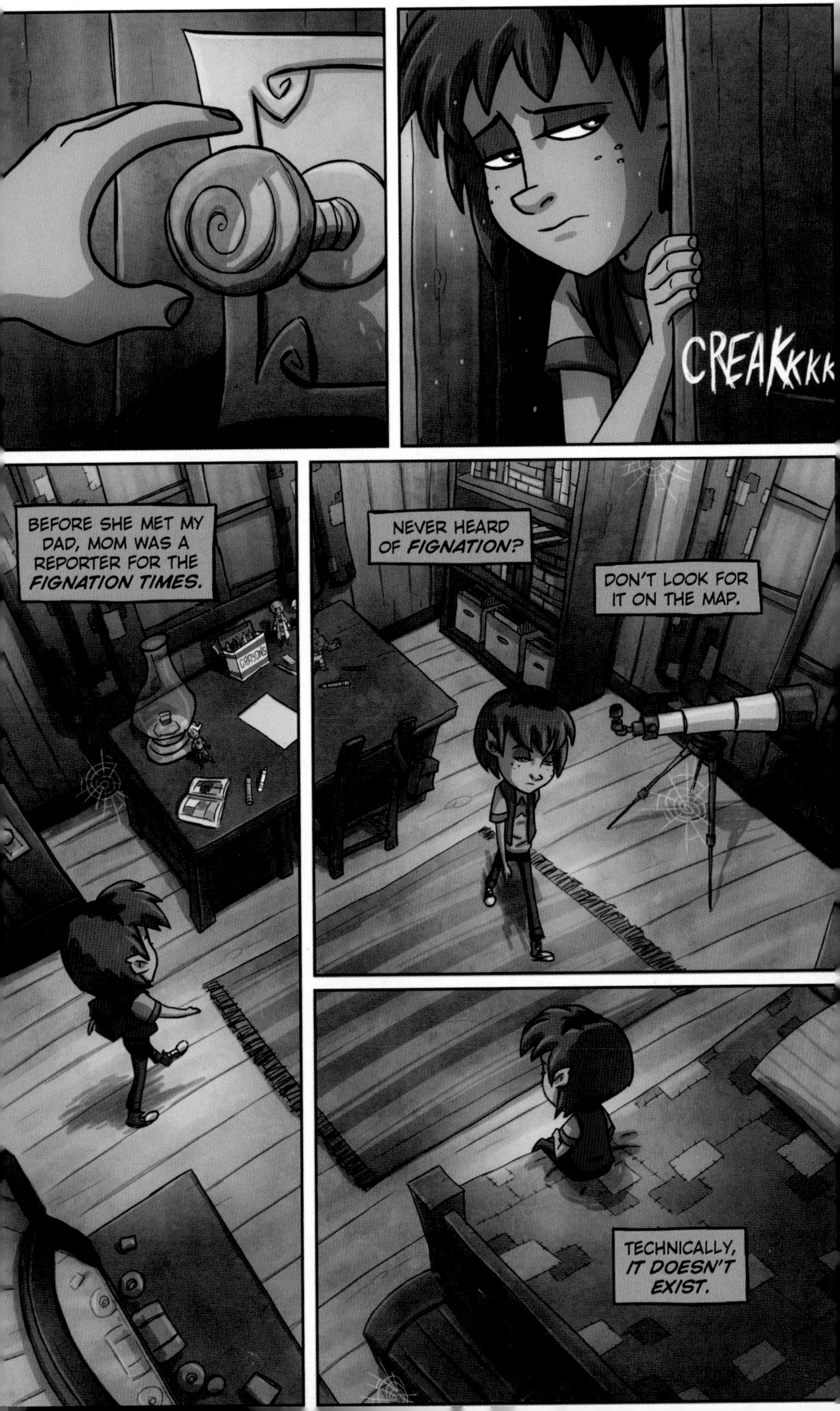
CREAKkkk
BEFORE SHE MET MY DAD, MOM WAS A REPORTER FOR THE *FIGNATION TIMES.*
CRAYONS
NEVER HEARD OF *FIGNATION?*
DON'T LOOK FOR IT ON THE MAP.
TECHNICALLY, *IT DOESN'T EXIST.*

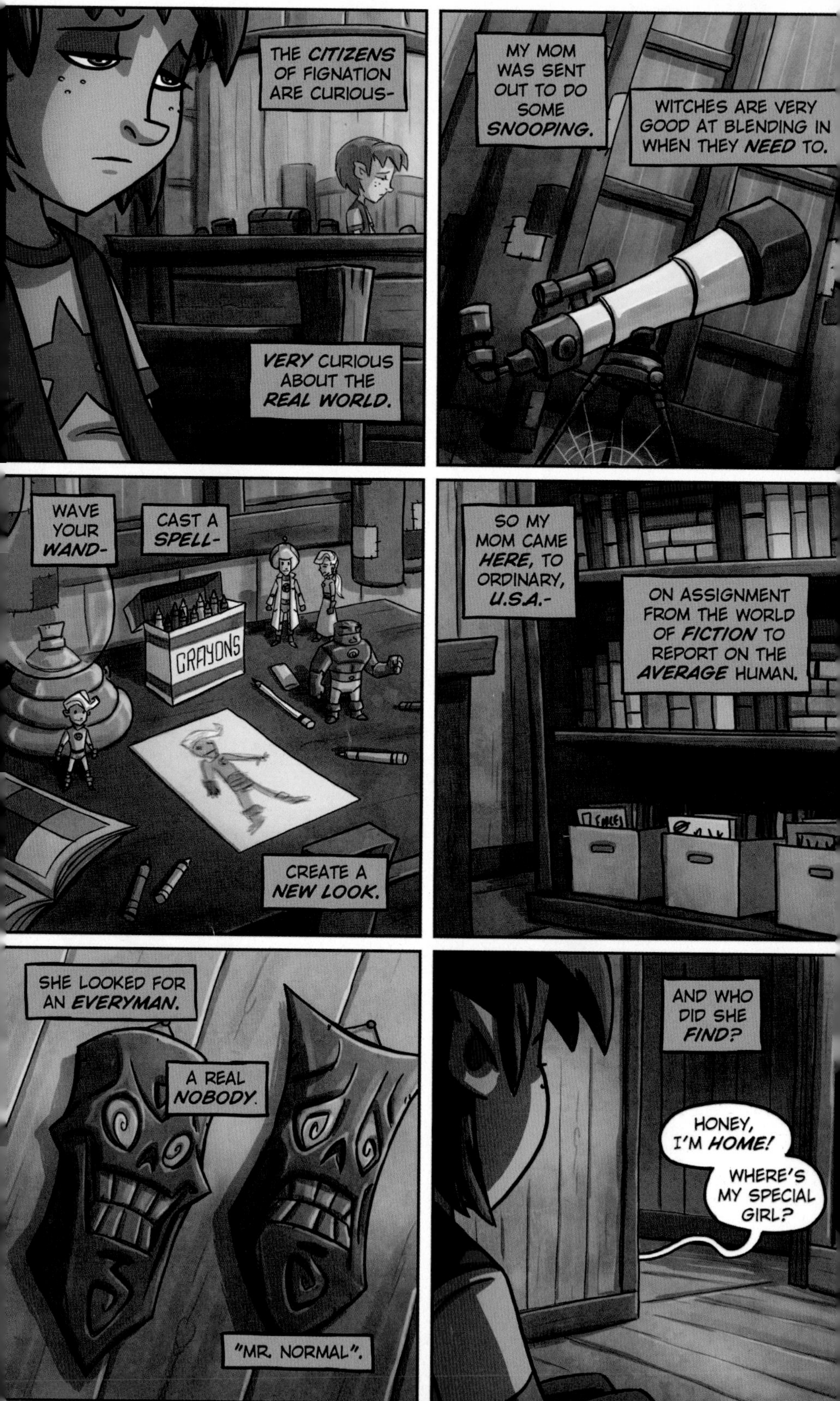
THE CITIZENS OF FIGNATION ARE CURIOUS-
VERY CURIOUS ABOUT THE REAL WORLD.
MY MOM WAS SENT OUT TO DO SOME SNOOPING.
WITCHES ARE VERY GOOD AT BLENDING IN WHEN THEY NEED TO.
WAVE YOUR WAND-
CAST A SPELL-
CRAYONS
CREATE A NEW LOOK.
SO MY MOM CAME HERE, TO ORDINARY, U.S.A.-
ON ASSIGNMENT FROM THE WORLD OF FICTION TO REPORT ON THE AVERAGE HUMAN.
SHE LOOKED FOR AN EVERYMAN.
A REAL NOBODY.
"MR. NORMAL".
AND WHO DID SHE FIND?
HONEY, I'M HOME!
WHERE'S MY SPECIAL GIRL?

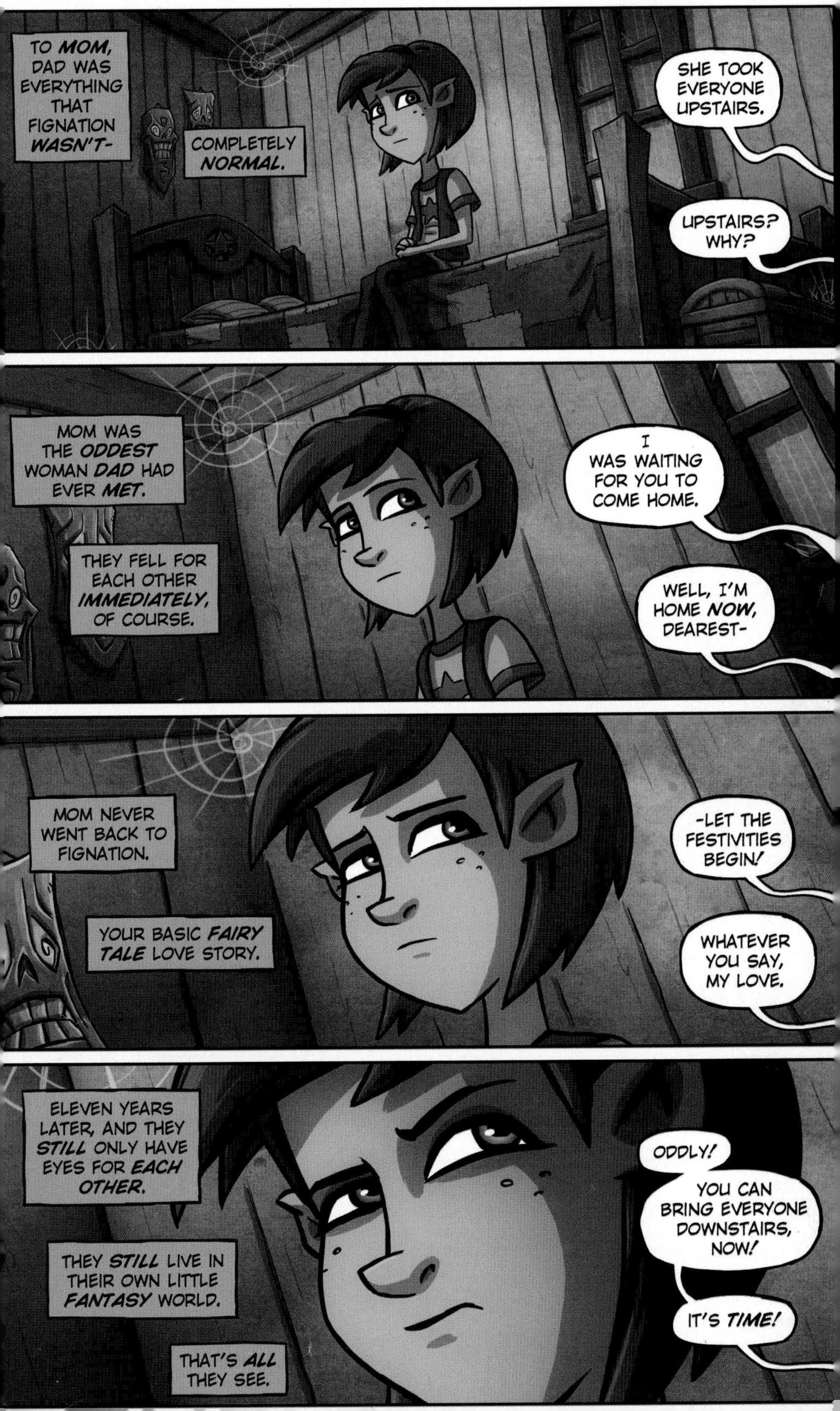
TO MOM, DAD WAS EVERYTHING THAT FIGNATION WASN'T-
COMPLETELY NORMAL.
SHE TOOK EVERYONE UPSTAIRS.
UPSTAIRS? WHY?
MOM WAS THE ODDEST WOMAN DAD HAD EVER MET.
THEY FELL FOR EACH OTHER IMMEDIATELY, OF COURSE.
I WAS WAITING FOR YOU TO COME HOME.
WELL, I'M HOME NOW, DEAREST-
MOM NEVER WENT BACK TO FIGNATION.
YOUR BASIC FAIRY TALE LOVE STORY.
-LET THE FESTIVITIES BEGIN!
WHATEVER YOU SAY, MY LOVE.
ELEVEN YEARS LATER, AND THEY STILL ONLY HAVE EYES FOR EACH OTHER.
THEY STILL LIVE IN THEIR OWN LITTLE FANTASY WORLD.
THAT'S ALL THEY SEE.
ODDLY!
YOU CAN BRING EVERYONE DOWNSTAIRS, NOW!
IT'S TIME!

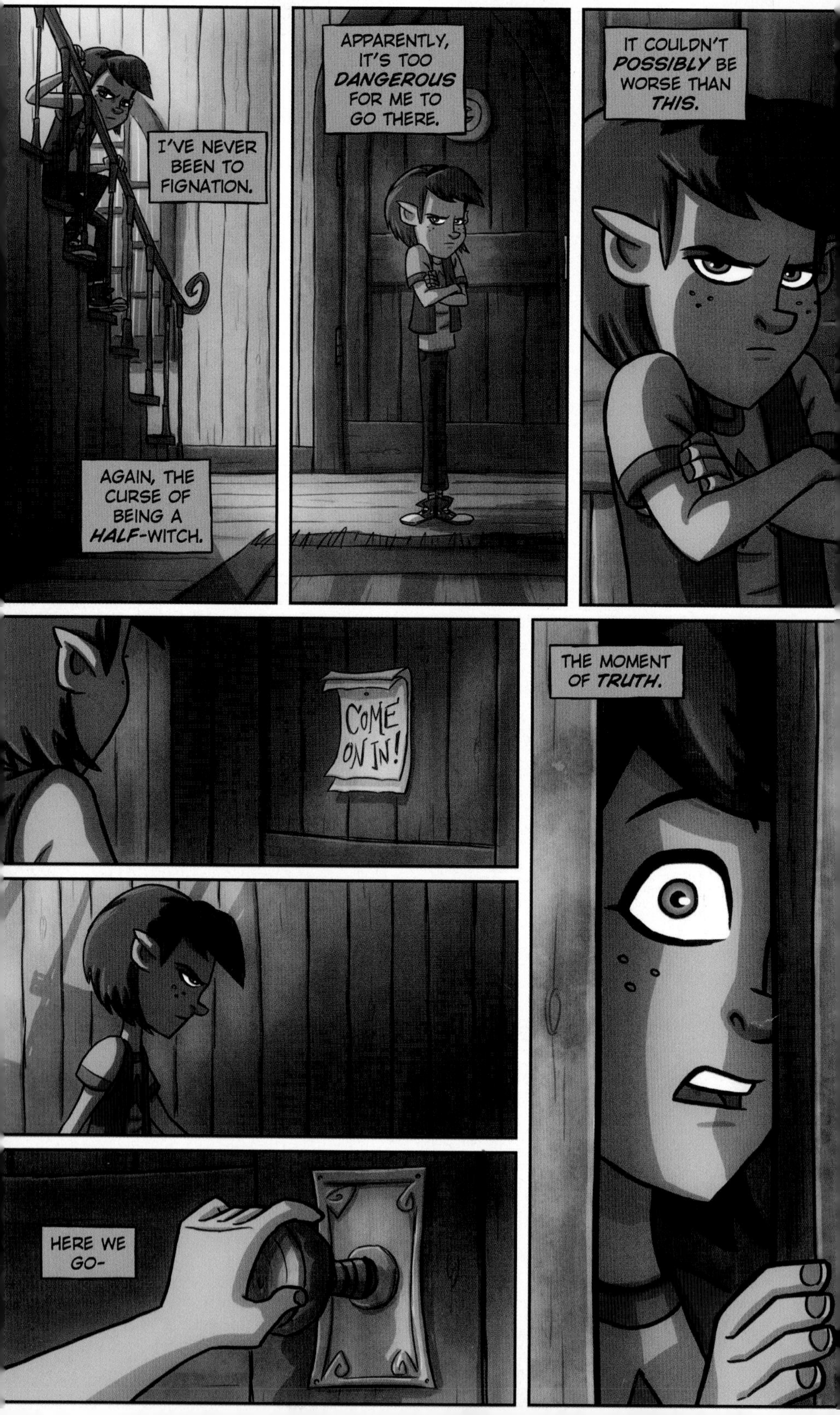
I'VE NEVER BEEN TO FIGNATION.
AGAIN, THE CURSE OF BEING A HALF-WITCH.
APPARENTLY, IT'S TOO DANGEROUS FOR ME TO GO THERE.
IT COULDN'T POSSIBLY BE WORSE THAN THIS.
COME ON IN!
THE MOMENT OF TRUTH.
HERE WE GO-

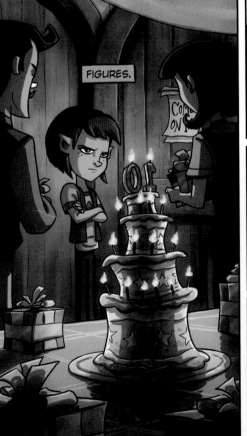

FIGURES.

WHERE IS EVERYONE?

WHERE ARE YOUR *FRIENDS*?

ARE THEY UPSTAIRS?

ARE THEY OUTSIDE?

ARE THEY HIDING?

ARE THEY LATE?

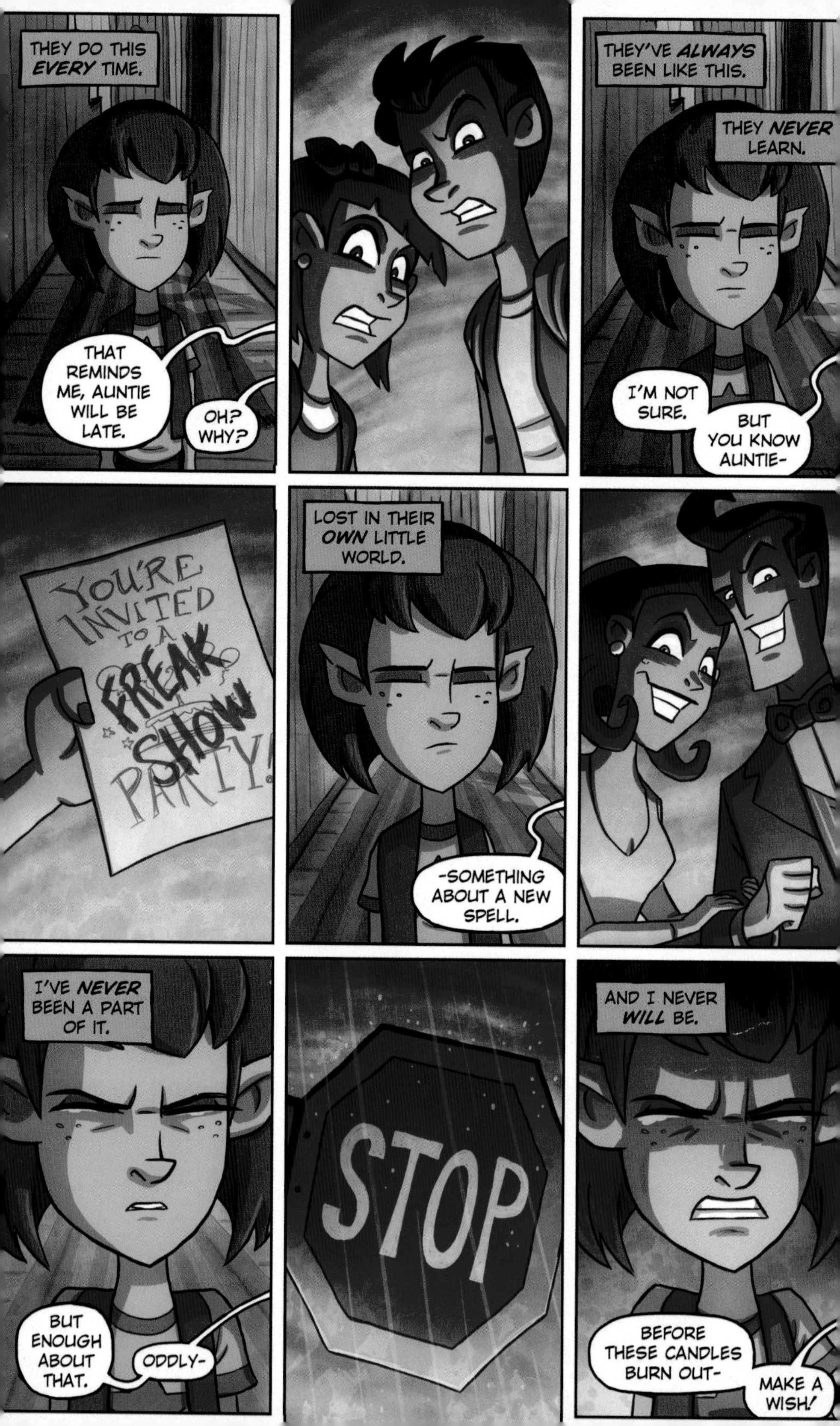
THEY DO THIS EVERY TIME.
THAT REMINDS ME, AUNTIE WILL BE LATE.
OH? WHY?
THEY'VE ALWAYS BEEN LIKE THIS.
THEY NEVER LEARN.
I'M NOT SURE.
BUT YOU KNOW AUNTIE-
YOU'RE INVITED TO A FREAK SHOW PARTY!
LOST IN THEIR OWN LITTLE WORLD.
-SOMETHING ABOUT A NEW SPELL.
I'VE NEVER BEEN A PART OF IT.
BUT ENOUGH ABOUT THAT.
ODDLY-
STOP
AND I NEVER WILL BE.
BEFORE THESE CANDLES BURN OUT-
MAKE A WISH!

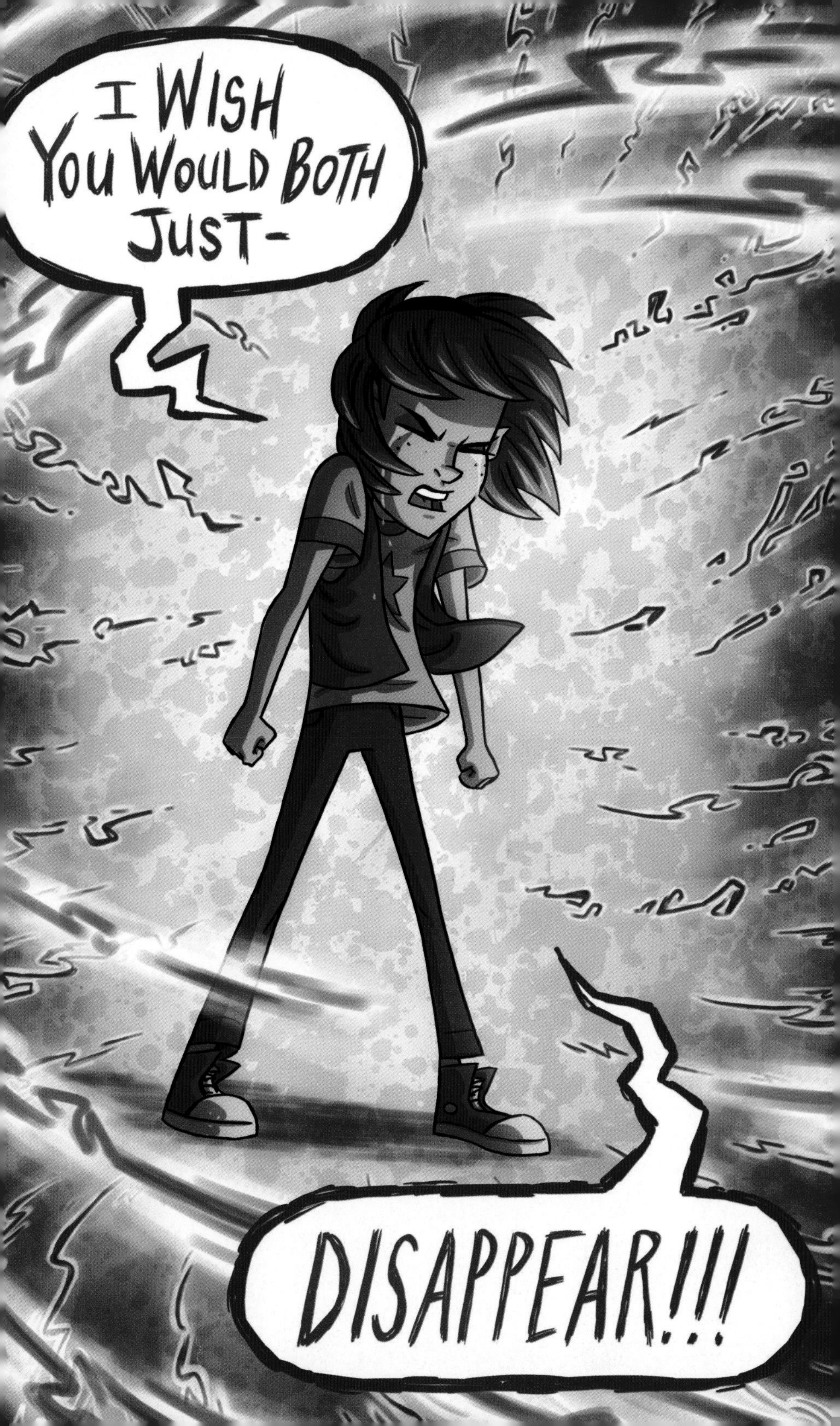
I WISH YOU WOULD BOTH JUST-
DISAPPEAR!!!

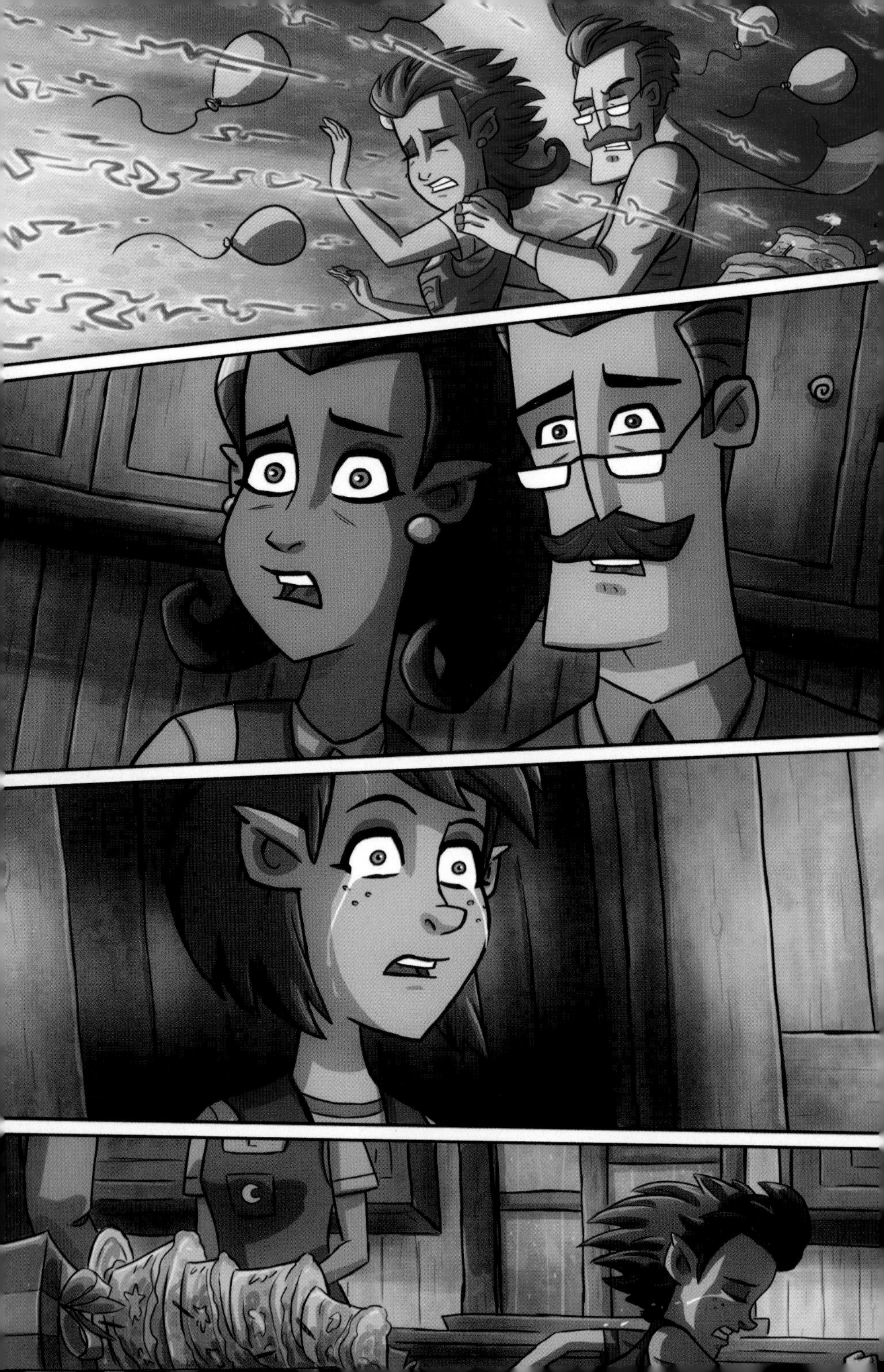

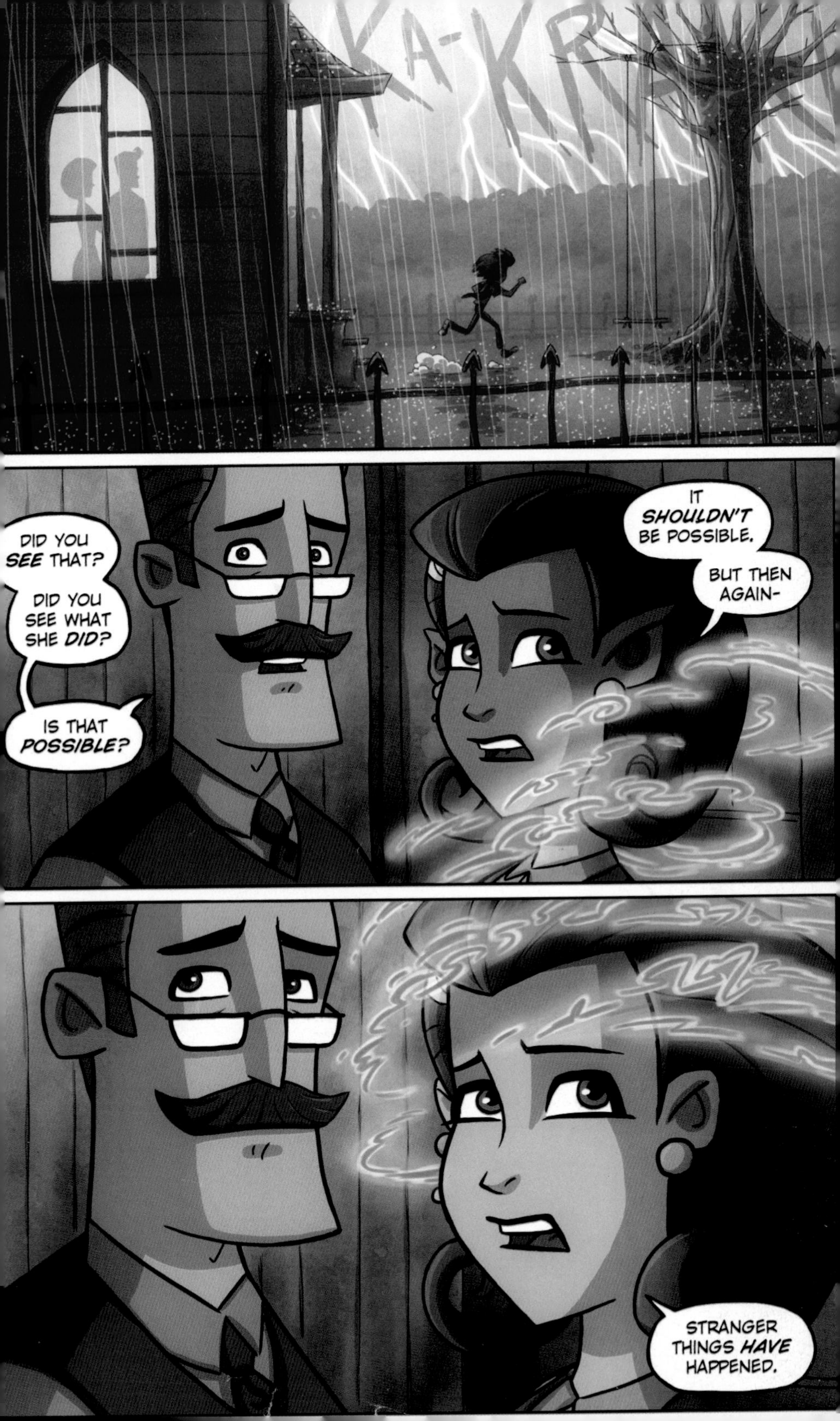
KA-KR
DID YOU SEE THAT?
DID YOU SEE WHAT SHE DID?
IS THAT POSSIBLE?
IT SHOULDN'T BE POSSIBLE.
BUT THEN AGAIN-
STRANGER THINGS HAVE HAPPENED.

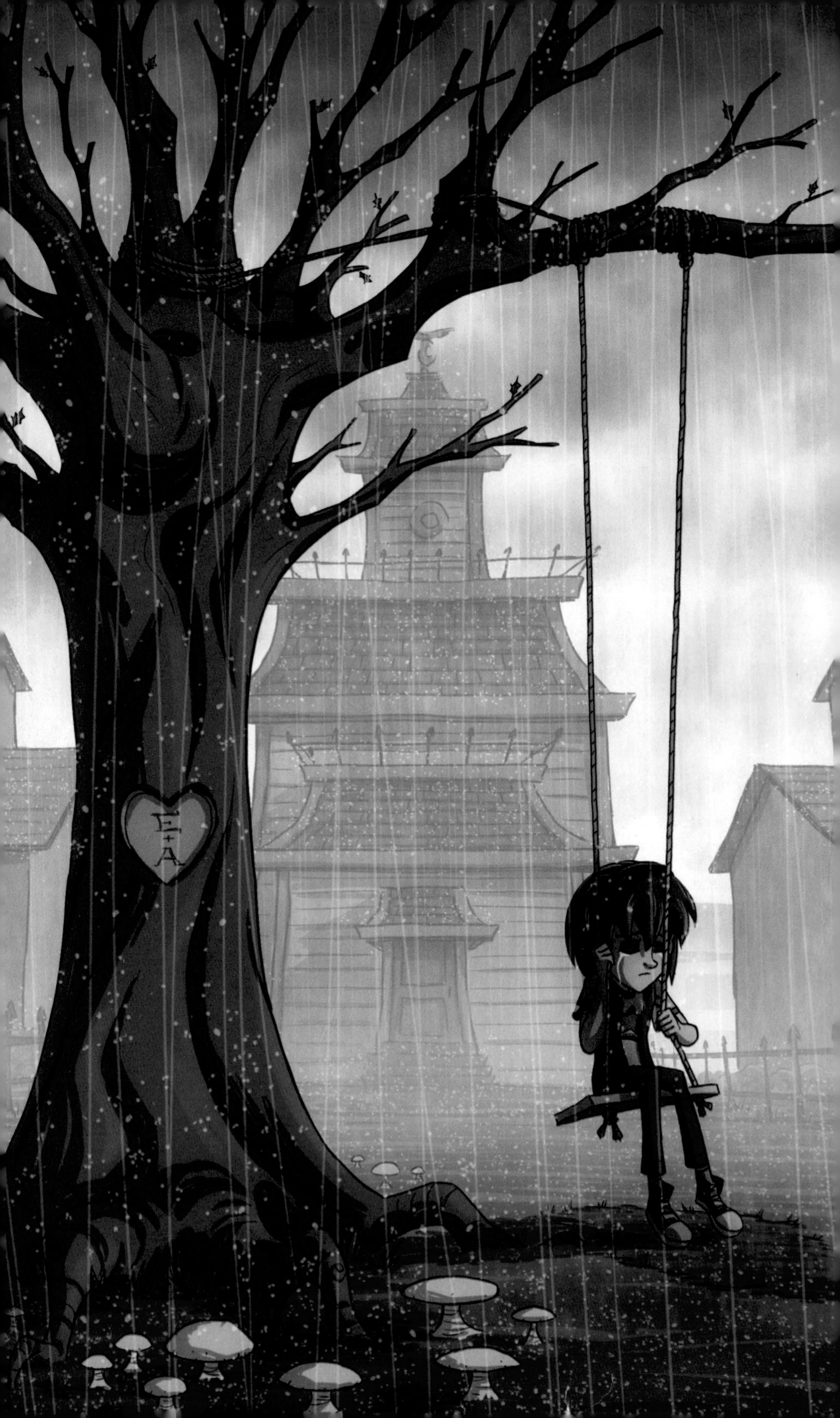
E
+
A

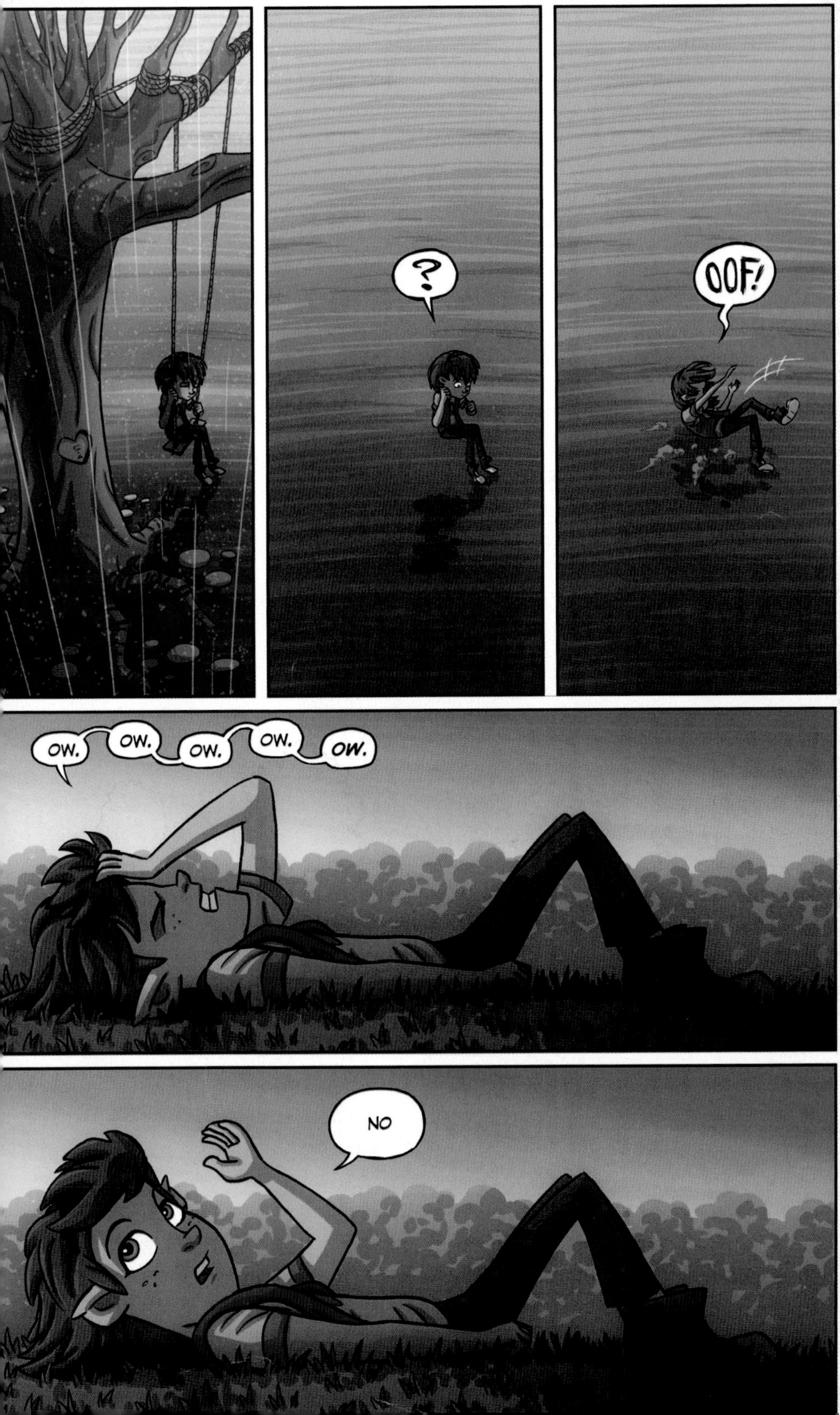
?
OOF!
OW. OW. OW. OW. OW.
NO

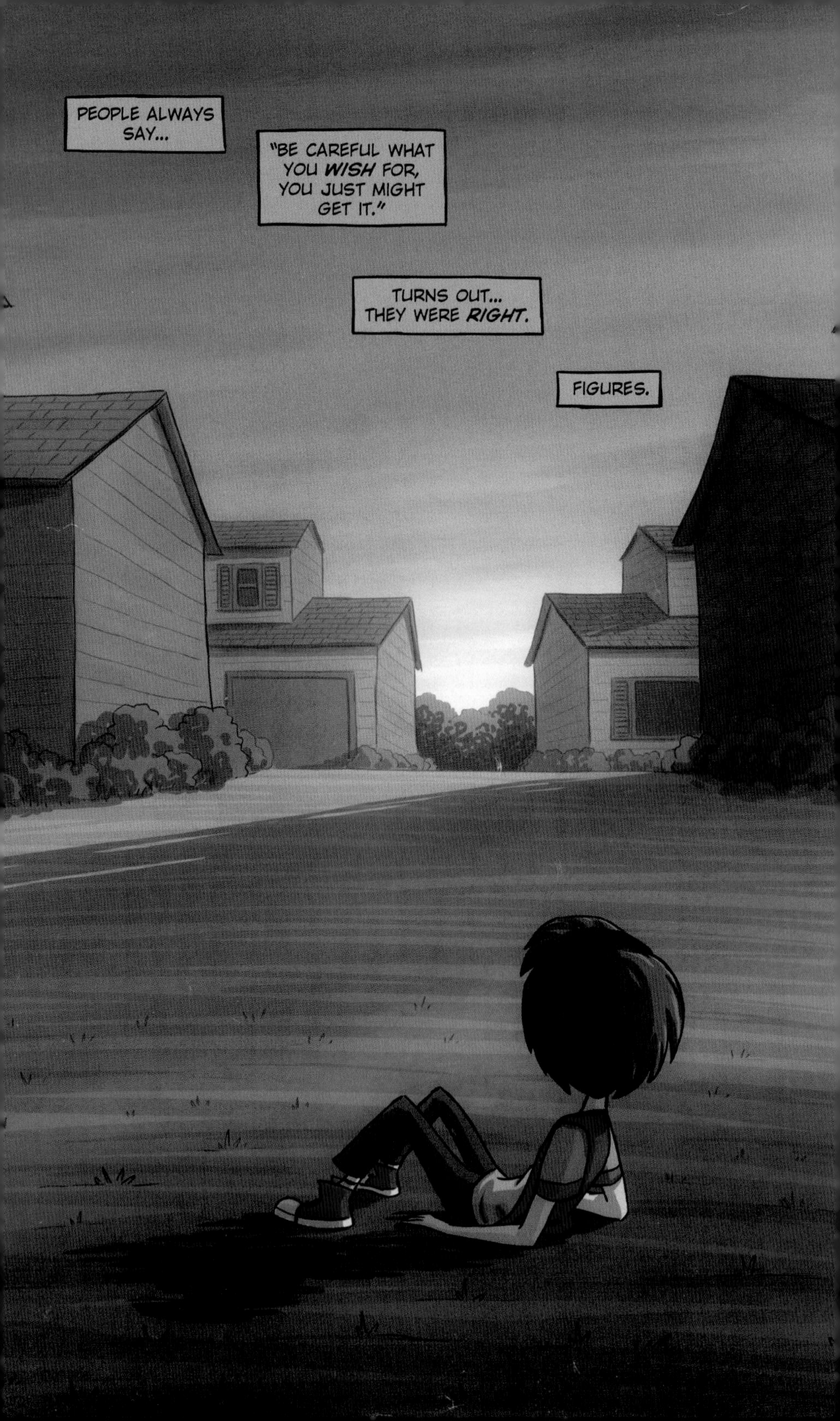
PEOPLE ALWAYS SAY...
"BE CAREFUL WHAT YOU *WISH* FOR, YOU JUST MIGHT GET IT."
TURNS OUT... THEY WERE *RIGHT*.
FIGURES.

Chapter 2

A Figment Of Your Imagination

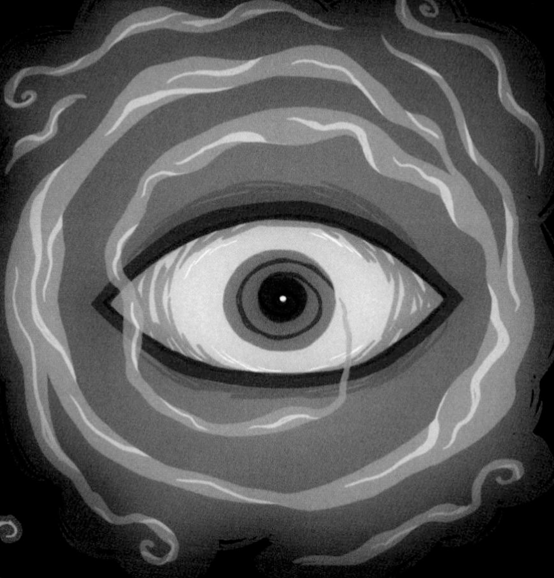

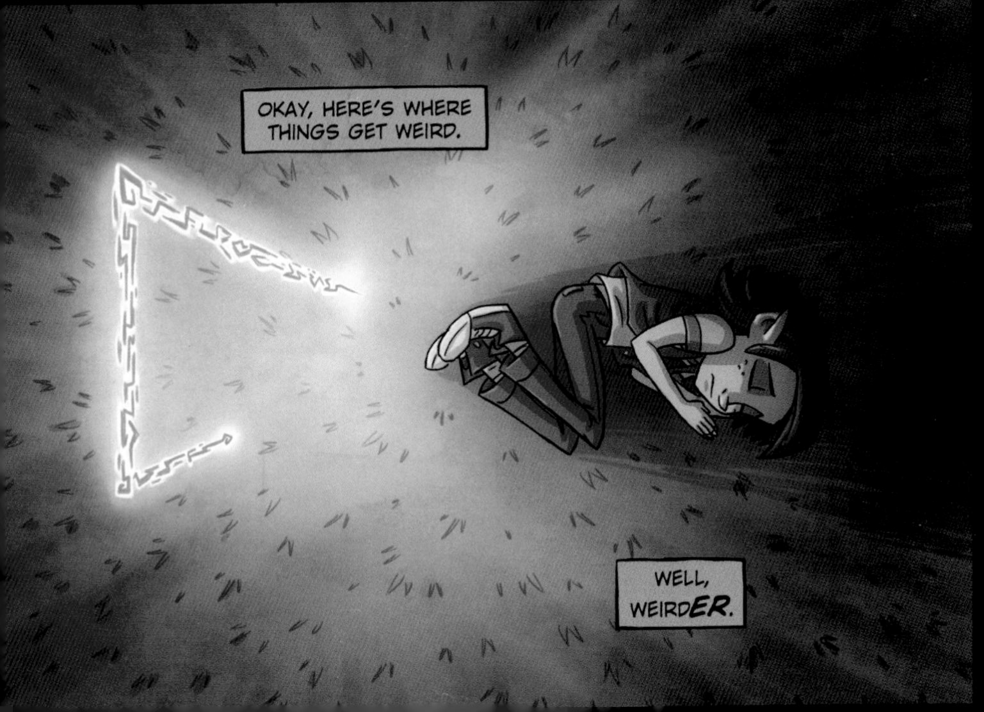
OKAY, HERE'S WHERE THINGS GET WEIRD.
WELL, WEIRDER.

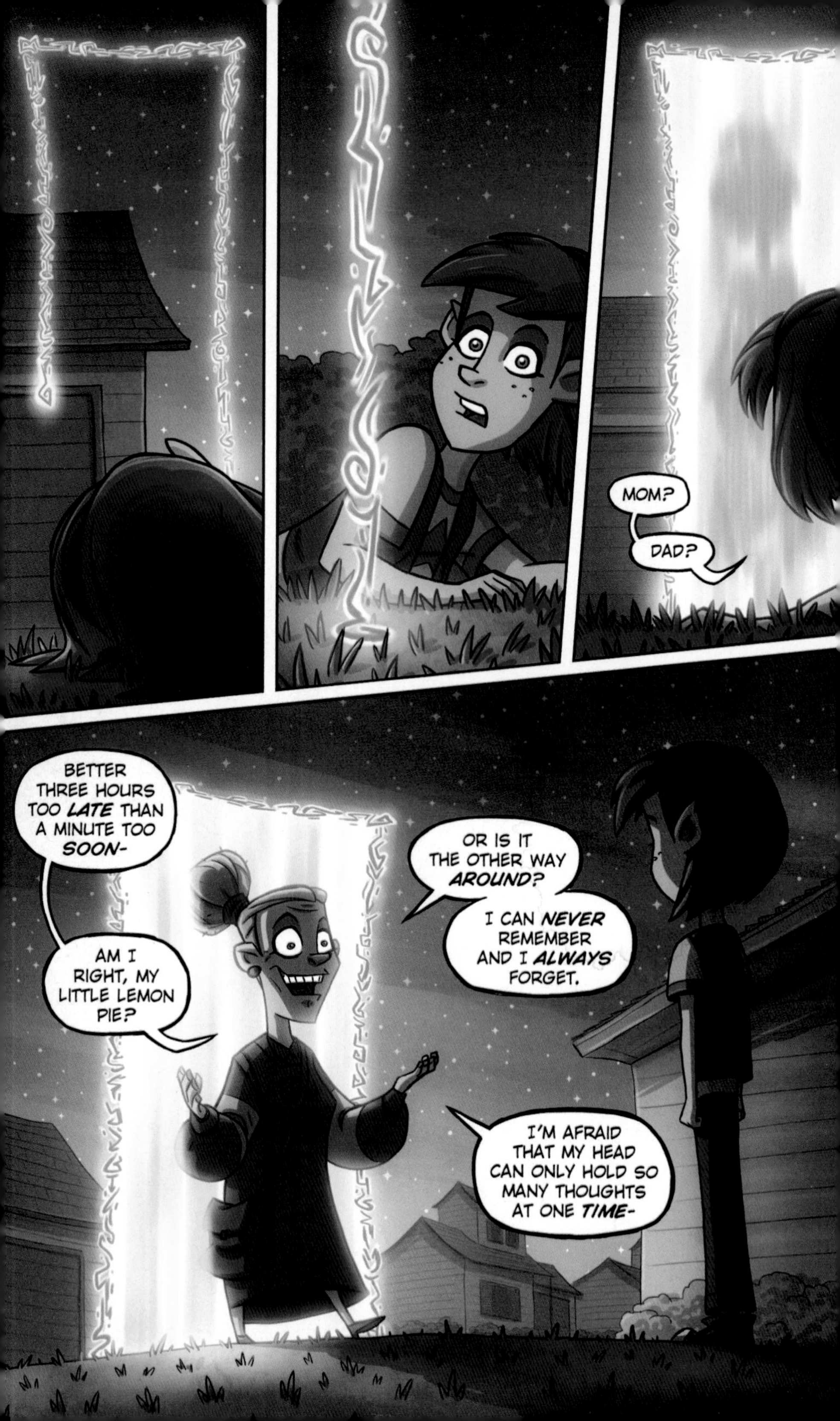
MOM?
DAD?
BETTER THREE HOURS TOO **LATE** THAN A MINUTE TOO **SOON-**
AM I RIGHT, MY LITTLE LEMON PIE?
OR IS IT THE OTHER WAY **AROUND?**
I CAN **NEVER** REMEMBER AND I **ALWAYS** FORGET.
I'M AFRAID THAT MY HEAD CAN ONLY HOLD SO MANY THOUGHTS AT ONE **TIME-**

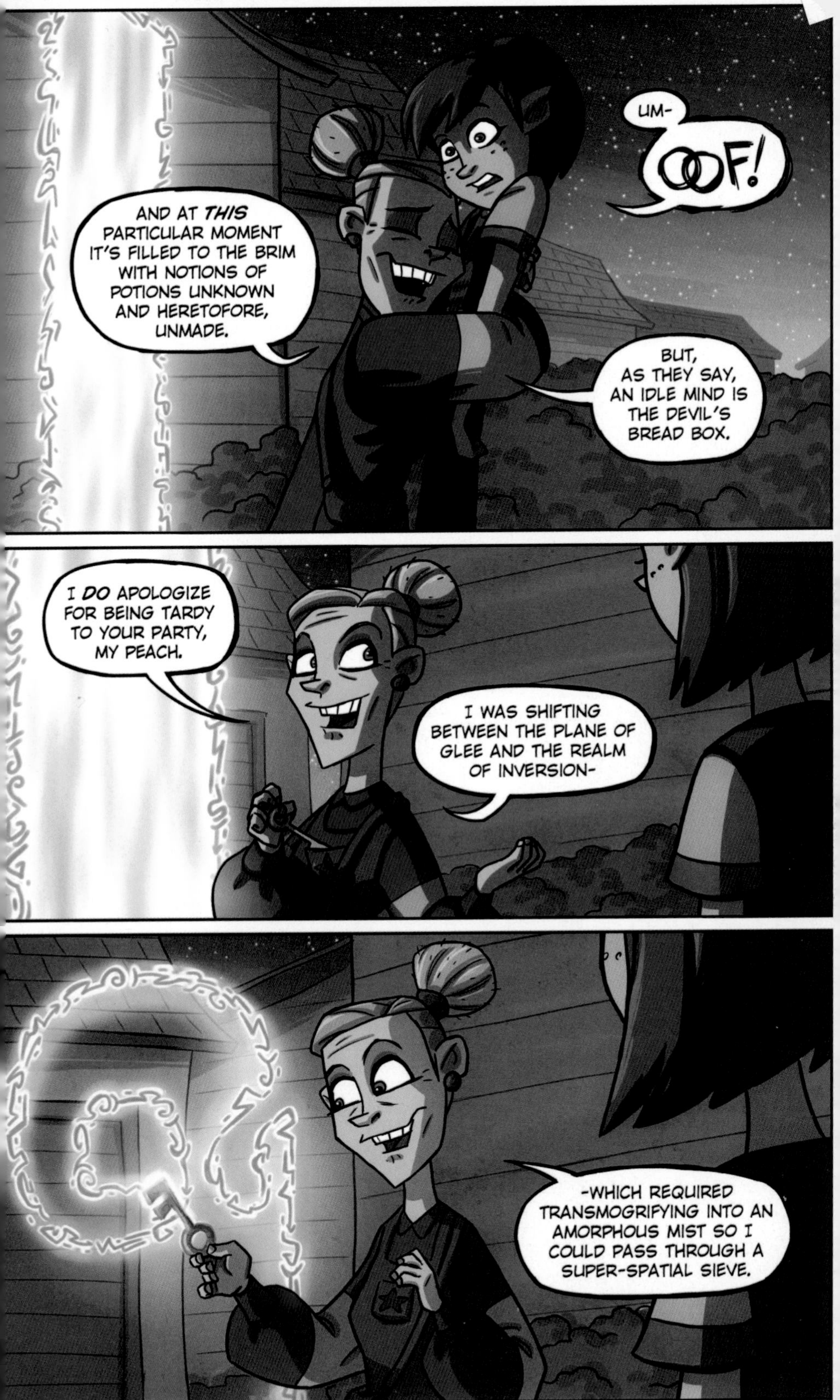
AND AT THIS PARTICULAR MOMENT IT'S FILLED TO THE BRIM WITH NOTIONS OF POTIONS UNKNOWN AND HERETOFORE, UNMADE.
UM-
OOF!
BUT, AS THEY SAY, AN IDLE MIND IS THE DEVIL'S BREAD BOX.
I DO APOLOGIZE FOR BEING TARDY TO YOUR PARTY, MY PEACH.
I WAS SHIFTING BETWEEN THE PLANE OF GLEE AND THE REALM OF INVERSION-
-WHICH REQUIRED TRANSMOGRIFYING INTO AN AMORPHOUS MIST SO I COULD PASS THROUGH A SUPER-SPATIAL SIEVE.

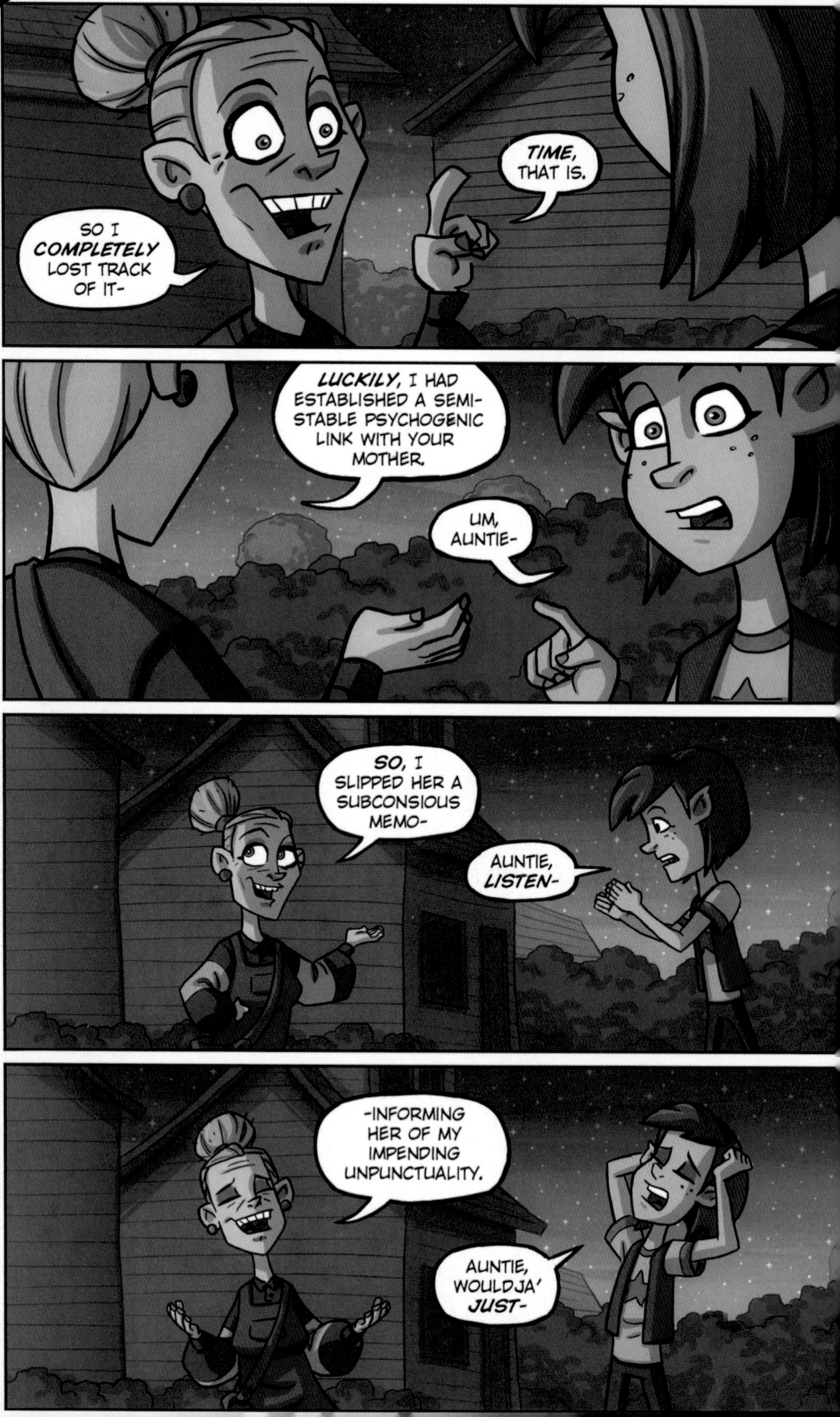
TIME, THAT IS.
SO I COMPLETELY LOST TRACK OF IT-
LUCKILY, I HAD ESTABLISHED A SEMI-STABLE PSYCHOGENIC LINK WITH YOUR MOTHER.
UM, AUNTIE-
SO, I SLIPPED HER A SUBCONSIOUS MEMO-
AUNTIE, LISTEN-
-INFORMING HER OF MY IMPENDING UNPUNCTUALITY.
AUNTIE, WOULDJA' JUST-

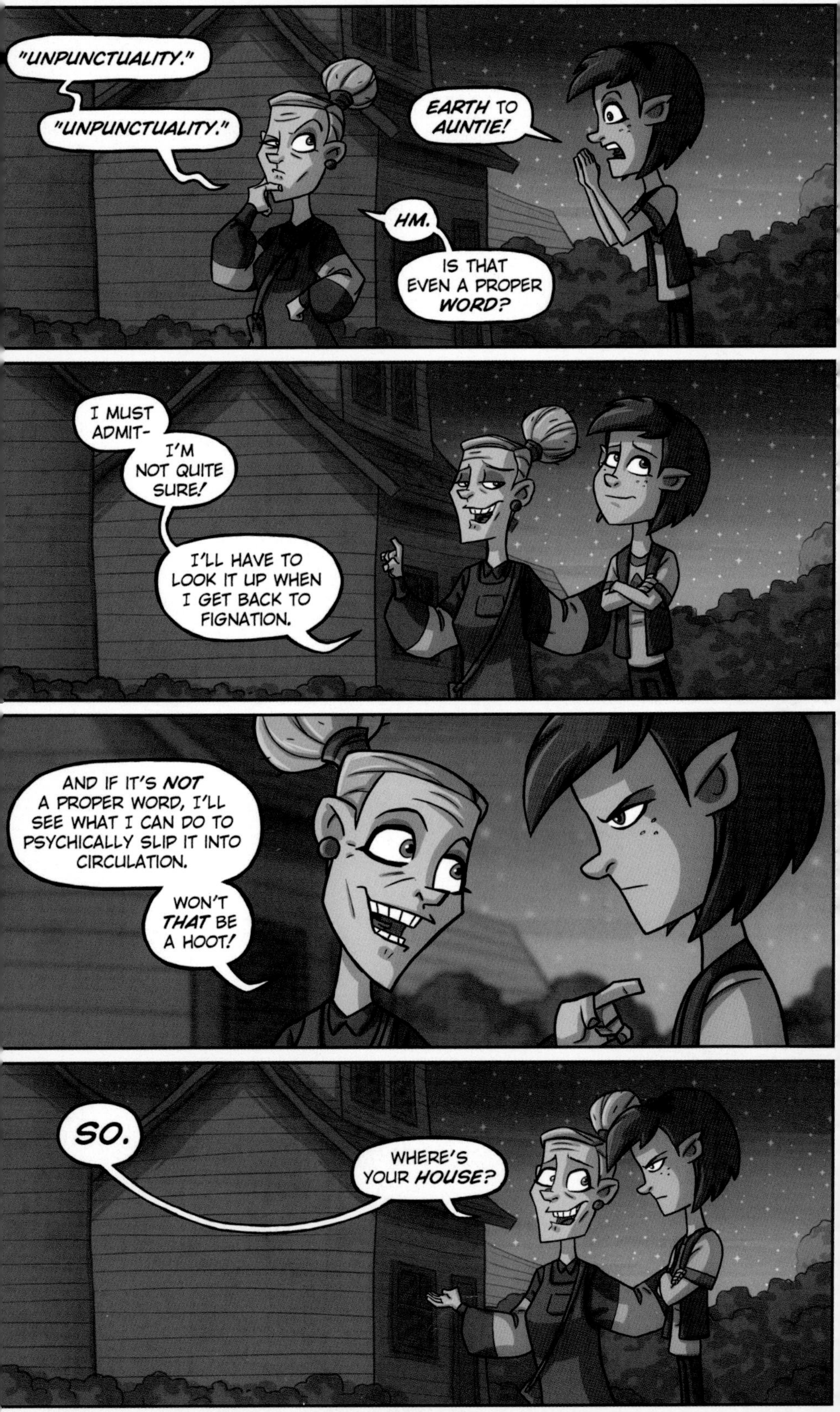
"UNPUNCTUALITY."
"UNPUNCTUALITY."
EARTH TO AUNTIE!
HM.
IS THAT EVEN A PROPER WORD?
I MUST ADMIT-
I'M NOT QUITE SURE!
I'LL HAVE TO LOOK IT UP WHEN I GET BACK TO FIGNATION.
AND IF IT'S NOT A PROPER WORD, I'LL SEE WHAT I CAN DO TO PSYCHICALLY SLIP IT INTO CIRCULATION.
WON'T THAT BE A HOOT!
SO.
WHERE'S YOUR HOUSE?

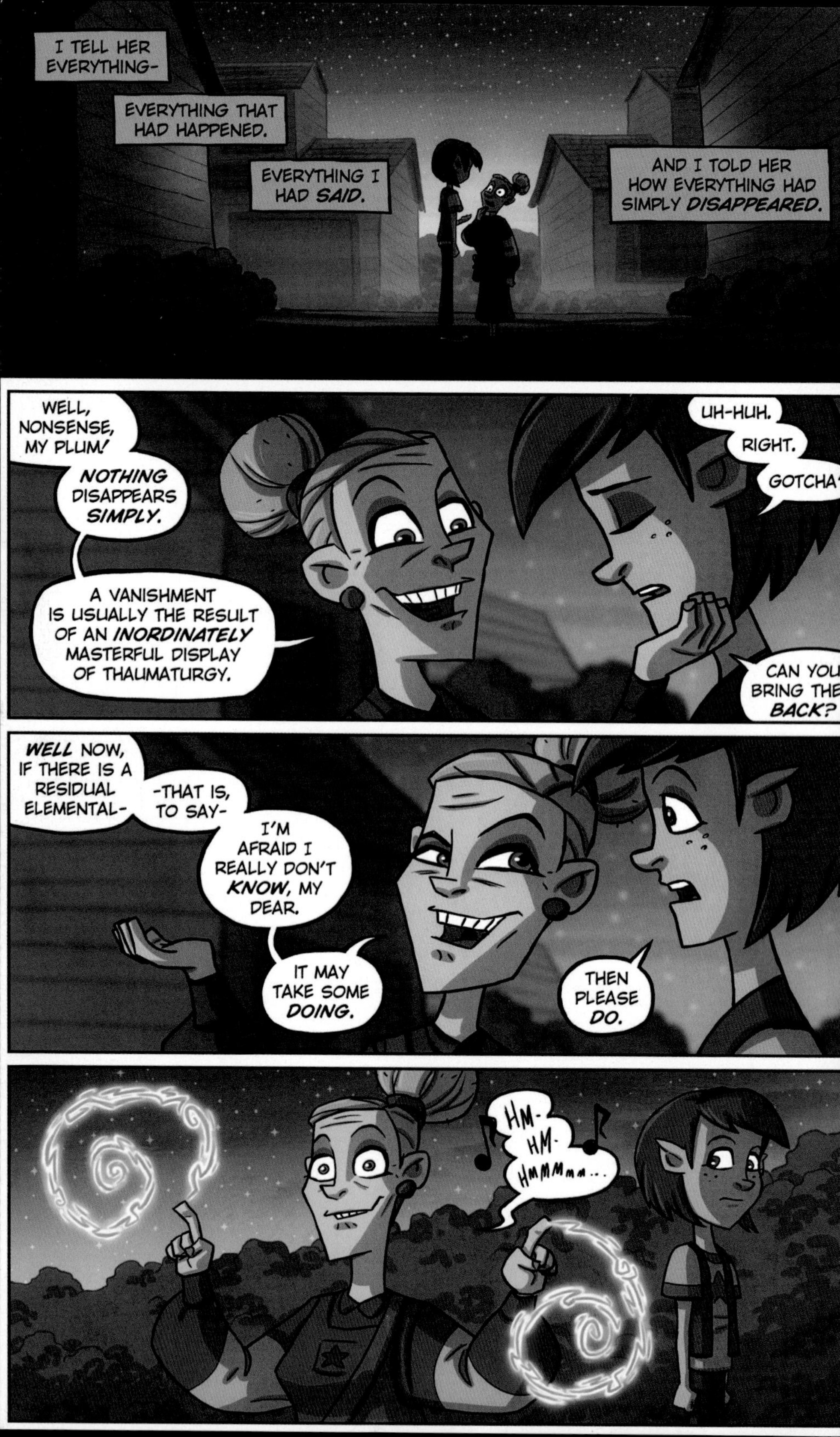
I TELL HER EVERYTHING-
EVERYTHING THAT HAD HAPPENED.
EVERYTHING I HAD SAID.
AND I TOLD HER HOW EVERYTHING HAD SIMPLY DISAPPEARED.
WELL, NONSENSE, MY PLUM!
NOTHING DISAPPEARS SIMPLY.
A VANISHMENT IS USUALLY THE RESULT OF AN INORDINATELY MASTERFUL DISPLAY OF THAUMATURGY.
UH-HUH.
RIGHT.
GOTCHA
CAN YOU BRING THE BACK?
WELL NOW, IF THERE IS A RESIDUAL ELEMENTAL-
-THAT IS, TO SAY-
I'M AFRAID I REALLY DON'T KNOW, MY DEAR.
IT MAY TAKE SOME DOING.
THEN PLEASE DO.
HM-HM-HMMMMM...

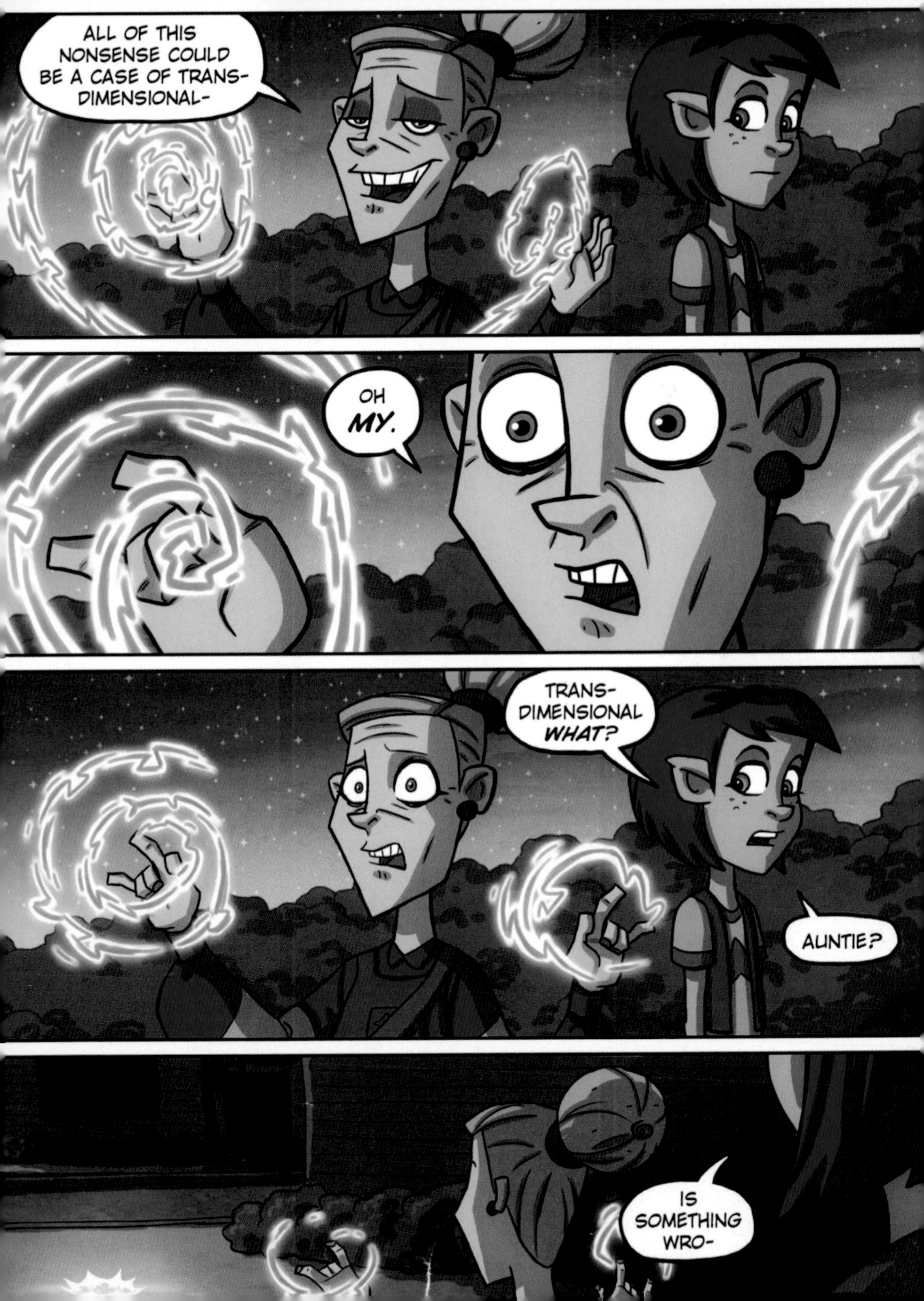
ALL OF THIS NONSENSE COULD BE A CASE OF TRANS-DIMENSIONAL-
OH *MY.*
TRANS-DIMENSIONAL *WHAT?*
AUNTIE?
IS SOMETHING WRO-

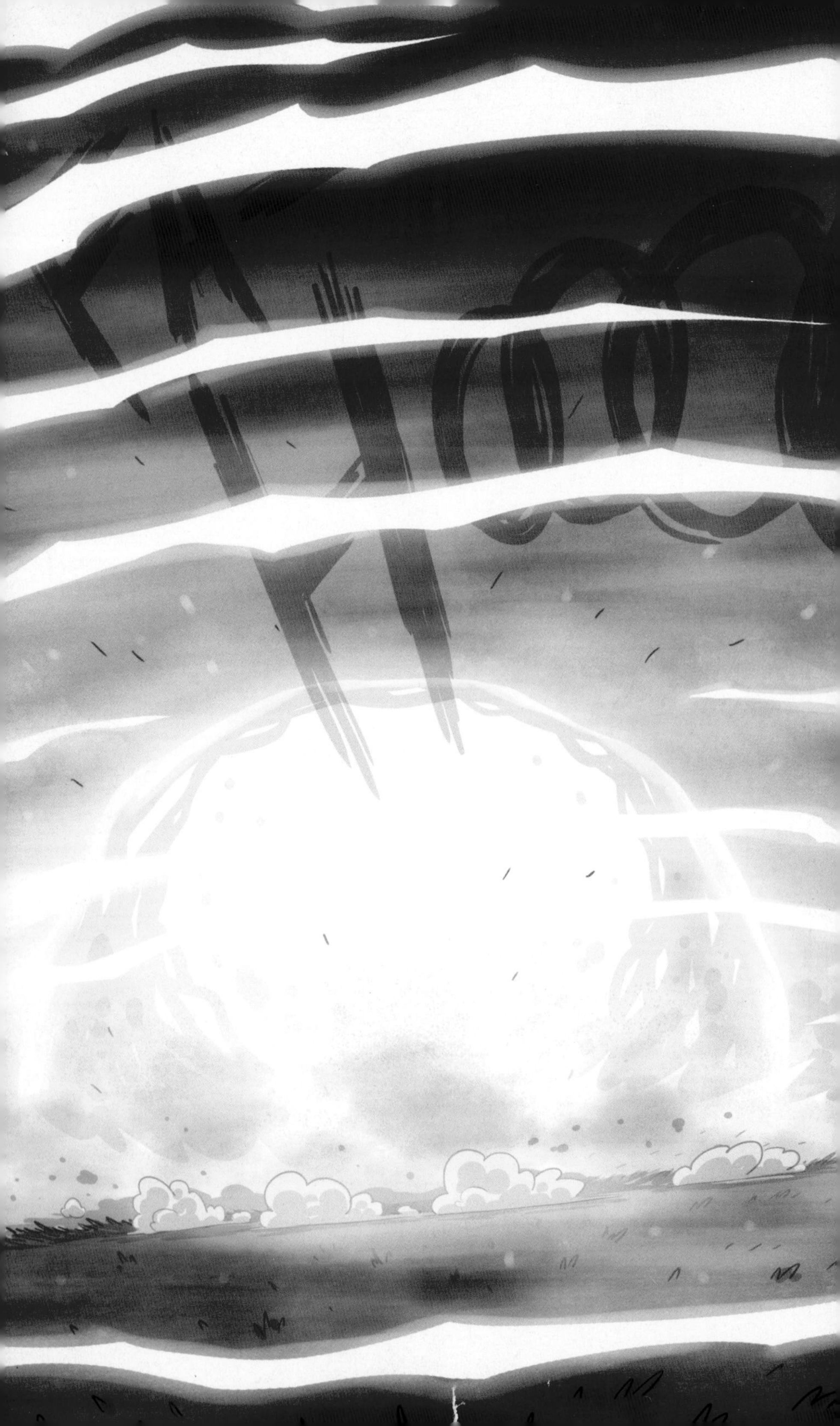

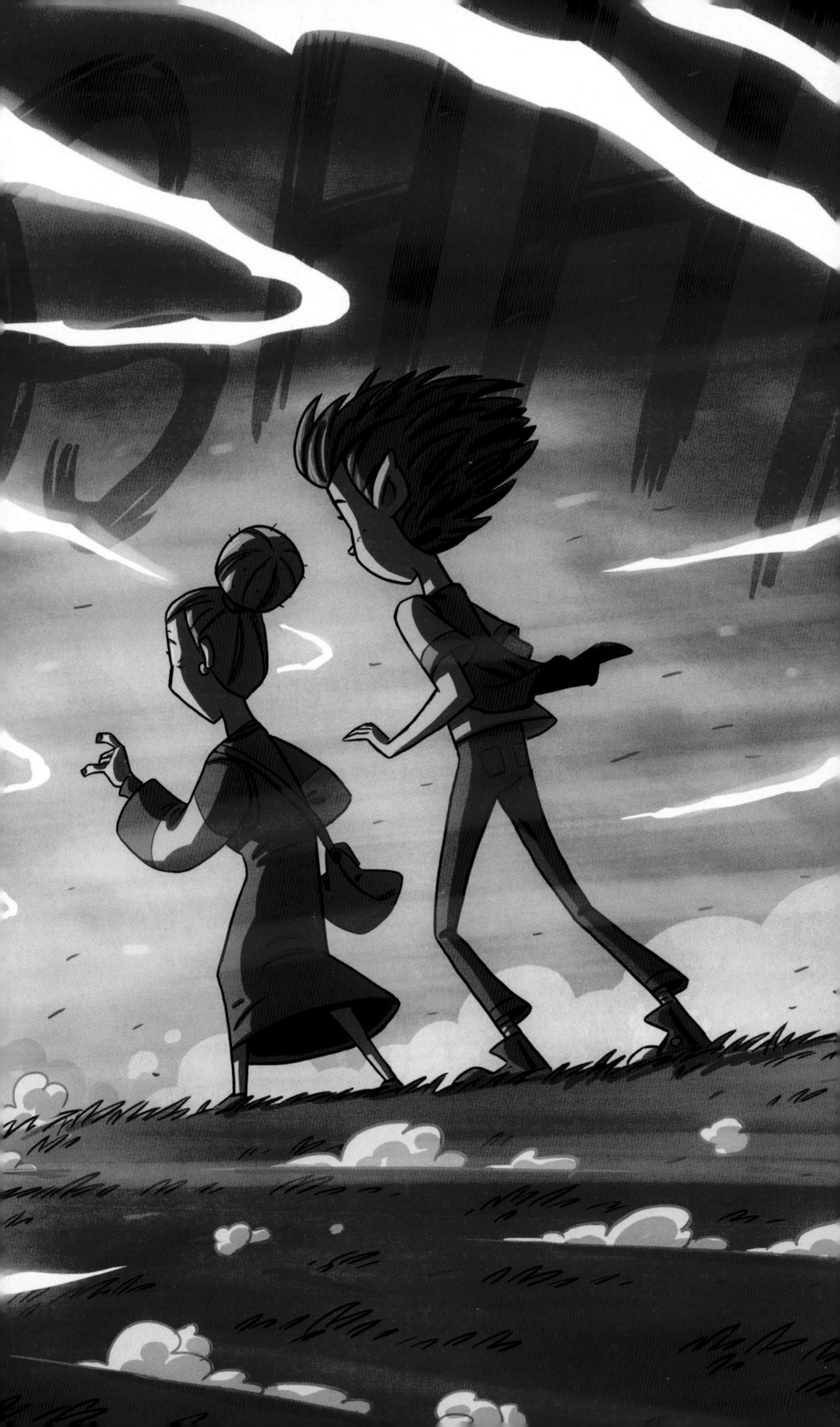

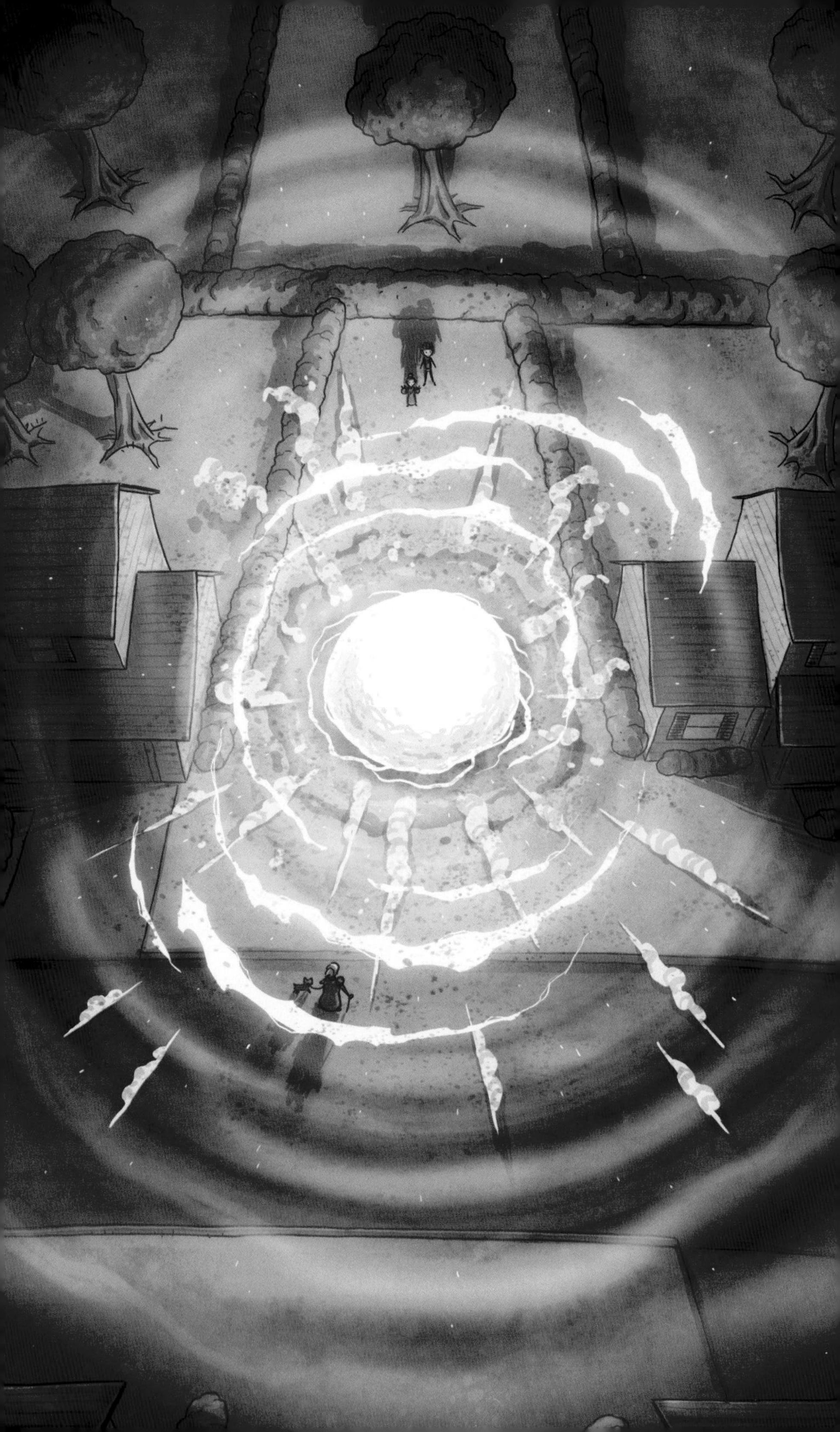

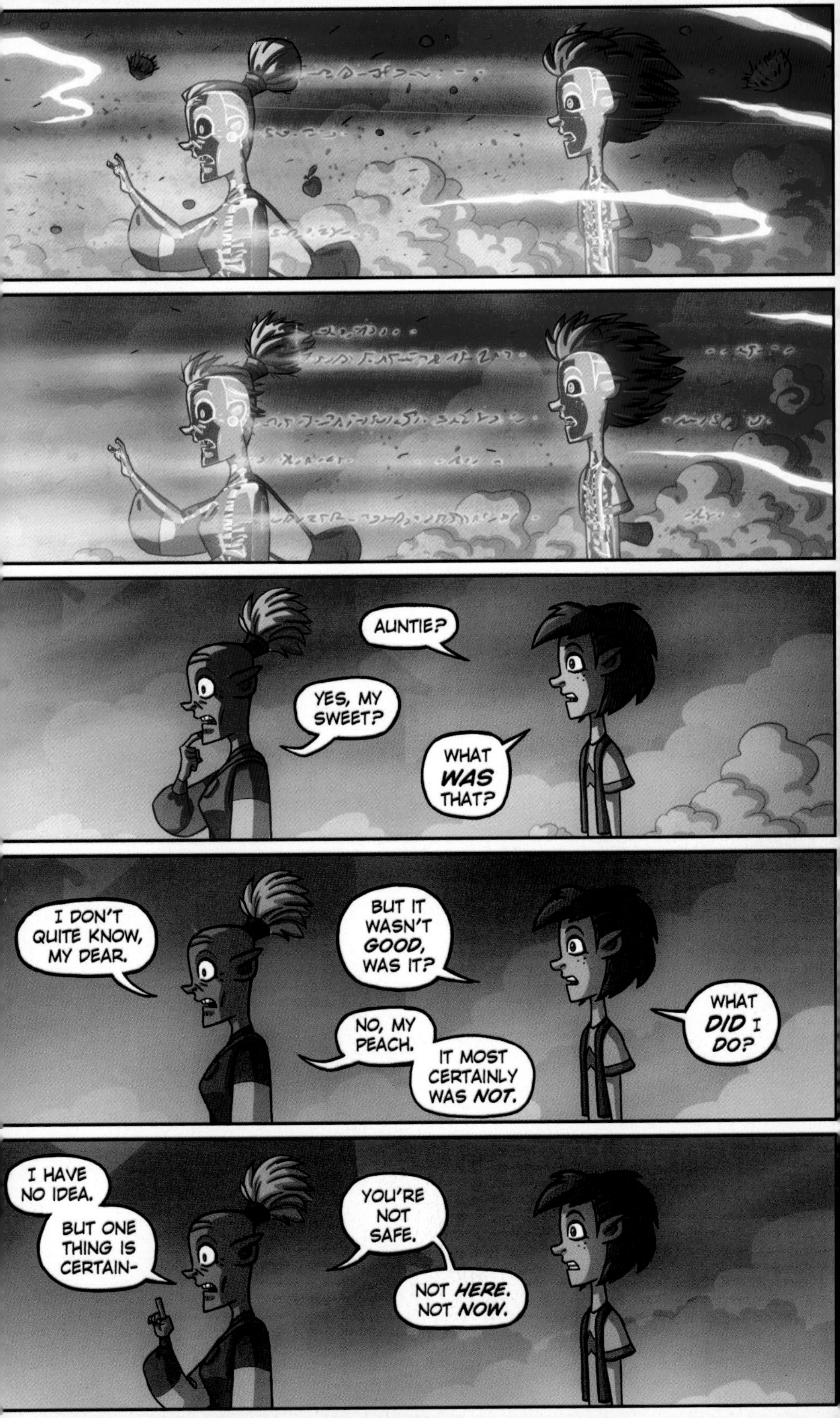
AUNTIE?
YES, MY SWEET?
WHAT WAS THAT?
I DON'T QUITE KNOW, MY DEAR.
BUT IT WASN'T GOOD, WAS IT?
NO, MY PEACH.
IT MOST CERTAINLY WAS NOT.
WHAT DID I DO?
I HAVE NO IDEA.
BUT ONE THING IS CERTAIN-
YOU'RE NOT SAFE.
NOT HERE. NOT NOW.

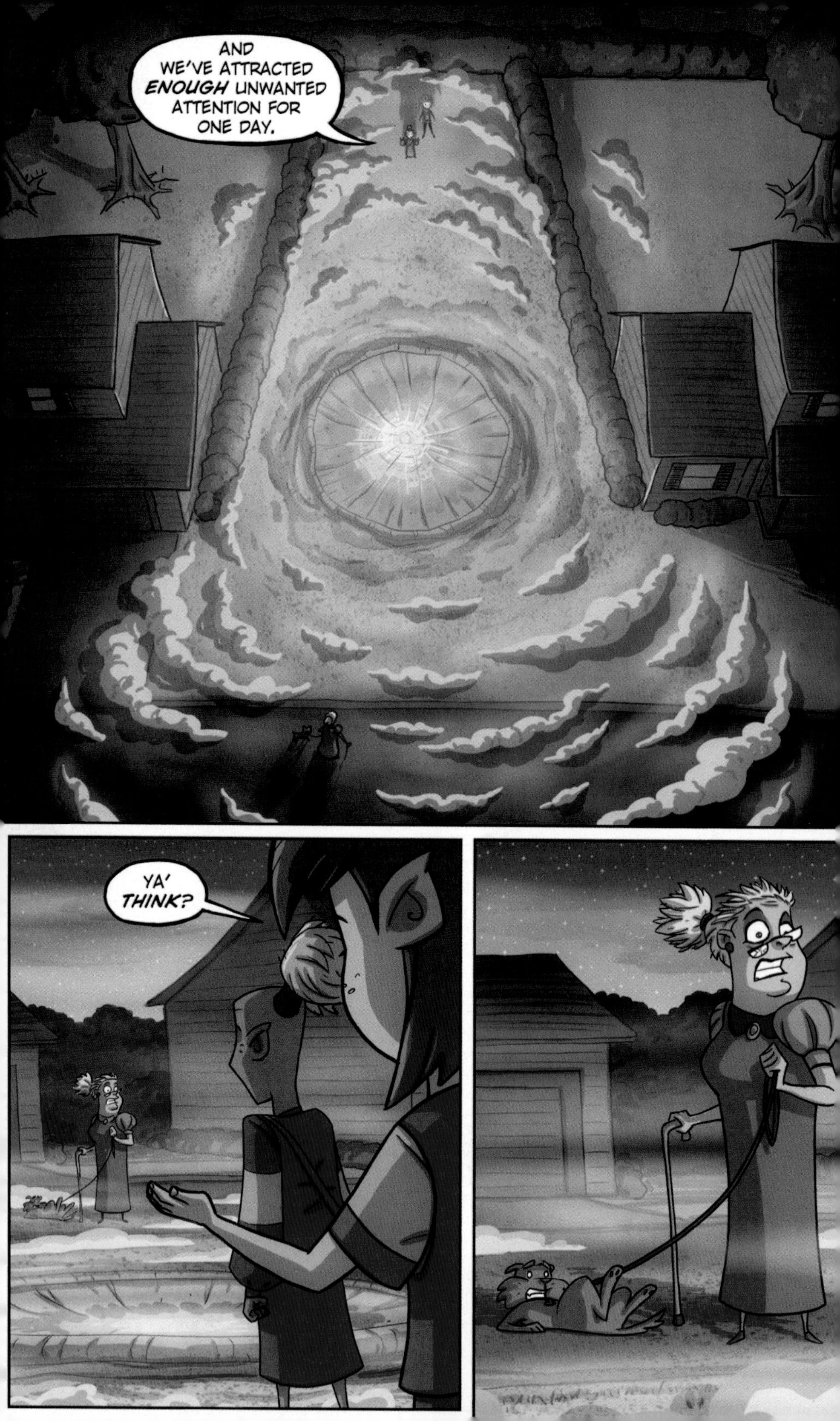
AND WE'VE ATTRACTED *ENOUGH* UNWANTED ATTENTION FOR ONE DAY.
YA' *THINK?*

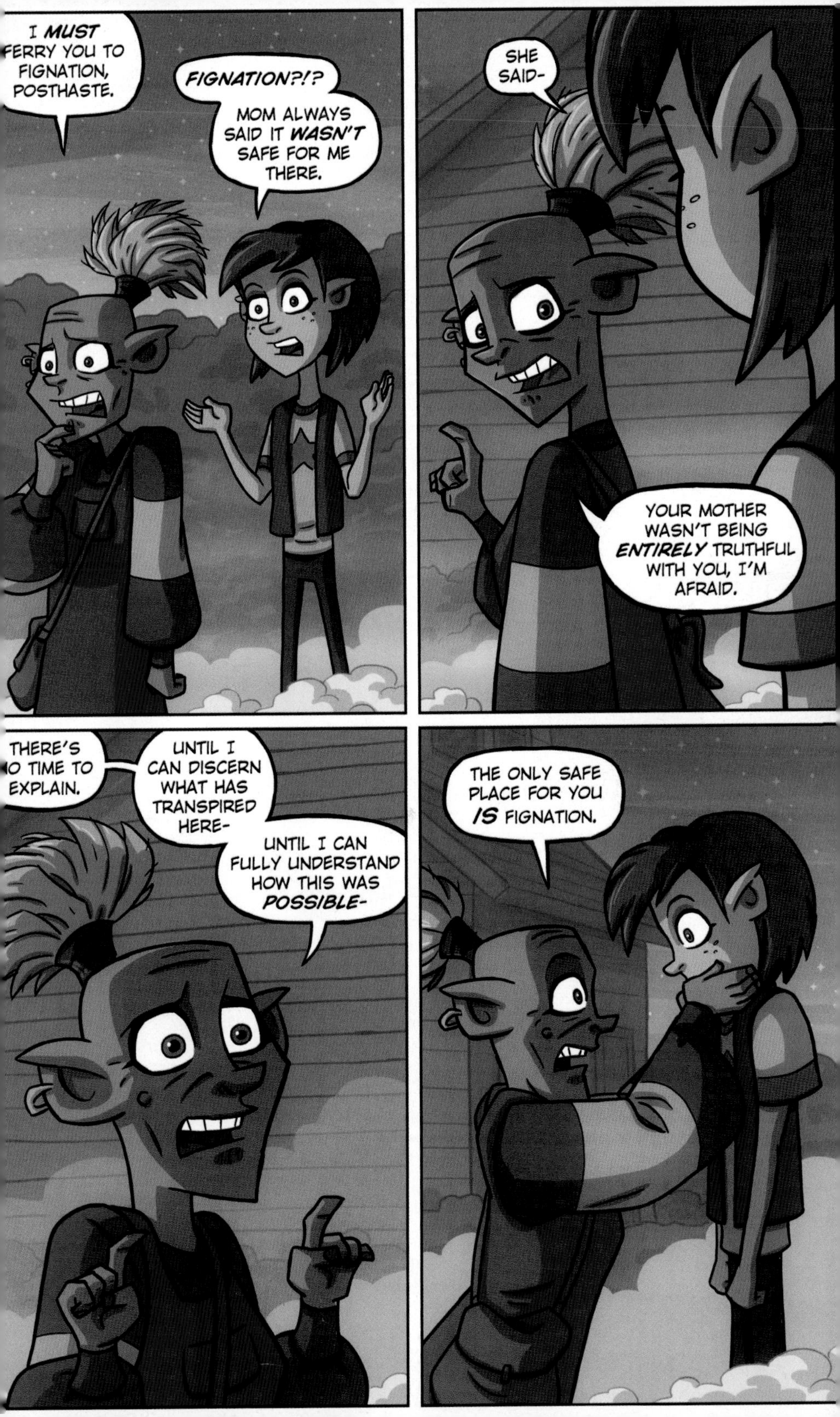
I MUST FERRY YOU TO FIGNATION, POSTHASTE.
FIGNATION?!? MOM ALWAYS SAID IT WASN'T SAFE FOR ME THERE.
SHE SAID-
YOUR MOTHER WASN'T BEING ENTIRELY TRUTHFUL WITH YOU, I'M AFRAID.
THERE'S O TIME TO EXPLAIN.
UNTIL I CAN DISCERN WHAT HAS TRANSPIRED HERE-
UNTIL I CAN FULLY UNDERSTAND HOW THIS WAS POSSIBLE-
THE ONLY SAFE PLACE FOR YOU IS FIGNATION.

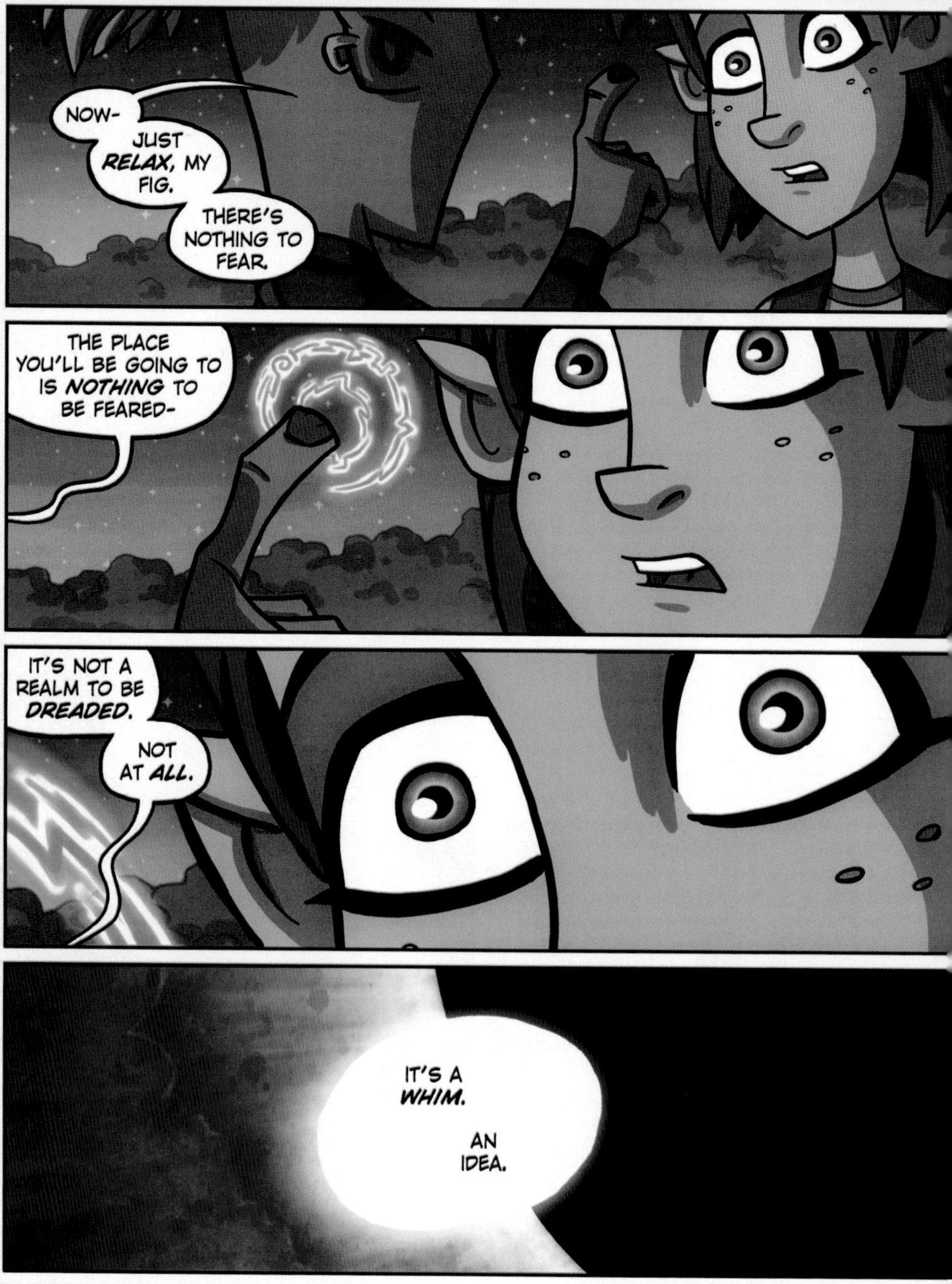
NOW-
JUST *RELAX*, MY FIG.
THERE'S NOTHING TO FEAR.
THE PLACE YOU'LL BE GOING TO IS *NOTHING* TO BE FEARED-
IT'S NOT A REALM TO BE *DREADED*.
NOT AT *ALL*.
IT'S A *WHIM*.
AN IDEA.

A SIMPLE
THOUGHT.

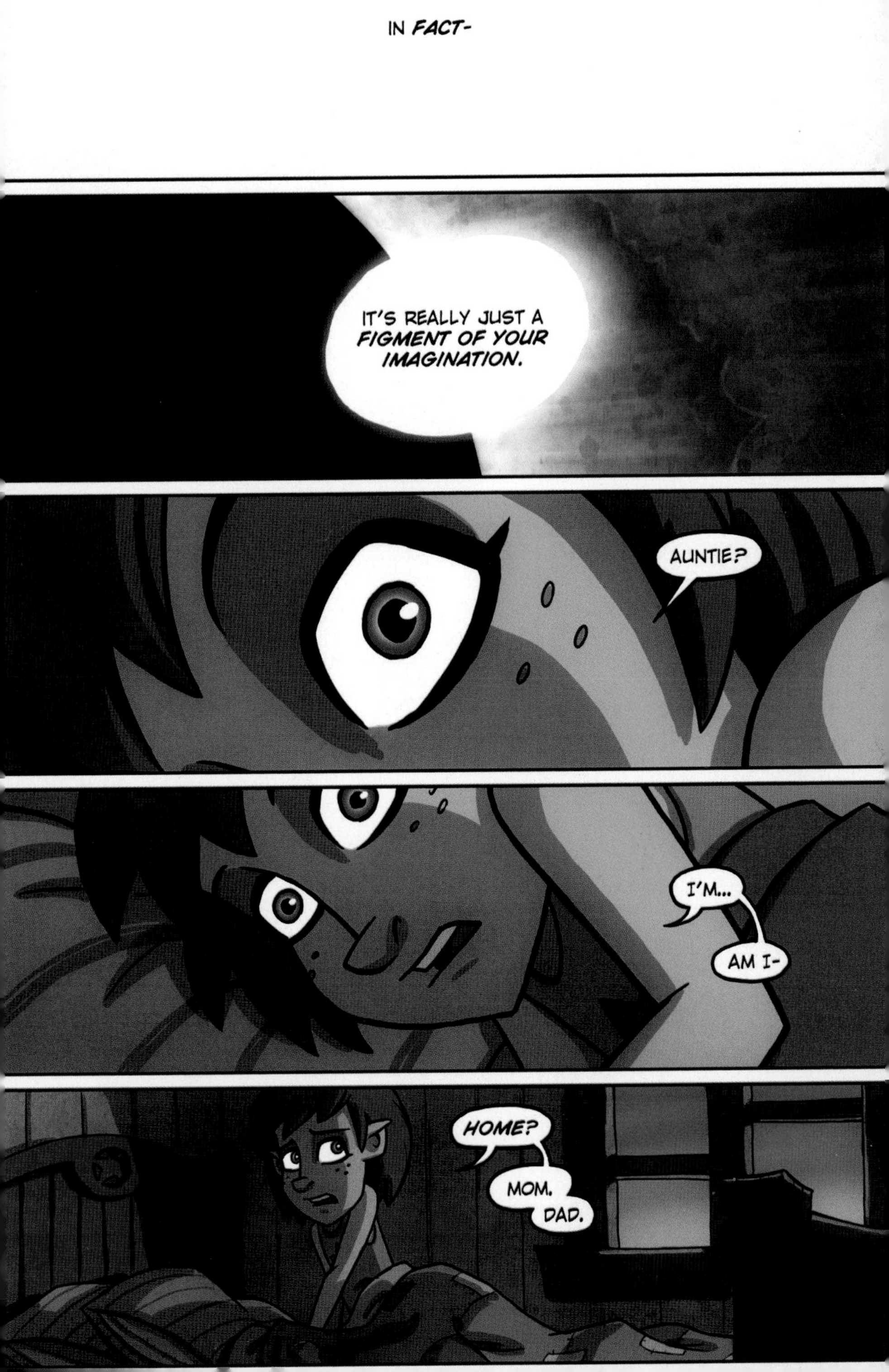
IN *FACT*-
IT'S REALLY JUST A *FIGMENT OF YOUR IMAGINATION.*
AUNTIE?
I'M...
AM I-
HOME?
MOM.
DAD.

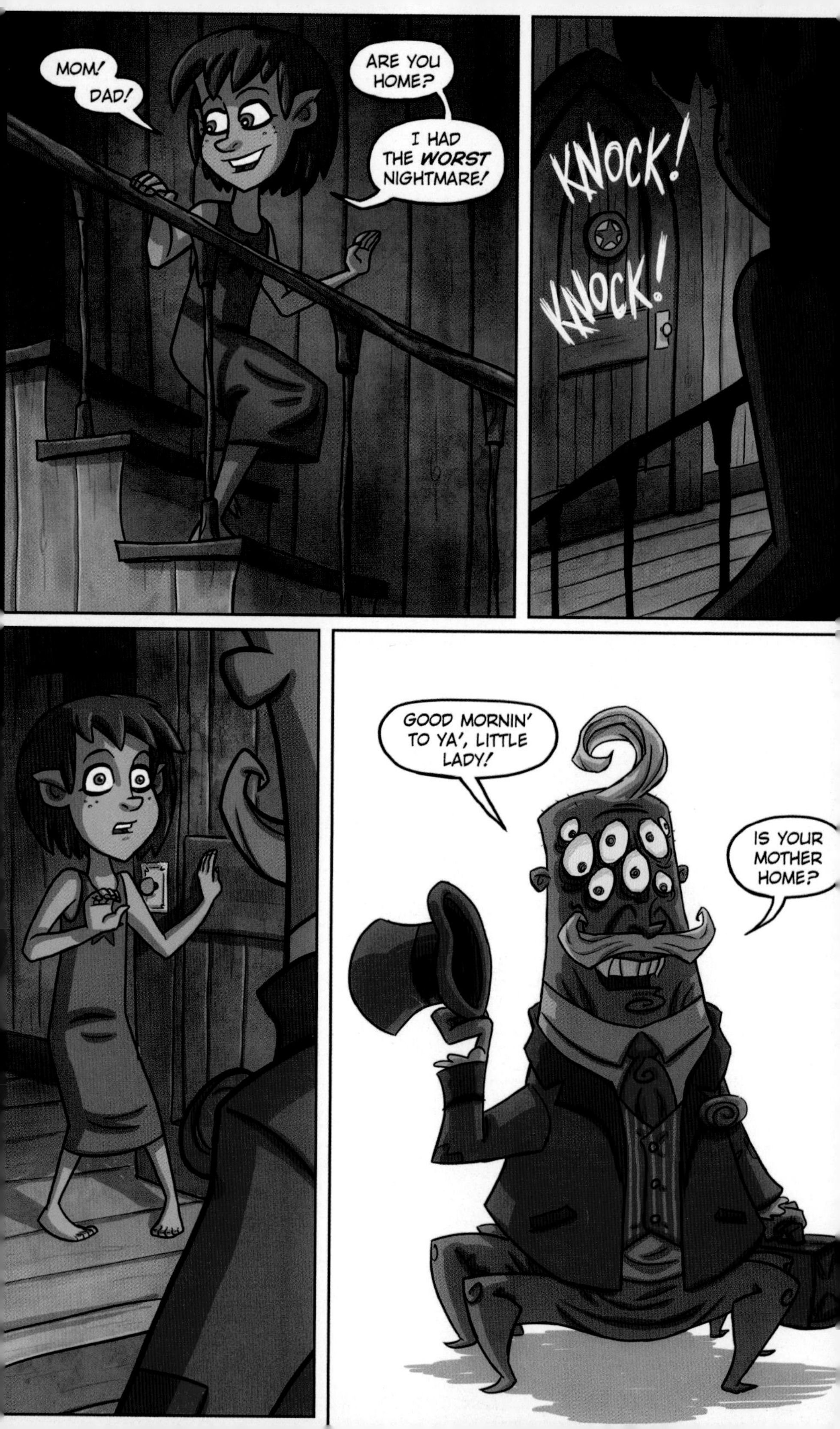
MOM! DAD!
ARE YOU HOME?
I HAD THE **WORST** NIGHTMARE!
KNOCK!
KNOCK!
GOOD MORNIN' TO YA', LITTLE LADY!
IS YOUR MOTHER HOME?

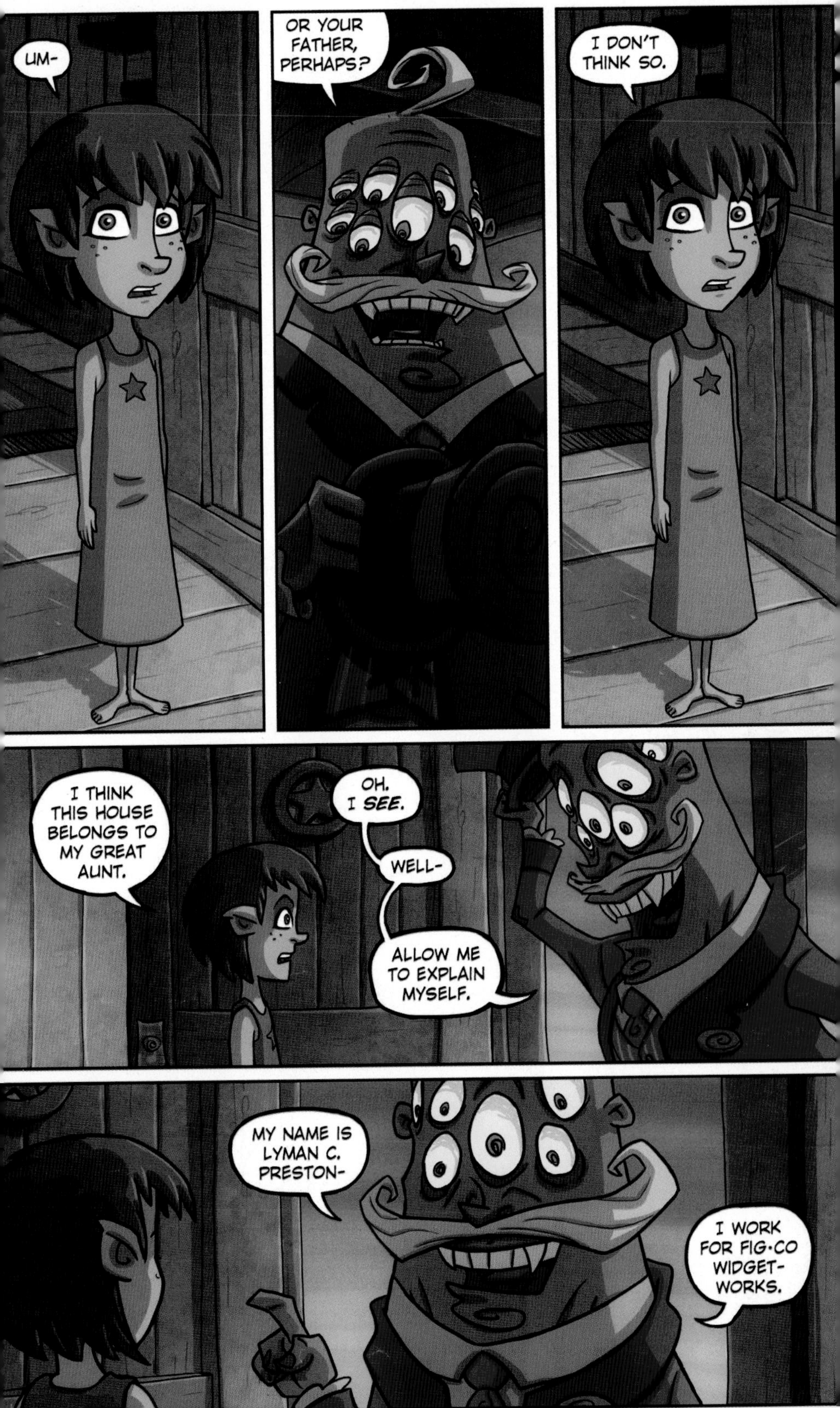
UM-
OR YOUR FATHER, PERHAPS?
I DON'T THINK SO.
I THINK THIS HOUSE BELONGS TO MY GREAT AUNT.
OH. I *SEE*.
WELL-
ALLOW ME TO EXPLAIN MYSELF.
MY NAME IS LYMAN C. PRESTON-
I WORK FOR FIG·CO WIDGET-WORKS.

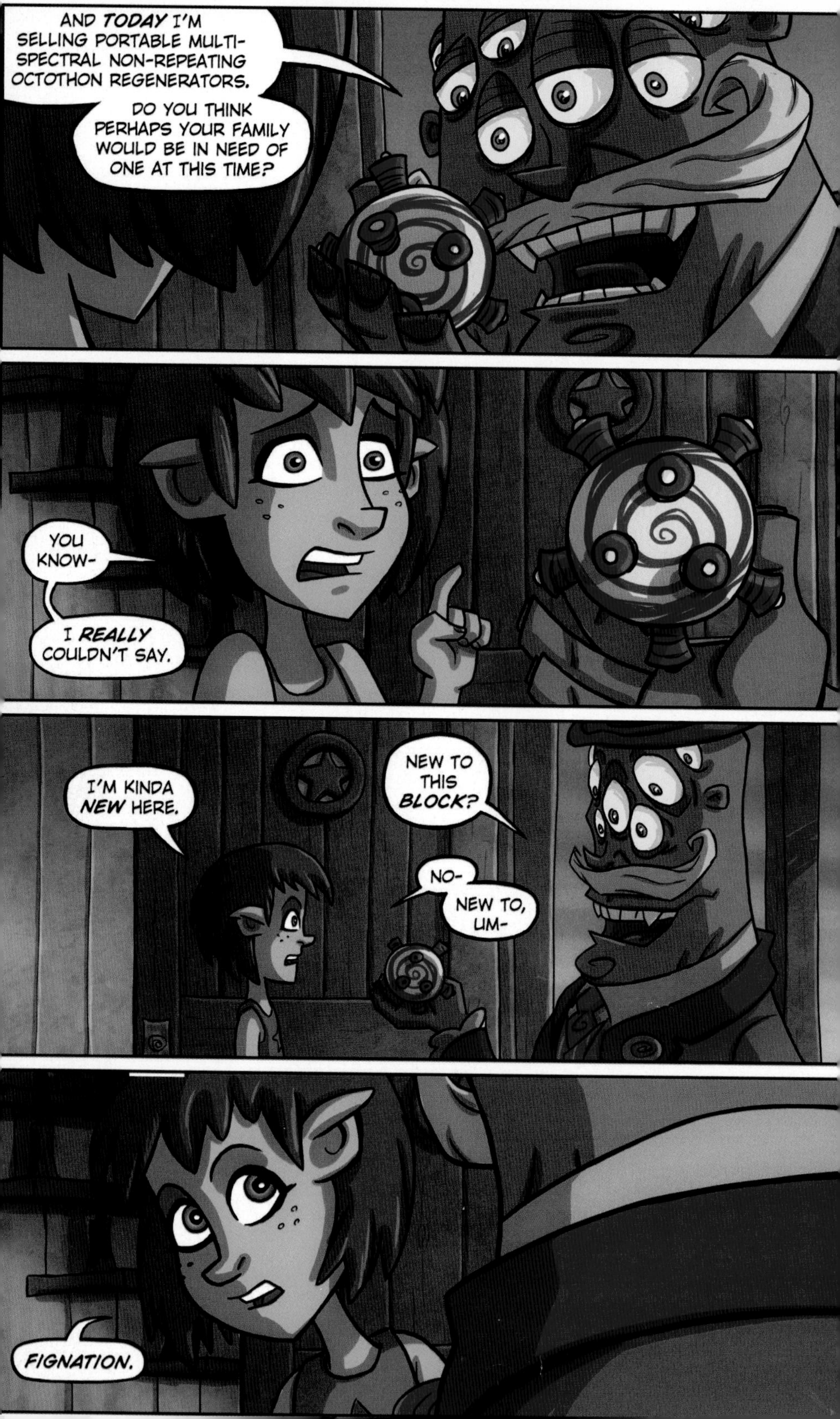
AND TODAY I'M SELLING PORTABLE MULTI-SPECTRAL NON-REPEATING OCTOTHON REGENERATORS.
DO YOU THINK PERHAPS YOUR FAMILY WOULD BE IN NEED OF ONE AT THIS TIME?
YOU KNOW-
I REALLY COULDN'T SAY.
I'M KINDA NEW HERE.
NEW TO THIS BLOCK?
NO-
NEW TO, UM-
FIGNATION.

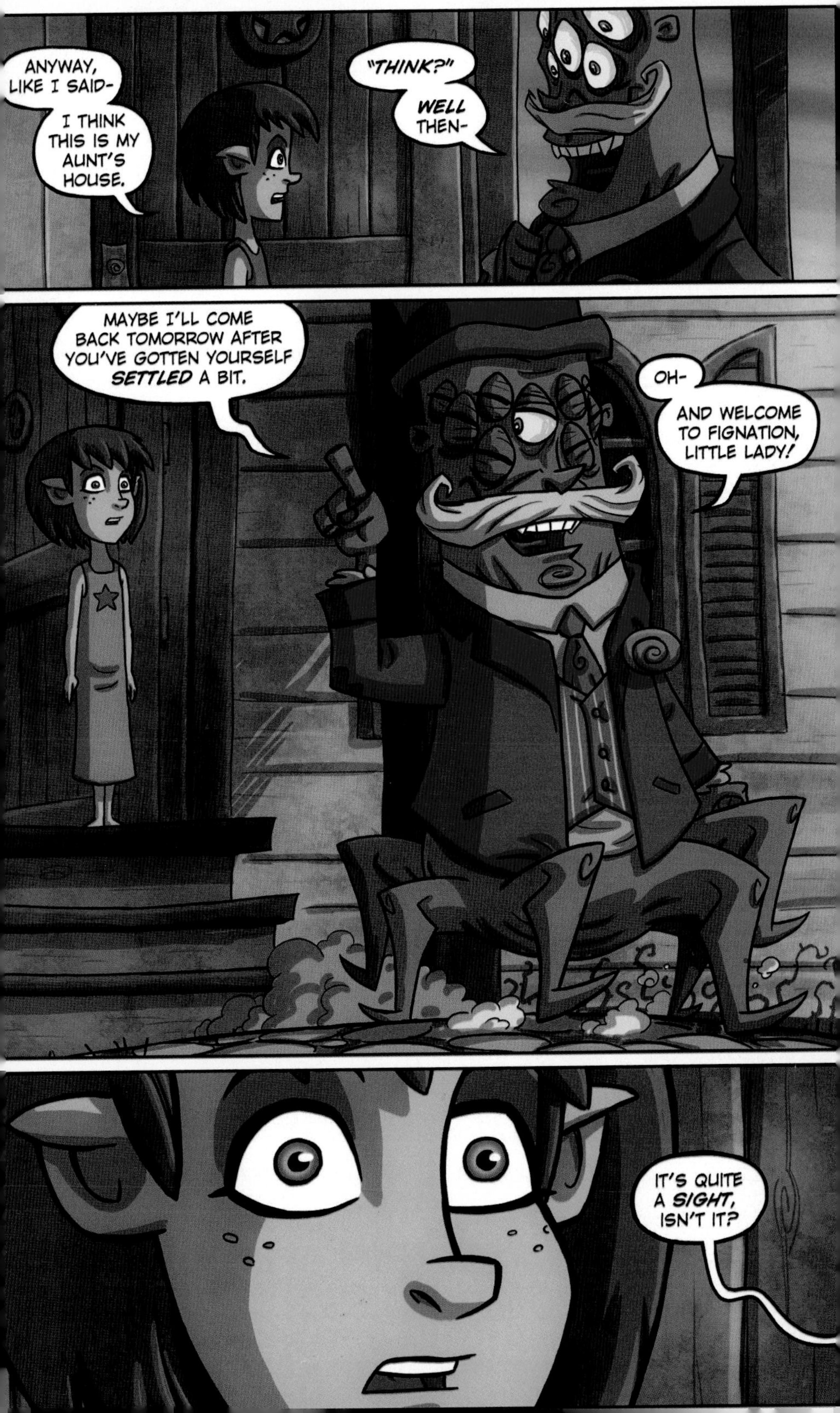

ANYWAY, LIKE I SAID-
I THINK THIS IS MY AUNT'S HOUSE.
"THINK?"
WELL THEN-
MAYBE I'LL COME BACK TOMORROW AFTER YOU'VE GOTTEN YOURSELF SETTLED A BIT.
OH-
AND WELCOME TO FIGNATION, LITTLE LADY!
IT'S QUITE A SIGHT, ISN'T IT?

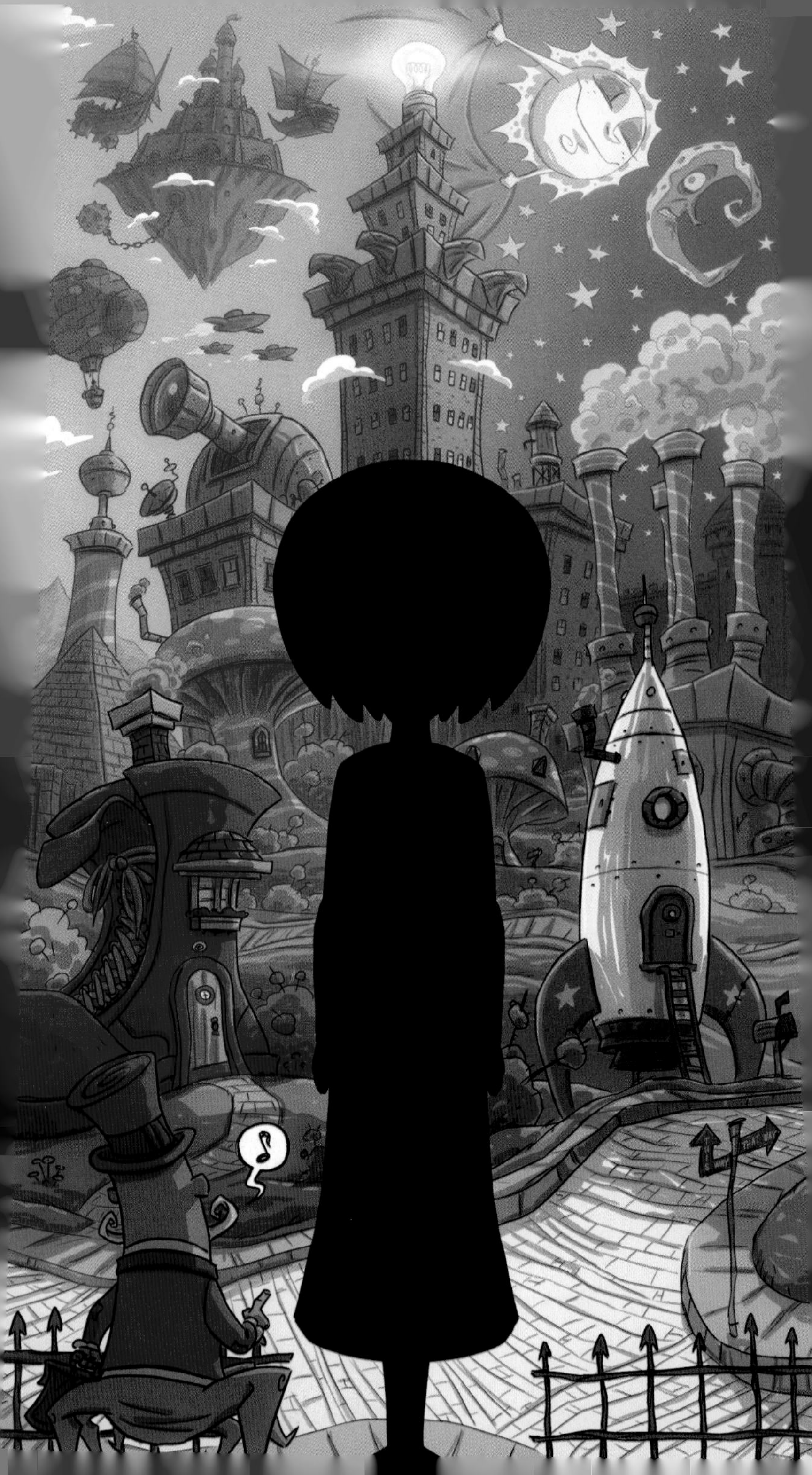
THAT WAY

Chapter 3
Strange New World

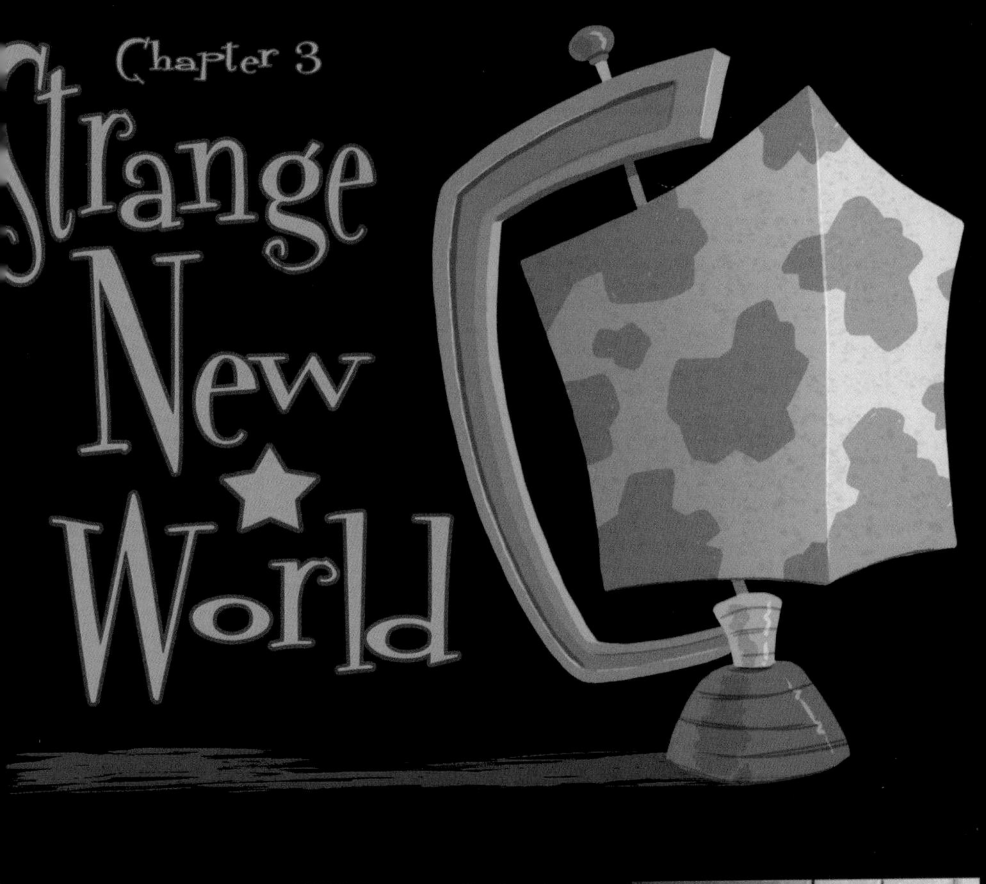

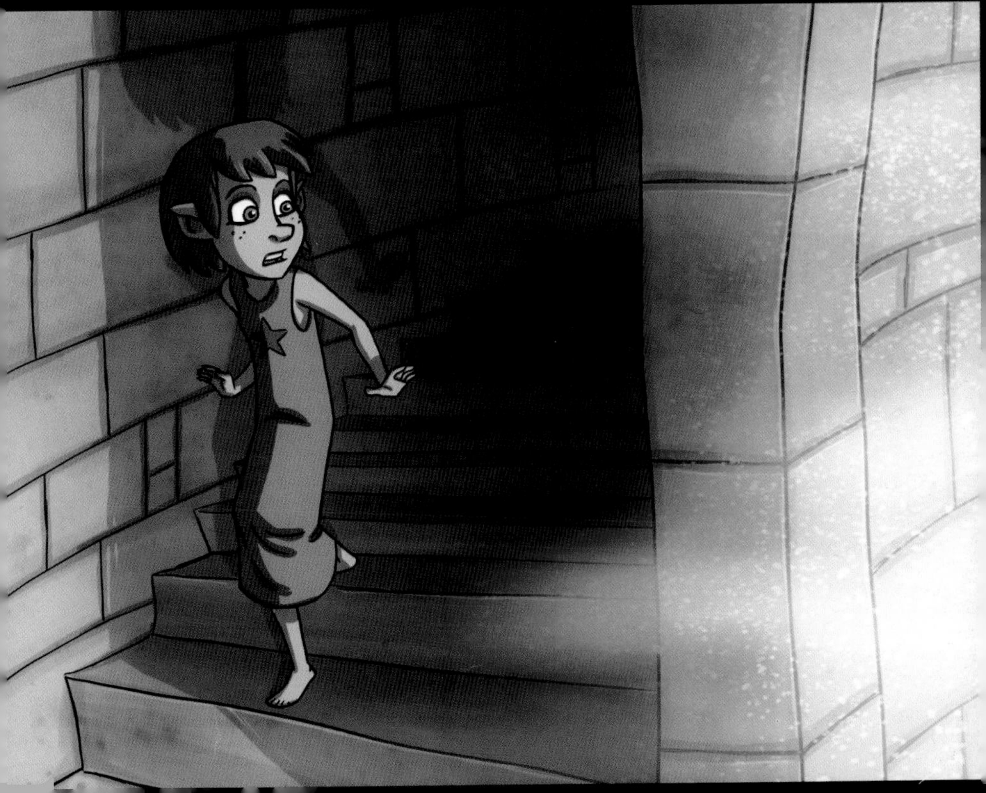

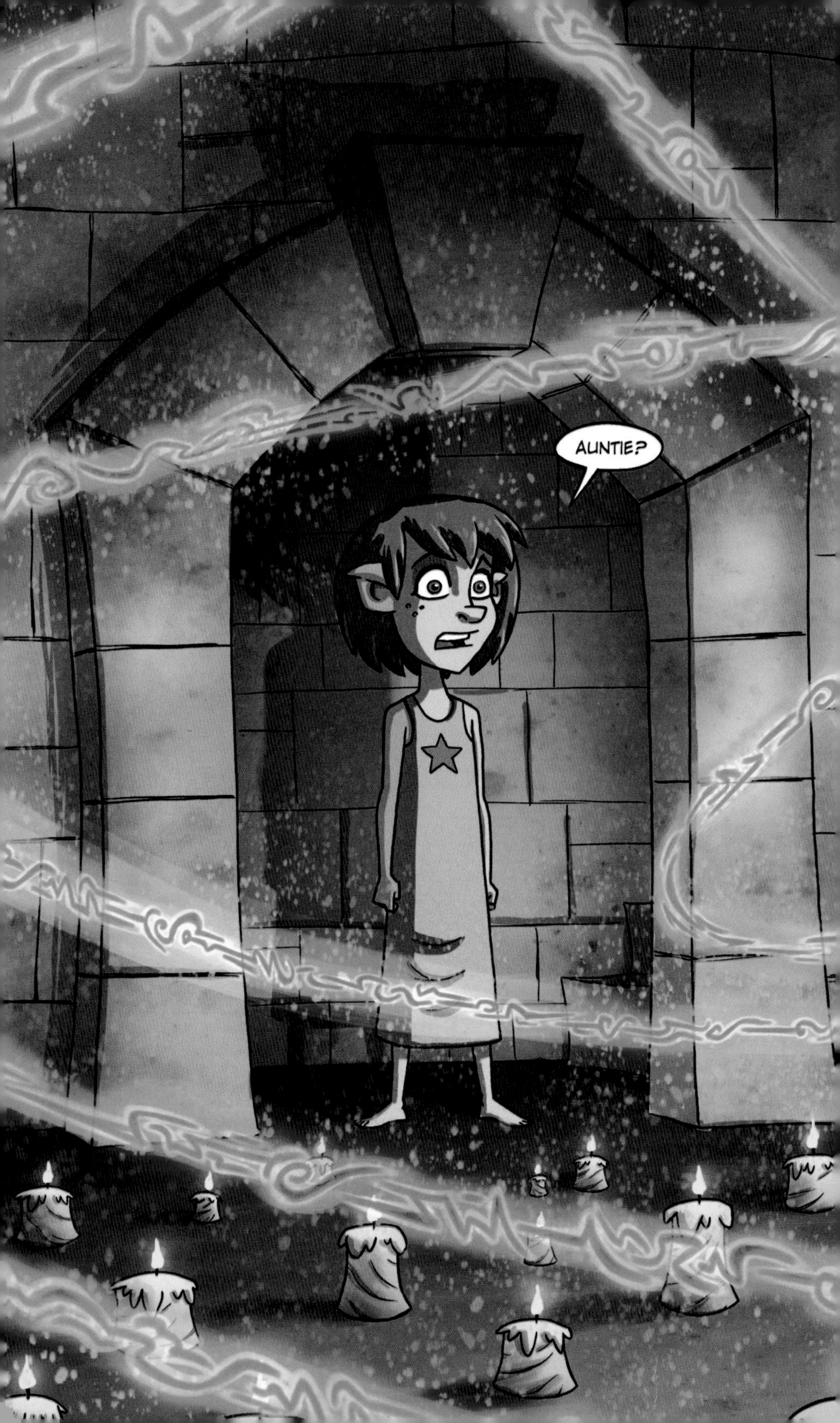
AUNTIE?

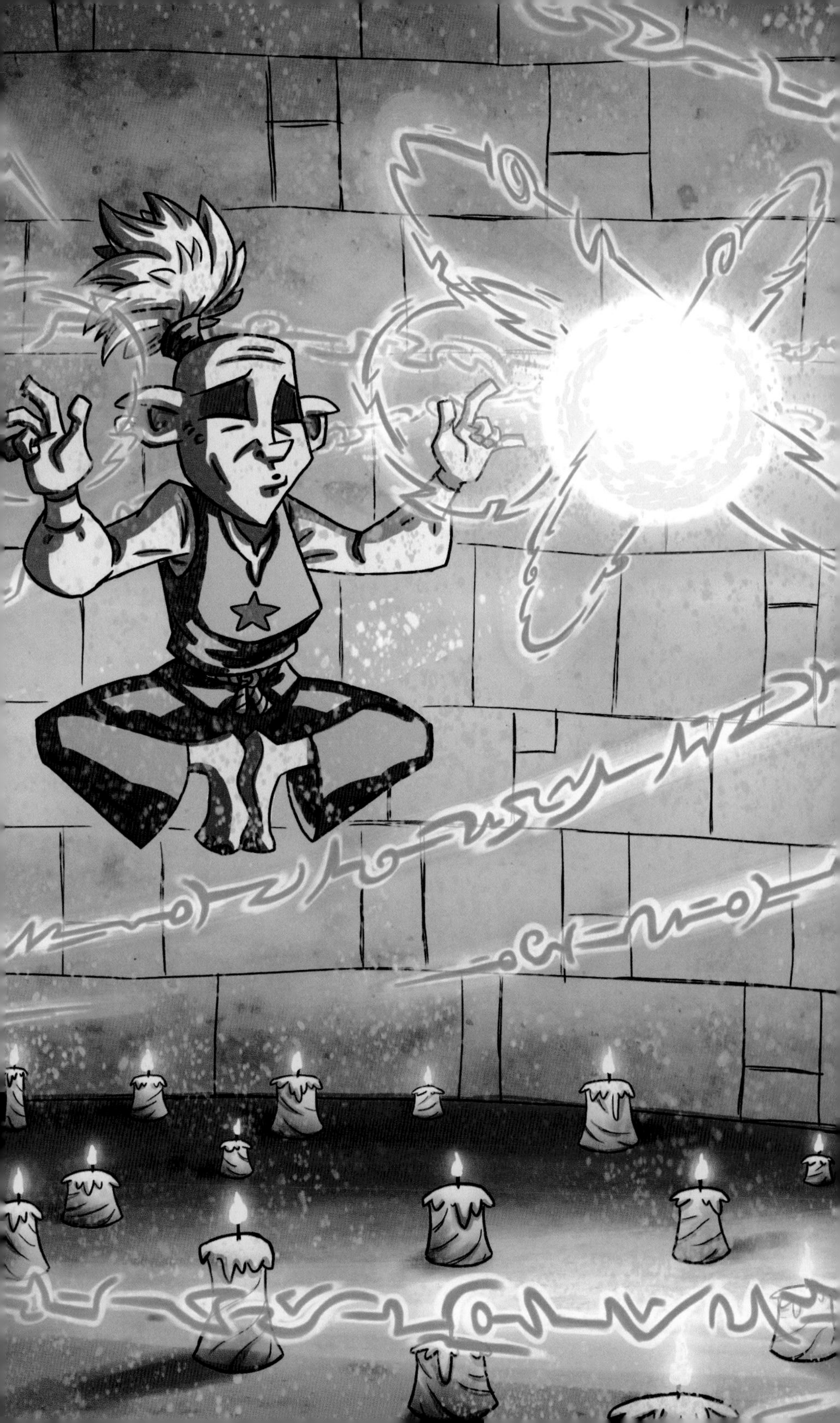

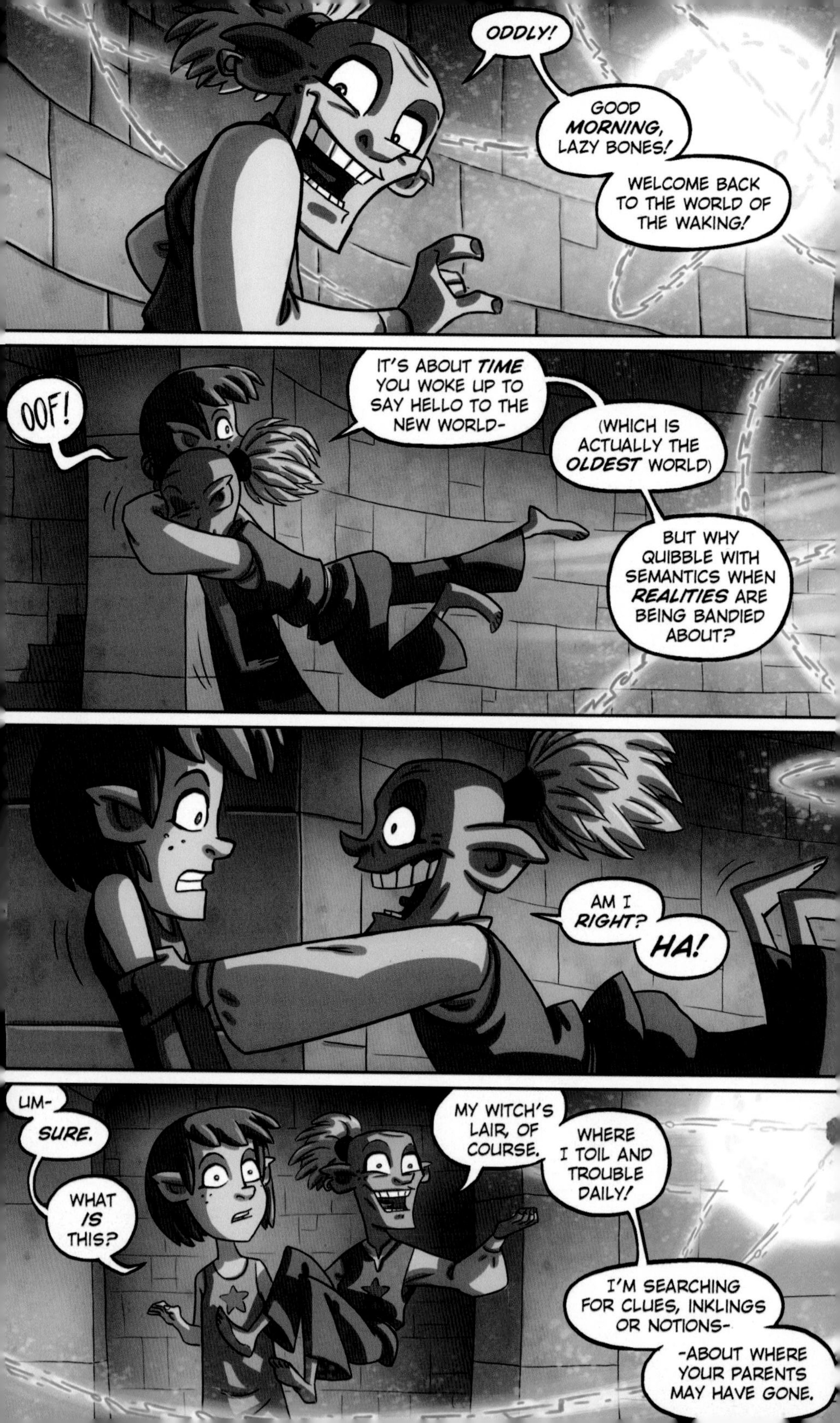
ODDLY!
GOOD MORNING, LAZY BONES!
WELCOME BACK TO THE WORLD OF THE WAKING!
OOF!
IT'S ABOUT TIME YOU WOKE UP TO SAY HELLO TO THE NEW WORLD-
(WHICH IS ACTUALLY THE OLDEST WORLD)
BUT WHY QUIBBLE WITH SEMANTICS WHEN REALITIES ARE BEING BANDIED ABOUT?
AM I RIGHT?
HA!
UM-
SURE.
WHAT IS THIS?
MY WITCH'S LAIR, OF COURSE.
WHERE I TOIL AND TROUBLE DAILY!
I'M SEARCHING FOR CLUES, INKLINGS OR NOTIONS-
-ABOUT WHERE YOUR PARENTS MAY HAVE GONE.

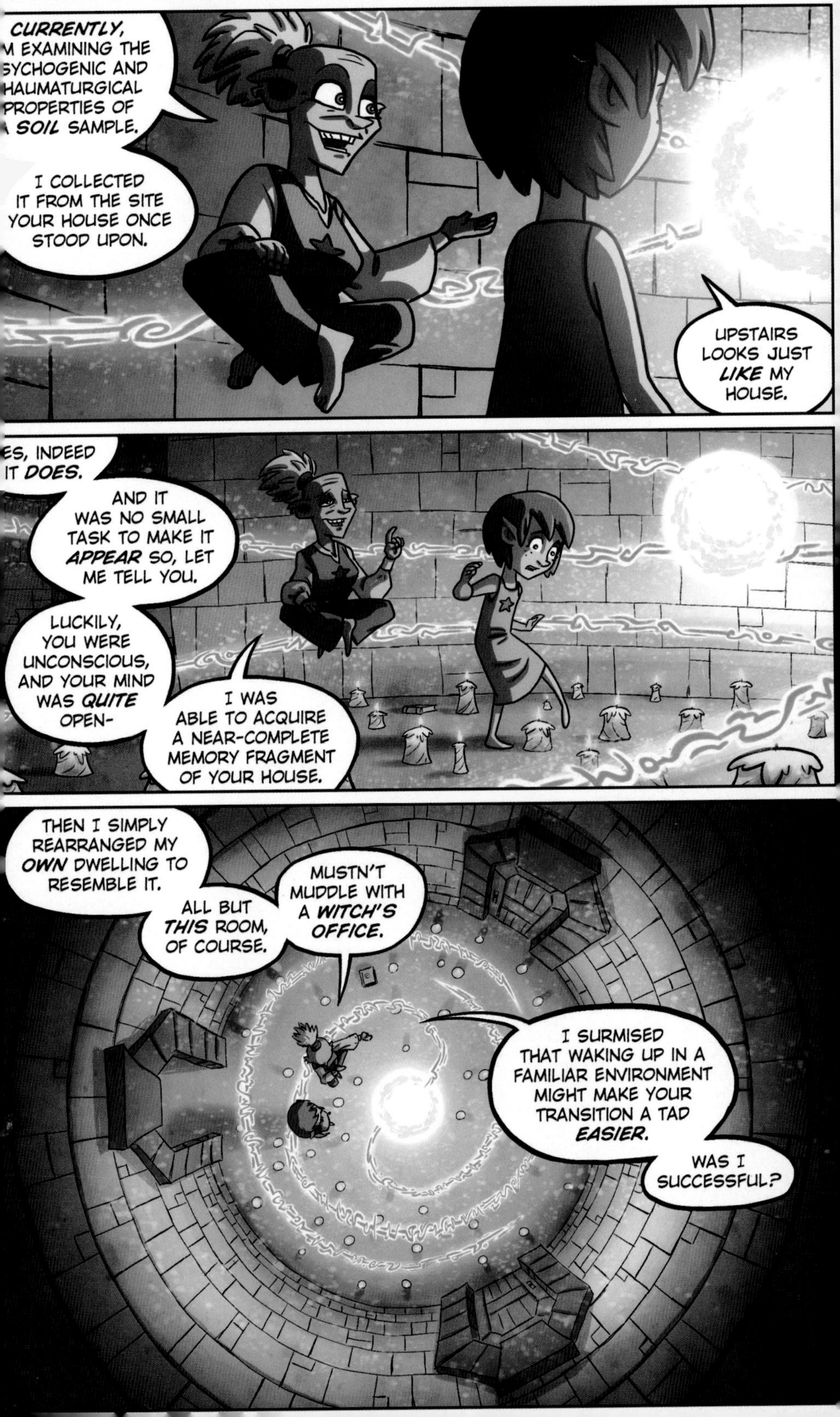
CURRENTLY, M EXAMINING THE SYCHOGENIC AND HAUMATURGICAL PROPERTIES OF A SOIL SAMPLE.
I COLLECTED IT FROM THE SITE YOUR HOUSE ONCE STOOD UPON.
UPSTAIRS LOOKS JUST LIKE MY HOUSE.
ES, INDEED IT DOES.
AND IT WAS NO SMALL TASK TO MAKE IT APPEAR SO, LET ME TELL YOU.
LUCKILY, YOU WERE UNCONSCIOUS, AND YOUR MIND WAS QUITE OPEN-
I WAS ABLE TO ACQUIRE A NEAR-COMPLETE MEMORY FRAGMENT OF YOUR HOUSE.
THEN I SIMPLY REARRANGED MY OWN DWELLING TO RESEMBLE IT.
ALL BUT THIS ROOM, OF COURSE.
MUSTN'T MUDDLE WITH A WITCH'S OFFICE.
I SURMISED THAT WAKING UP IN A FAMILIAR ENVIRONMENT MIGHT MAKE YOUR TRANSITION A TAD EASIER.
WAS I SUCCESSFUL?

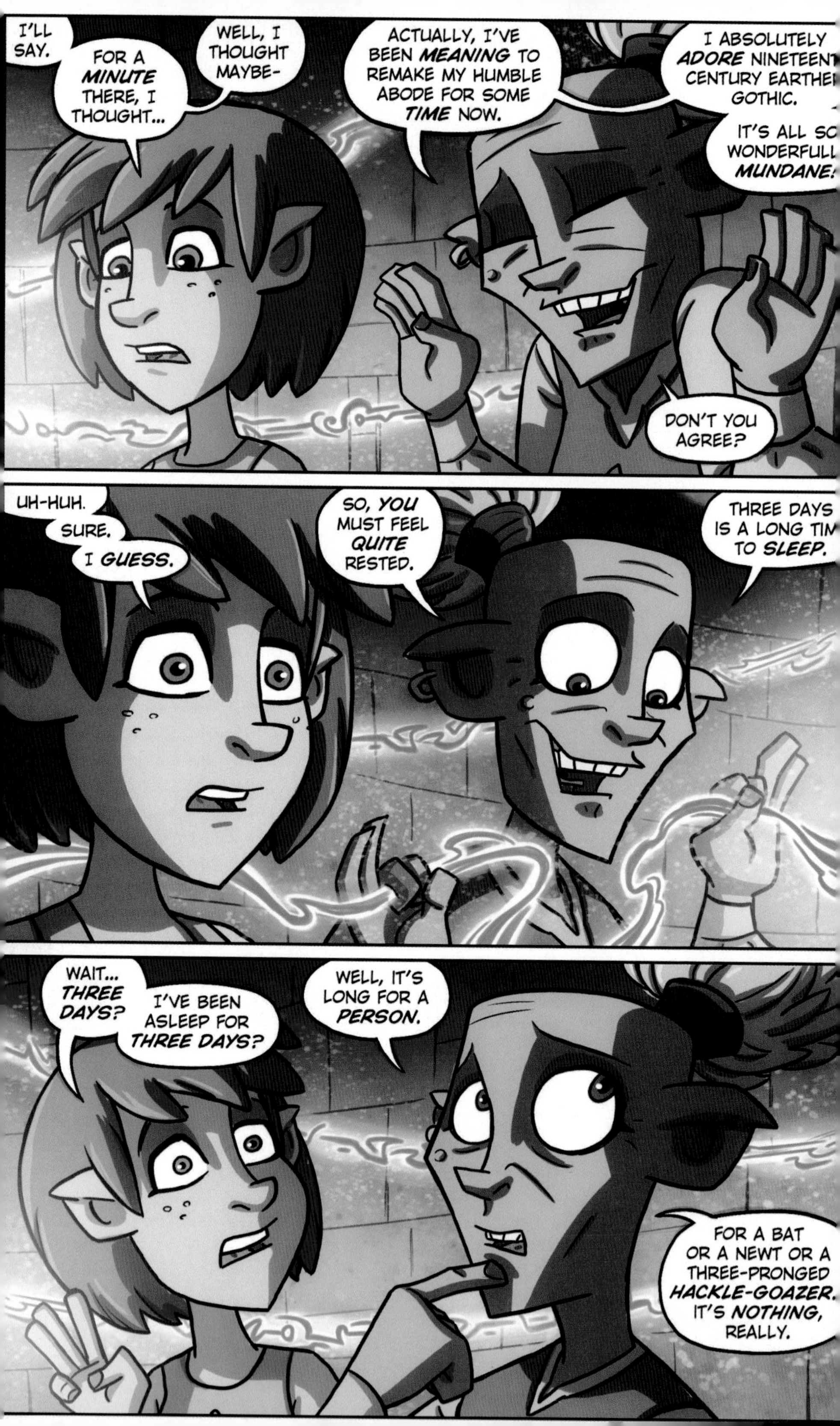
I'LL SAY.
FOR A MINUTE THERE, I THOUGHT...
WELL, I THOUGHT MAYBE-
ACTUALLY, I'VE BEEN MEANING TO REMAKE MY HUMBLE ABODE FOR SOME TIME NOW.
I ABSOLUTELY ADORE NINETEENT CENTURY EARTHE GOTHIC.
IT'S ALL SO WONDERFULL MUNDANE!
DON'T YOU AGREE?
UH-HUH.
SURE.
I GUESS.
SO, YOU MUST FEEL QUITE RESTED.
THREE DAYS IS A LONG TIM TO SLEEP.
WAIT... THREE DAYS?
I'VE BEEN ASLEEP FOR THREE DAYS?
WELL, IT'S LONG FOR A PERSON.
FOR A BAT OR A NEWT OR A THREE-PRONGED HACKLE-GOAZER. IT'S NOTHING, REALLY.

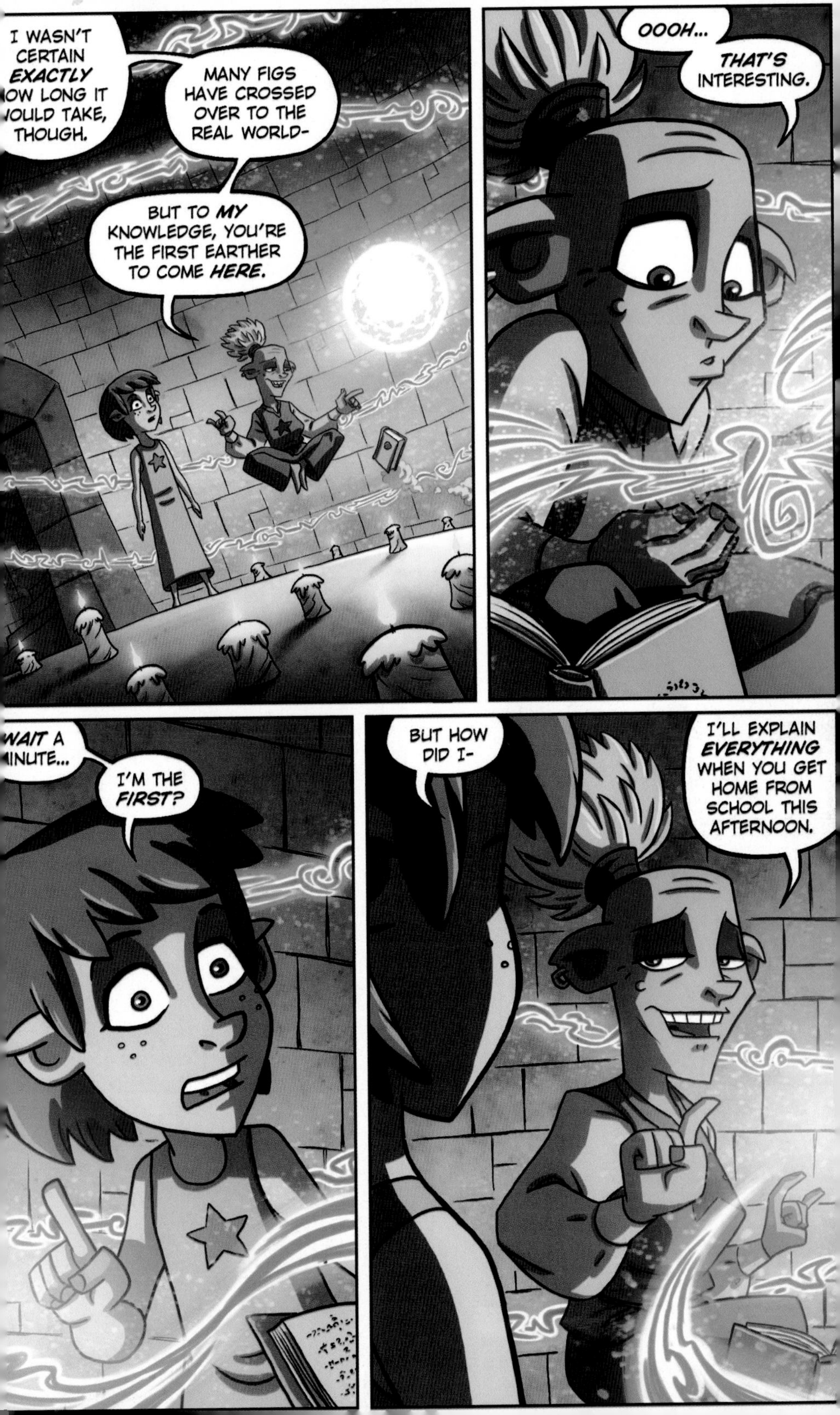
I WASN'T CERTAIN EXACTLY OW LONG IT VOULD TAKE, THOUGH.
MANY FIGS HAVE CROSSED OVER TO THE REAL WORLD-
BUT TO MY KNOWLEDGE, YOU'RE THE FIRST EARTHER TO COME HERE.
OOOH... THAT'S INTERESTING.
WAIT A INUTE...
I'M THE FIRST?
BUT HOW DID I-
I'LL EXPLAIN EVERYTHING WHEN YOU GET HOME FROM SCHOOL THIS AFTERNOON.

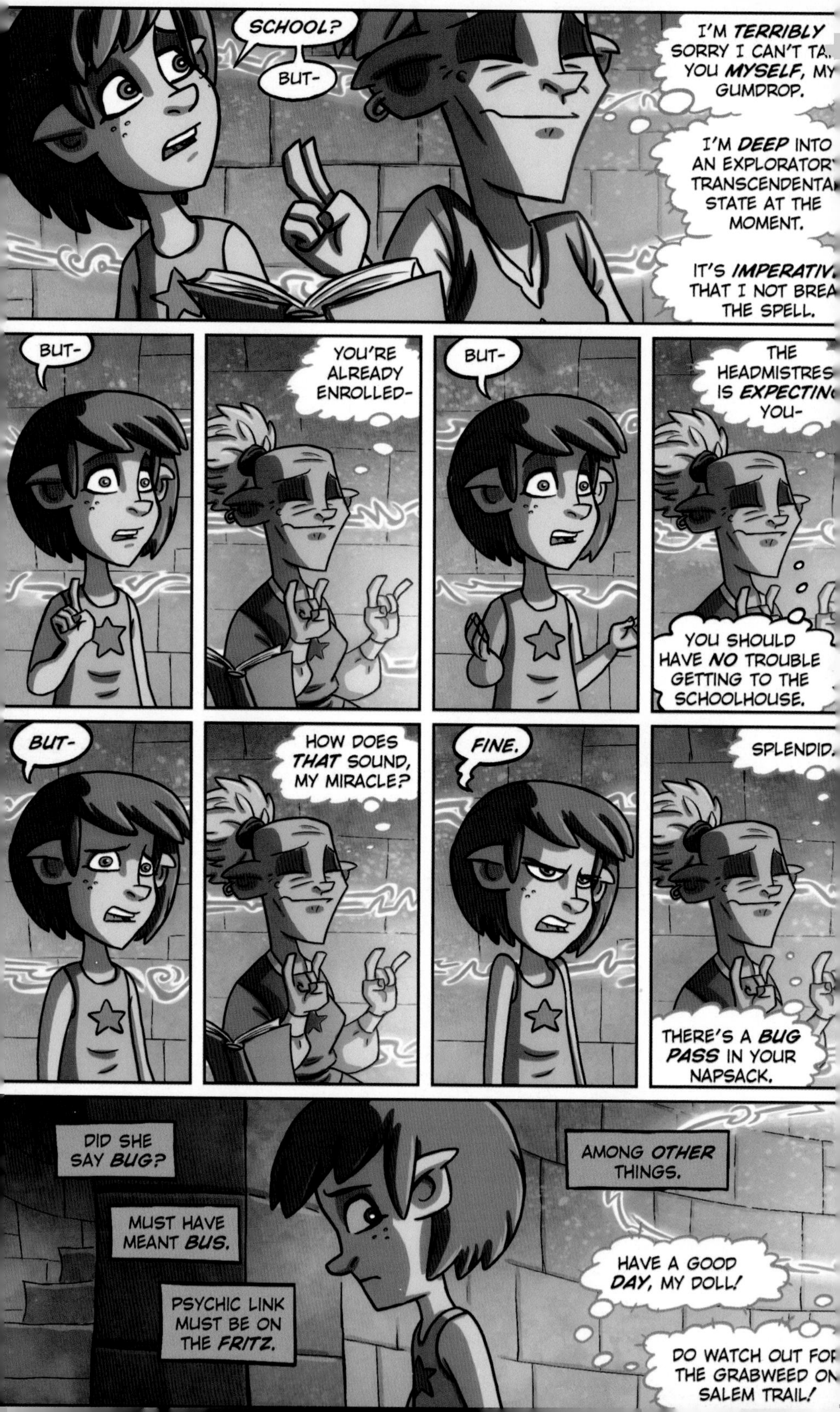
SCHOOL?
BUT-
I'M TERRIBLY SORRY I CAN'T TA YOU MYSELF, MY GUMDROP.
I'M DEEP INTO AN EXPLORATOR TRANSCENDENTA STATE AT THE MOMENT.
IT'S IMPERATIV THAT I NOT BREA THE SPELL.
BUT-
YOU'RE ALREADY ENROLLED-
BUT-
THE HEADMISTRES IS EXPECTIN YOU-
YOU SHOULD HAVE NO TROUBLE GETTING TO THE SCHOOLHOUSE.
BUT-
HOW DOES THAT SOUND, MY MIRACLE?
FINE.
SPLENDID.
THERE'S A BUG PASS IN YOUR NAPSACK.
DID SHE SAY BUG?
MUST HAVE MEANT BUS.
PSYCHIC LINK MUST BE ON THE FRITZ.
AMONG OTHER THINGS.
HAVE A GOOD DAY, MY DOLL!
DO WATCH OUT FO THE GRABWEED O SALEM TRAIL!

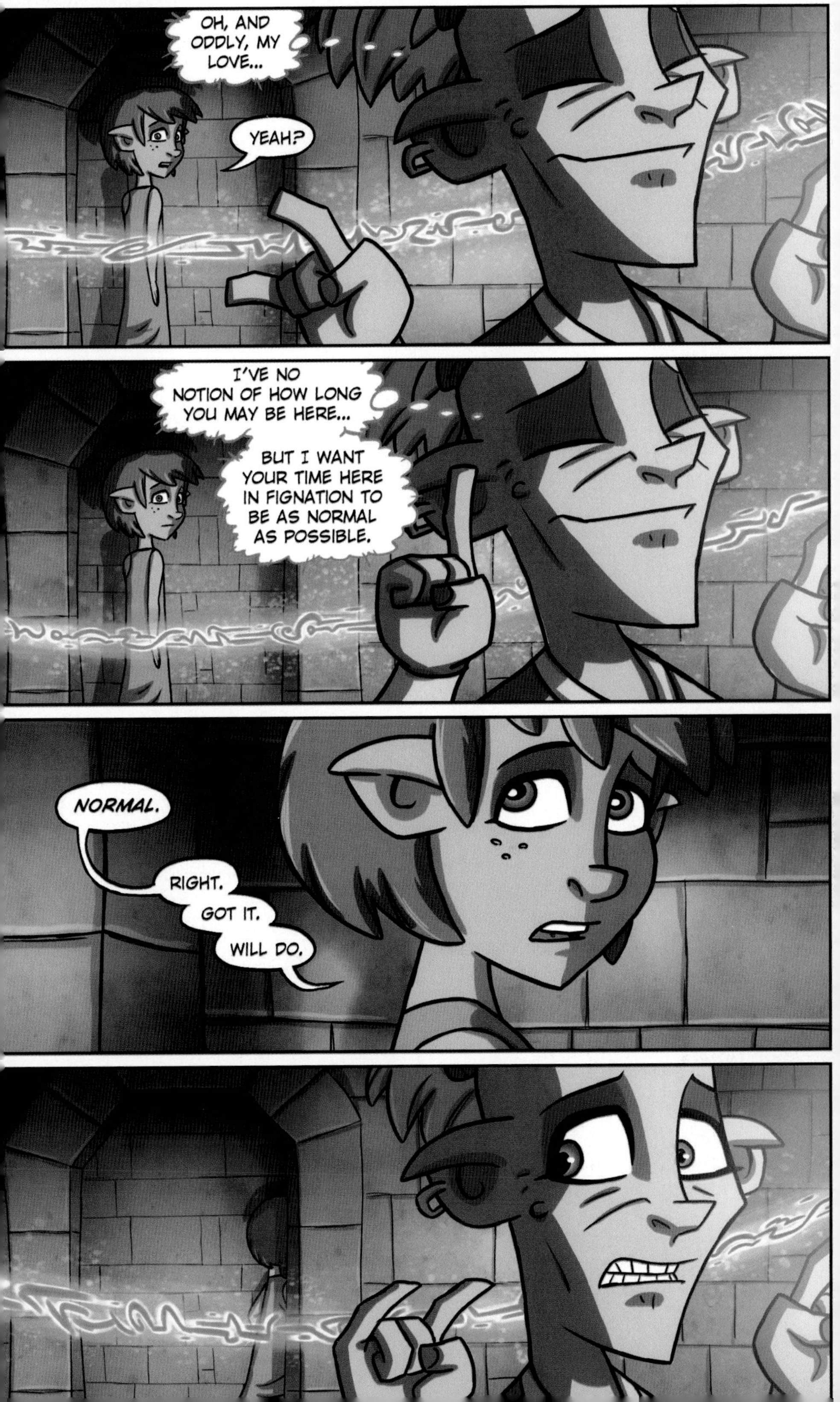
OH, AND ODDLY, MY LOVE...
YEAH?
I'VE NO NOTION OF HOW LONG YOU MAY BE HERE...
BUT I WANT YOUR TIME HERE IN FIGNATION TO BE AS NORMAL AS POSSIBLE.
NORMAL.
RIGHT.
GOT IT.
WILL DO.

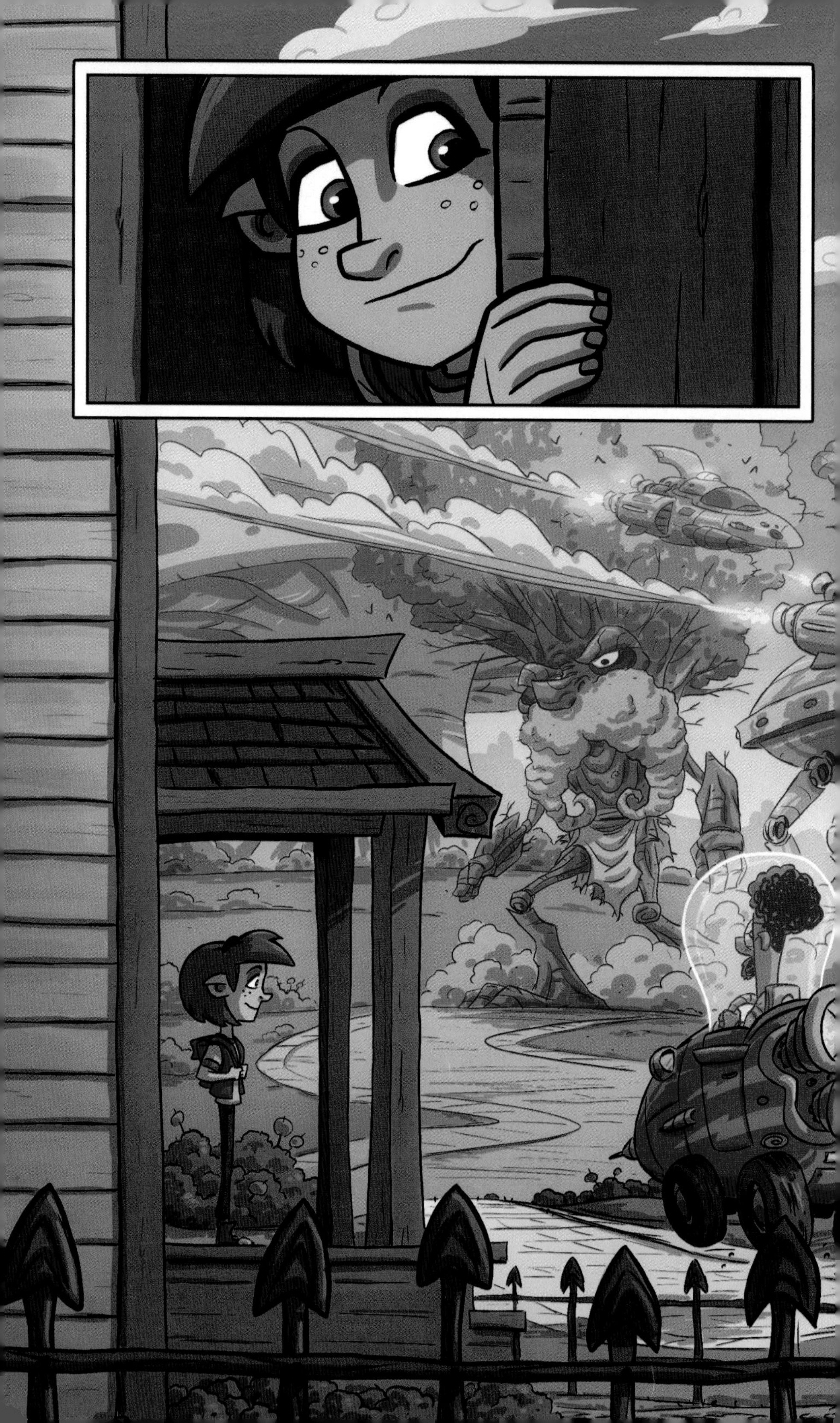

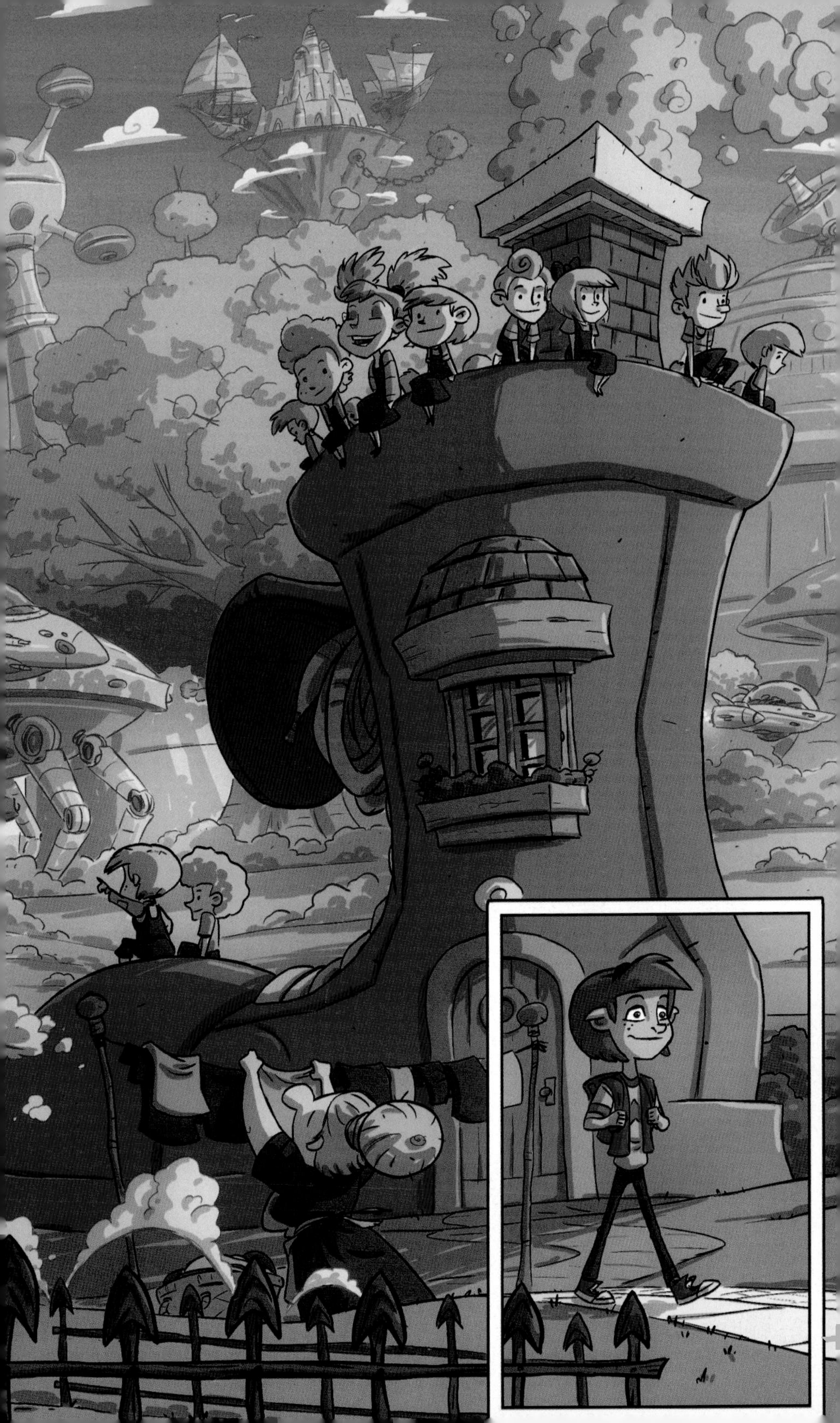

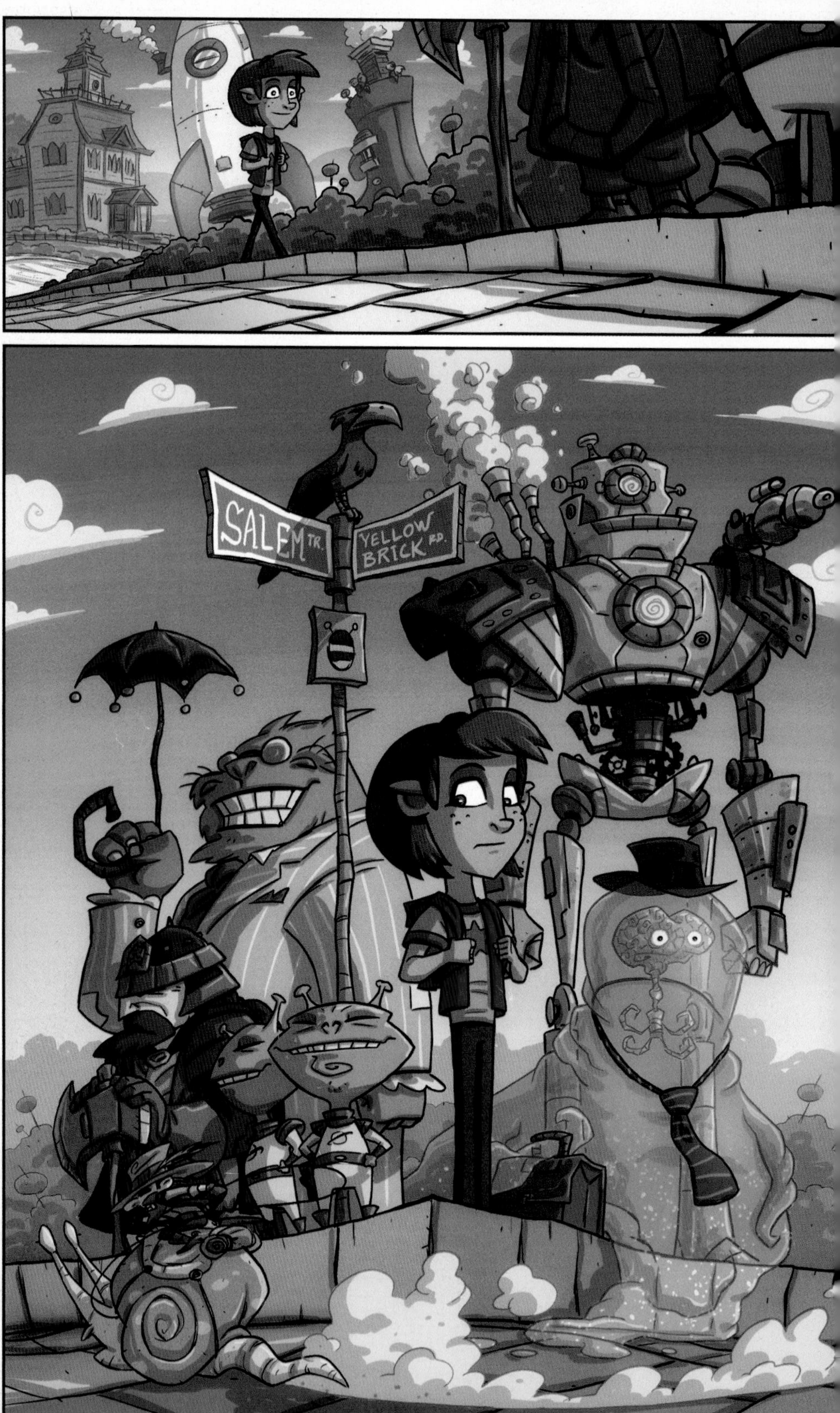
SALEM TR.
YELLOW BRICK RD.

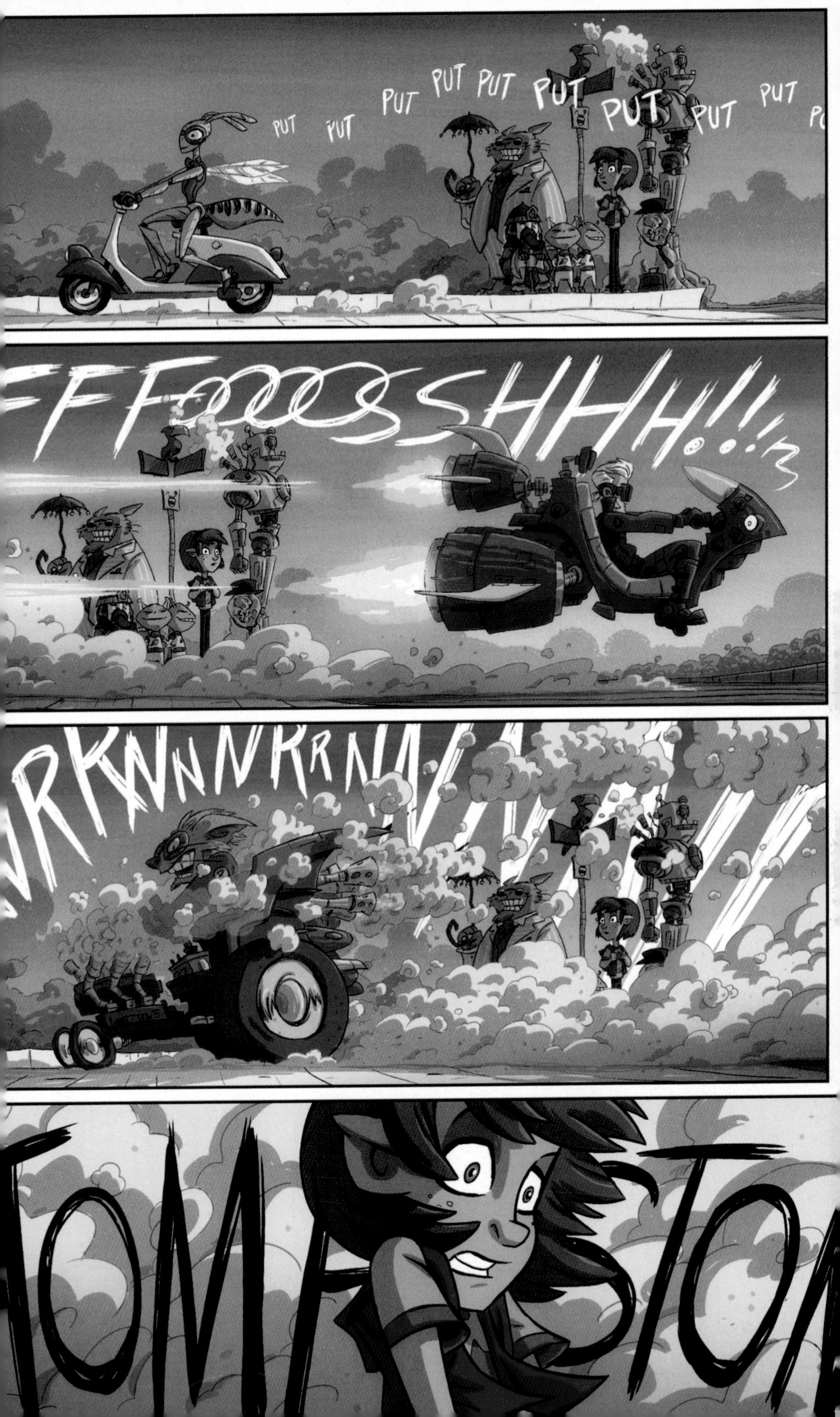
PUT PUT PUT PUT PUT PUT PUT PUT PUT PUT
FFFOOOSSHHH!!!
TOM

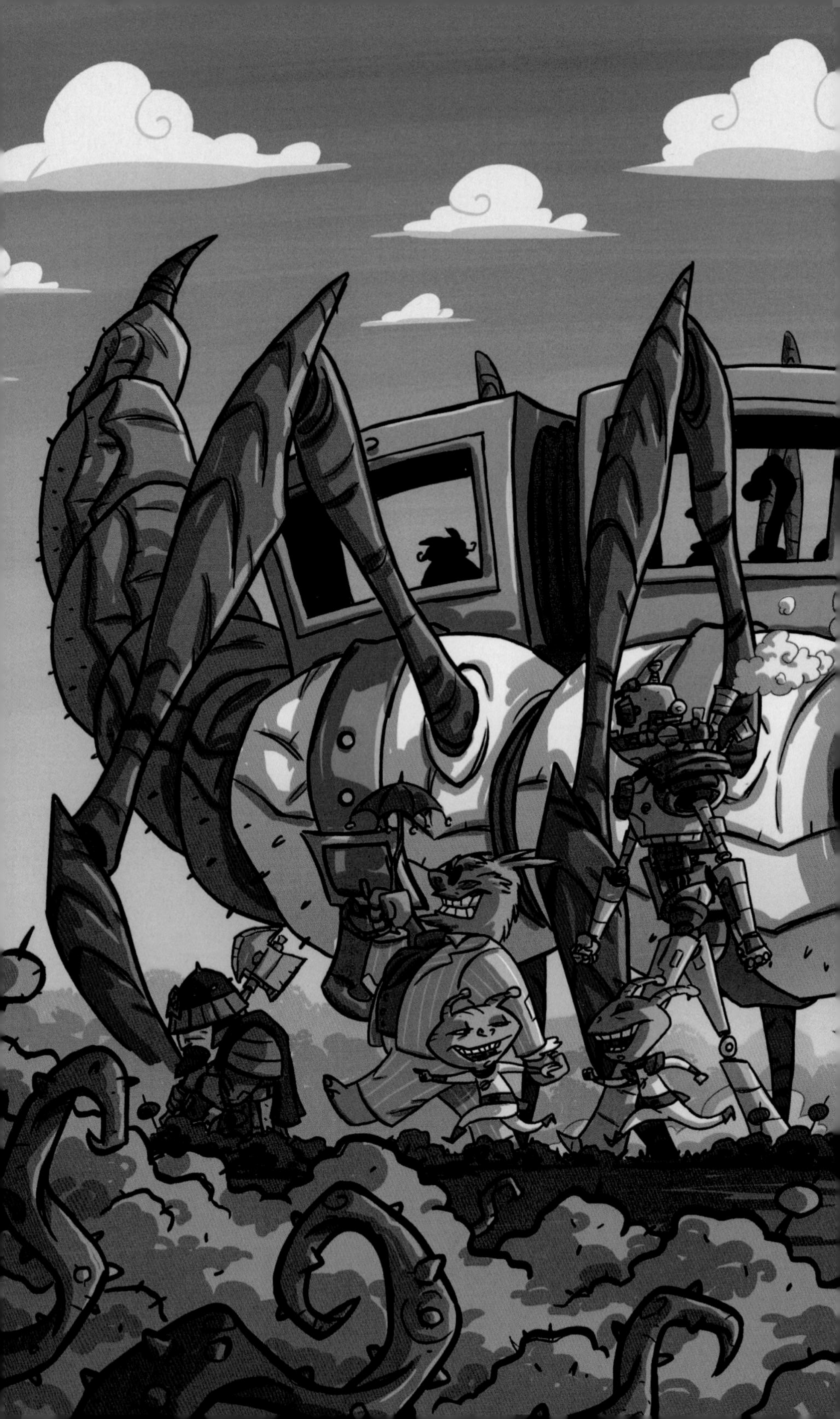

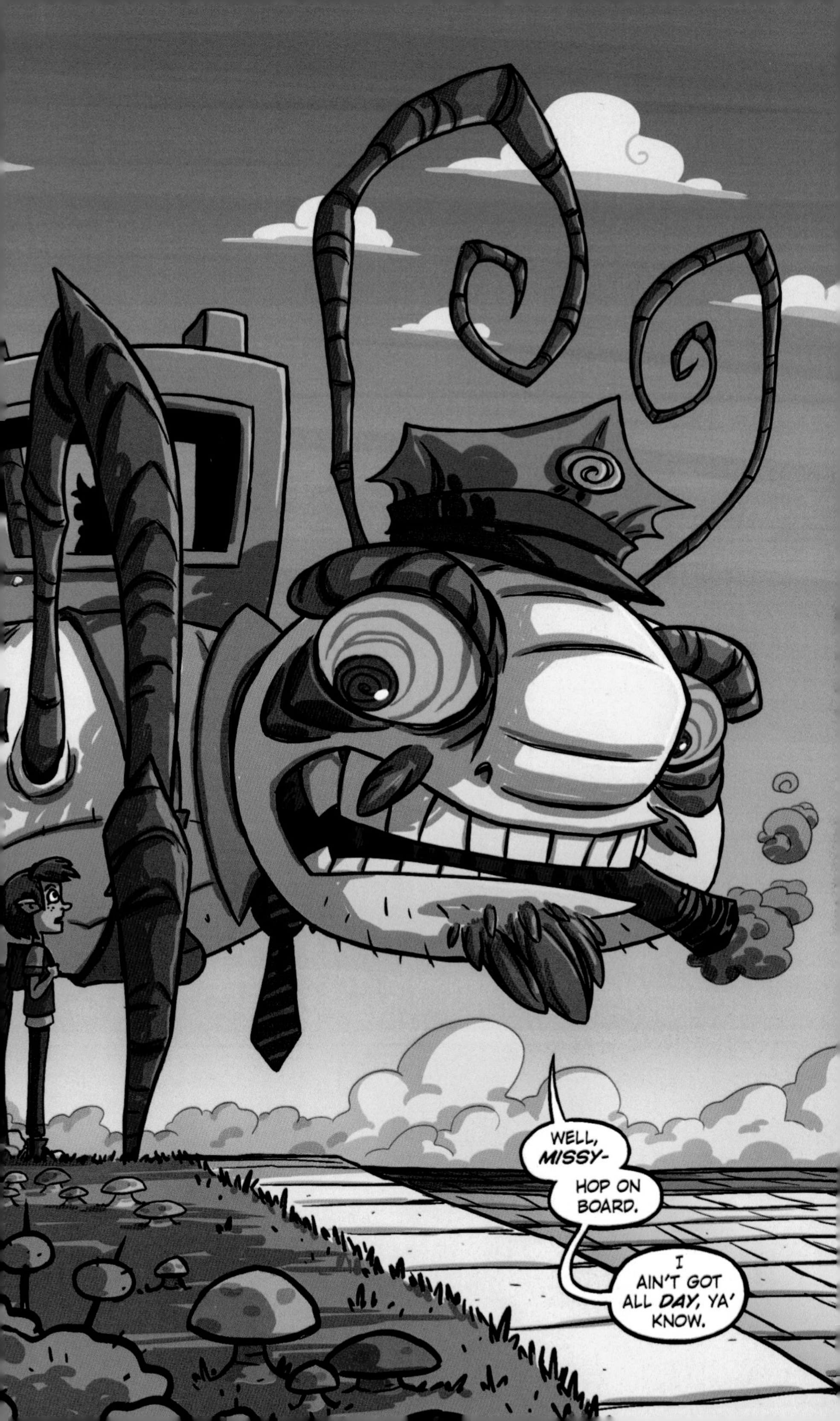
WELL, *MISSY*-
HOP ON BOARD.
I AIN'T GOT ALL *DAY*, YA' KNOW.

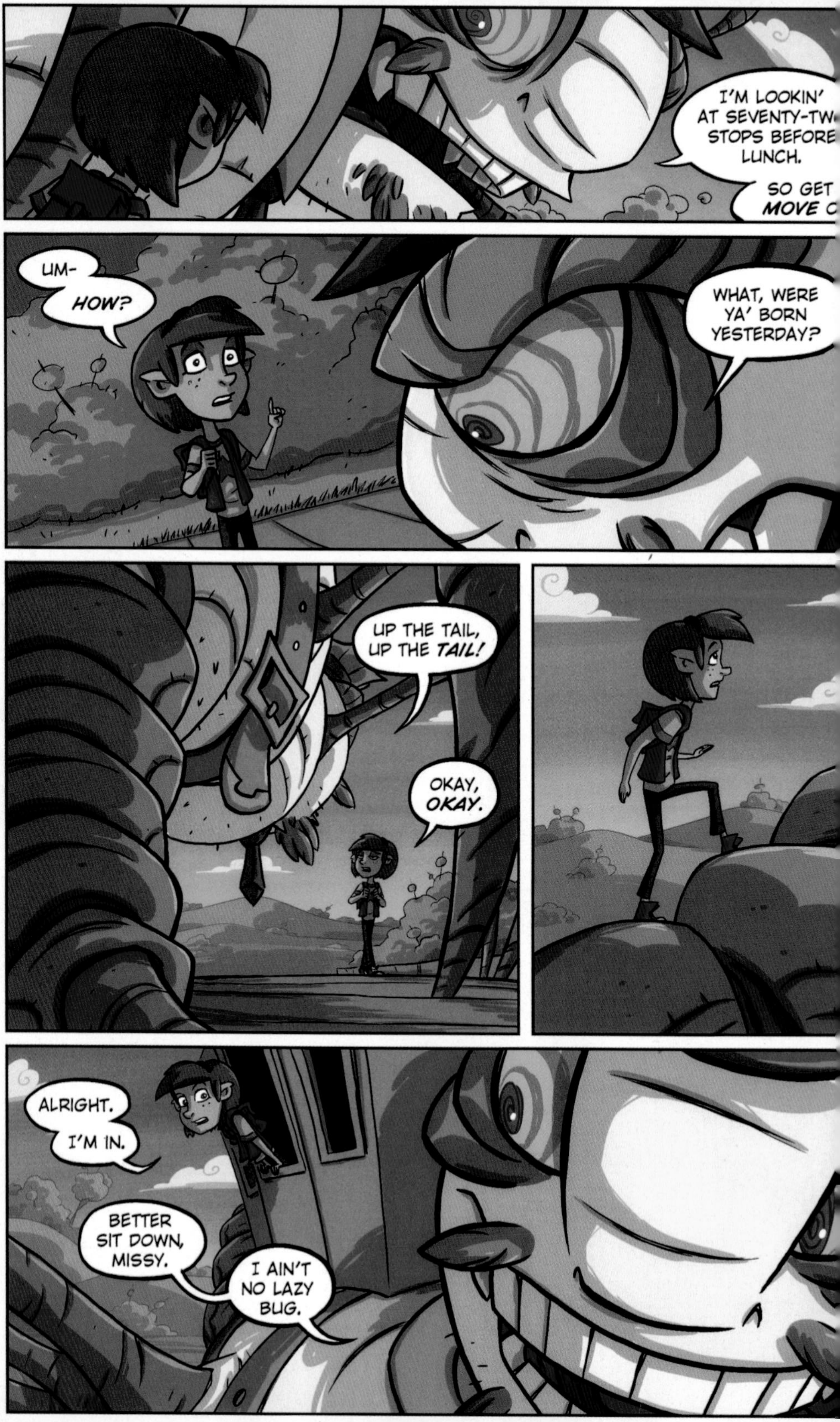
I'M LOOKIN' AT SEVENTY-TW STOPS BEFORE LUNCH.
SO GET MOVE
UM- HOW?
WHAT, WERE YA' BORN YESTERDAY?
UP THE TAIL, UP THE TAIL!
OKAY, OKAY.
ALRIGHT.
I'M IN.
BETTER SIT DOWN, MISSY.
I AIN'T NO LAZY BUG.

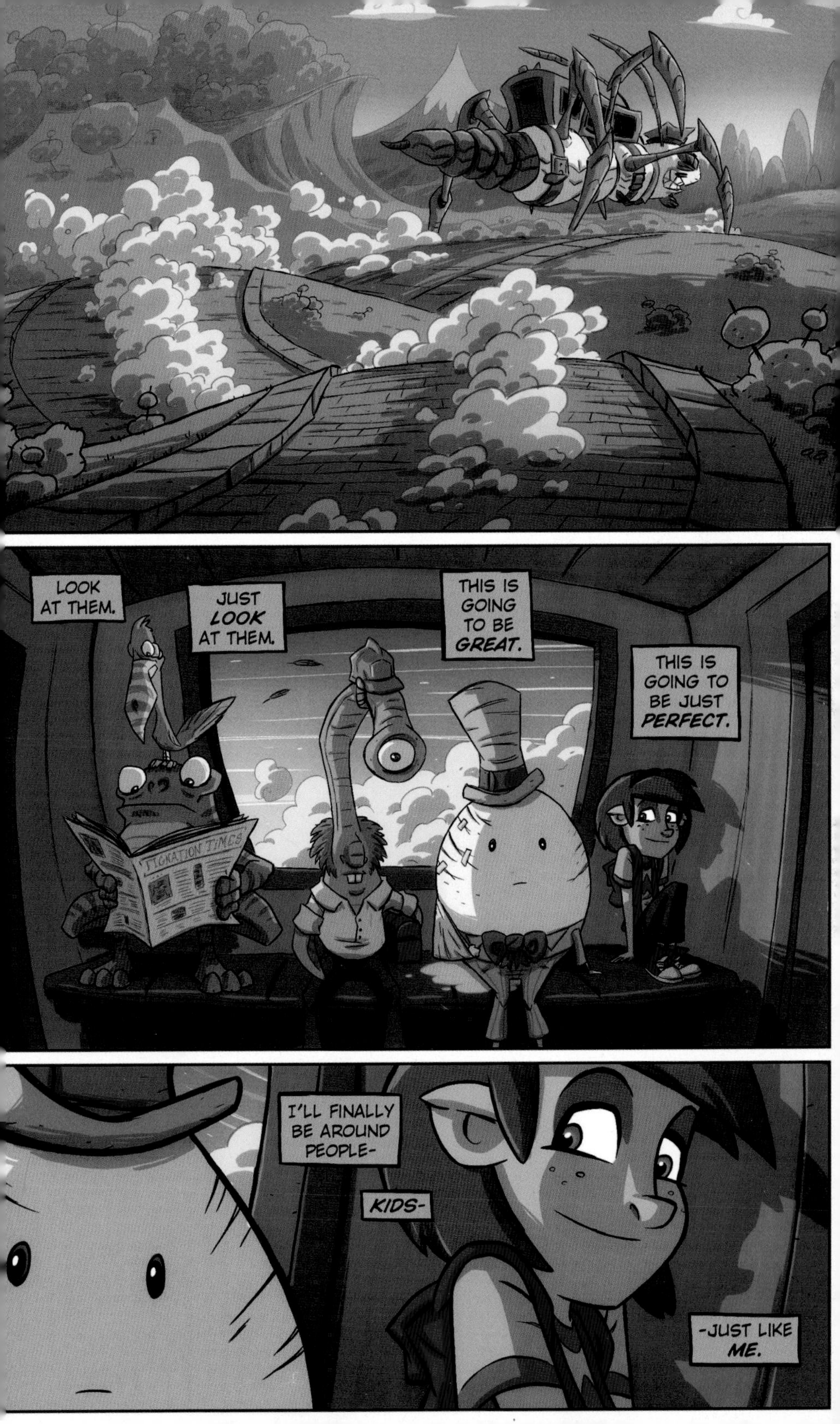
LOOK AT THEM.
JUST *LOOK* AT THEM.
THIS IS GOING TO BE *GREAT*.
THIS IS GOING TO BE JUST *PERFECT*.
I'LL FINALLY BE AROUND PEOPLE-
KIDS-
-JUST LIKE *ME*.

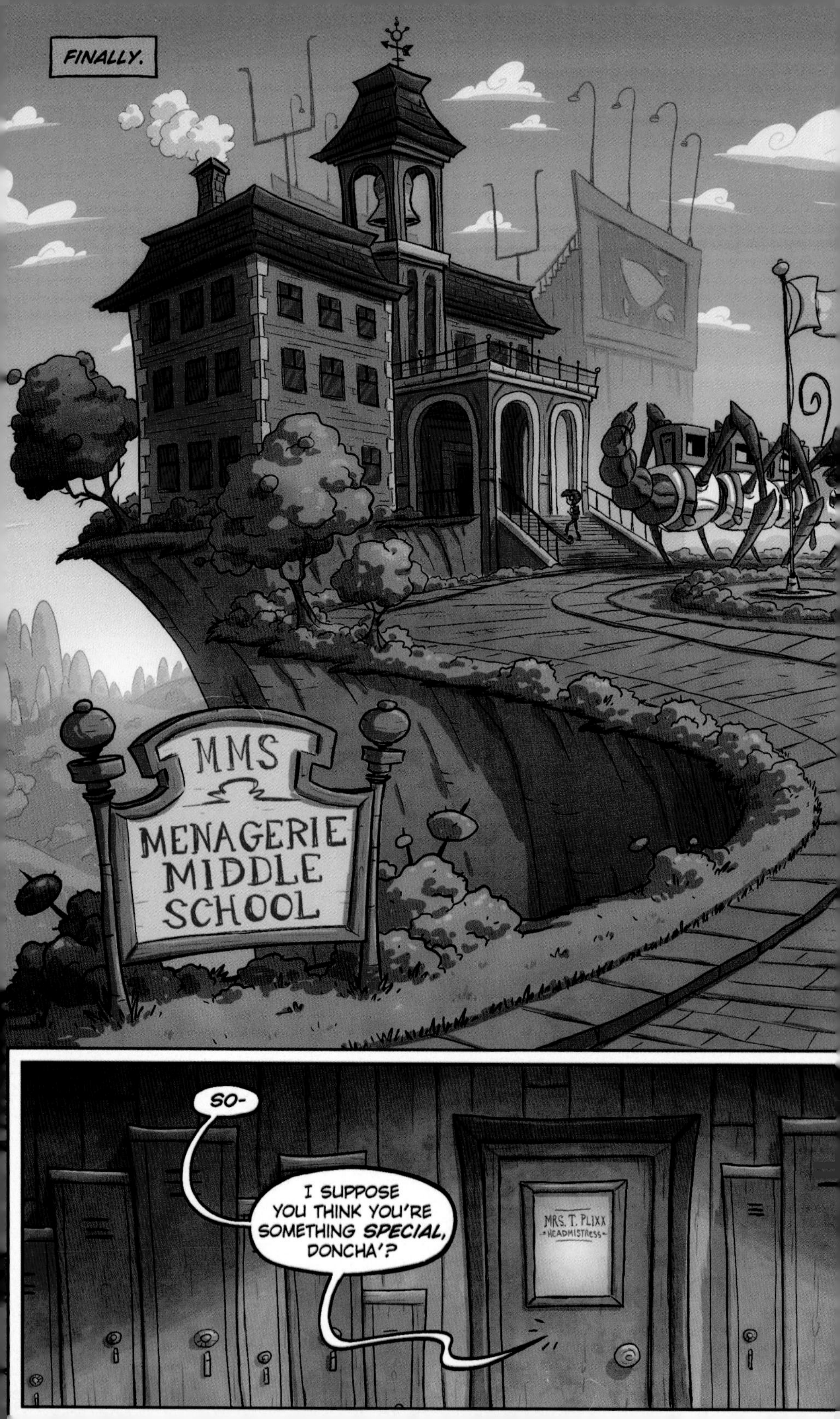
FINALLY.
MMS
MENAGERIE MIDDLE SCHOOL
SO-
I SUPPOSE YOU THINK YOU'RE SOMETHING *SPECIAL*, DONCHA'?
MRS. T. PLIXX
HEADMISTRESS

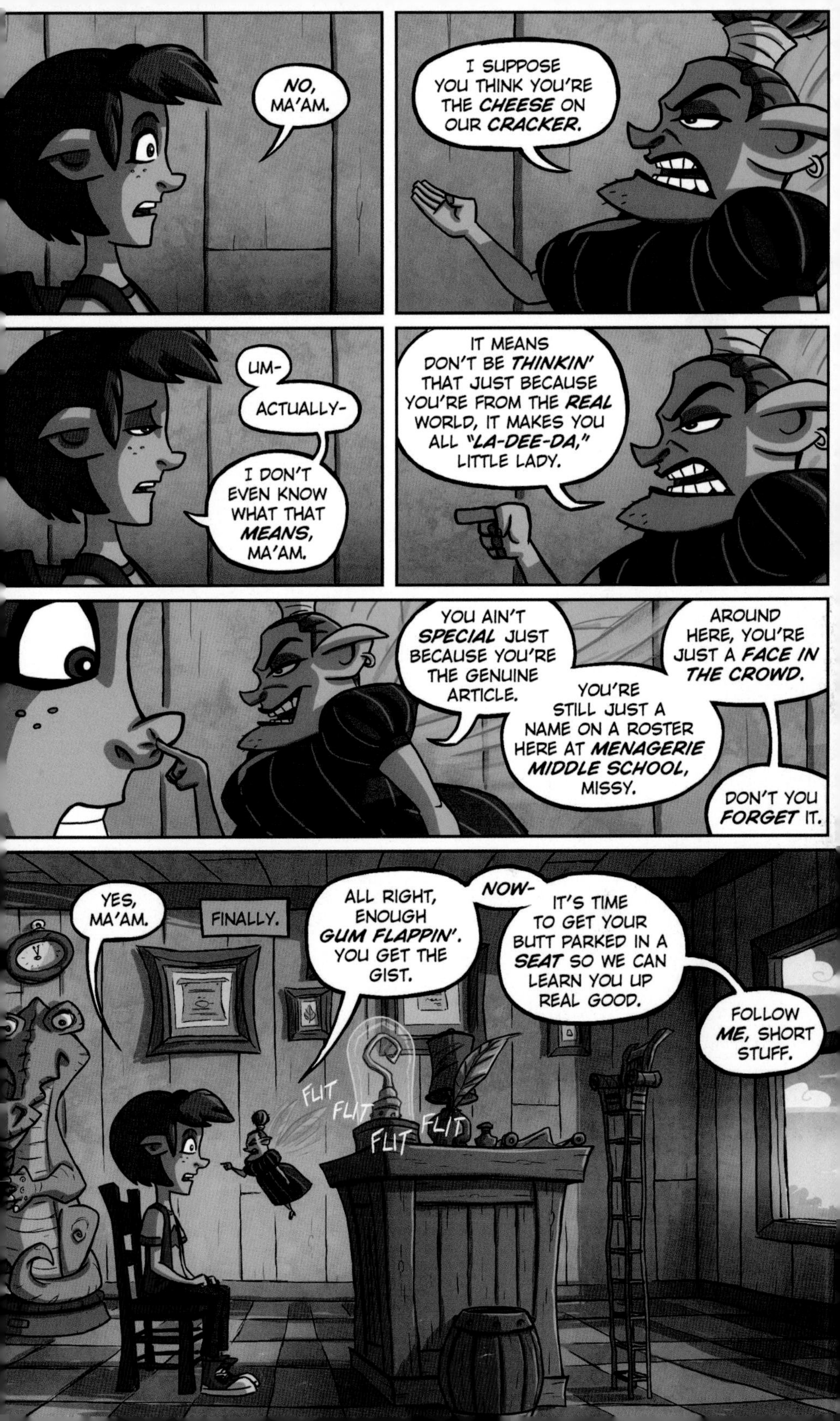
NO, MA'AM.
I SUPPOSE YOU THINK YOU'RE THE CHEESE ON OUR CRACKER.
UM-
ACTUALLY-
I DON'T EVEN KNOW WHAT THAT MEANS, MA'AM.
IT MEANS DON'T BE THINKIN' THAT JUST BECAUSE YOU'RE FROM THE REAL WORLD, IT MAKES YOU ALL "LA-DEE-DA," LITTLE LADY.
YOU AIN'T SPECIAL JUST BECAUSE YOU'RE THE GENUINE ARTICLE.
YOU'RE STILL JUST A NAME ON A ROSTER HERE AT MENAGERIE MIDDLE SCHOOL, MISSY.
AROUND HERE, YOU'RE JUST A FACE IN THE CROWD.
DON'T YOU FORGET IT.
YES, MA'AM.
FINALLY.
ALL RIGHT, ENOUGH GUM FLAPPIN'. YOU GET THE GIST.
NOW-
IT'S TIME TO GET YOUR BUTT PARKED IN A SEAT SO WE CAN LEARN YOU UP REAL GOOD.
FOLLOW ME, SHORT STUFF.
FLIT FLIT FLIT FLIT

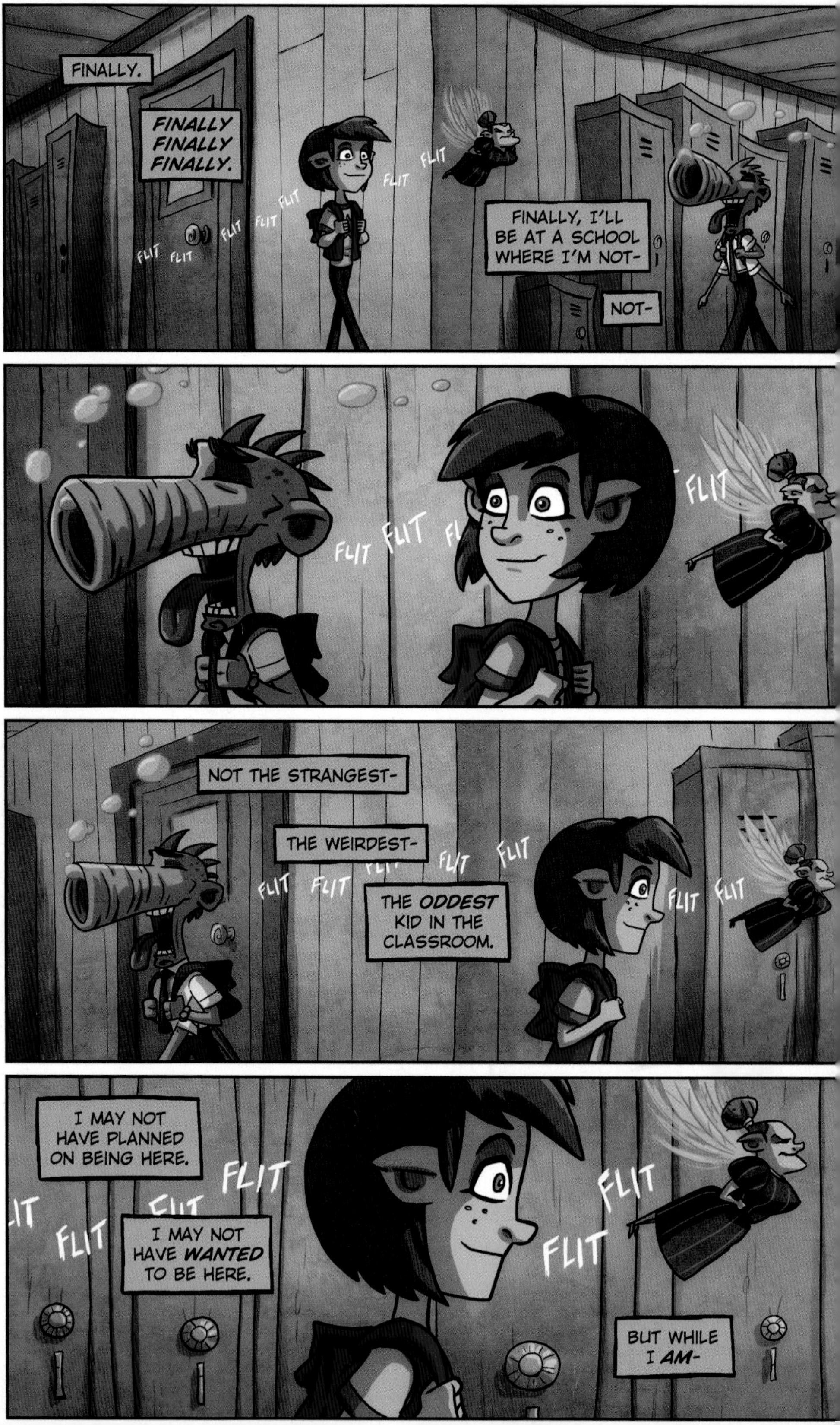
FINALLY.
FINALLY FINALLY FINALLY.
FLIT FLIT FLIT FLIT FLIT FLIT FLIT FLIT
FINALLY, I'LL BE AT A SCHOOL WHERE I'M NOT-
NOT-
FLIT FLIT FLIT
NOT THE STRANGEST-
THE WEIRDEST-
FLIT FLIT FLIT FLIT FLIT FLIT
THE *ODDEST* KID IN THE CLASSROOM.
I MAY NOT HAVE PLANNED ON BEING HERE.
FLIT FLIT FLIT FLIT
I MAY NOT HAVE *WANTED* TO BE HERE.
BUT WHILE I *AM*-

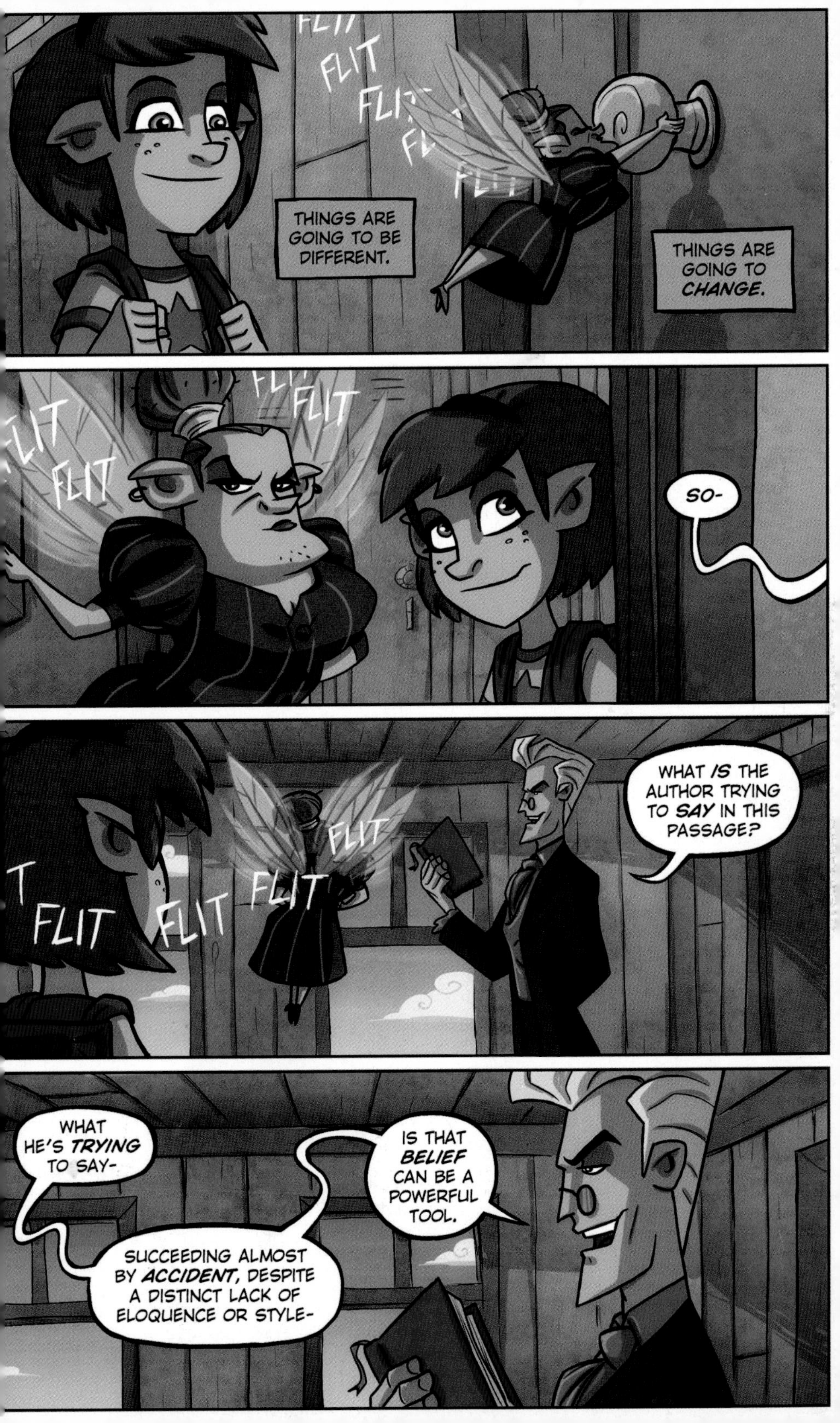
FLIT FLIT FLIT FLIT FLIT
THINGS ARE GOING TO BE DIFFERENT.
THINGS ARE GOING TO CHANGE.
FLIT FLIT FLIT FLIT
SO-
FLIT FLIT FLIT FLIT FLIT
WHAT IS THE AUTHOR TRYING TO SAY IN THIS PASSAGE?
WHAT HE'S TRYING TO SAY-
SUCCEEDING ALMOST BY ACCIDENT, DESPITE A DISTINCT LACK OF ELOQUENCE OR STYLE-
IS THAT BELIEF CAN BE A POWERFUL TOOL.

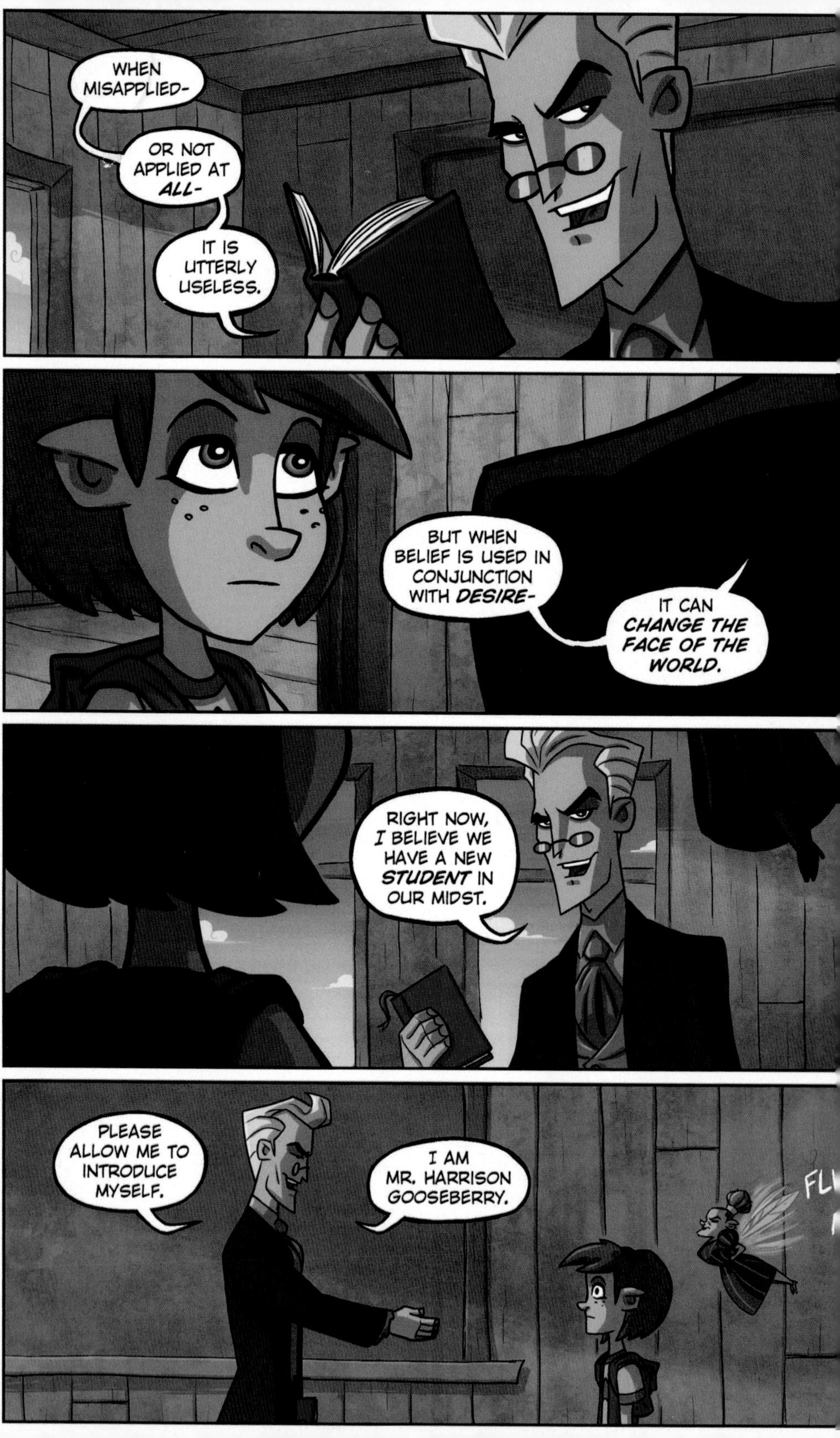
WHEN MISAPPLIED-
OR NOT APPLIED AT ALL-
IT IS UTTERLY USELESS.
BUT WHEN BELIEF IS USED IN CONJUNCTION WITH DESIRE-
IT CAN CHANGE THE FACE OF THE WORLD.
RIGHT NOW, I BELIEVE WE HAVE A NEW STUDENT IN OUR MIDST.
PLEASE ALLOW ME TO INTRODUCE MYSELF.
I AM MR. HARRISON GOOSEBERRY.

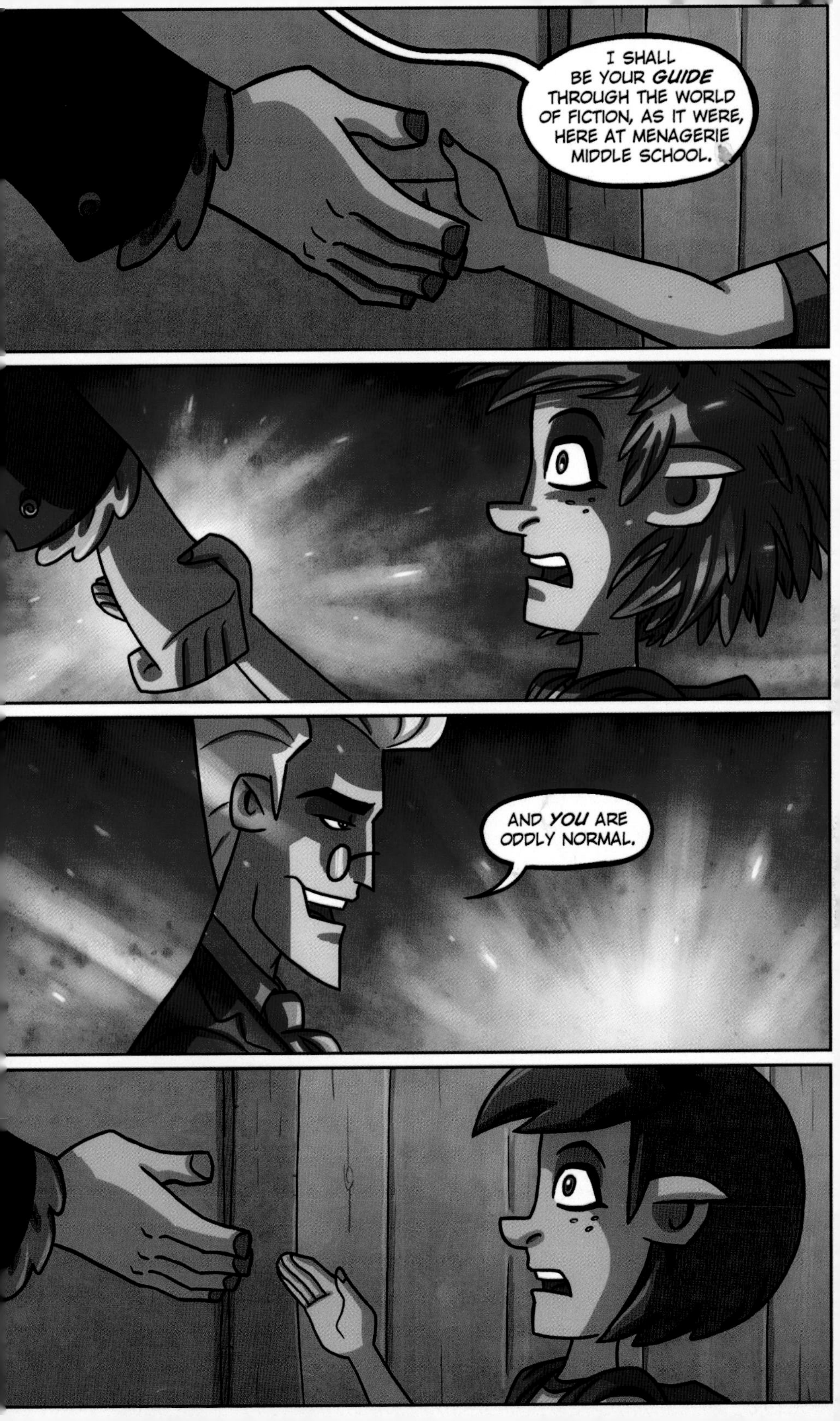
I SHALL BE YOUR GUIDE THROUGH THE WORLD OF FICTION, AS IT WERE, HERE AT MENAGERIE MIDDLE SCHOOL.
AND YOU ARE ODDLY NORMAL.

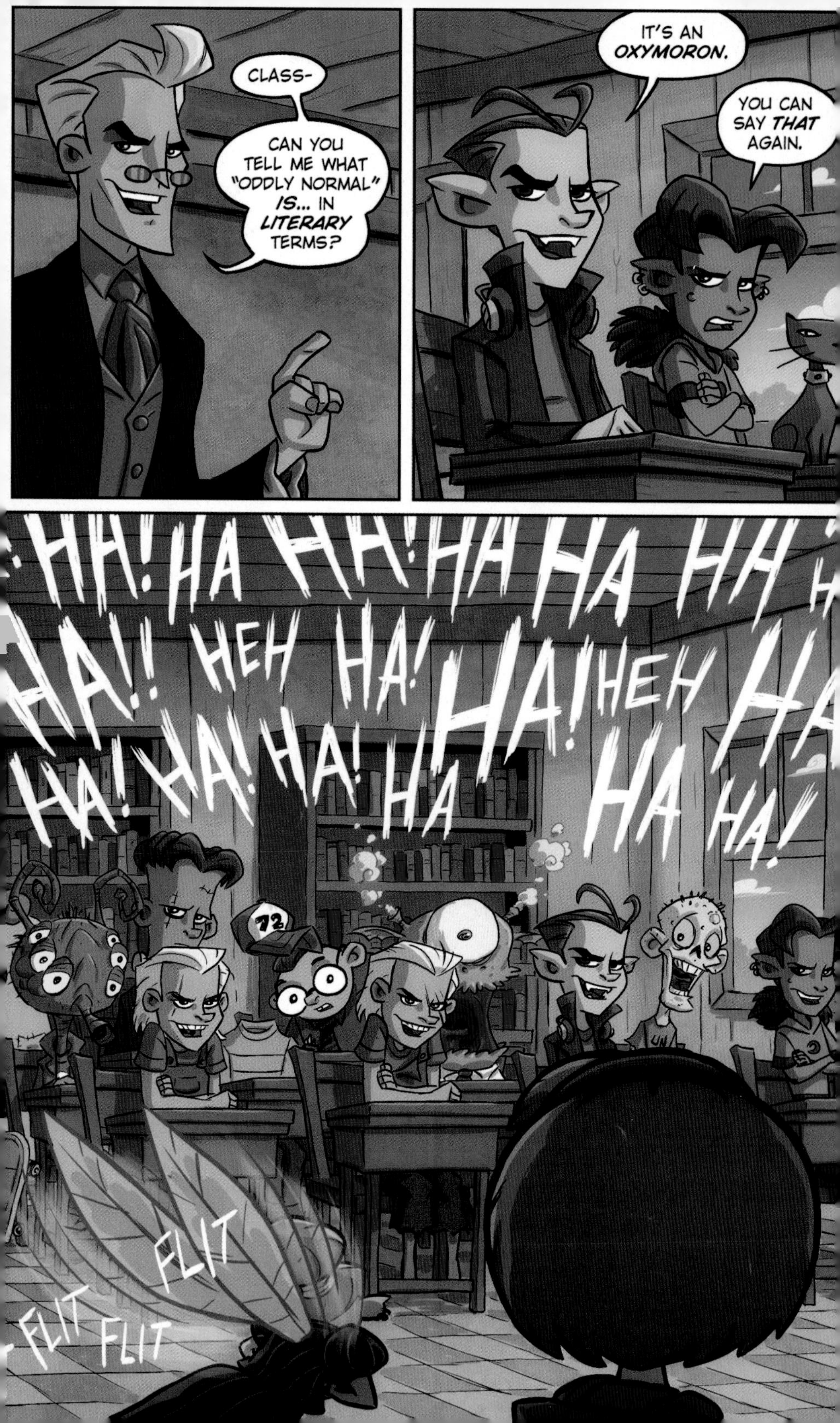
CLASS-
CAN YOU TELL ME WHAT "ODDLY NORMAL" IS... IN LITERARY TERMS?
IT'S AN OXYMORON.
YOU CAN SAY THAT AGAIN.
HA! HA HA! HA HA HA
HA!! HEH HA! HA! HEH HA
HA! HA! HA! HA HA HA HA!
FLIT
FLIT FLIT

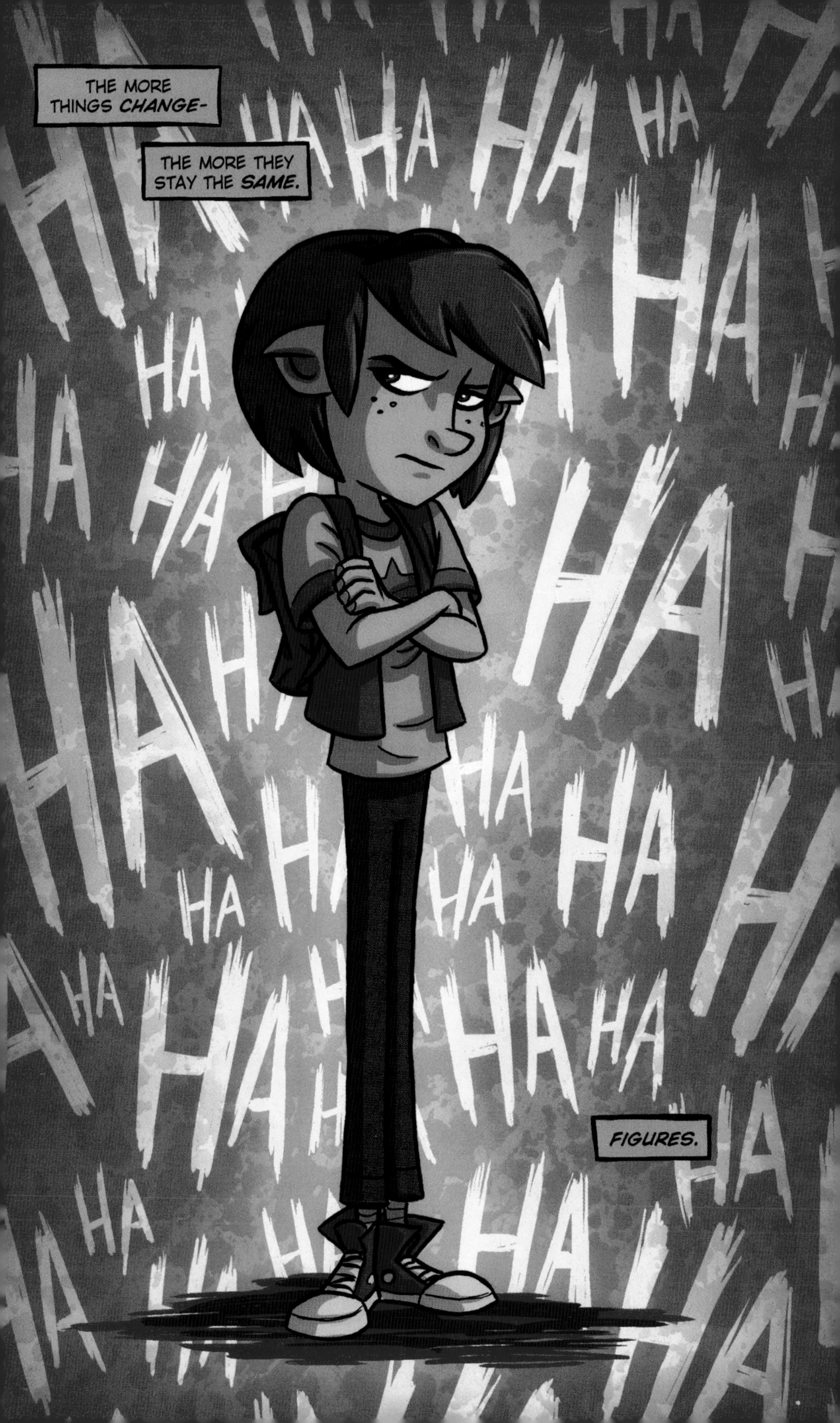
THE MORE THINGS CHANGE-
THE MORE THEY STAY THE SAME.
FIGURES.

Chapter 4 The Class Menagerie

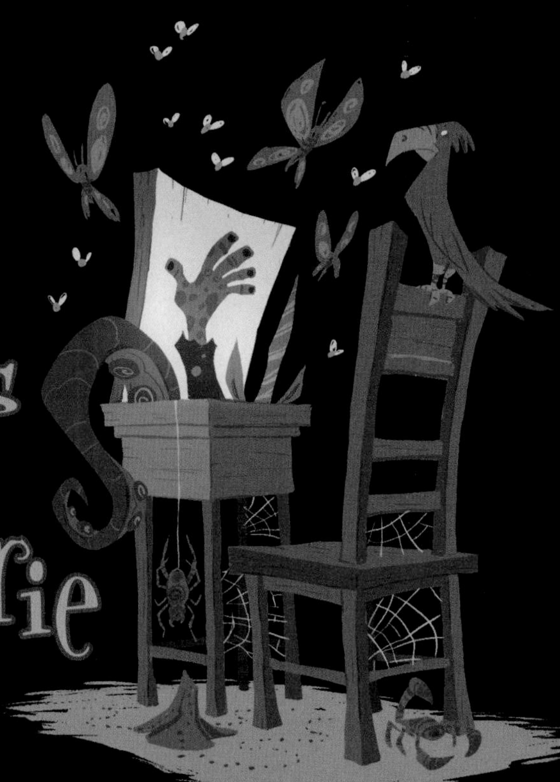

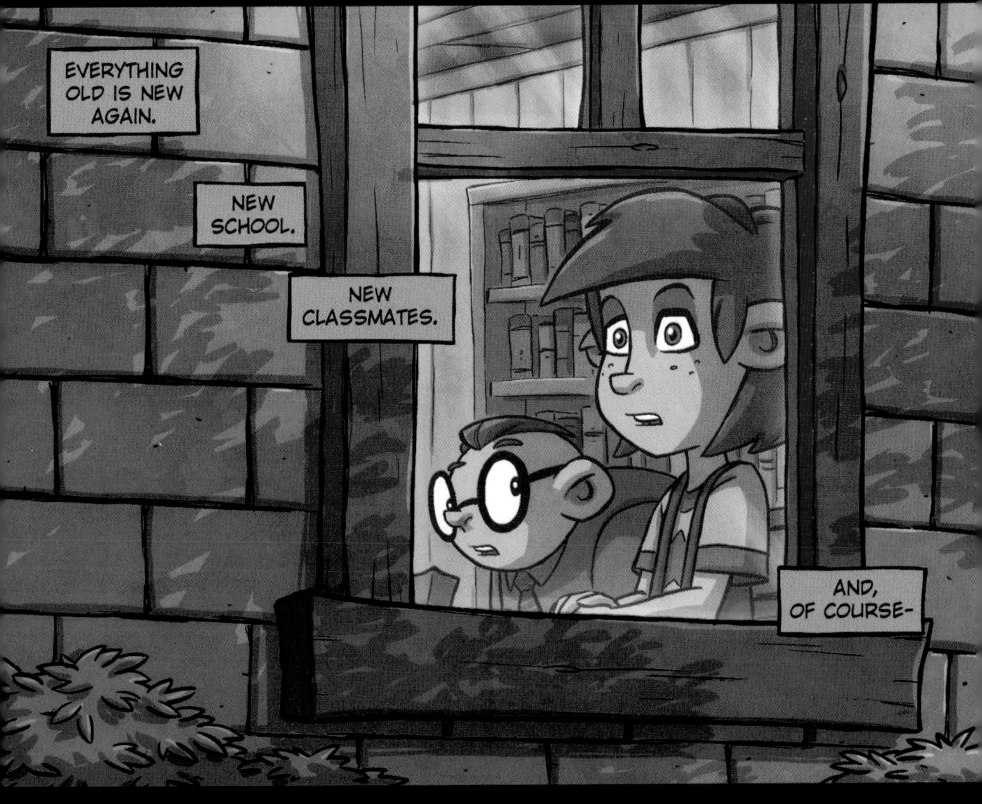
EVERYTHING OLD IS NEW AGAIN.
NEW SCHOOL.
NEW CLASSMATES.
AND, OF COURSE-

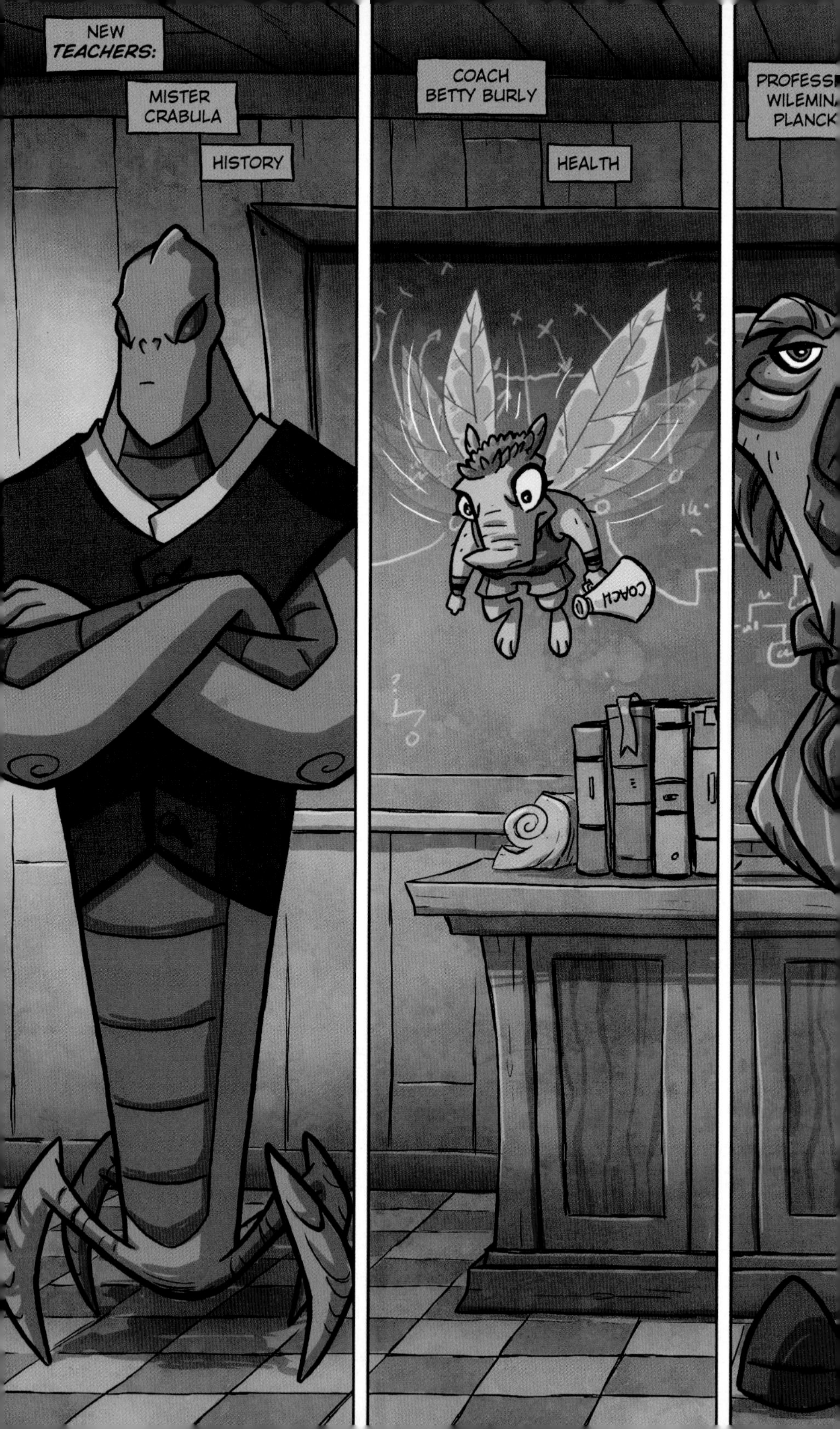
NEW *TEACHERS*:
MISTER CRABULA
HISTORY
COACH BETTY BURLY
HEALTH
COACH
PROFESS
WILEMIN
PLANCK

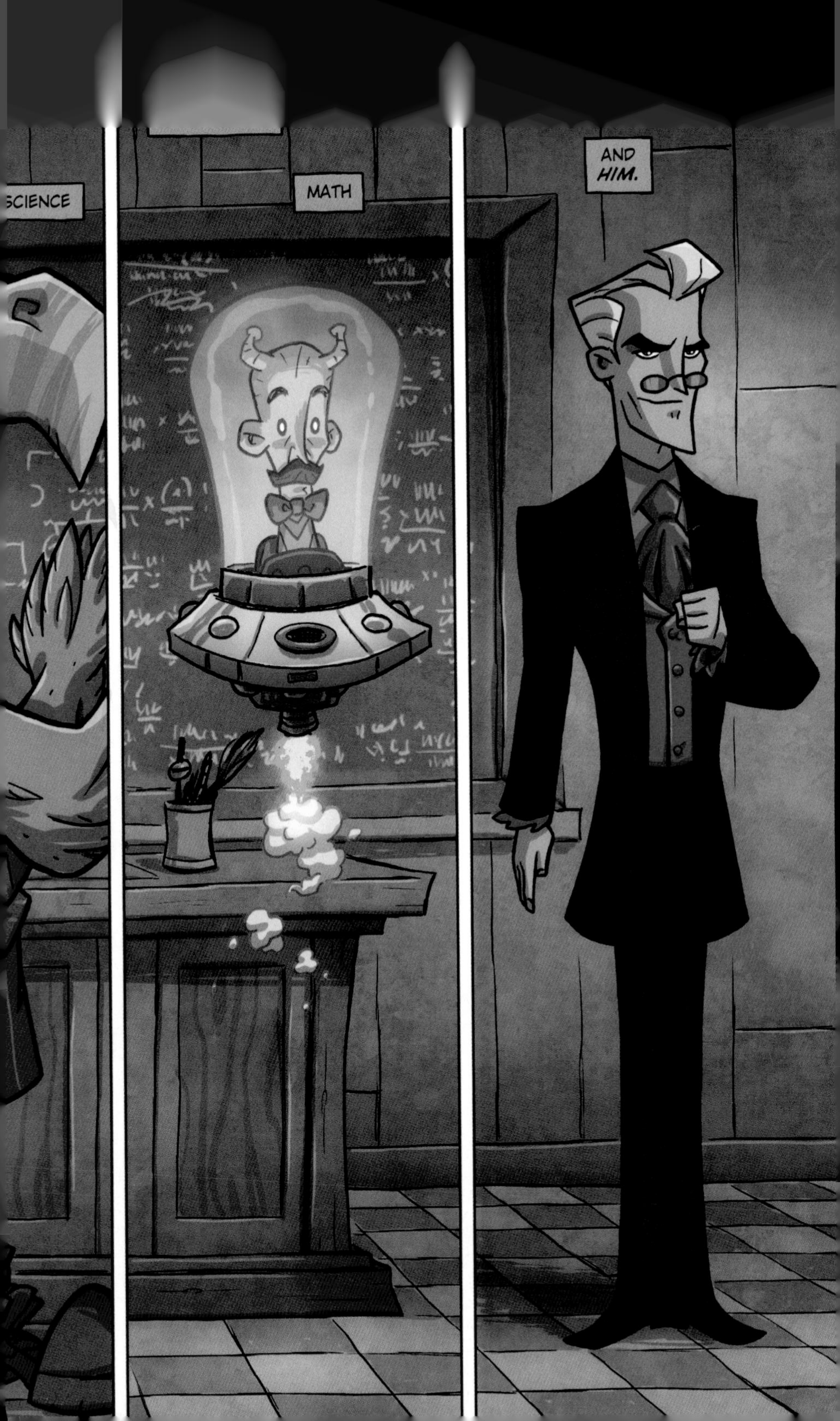

SCIENCE
MATH
AND *HIM.*

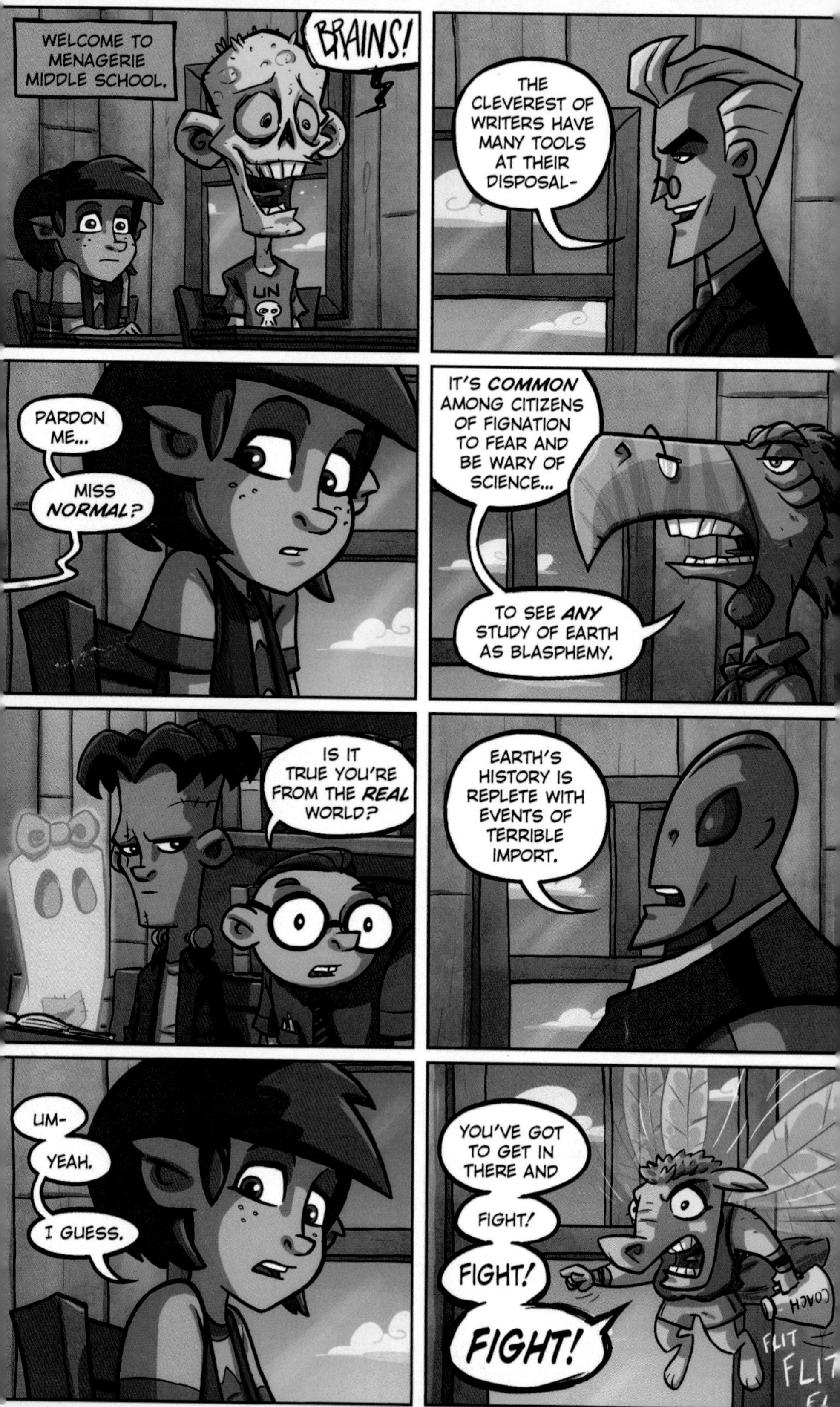
WELCOME TO MENAGERIE MIDDLE SCHOOL.
BRAINS!
THE CLEVEREST OF WRITERS HAVE MANY TOOLS AT THEIR DISPOSAL-
PARDON ME...
MISS *NORMAL*?
IT'S *COMMON* AMONG CITIZENS OF FIGNATION TO FEAR AND BE WARY OF SCIENCE...
TO SEE *ANY* STUDY OF EARTH AS BLASPHEMY.
IS IT TRUE YOU'RE FROM THE *REAL* WORLD?
EARTH'S HISTORY IS REPLETE WITH EVENTS OF TERRIBLE IMPORT.
UM-
YEAH.
I GUESS.
YOU'VE GOT TO GET IN THERE AND
FIGHT!
FIGHT!
FIGHT!
COACH
FLIT
FLIT

SCINATING! HOW IS *THAT* POSSIBLE?

WAS IT MAGIC?

PUNS, PALINDROMES, ALLITERATION, MALAPROPISMS, REPETITION, AND THE EVER RELIABLE *ANAGRAM*.

MY PERSONAL FAVORITE.

YES, BUT NOT MINE.

I'M ONLY A *HALF*-WITCH, I CAN'T DO MAGIC.

BUT SOMEHOW, I —

DID SOMETHING *BAD*.

WARS OF CONQUEST—

GENOCIDE—

EVEN FAMINE AND DISEASE ARE ALLOWED TO PROSPER...

WHILE THE ABLE STAND IDLY BY...

SOMEHOW I ENDED UP *HERE*.

IT JUST DOESN'T ADD *UP*.

SIXTEEN TIMES TWELVE IS...

ONE HUNDRED AND NINETY -SIX...

NO, THAT'S NOT RIGHT.

BEEP BOOP BEEP

BRAINS! BRAINS!

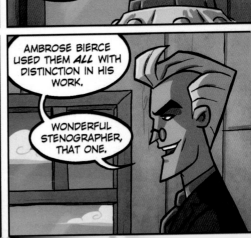

AMBROSE BIERCE USED THEM *ALL* WITH DISTINCTION IN HIS WORK.

WONDERFUL STENOGRAPHER, THAT ONE.

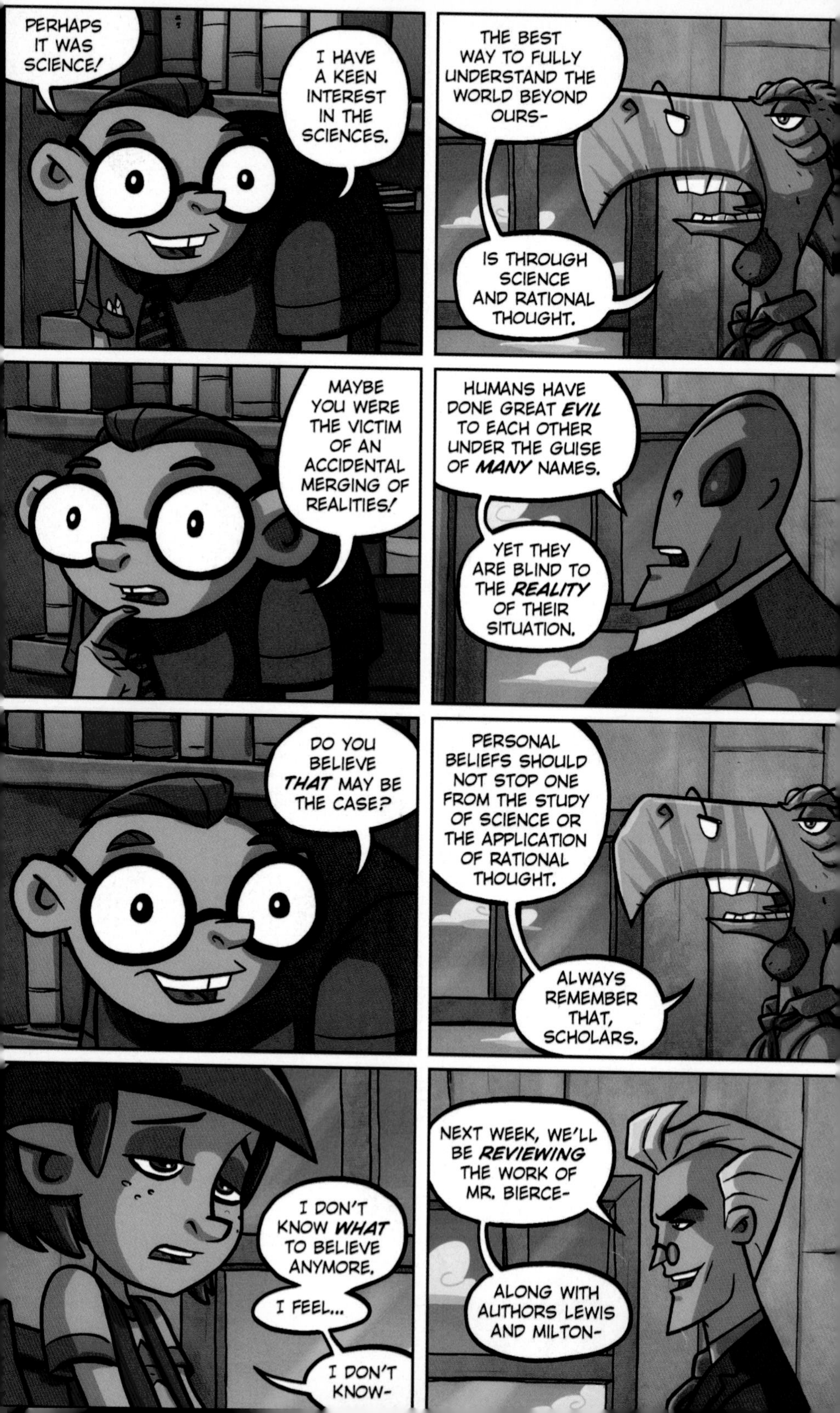
PERHAPS IT WAS SCIENCE!
I HAVE A KEEN INTEREST IN THE SCIENCES.
THE BEST WAY TO FULLY UNDERSTAND THE WORLD BEYOND OURS-
IS THROUGH SCIENCE AND RATIONAL THOUGHT.
MAYBE YOU WERE THE VICTIM OF AN ACCIDENTAL MERGING OF REALITIES!
HUMANS HAVE DONE GREAT *EVIL* TO EACH OTHER UNDER THE GUISE OF *MANY* NAMES.
YET THEY ARE BLIND TO THE *REALITY* OF THEIR SITUATION.
DO YOU BELIEVE *THAT* MAY BE THE CASE?
PERSONAL BELIEFS SHOULD NOT STOP ONE FROM THE STUDY OF SCIENCE OR THE APPLICATION OF RATIONAL THOUGHT.
ALWAYS REMEMBER THAT, SCHOLARS.
I DON'T KNOW *WHAT* TO BELIEVE ANYMORE.
I FEEL...
I DON'T KNOW-
NEXT WEEK, WE'LL BE *REVIEWING* THE WORK OF MR. BIERCE-
ALONG WITH AUTHORS LEWIS AND MILTON-

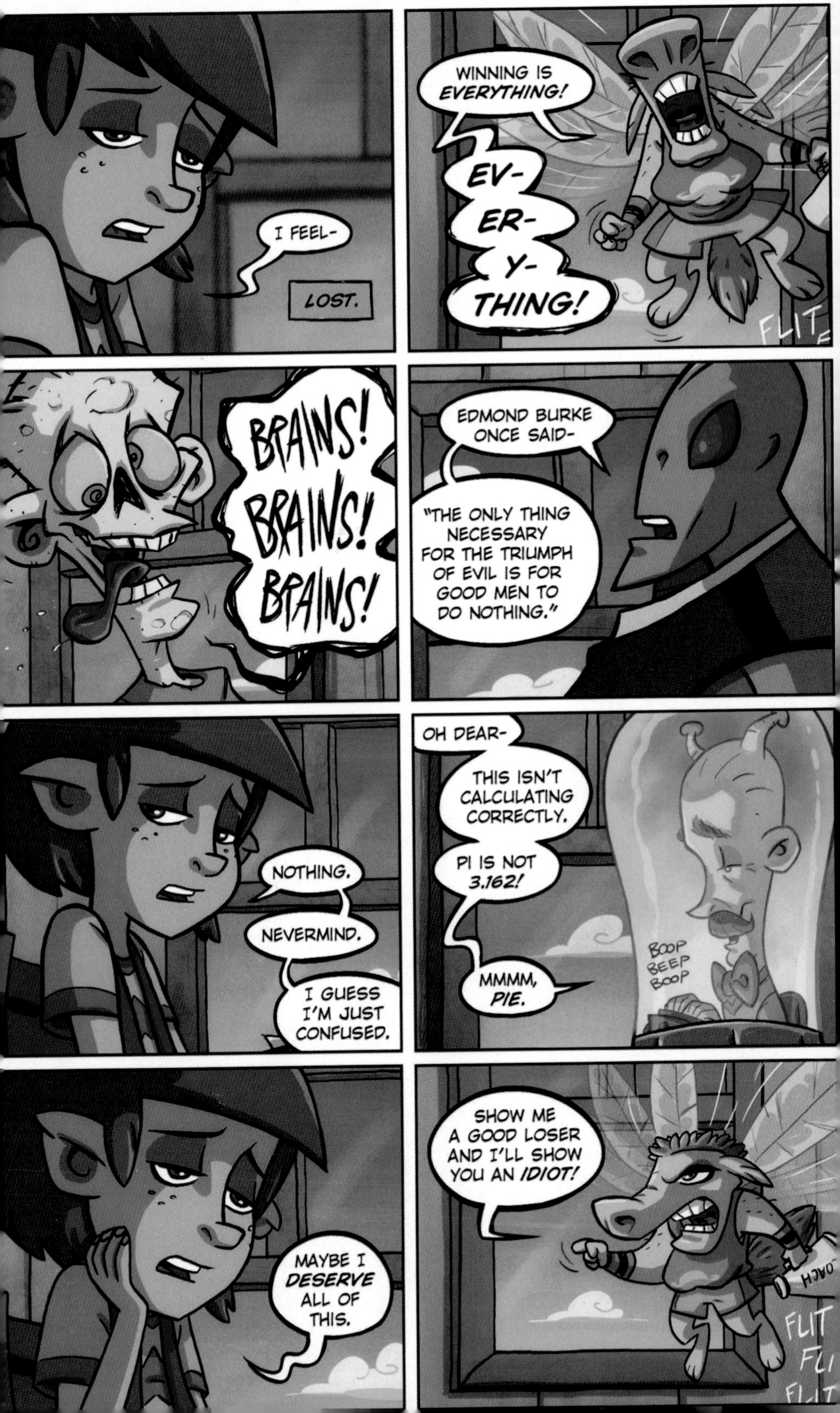
I FEEL-
LOST.
WINNING IS EVERYTHING!
EV-
ER-
Y-
THING!
FLIT
BRAINS! BRAINS! BRAINS!
EDMOND BURKE ONCE SAID-
"THE ONLY THING NECESSARY FOR THE TRIUMPH OF EVIL IS FOR GOOD MEN TO DO NOTHING."
NOTHING.
NEVERMIND.
I GUESS I'M JUST CONFUSED.
OH DEAR-
THIS ISN'T CALCULATING CORRECTLY.
PI IS NOT 3.162!
BOOP BEEP BOOP
MMMM, PIE.
MAYBE I DESERVE ALL OF THIS.
SHOW ME A GOOD LOSER AND I'LL SHOW YOU AN IDIOT!
FLIT

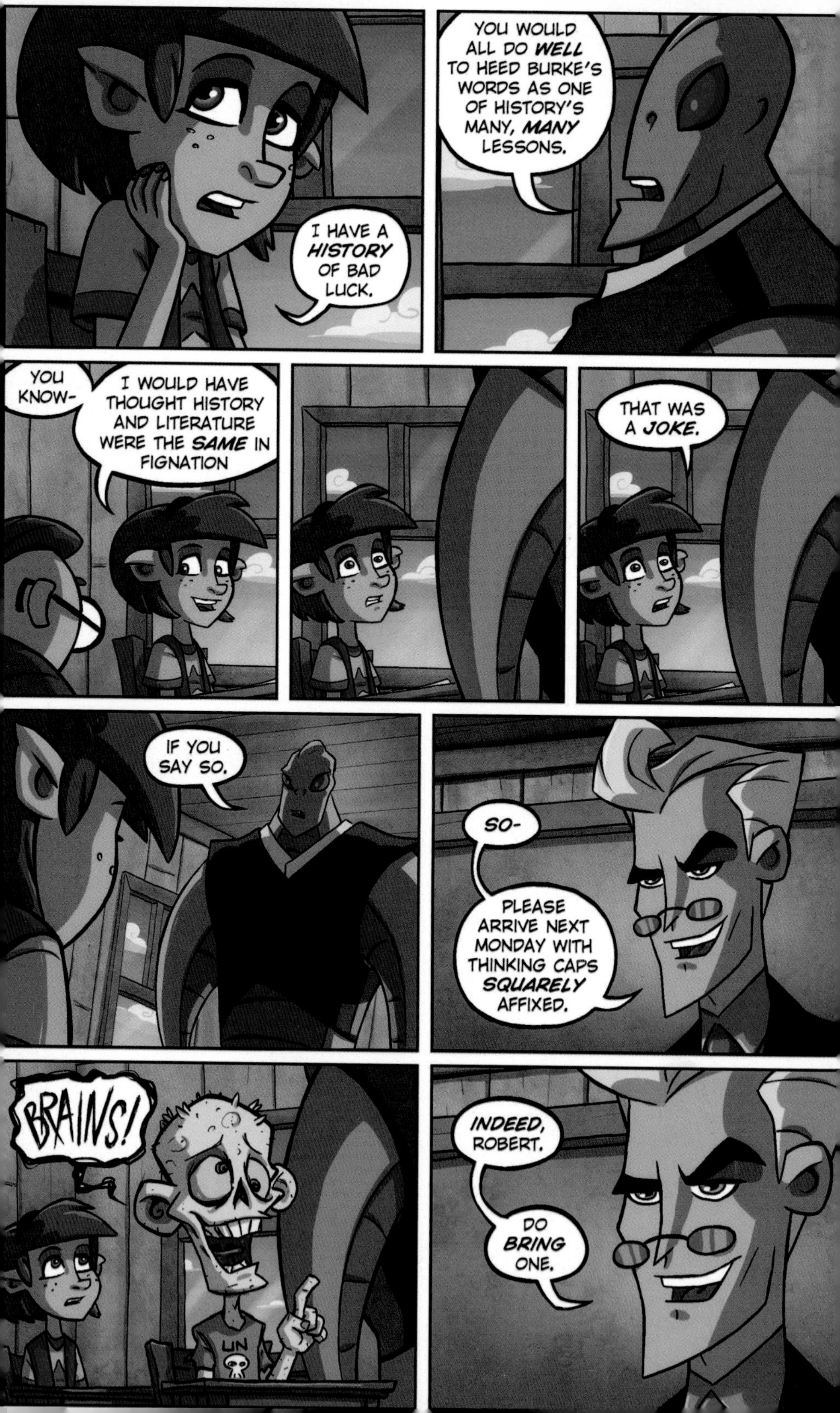

I HAVE A HISTORY OF BAD LUCK.
YOU WOULD ALL DO WELL TO HEED BURKE'S WORDS AS ONE OF HISTORY'S MANY, MANY LESSONS.
YOU KNOW-
I WOULD HAVE THOUGHT HISTORY AND LITERATURE WERE THE SAME IN FIGNATION
THAT WAS A JOKE.
IF YOU SAY SO.
SO-
PLEASE ARRIVE NEXT MONDAY WITH THINKING CAPS SQUARELY AFFIXED.
BRAINS!
UN
INDEED, ROBERT.
DO BRING ONE.

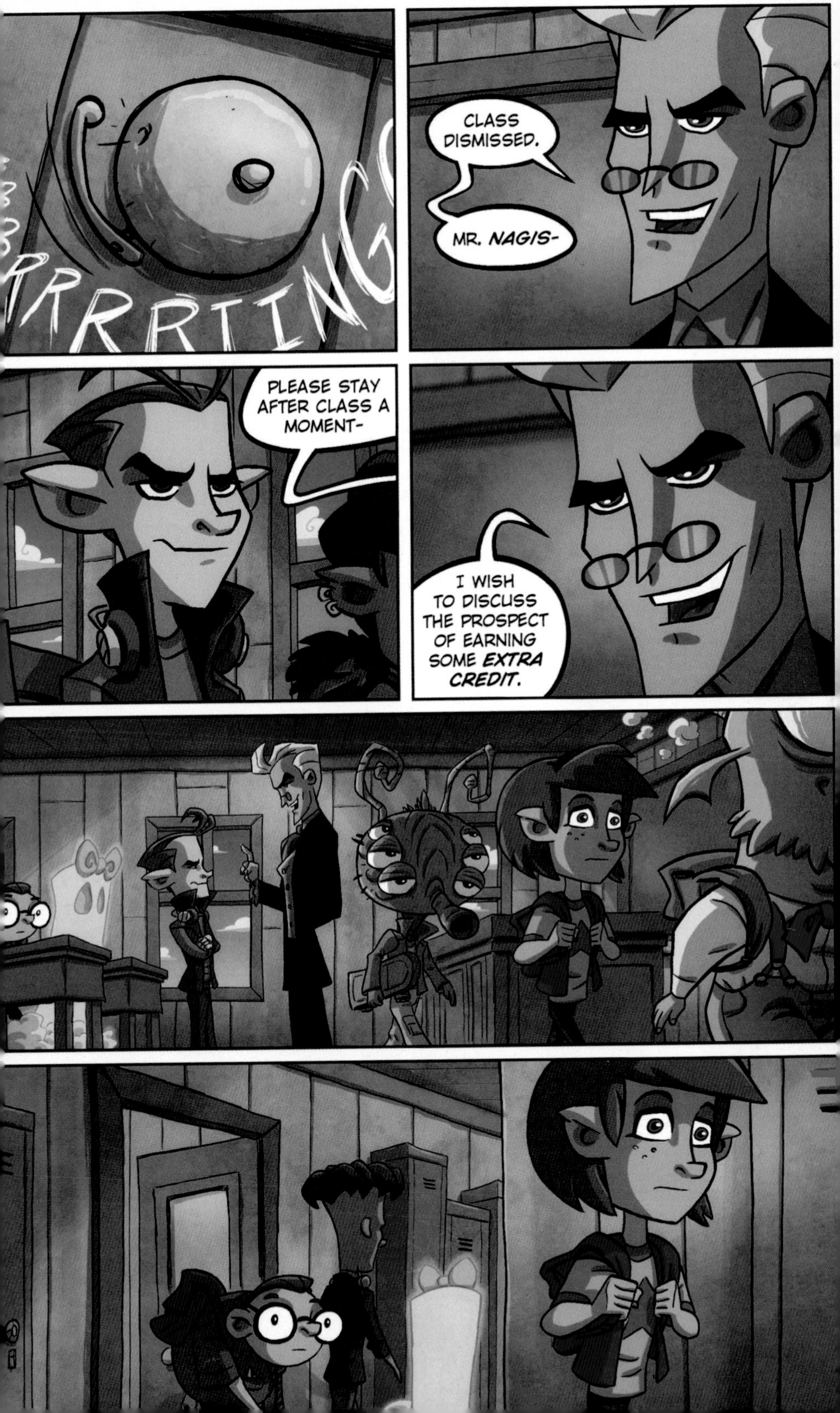
BRRRRRRRTING
CLASS DISMISSED.
MR. NAGIS-
PLEASE STAY AFTER CLASS A MOMENT-
I WISH TO DISCUSS THE PROSPECT OF EARNING SOME EXTRA CREDIT.

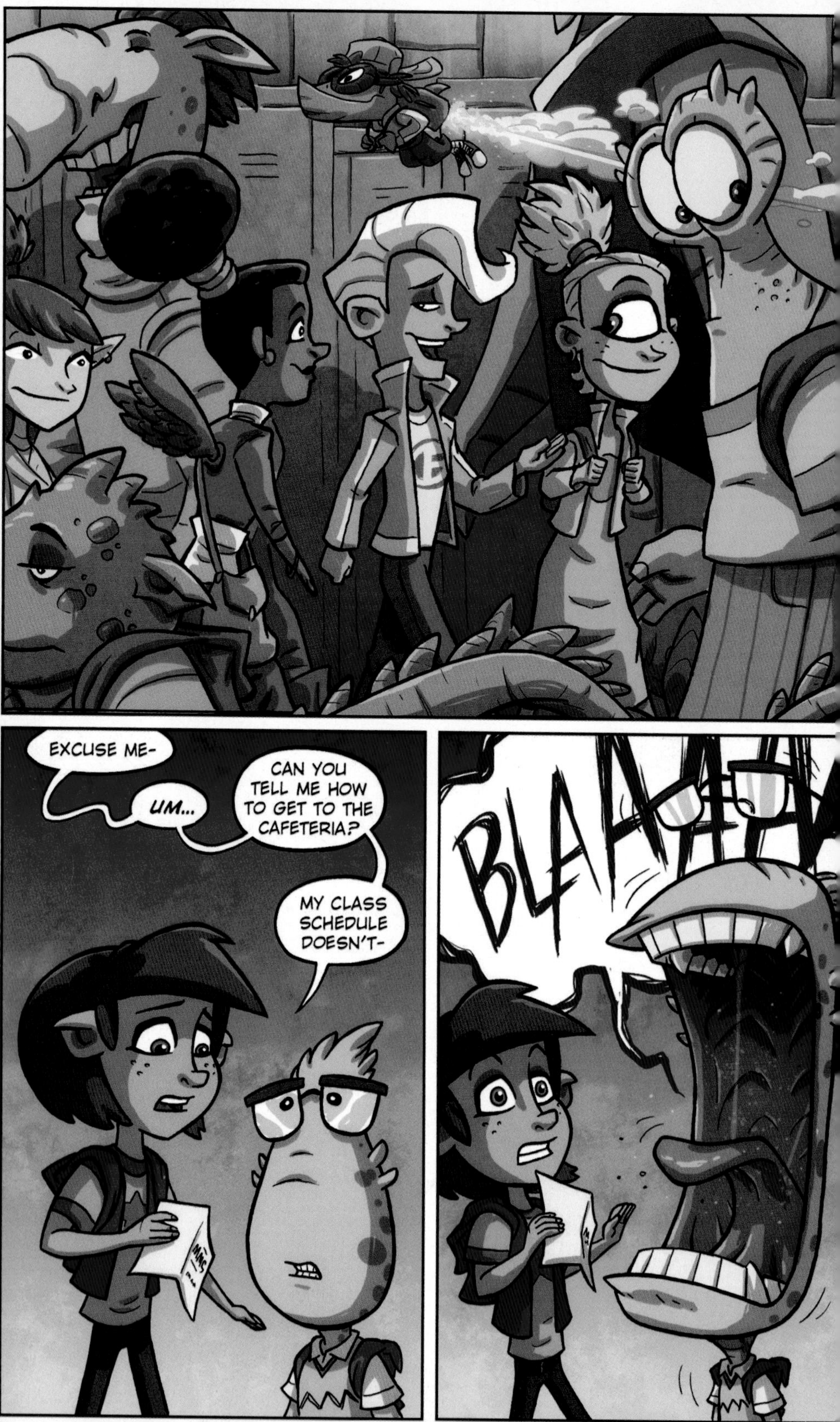
EXCUSE ME-
UM...
CAN YOU TELL ME HOW TO GET TO THE CAFETERIA?
MY CLASS SCHEDULE DOESN'T-
BLAAAA

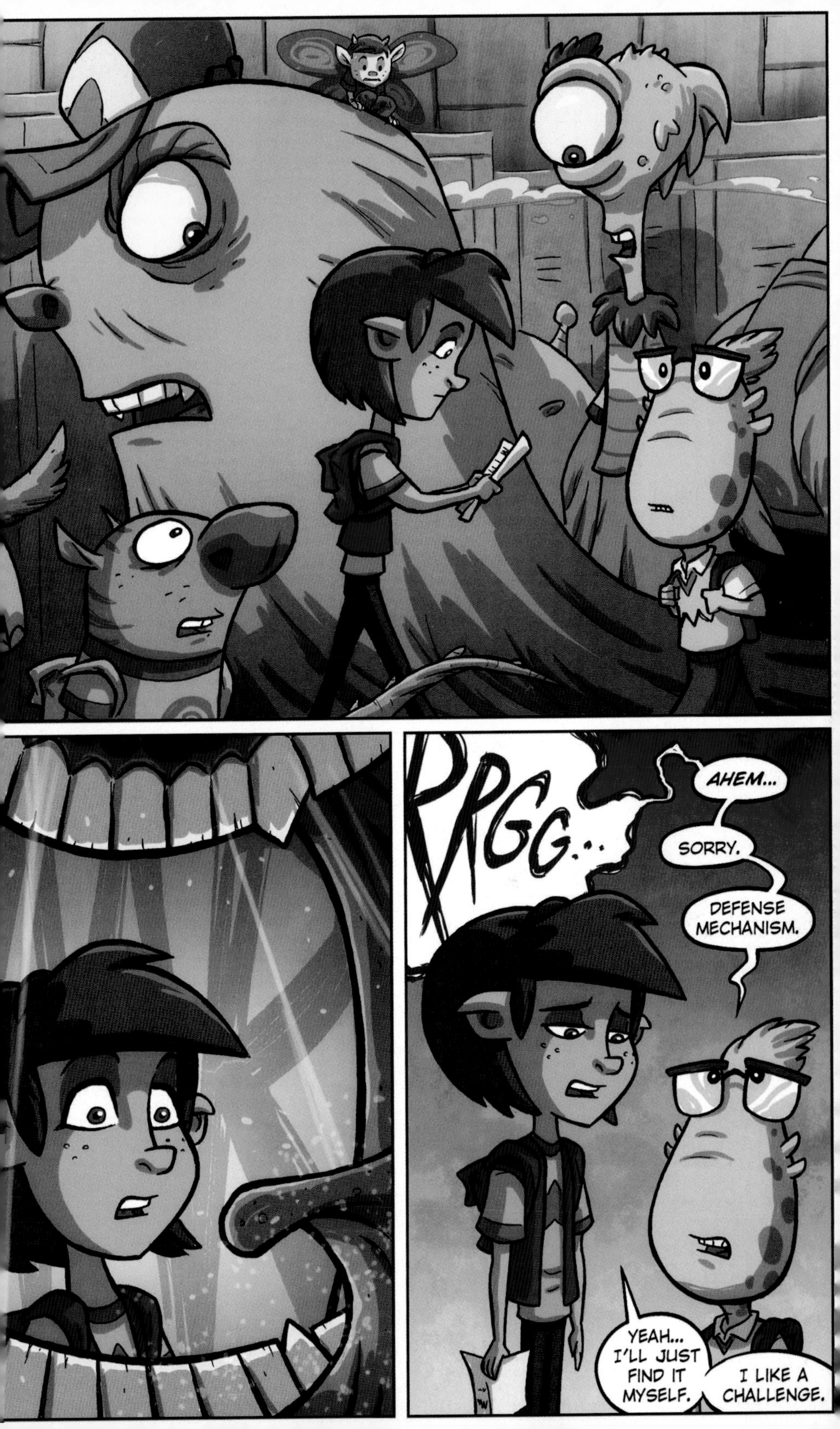
PRGG...
AHEM...
SORRY.
DEFENSE MECHANISM.
YEAH... I'LL JUST FIND IT MYSELF.
I LIKE A CHALLENGE.

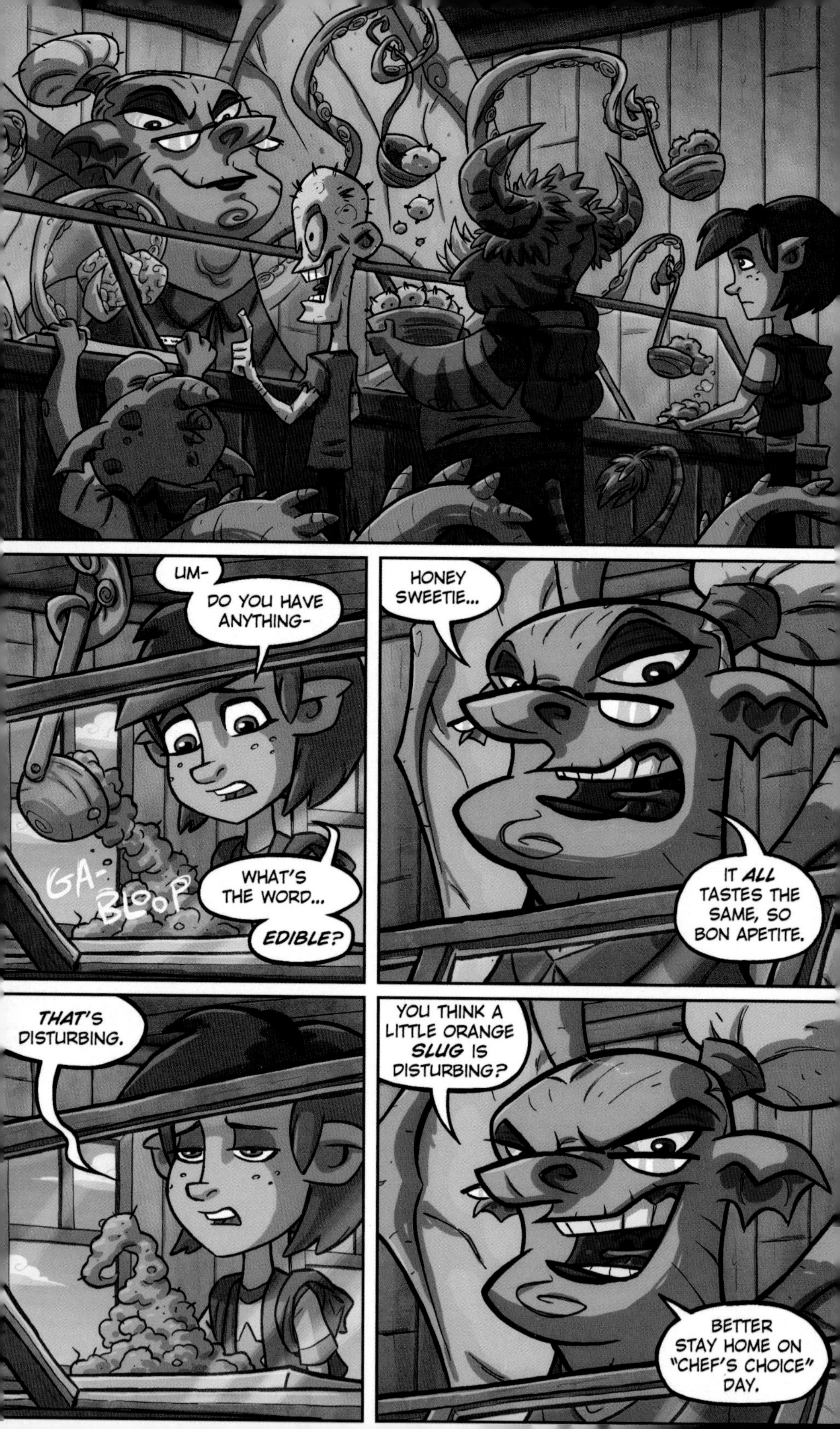
UM-
DO YOU HAVE ANYTHING-
GA-BLOOP
WHAT'S THE WORD...
EDIBLE?
HONEY SWEETIE...
IT *ALL* TASTES THE SAME, SO BON APETITE.
THAT'S DISTURBING.
YOU THINK A LITTLE ORANGE *SLUG* IS DISTURBING?
BETTER STAY HOME ON "CHEF'S CHOICE" DAY.

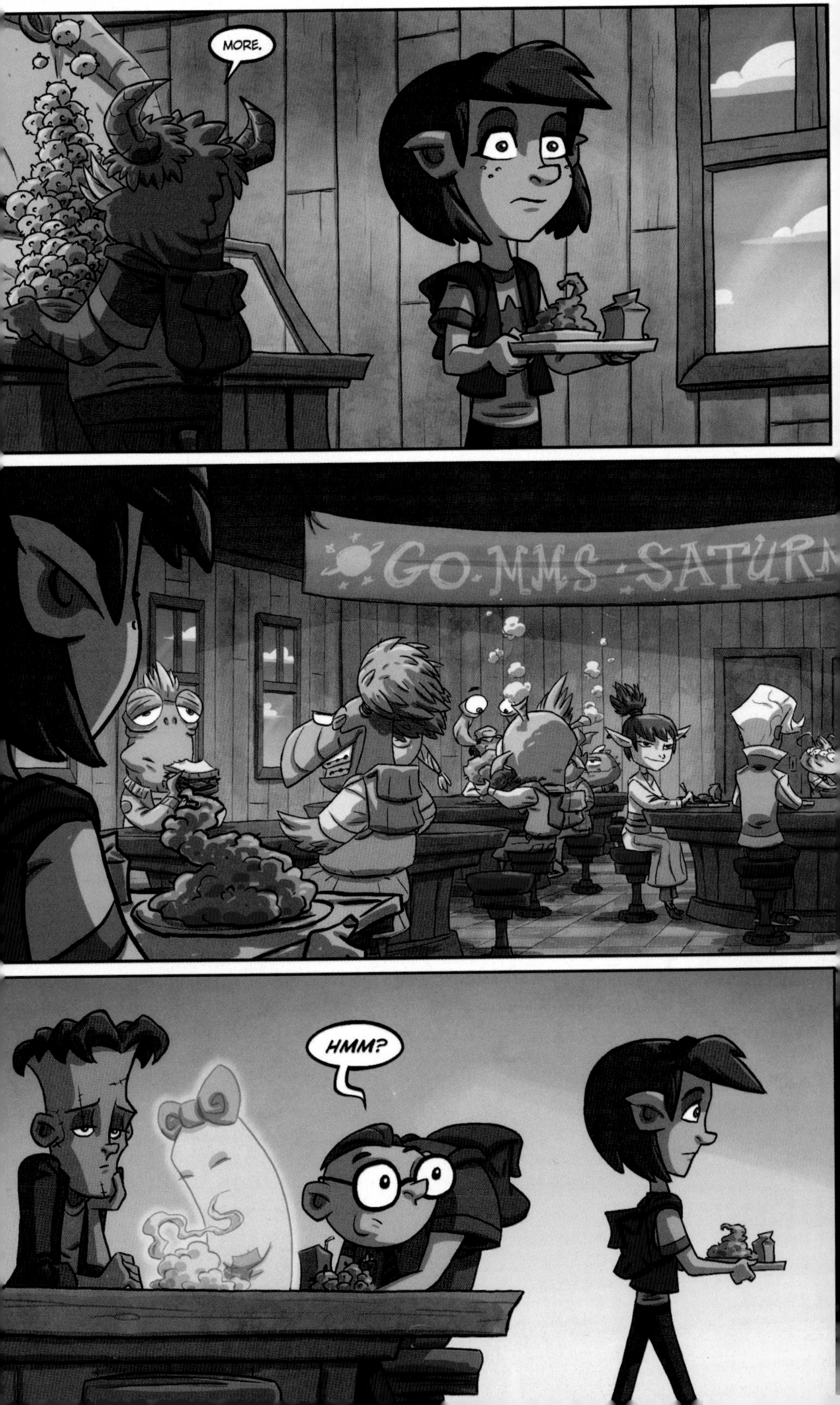
MORE.
GO MMS SATUR
HMM?

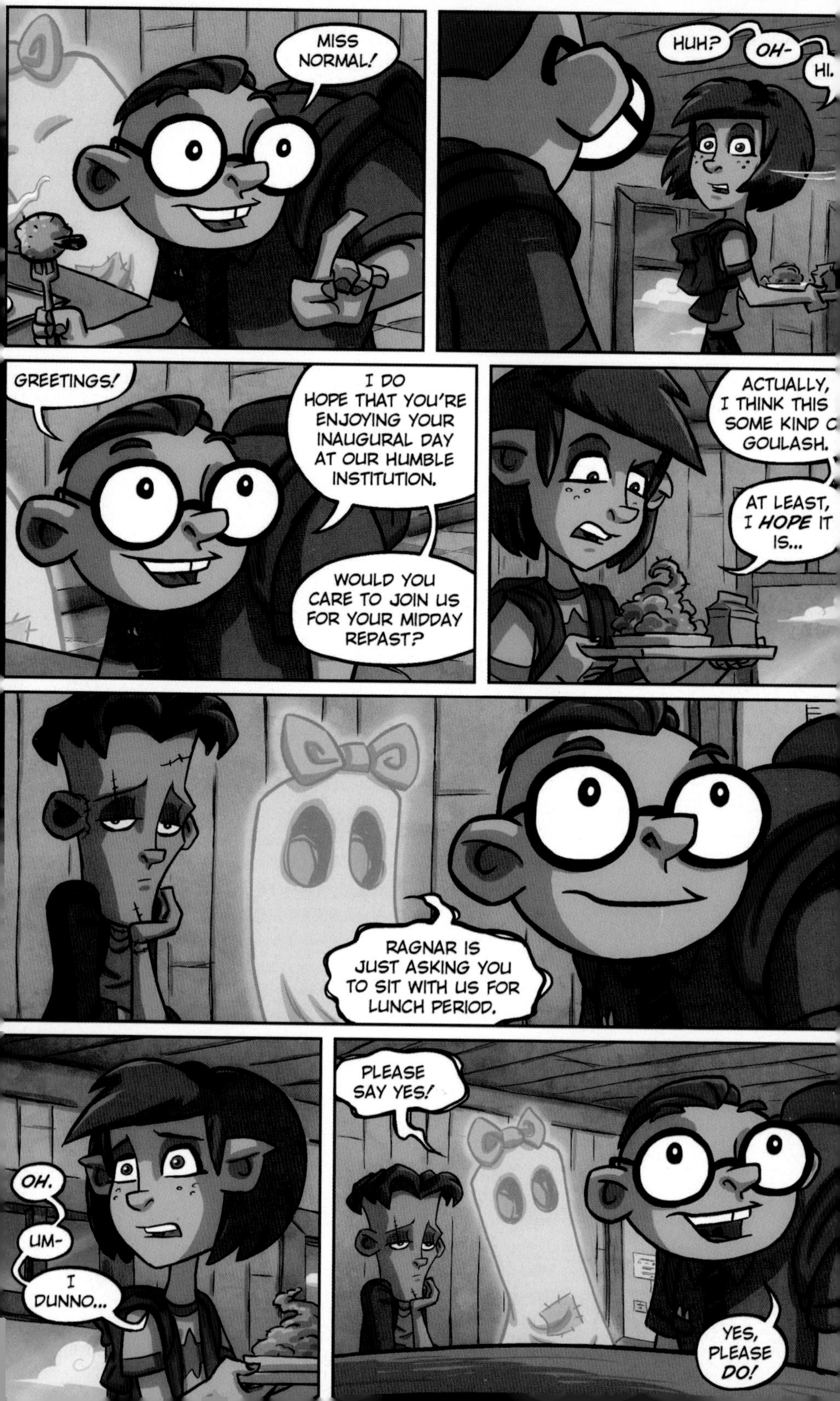

MISS NORMAL!
HUH?
OH-
HI.
GREETINGS!
I DO HOPE THAT YOU'RE ENJOYING YOUR INAUGURAL DAY AT OUR HUMBLE INSTITUTION.
WOULD YOU CARE TO JOIN US FOR YOUR MIDDAY REPAST?
ACTUALLY, I THINK THIS SOME KIND GOULASH.
AT LEAST, I *HOPE* IT IS...
RAGNAR IS JUST ASKING YOU TO SIT WITH US FOR LUNCH PERIOD.
OH.
UM-
I DUNNO...
PLEASE SAY YES!
YES, PLEASE *DO!*

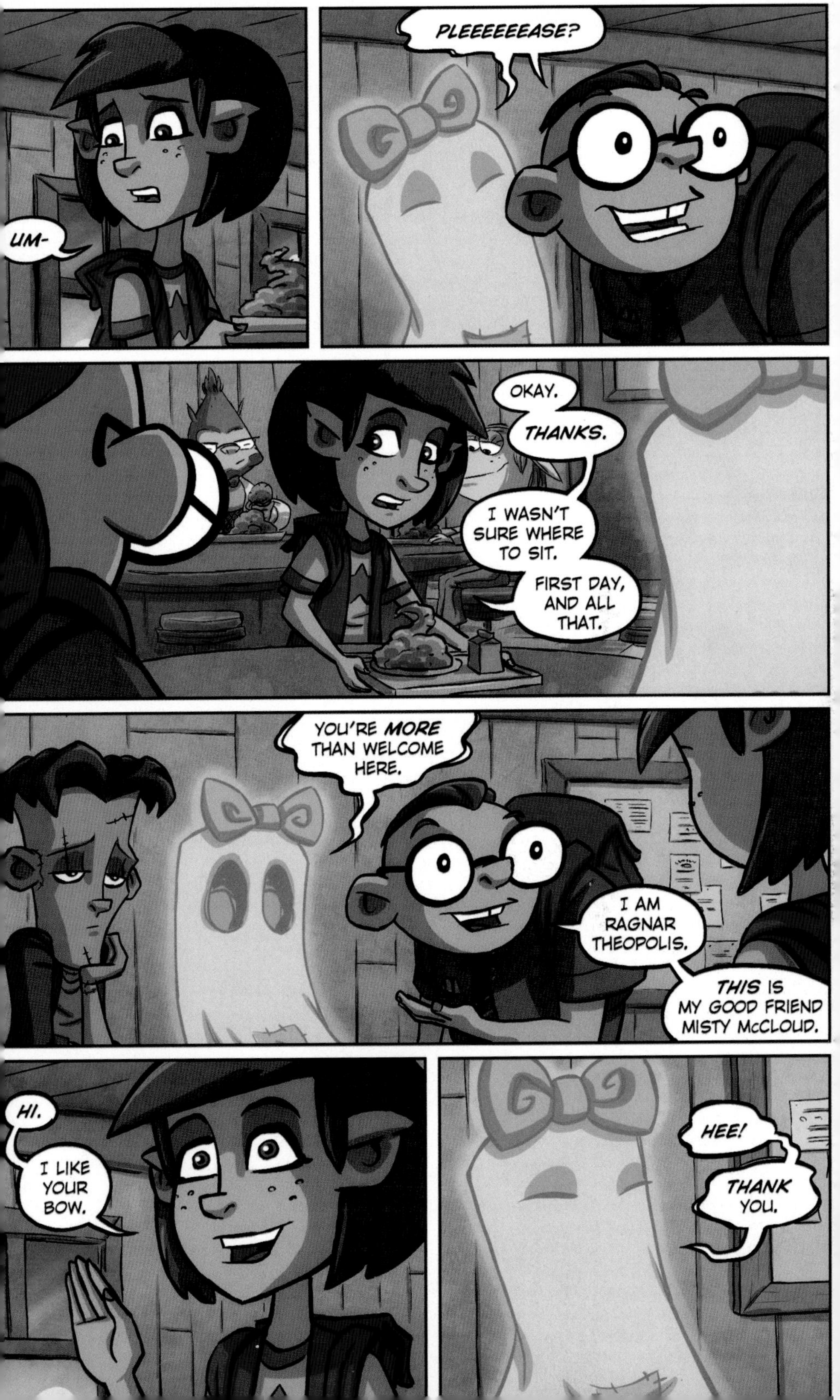
UM-
PLEEEEEEASE?
OKAY.
THANKS.
I WASN'T SURE WHERE TO SIT.
FIRST DAY, AND ALL THAT.
YOU'RE MORE THAN WELCOME HERE.
I AM RAGNAR THEOPOLIS.
THIS IS MY GOOD FRIEND MISTY McCLOUD.
HI.
I LIKE YOUR BOW.
HEE!
THANK YOU.

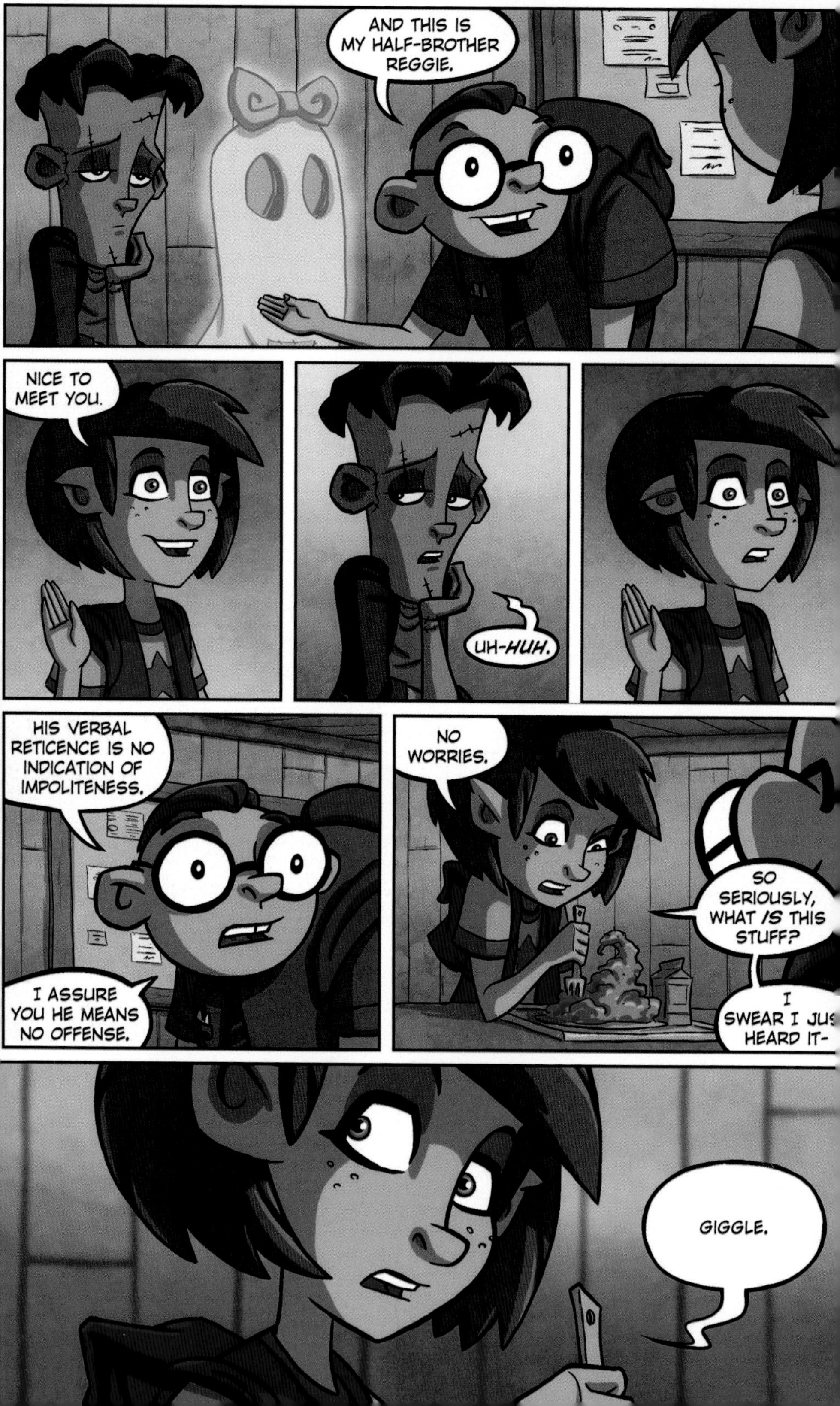
AND THIS IS MY HALF-BROTHER REGGIE.
NICE TO MEET YOU.
UH-HUH.
HIS VERBAL RETICENCE IS NO INDICATION OF IMPOLITENESS.
I ASSURE YOU HE MEANS NO OFFENSE.
NO WORRIES.
SO SERIOUSLY, WHAT IS THIS STUFF?
I SWEAR I JUS
HEARD IT-
GIGGLE.

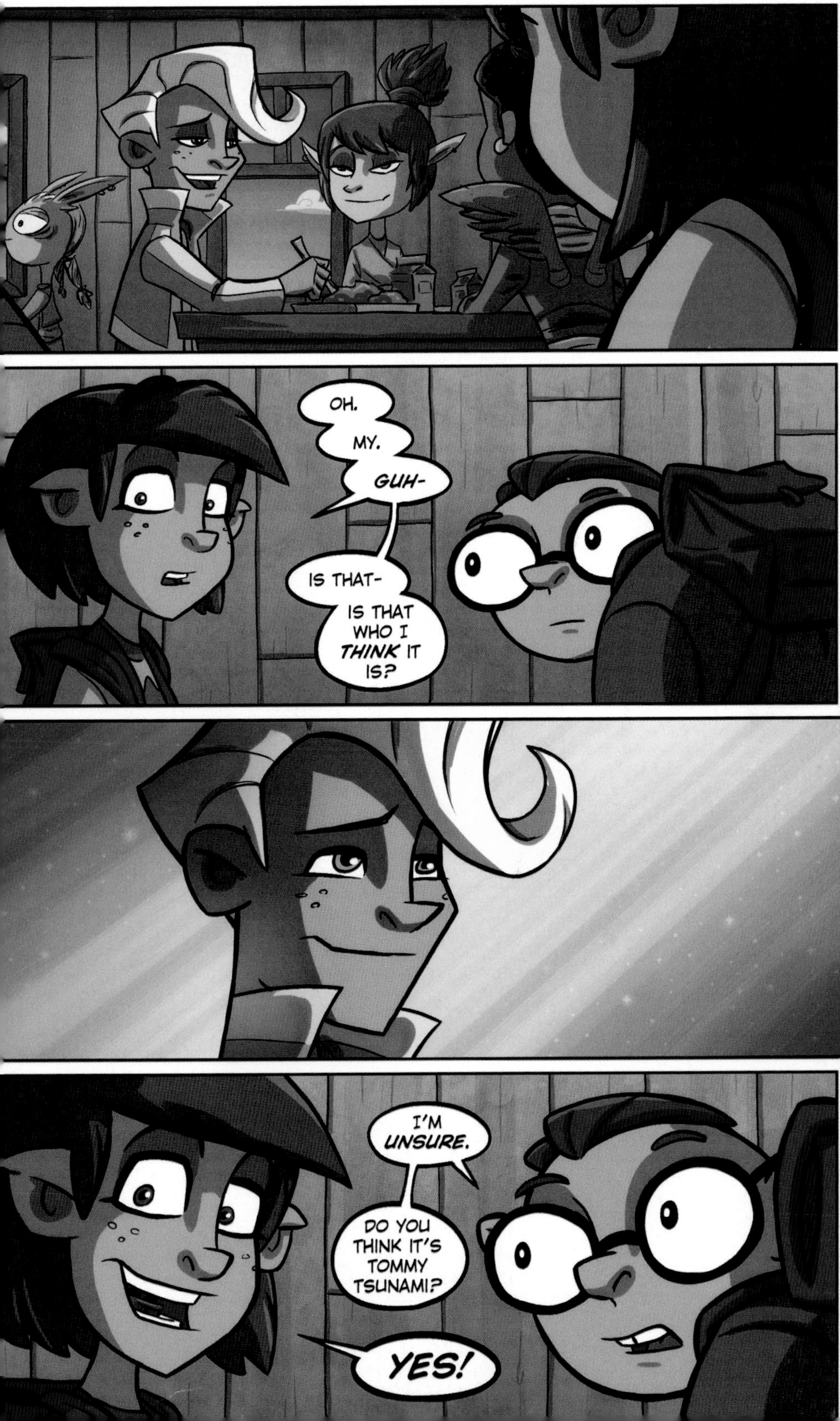
OH.
MY.
GUH-
IS THAT-
IS THAT WHO I THINK IT IS?
I'M UNSURE.
DO YOU THINK IT'S TOMMY TSUNAMI?
YES!

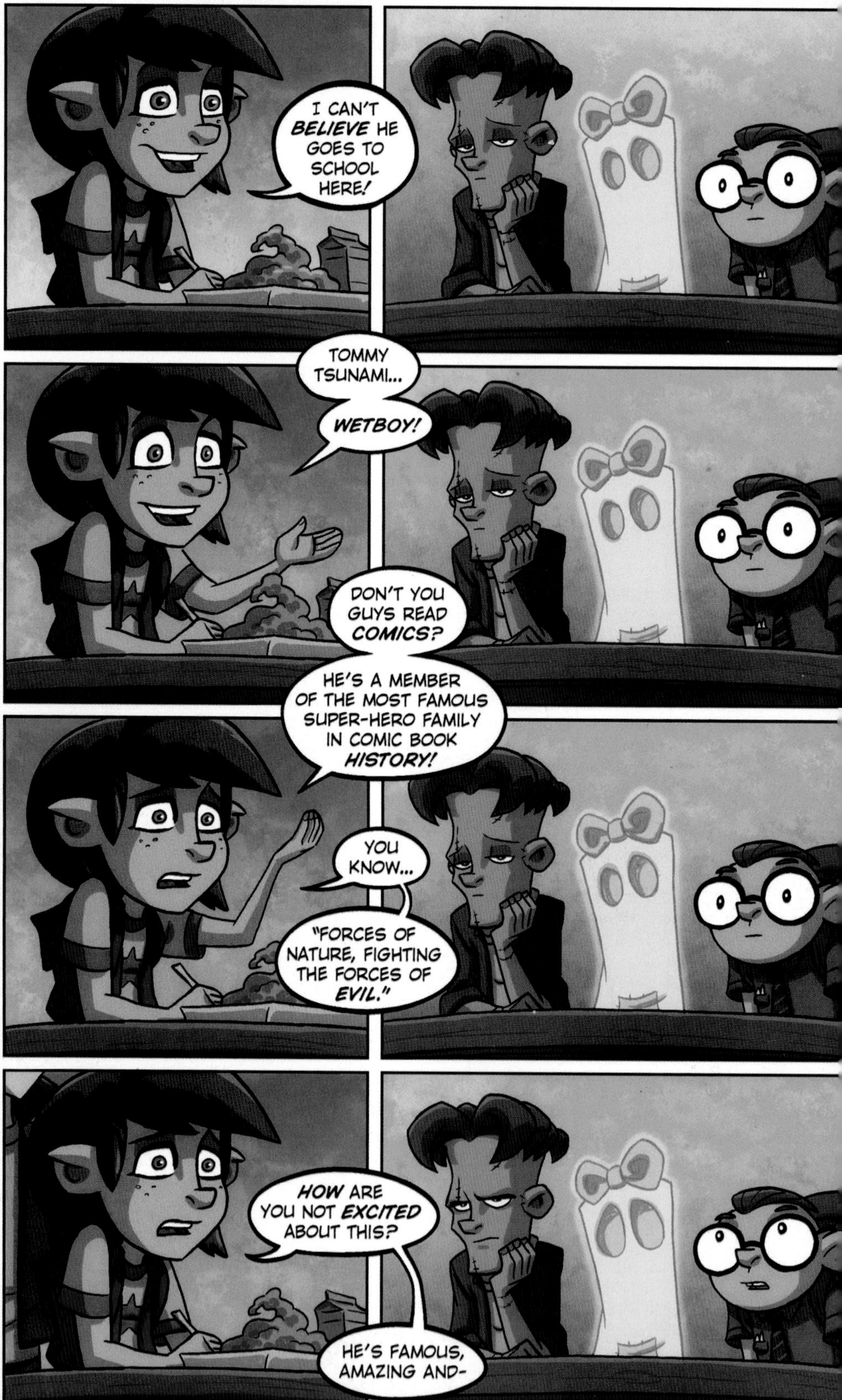
I CAN'T BELIEVE HE GOES TO SCHOOL HERE!
TOMMY TSUNAMI...
WETBOY!
DON'T YOU GUYS READ COMICS?
HE'S A MEMBER OF THE MOST FAMOUS SUPER-HERO FAMILY IN COMIC BOOK HISTORY!
YOU KNOW...
"FORCES OF NATURE, FIGHTING THE FORCES OF EVIL."
HOW ARE YOU NOT EXCITED ABOUT THIS?
HE'S FAMOUS, AMAZING AND-

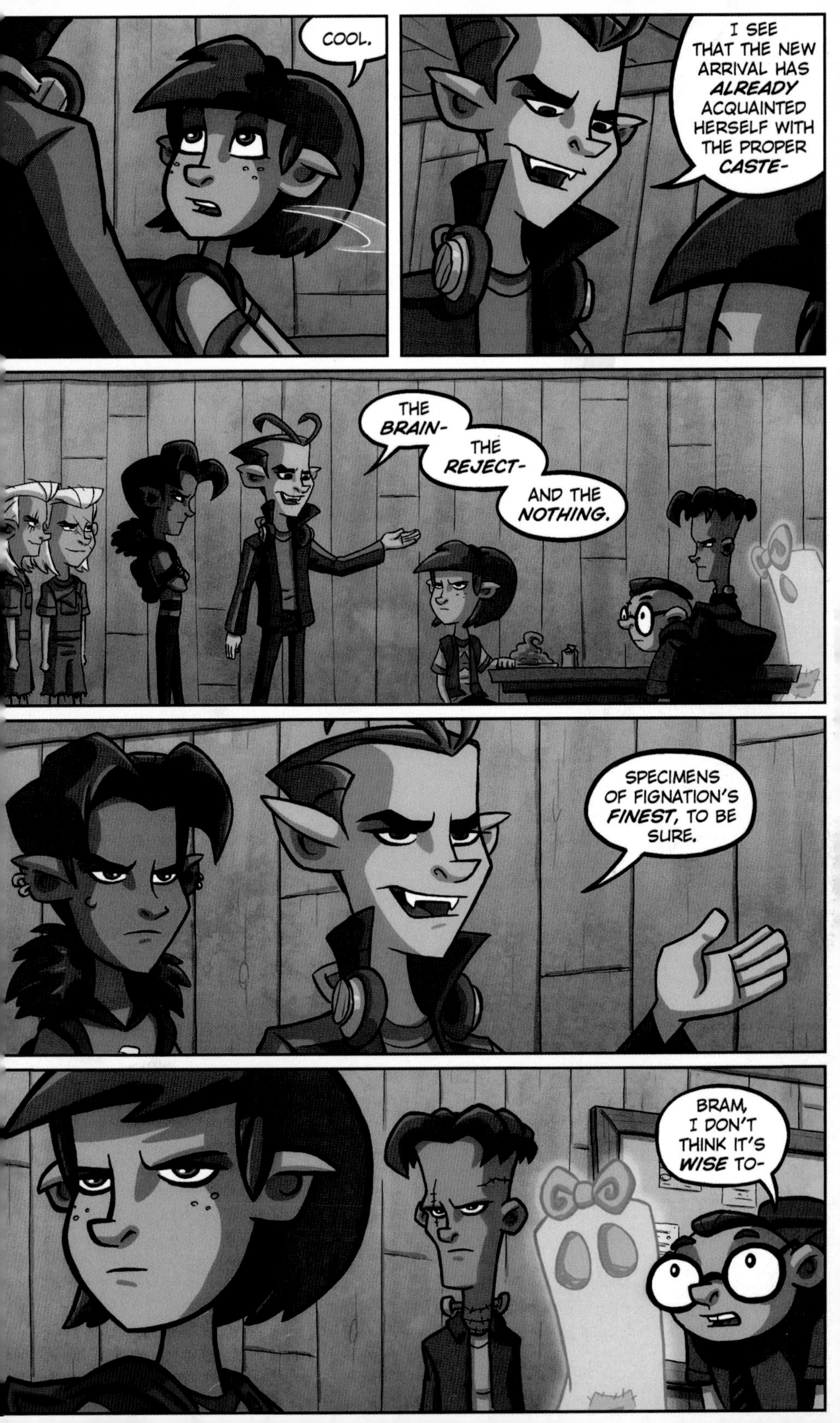
COOL.
I SEE THAT THE NEW ARRIVAL HAS ALREADY ACQUAINTED HERSELF WITH THE PROPER CASTE-
THE BRAIN-
THE REJECT-
AND THE NOTHING.
SPECIMENS OF FIGNATION'S FINEST, TO BE SURE.
BRAM, I DON'T THINK IT'S WISE TO-

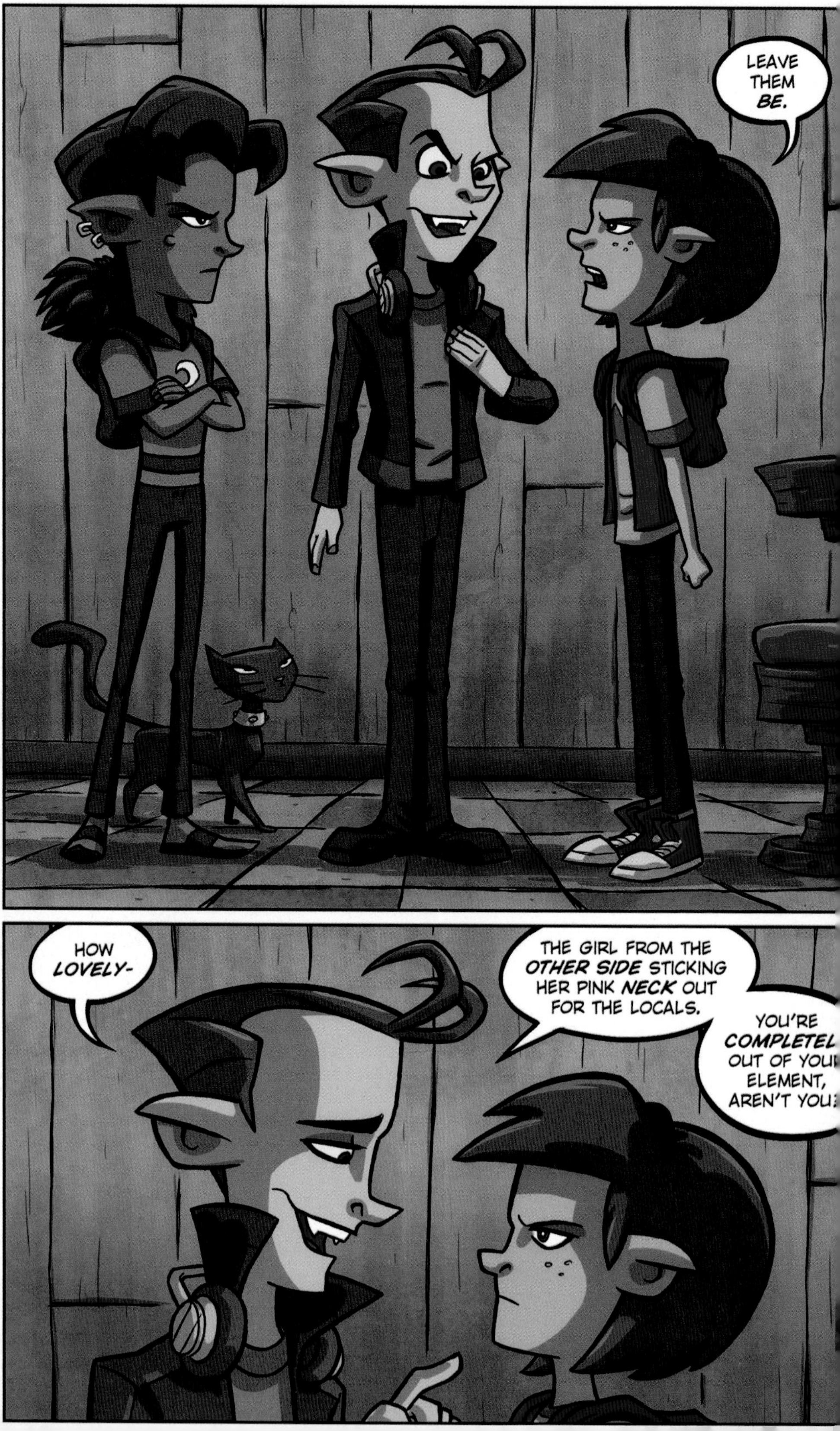
LEAVE THEM *BE.*
HOW *LOVELY-*
THE GIRL FROM THE *OTHER SIDE* STICKING HER PINK *NECK* OUT FOR THE LOCALS.
YOU'RE *COMPLETEL* OUT OF YOU ELEMENT, AREN'T YOU

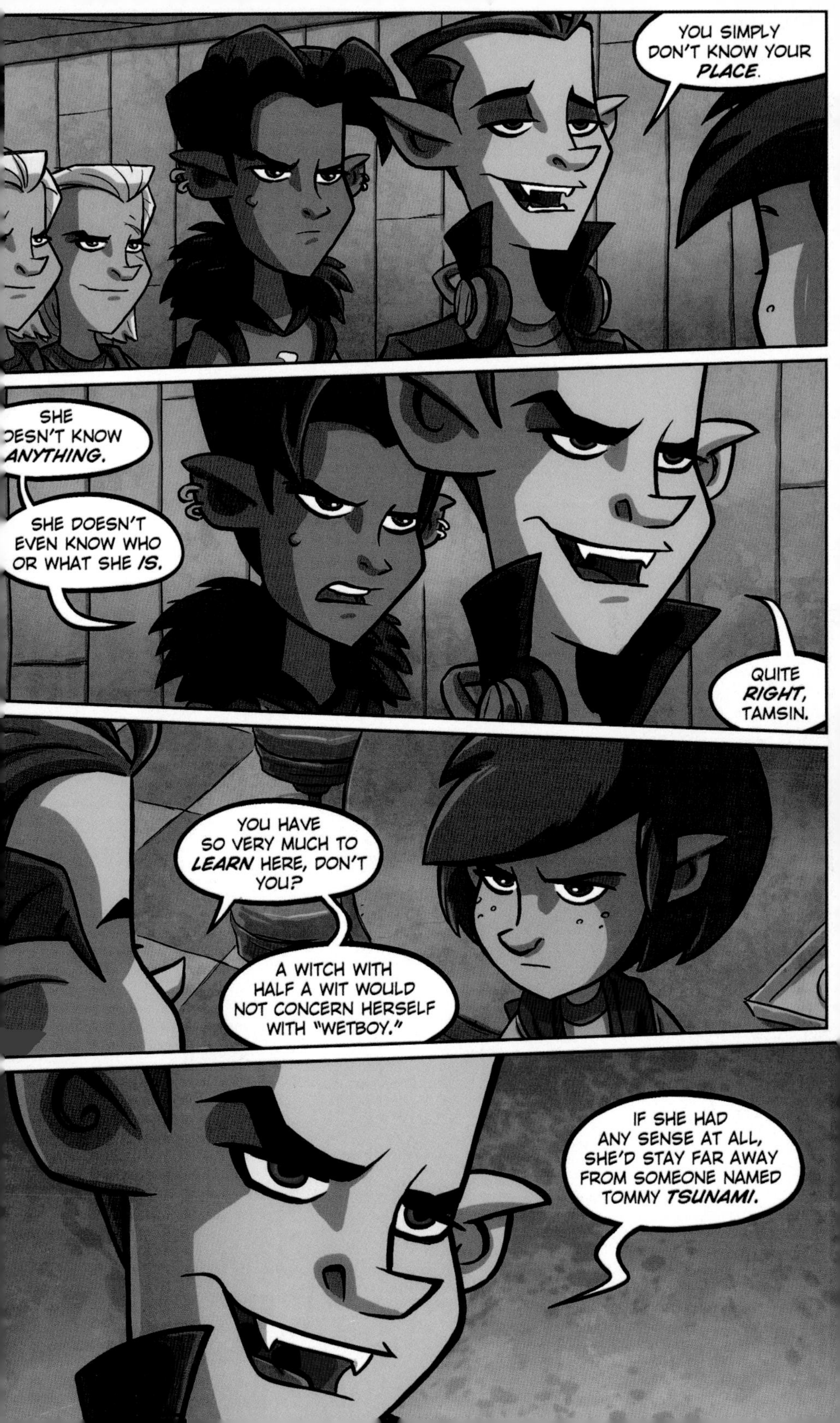
YOU SIMPLY DON'T KNOW YOUR *PLACE*.
SHE DOESN'T KNOW *ANYTHING*.
SHE DOESN'T EVEN KNOW WHO OR WHAT SHE *IS*.
QUITE *RIGHT*, TAMSIN.
YOU HAVE SO VERY MUCH TO *LEARN* HERE, DON'T YOU?
A WITCH WITH HALF A WIT WOULD NOT CONCERN HERSELF WITH "WETBOY."
IF SHE HAD ANY SENSE AT ALL, SHE'D STAY FAR AWAY FROM SOMEONE NAMED TOMMY *TSUNAMI*.

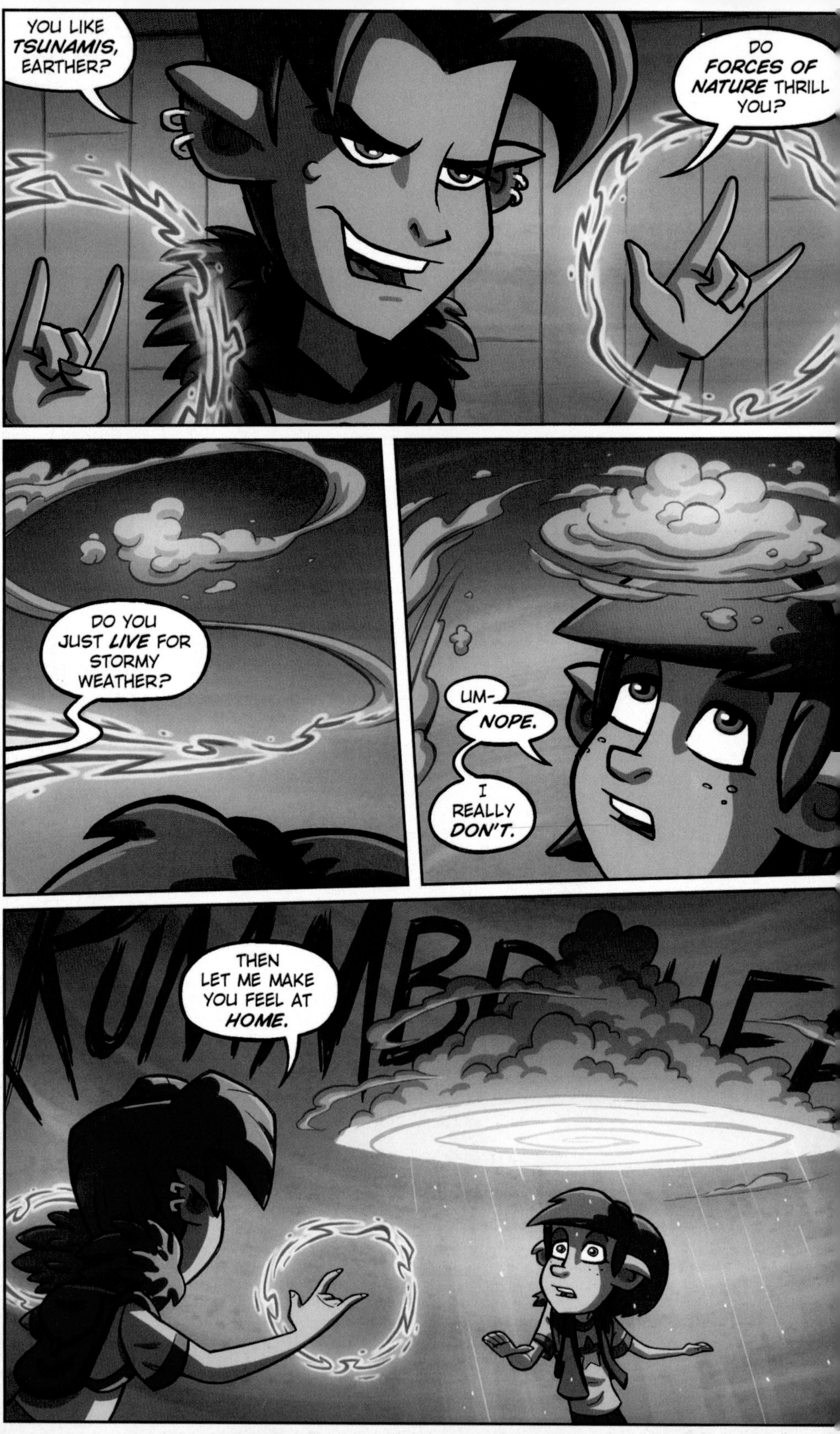
YOU LIKE TSUNAMIS, EARTHER?
DO FORCES OF NATURE THRILL YOU?
DO YOU JUST LIVE FOR STORMY WEATHER?
UM-
NOPE.
I REALLY DON'T.
THEN LET ME MAKE YOU FEEL AT HOME.

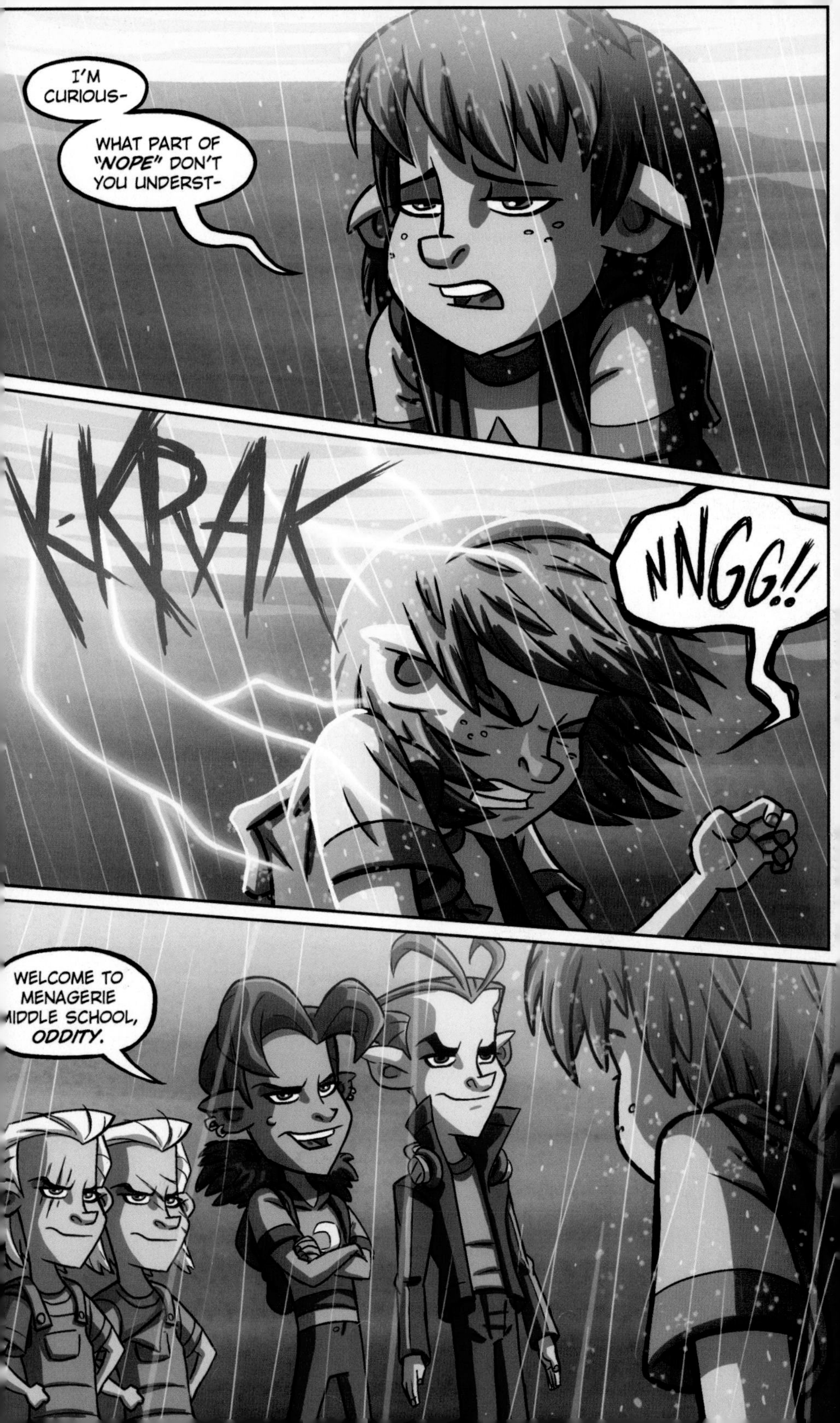
I'M CURIOUS-
WHAT PART OF "NOPE" DON'T YOU UNDERST-
K-KRAK
NNGG!!
WELCOME TO MENAGERIE MIDDLE SCHOOL, ODDITY.

Chapter 5
Sticks, Stones, Words & Bones

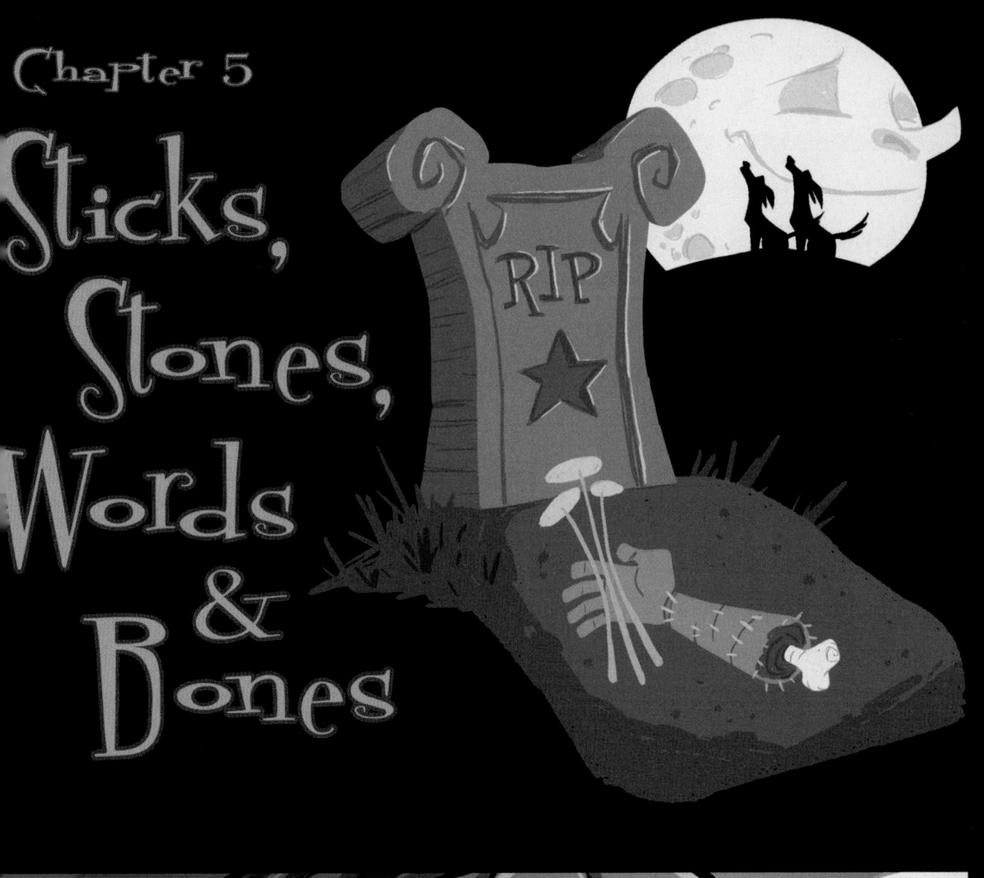
RIP

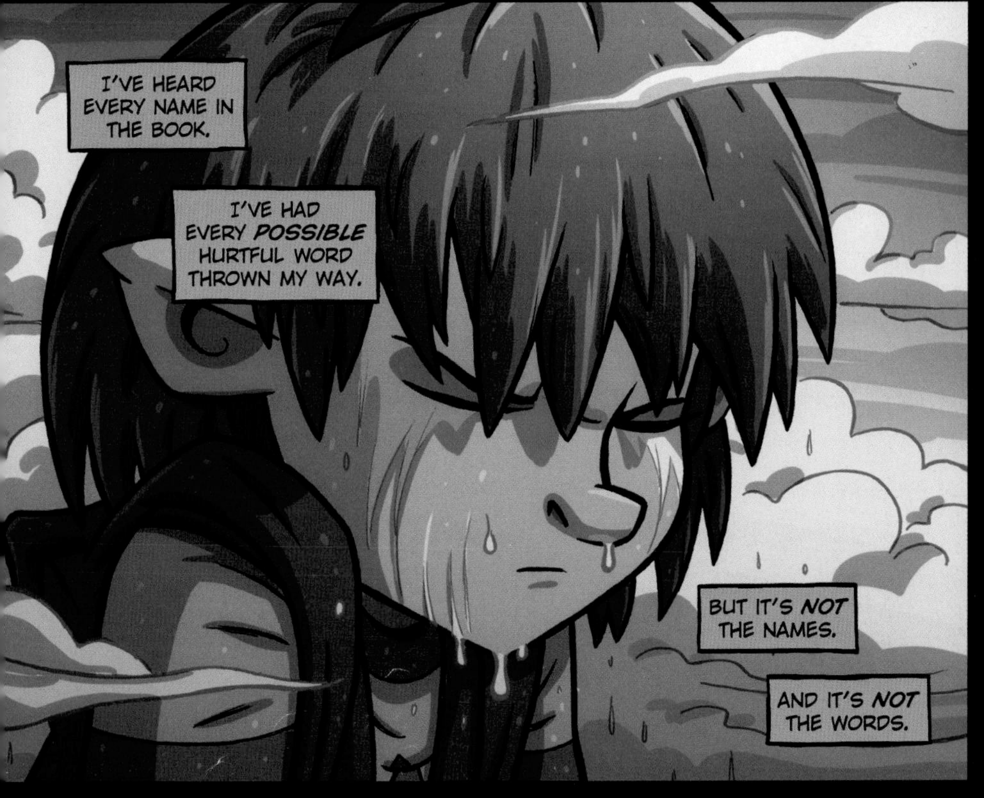
I'VE HEARD EVERY NAME IN THE BOOK.
I'VE HAD EVERY *POSSIBLE* HURTFUL WORD THROWN MY WAY.
BUT IT'S *NOT* THE NAMES.
AND IT'S *NOT* THE WORDS.

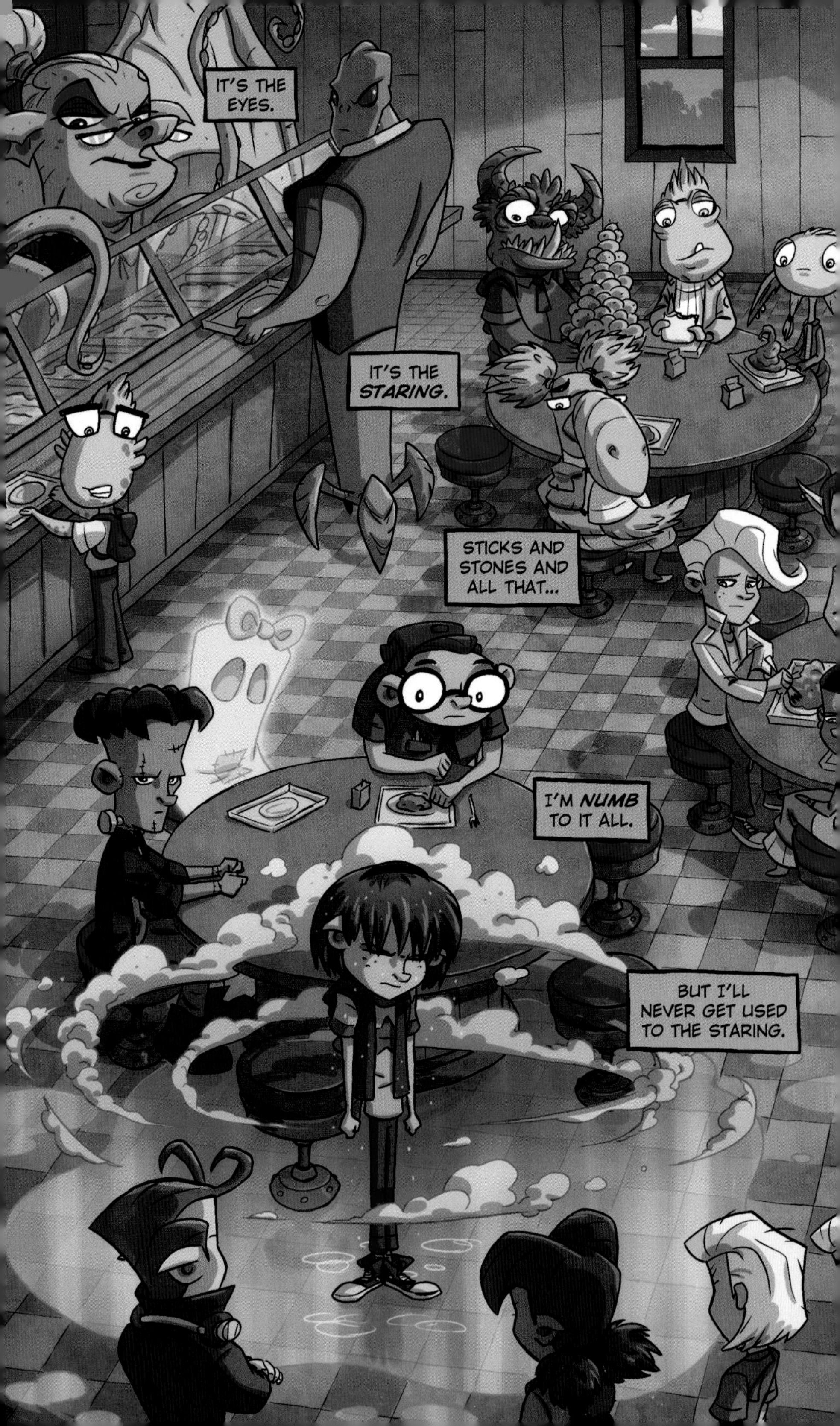
IT'S THE EYES.
IT'S THE *STARING.*
STICKS AND STONES AND ALL THAT...
I'M ***NUMB*** TO IT ALL.
BUT I'LL NEVER GET USED TO THE STARING.

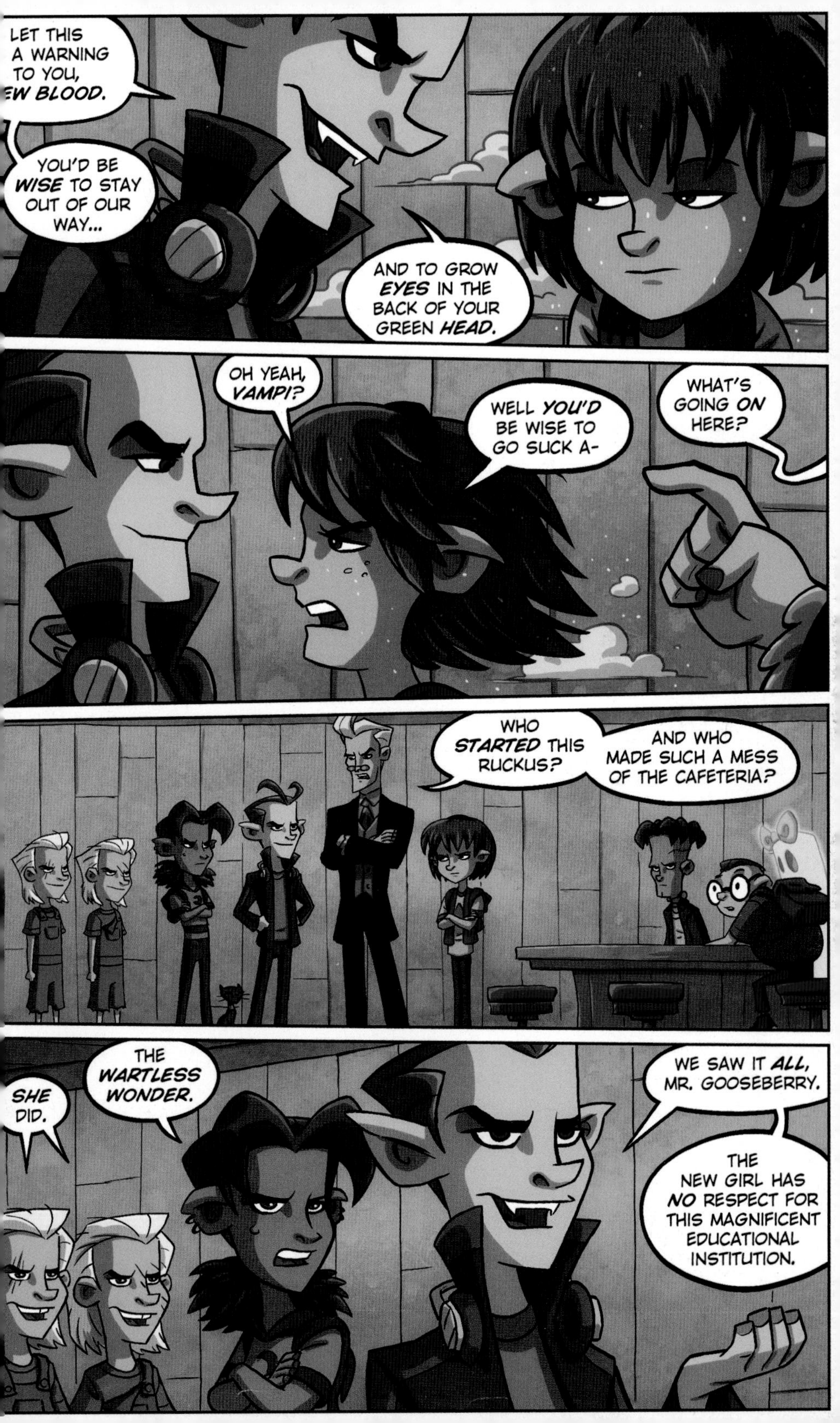
LET THIS A WARNING TO YOU, EW BLOOD.
YOU'D BE *WISE* TO STAY OUT OF OUR WAY...
AND TO GROW *EYES* IN THE BACK OF YOUR GREEN *HEAD.*
OH YEAH, *VAMPI?*
WELL *YOU'D* BE WISE TO GO SUCK A-
WHAT'S GOING *ON* HERE?
WHO *STARTED* THIS RUCKUS?
AND WHO MADE SUCH A MESS OF THE CAFETERIA?
SHE DID.
THE *WARTLESS WONDER.*
WE SAW IT *ALL*, MR. GOOSEBERRY.
THE NEW GIRL HAS *NO* RESPECT FOR THIS MAGNIFICENT EDUCATIONAL INSTITUTION.

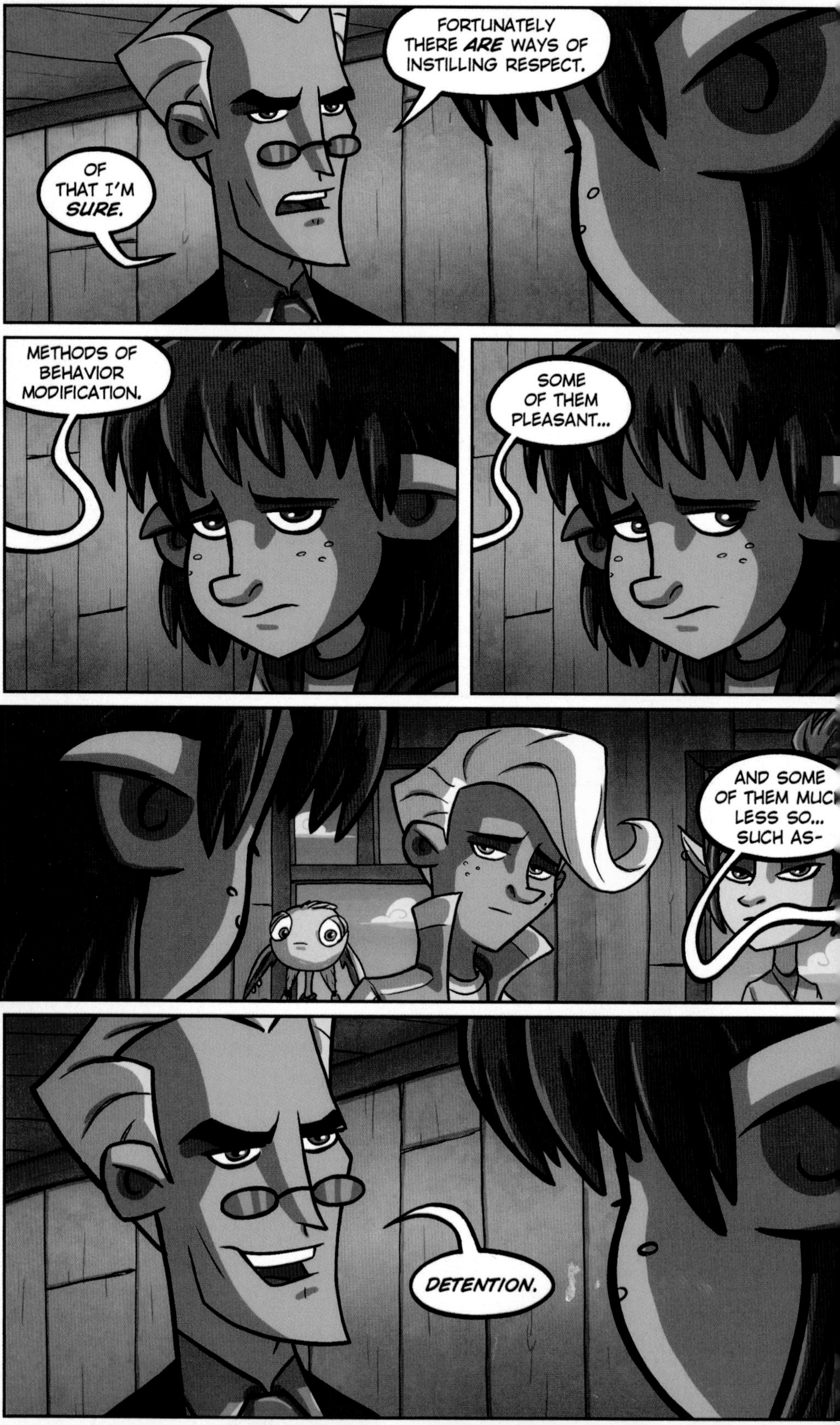
FORTUNATELY THERE *ARE* WAYS OF INSTILLING RESPECT.
OF THAT I'M *SURE.*
METHODS OF BEHAVIOR MODIFICATION.
SOME OF THEM PLEASANT...
AND SOME OF THEM MUC
LESS SO... SUCH AS-
DETENTION.

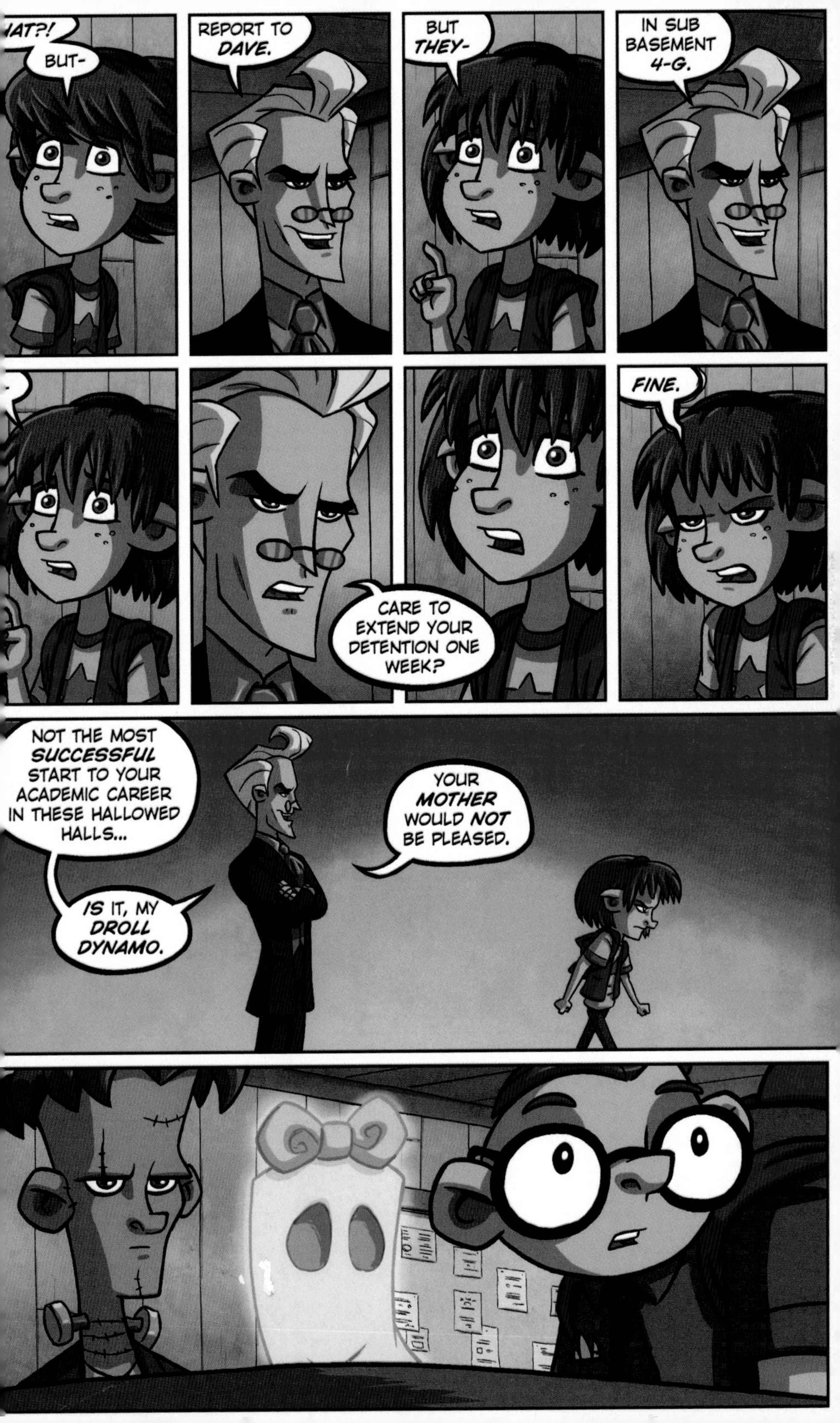

WHAT?! BUT-
REPORT TO DAVE.
BUT THEY-
IN SUB BASEMENT 4-G.
CARE TO EXTEND YOUR DETENTION ONE WEEK?
FINE.
NOT THE MOST SUCCESSFUL START TO YOUR ACADEMIC CAREER IN THESE HALLOWED HALLS...
IS IT, MY DROLL DYNAMO.
YOUR MOTHER WOULD NOT BE PLEASED.

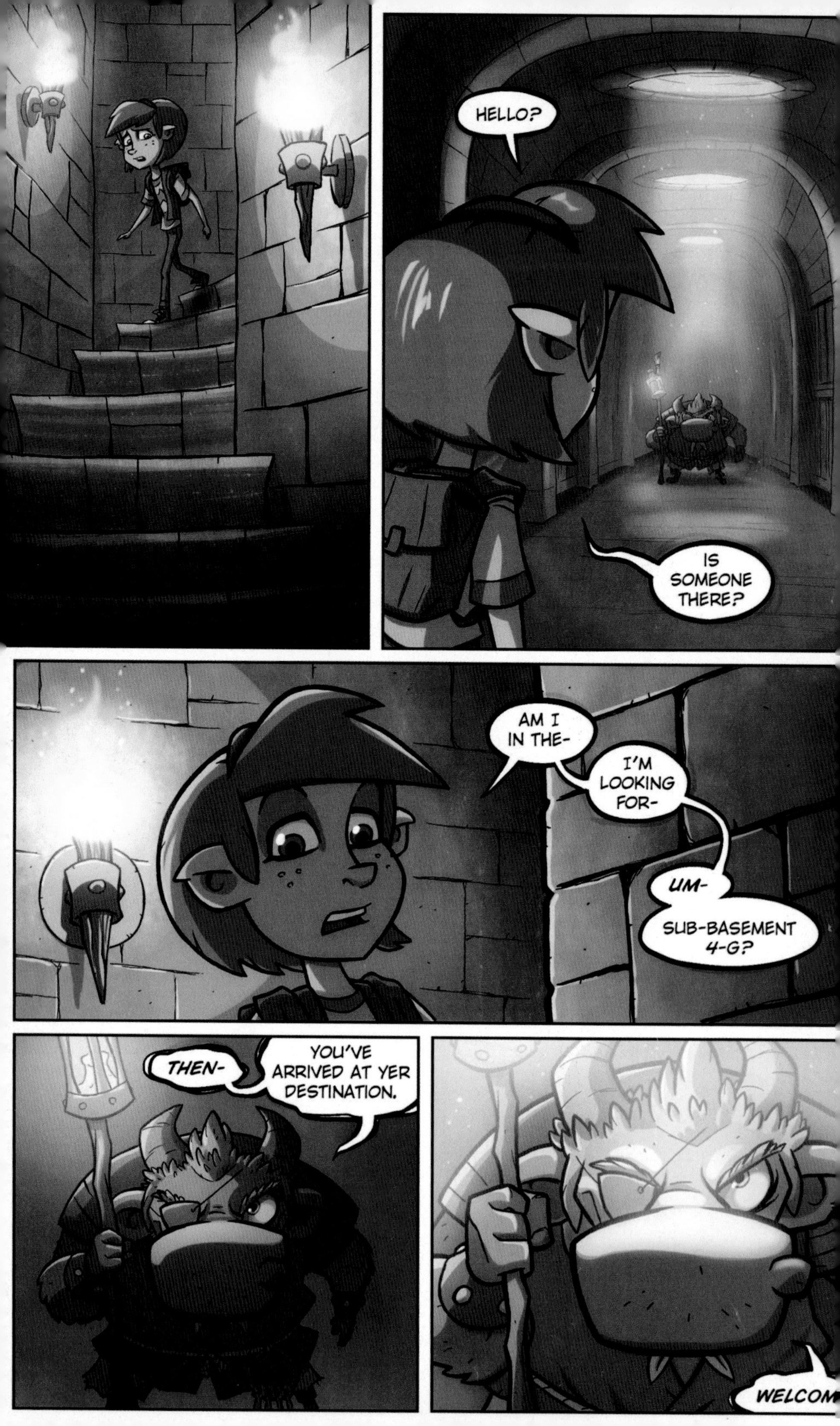
HELLO?
IS SOMEONE THERE?
AM I IN THE-
I'M LOOKING FOR-
UM-
SUB-BASEMENT 4-G?
THEN-
YOU'VE ARRIVED AT YER DESTINATION.
WELCOM

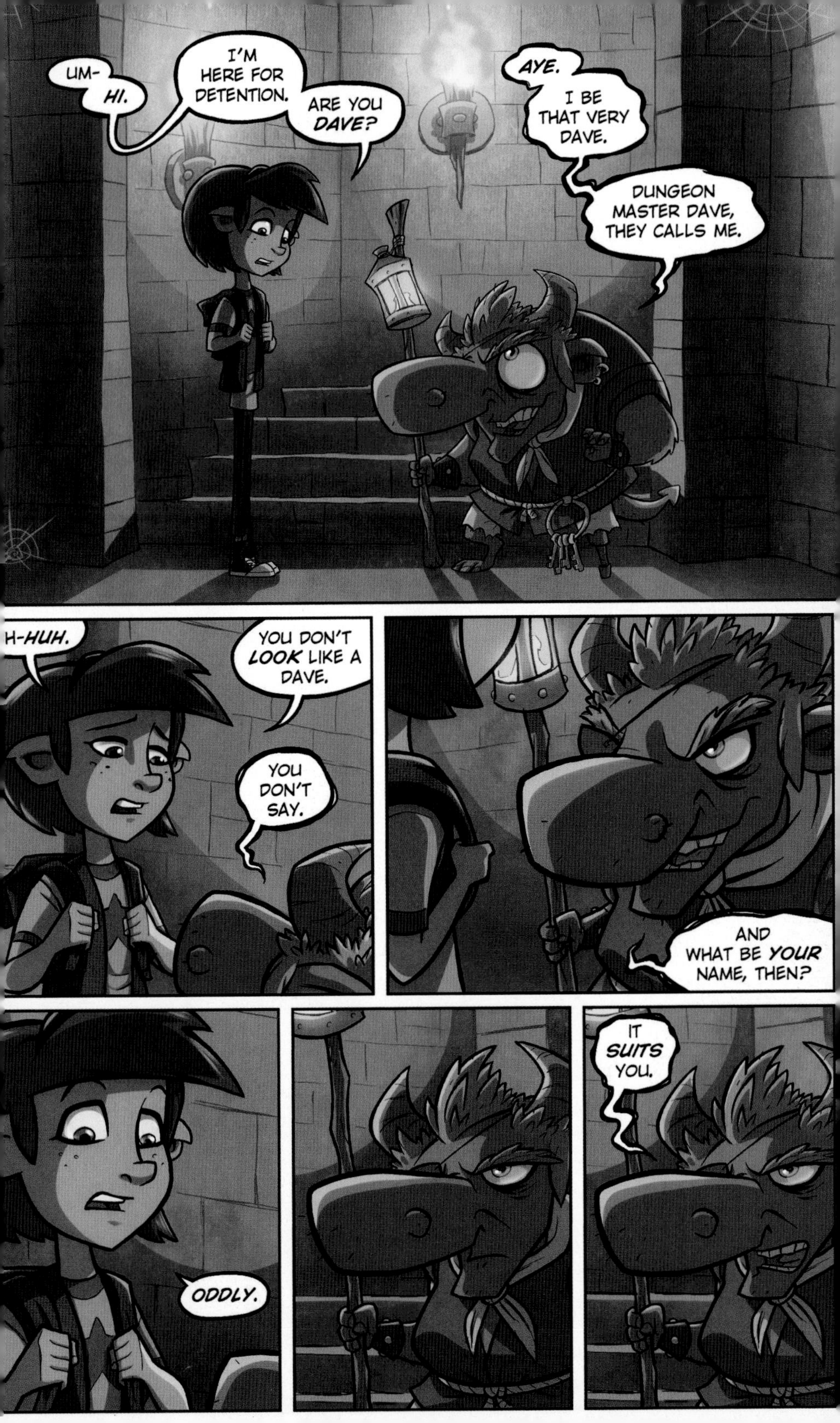
UM-
HI.
I'M HERE FOR DETENTION.
ARE YOU DAVE?
AYE.
I BE THAT VERY DAVE.
DUNGEON MASTER DAVE, THEY CALLS ME.
H-HUH.
YOU DON'T LOOK LIKE A DAVE.
YOU DON'T SAY.
AND WHAT BE YOUR NAME, THEN?
ODDLY.
IT SUITS YOU.

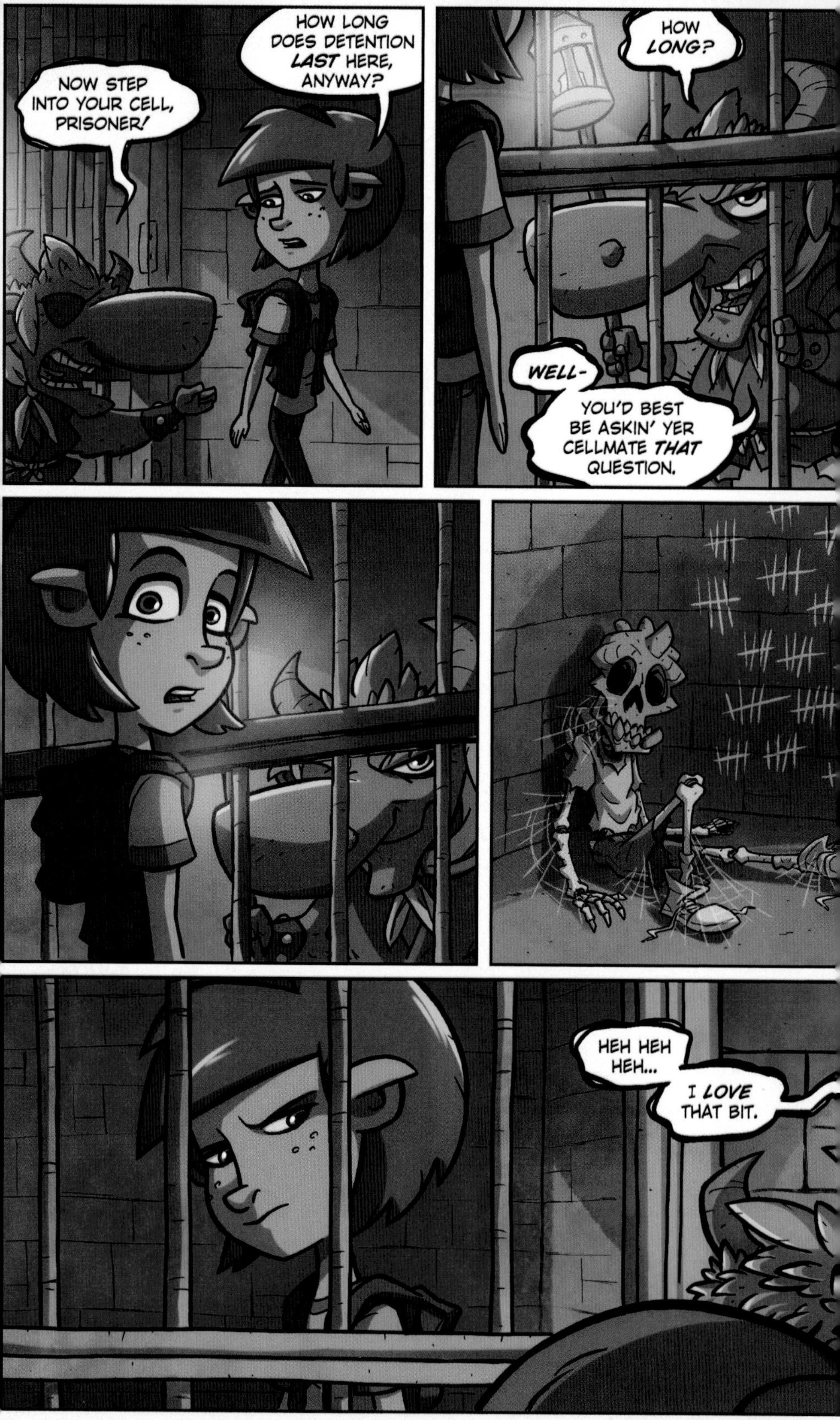
NOW STEP INTO YOUR CELL, PRISONER!
HOW LONG DOES DETENTION LAST HERE, ANYWAY?
HOW LONG?
WELL-
YOU'D BEST BE ASKIN' YER CELLMATE THAT QUESTION.
HEH HEH HEH...
I LOVE THAT BIT.

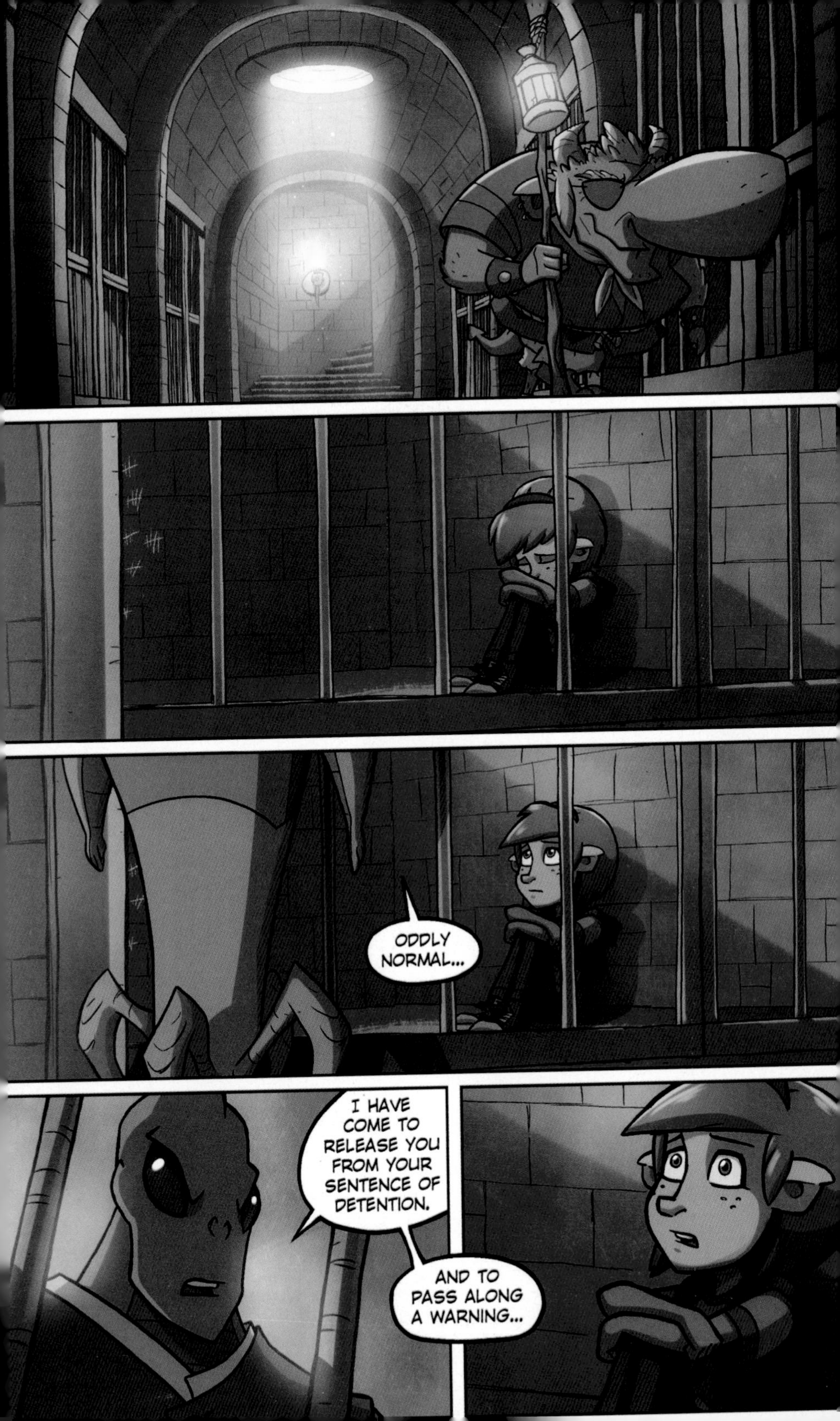
ODDLY NORMAL...
I HAVE COME TO RELEASE YOU FROM YOUR SENTENCE OF DETENTION.
AND TO PASS ALONG A WARNING...

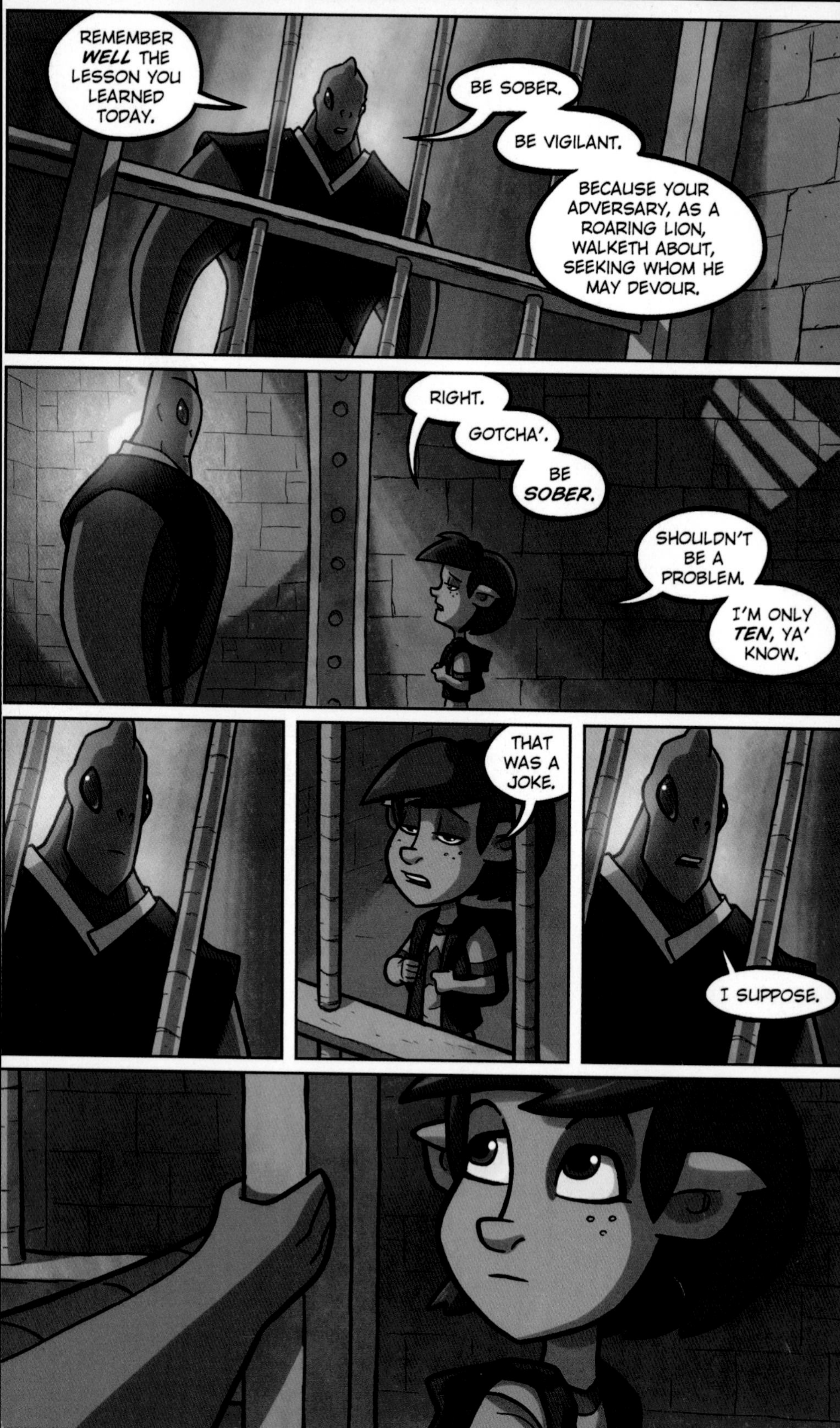

REMEMBER WELL THE LESSON YOU LEARNED TODAY.
BE SOBER.
BE VIGILANT.
BECAUSE YOUR ADVERSARY, AS A ROARING LION, WALKETH ABOUT, SEEKING WHOM HE MAY DEVOUR.
RIGHT.
GOTCHA'.
BE SOBER.
SHOULDN'T BE A PROBLEM.
I'M ONLY TEN, YA' KNOW.
THAT WAS A JOKE.
I SUPPOSE.

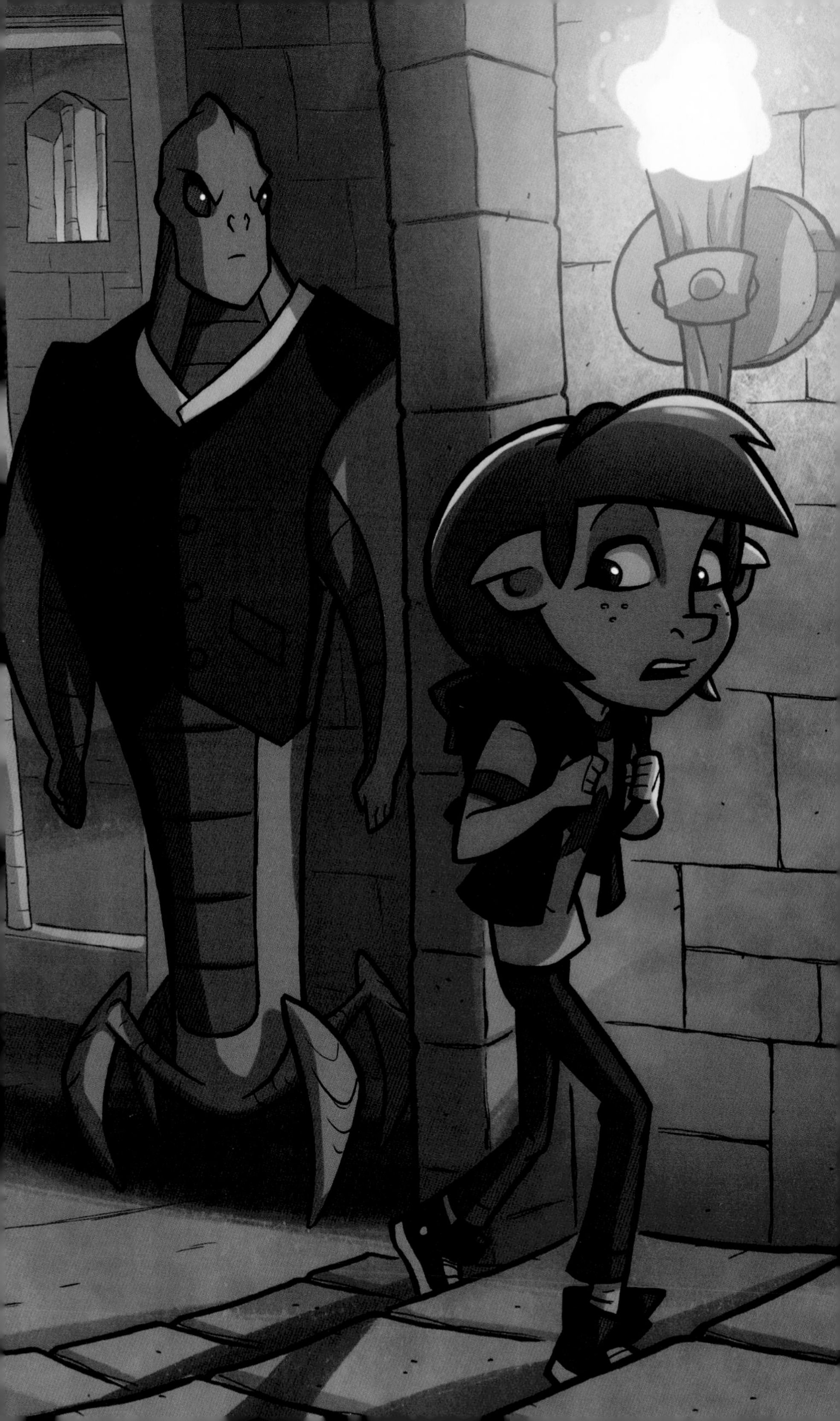

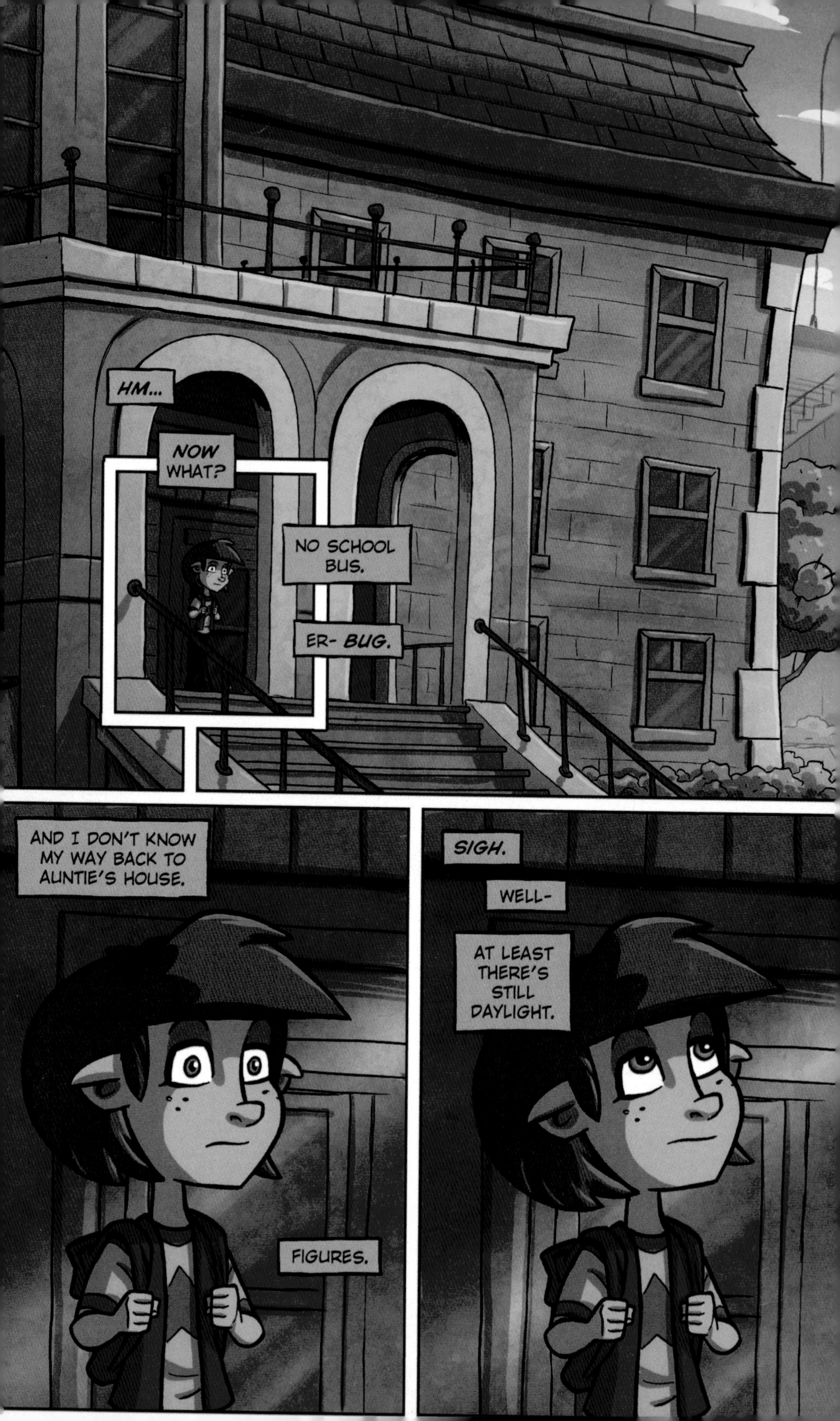
HM...
NOW WHAT?
NO SCHOOL BUS.
ER- *BUG.*
AND I DON'T KNOW MY WAY BACK TO AUNTIE'S HOUSE.
FIGURES.
SIGH.
WELL-
AT LEAST THERE'S STILL DAYLIGHT.

SORRY!

I HAVE A SCHEDULE TO KEEP!

FIGURES.
FIGURES.
FIGURES.
FIGURES.
FIGURES.
FIGURES.
FIGURES.
FIGURES.
FIGURES.
FIGURES.

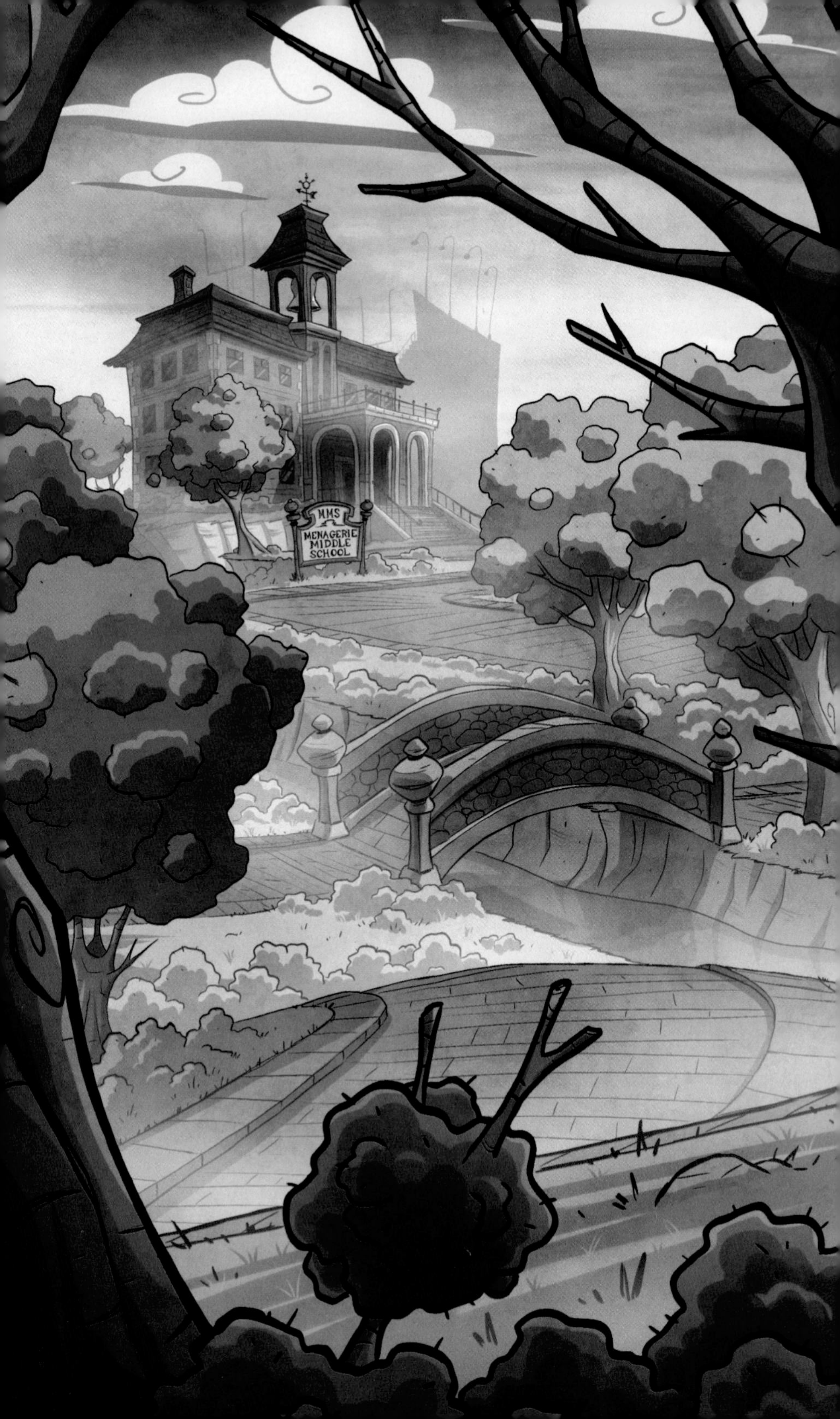
MMS
MENAGERIE
MIDDLE
SCHOOL

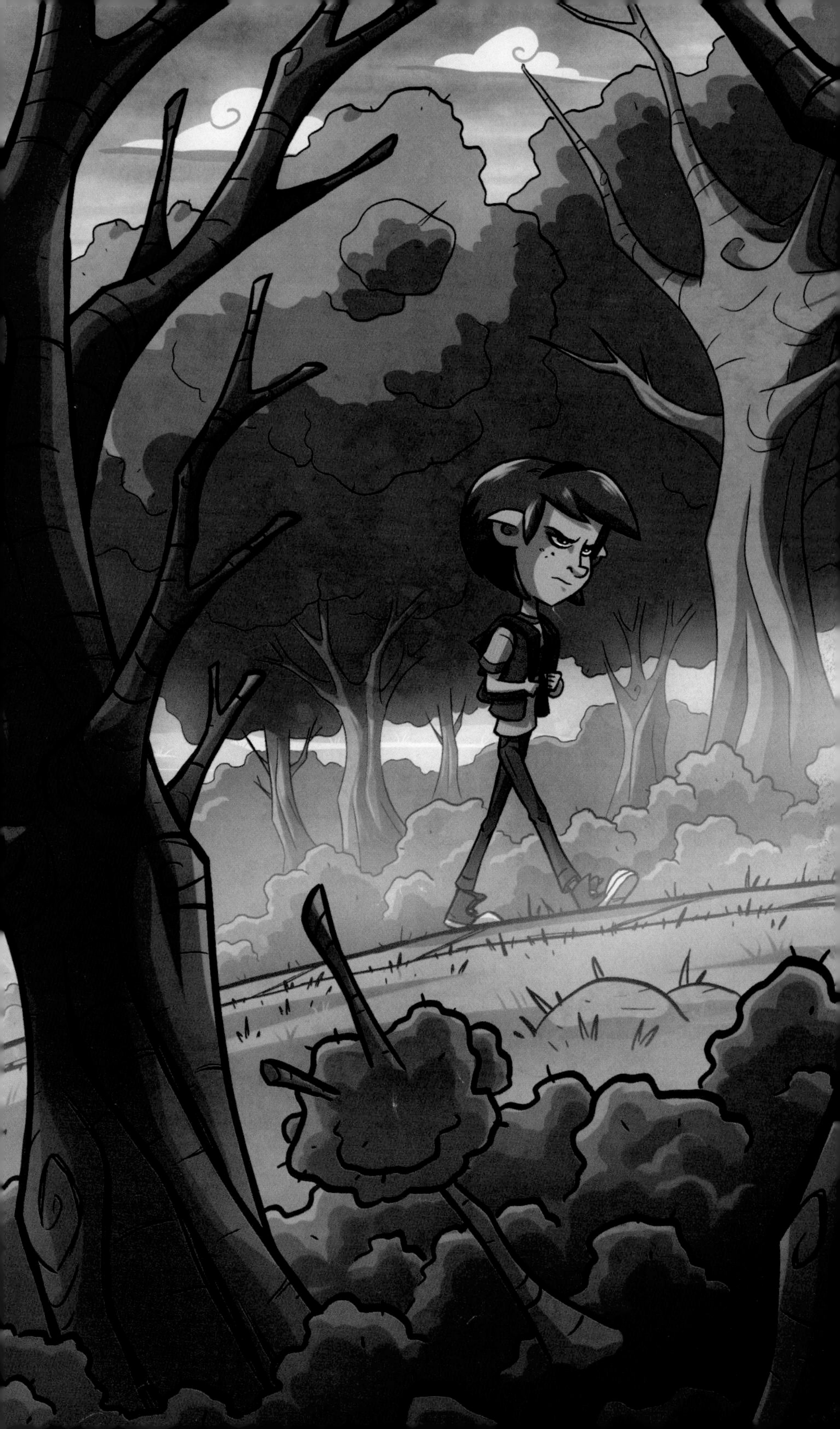

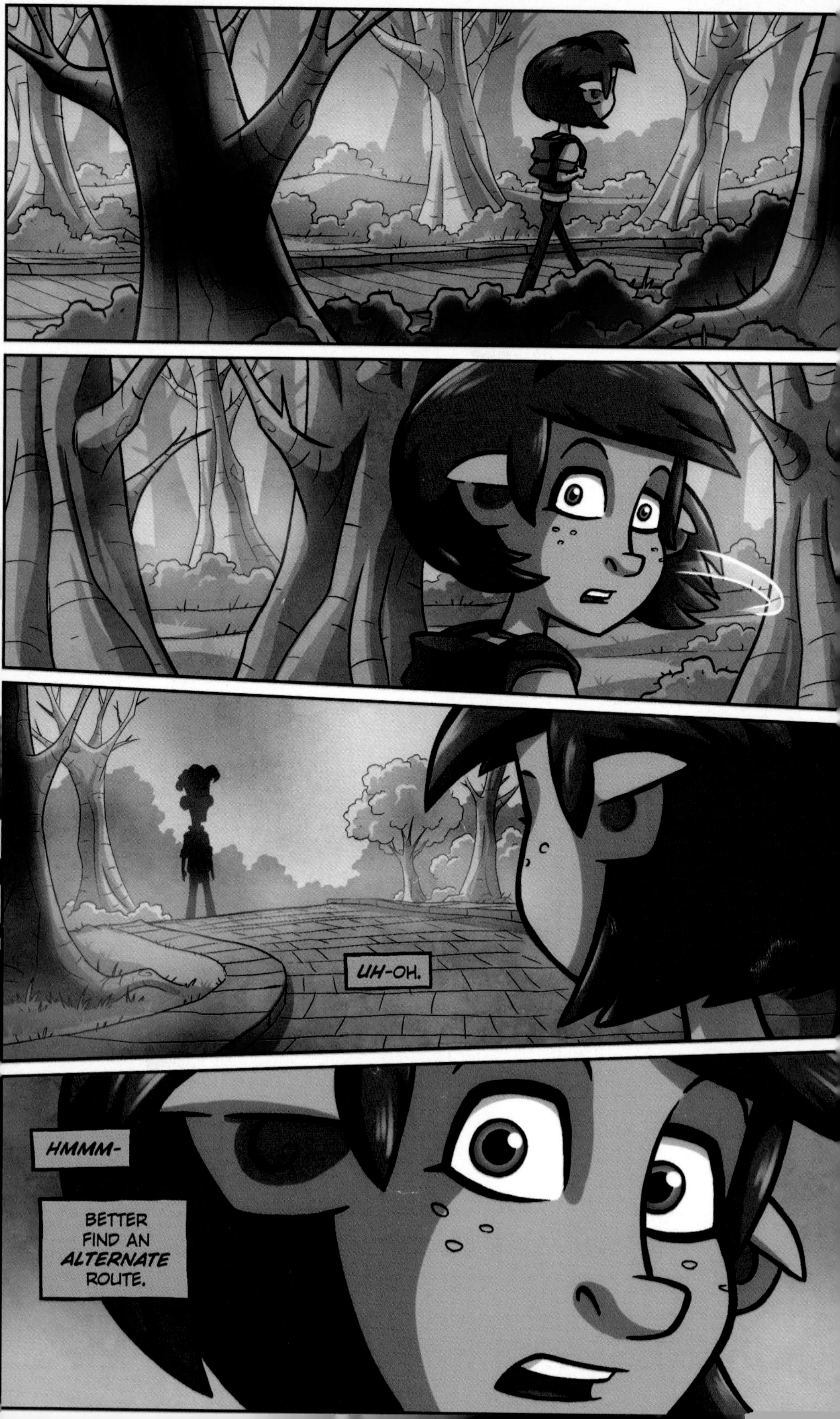
UH-OH.
HMMM-
BETTER FIND AN ALTERNATE ROUTE.

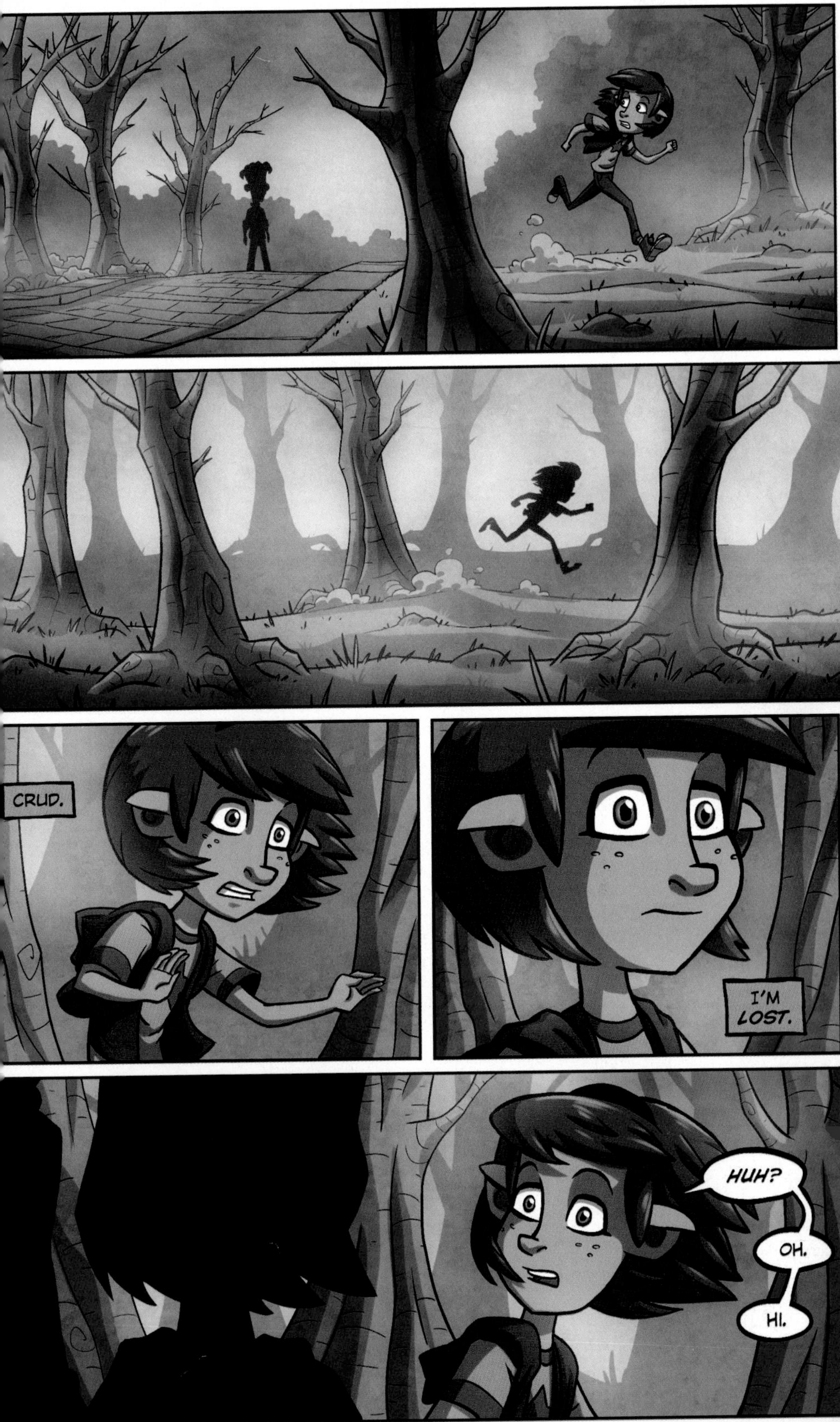
CRUD.
I'M LOST.
HUH?
OH.
HI.

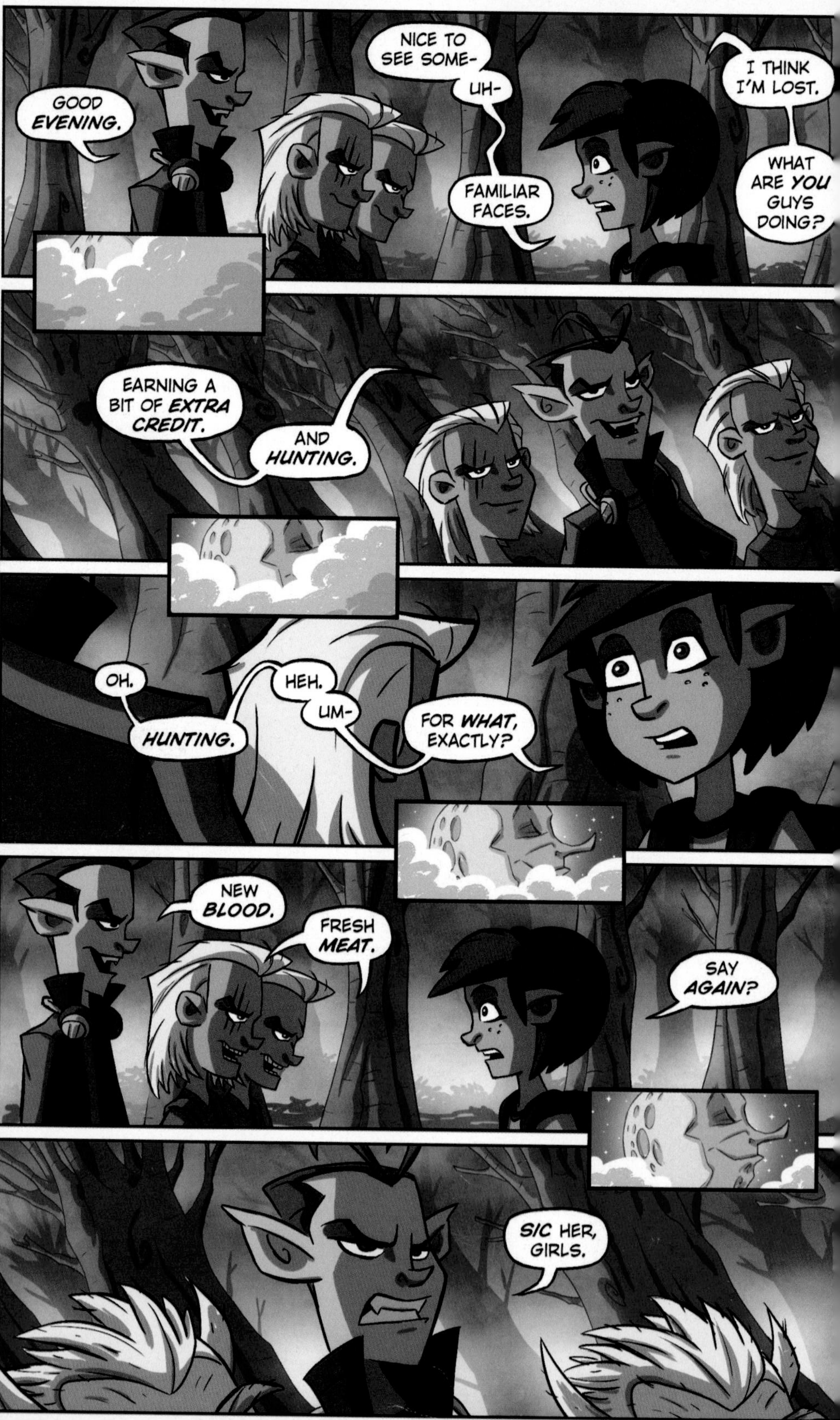
GOOD EVENING.
NICE TO SEE SOME-
UH-
FAMILIAR FACES.
I THINK I'M LOST.
WHAT ARE YOU GUYS DOING?
EARNING A BIT OF EXTRA CREDIT.
AND HUNTING.
OH.
HUNTING.
HEH.
UM-
FOR WHAT, EXACTLY?
NEW BLOOD.
FRESH MEAT.
SAY AGAIN?
SIC HER, GIRLS.

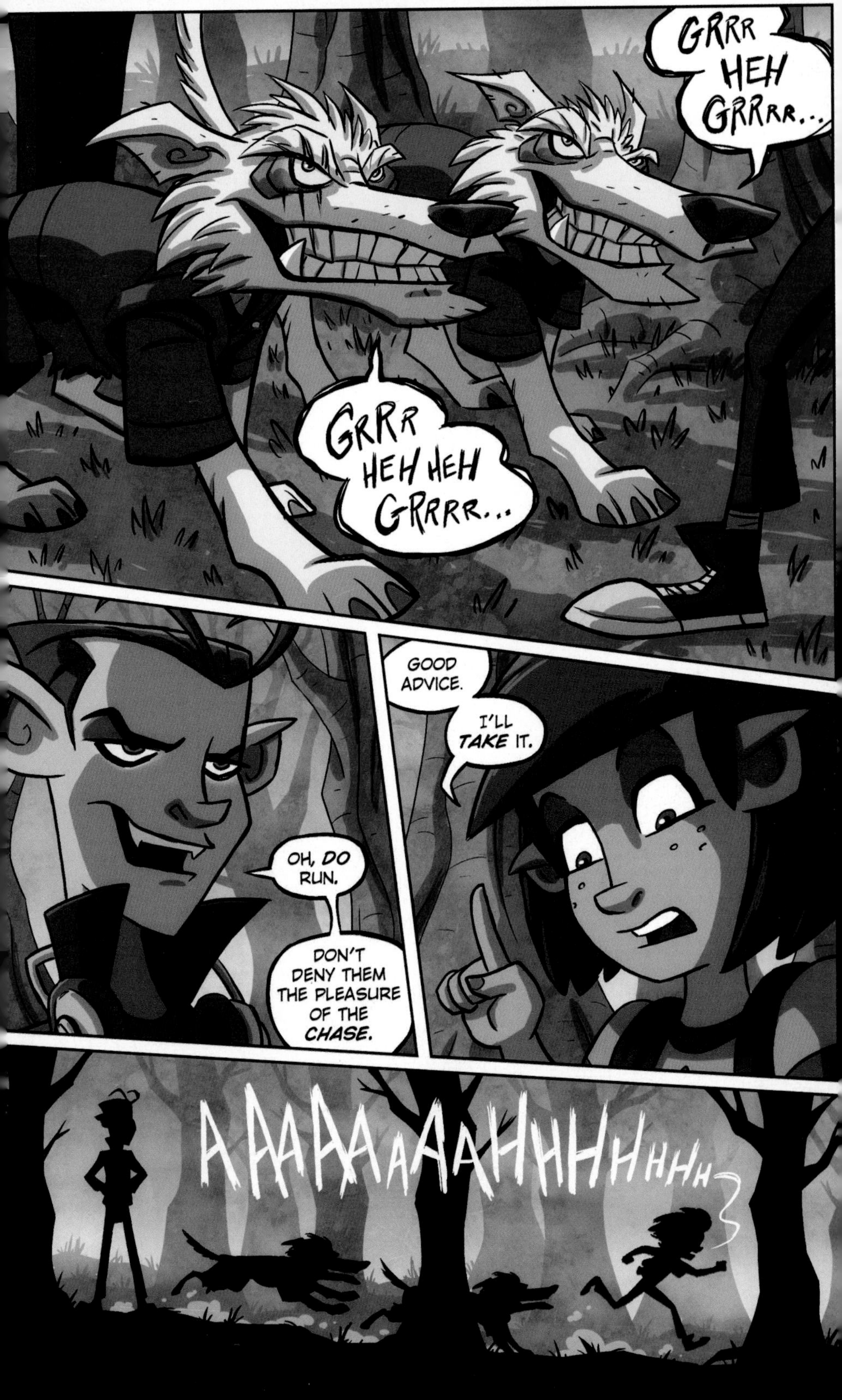
GRRR HEH GRRrr...
GRRR HEH HEH GRRRR...
OH, DO RUN.
DON'T DENY THEM THE PLEASURE OF THE CHASE.
GOOD ADVICE.
I'LL TAKE IT.
AAAAAAAAHHHHHHHH

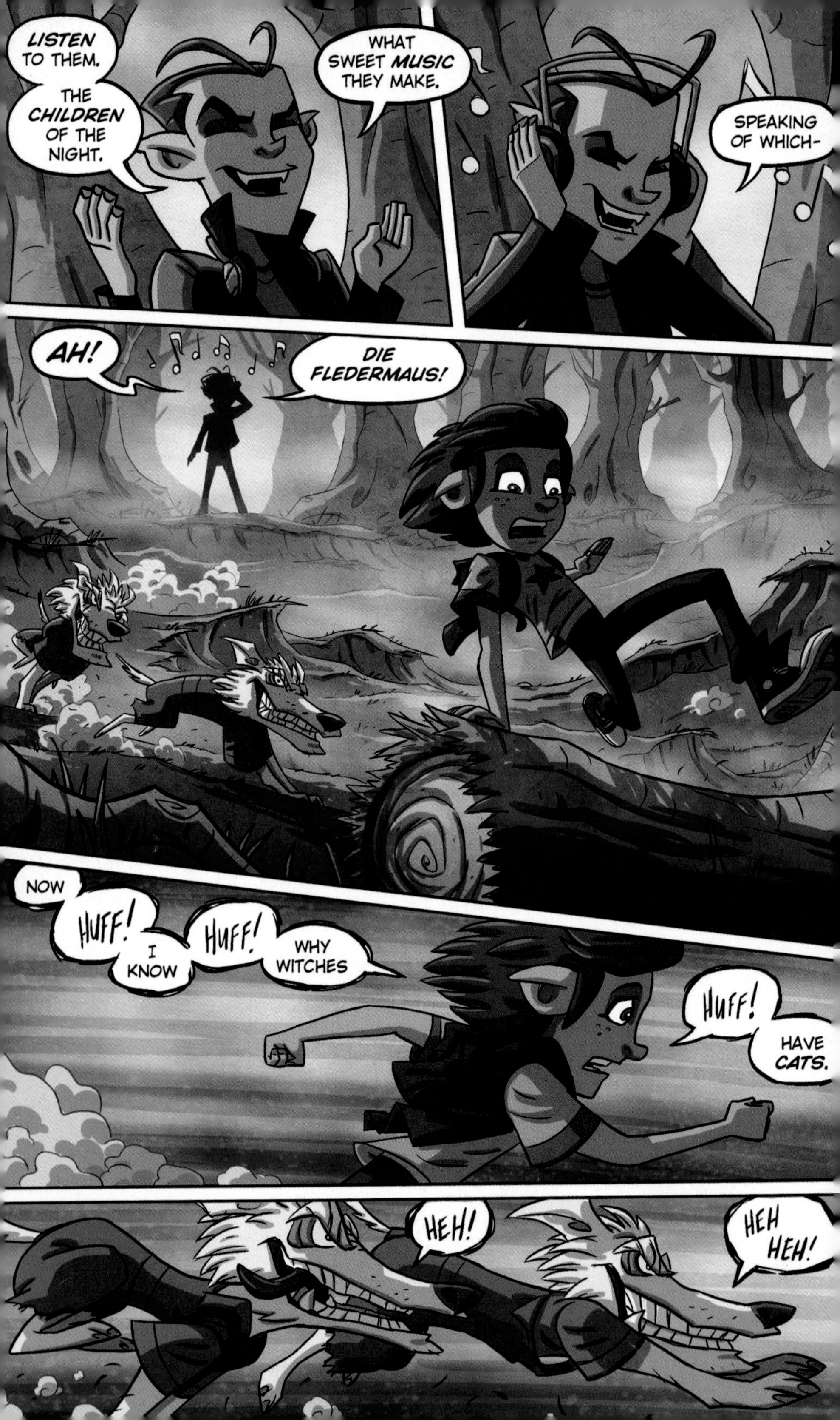
LISTEN TO THEM.
THE CHILDREN OF THE NIGHT.
WHAT SWEET MUSIC THEY MAKE.
SPEAKING OF WHICH-
AH!
DIE FLEDERMAUS!
NOW
HUFF!
I KNOW
HUFF!
WHY WITCHES
HUFF!
HAVE CATS.
HEH!
HEH HEH!

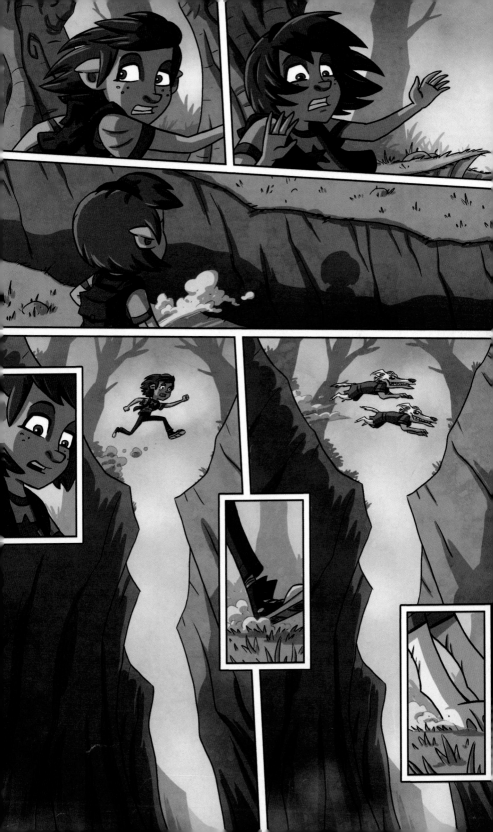

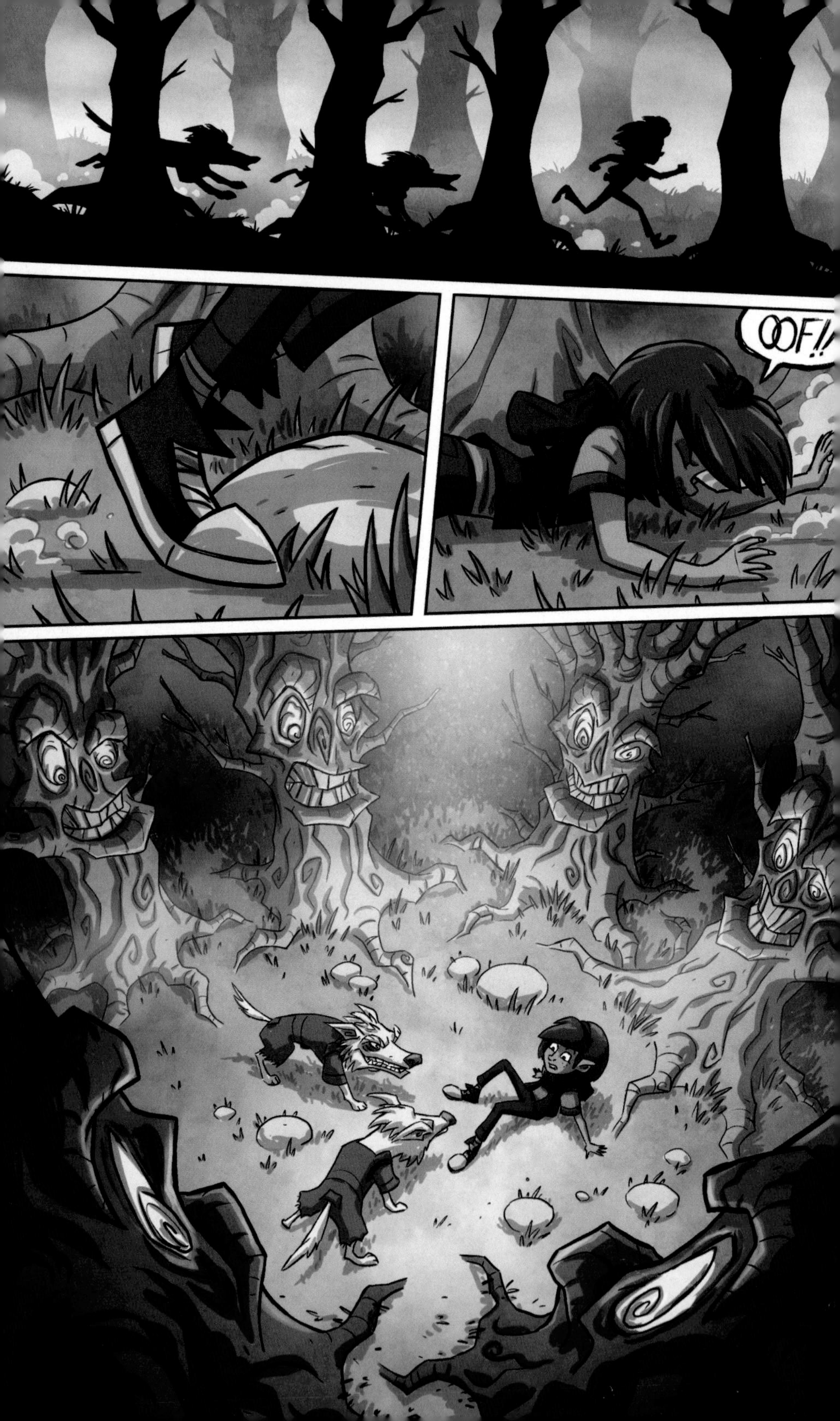
OOF!!

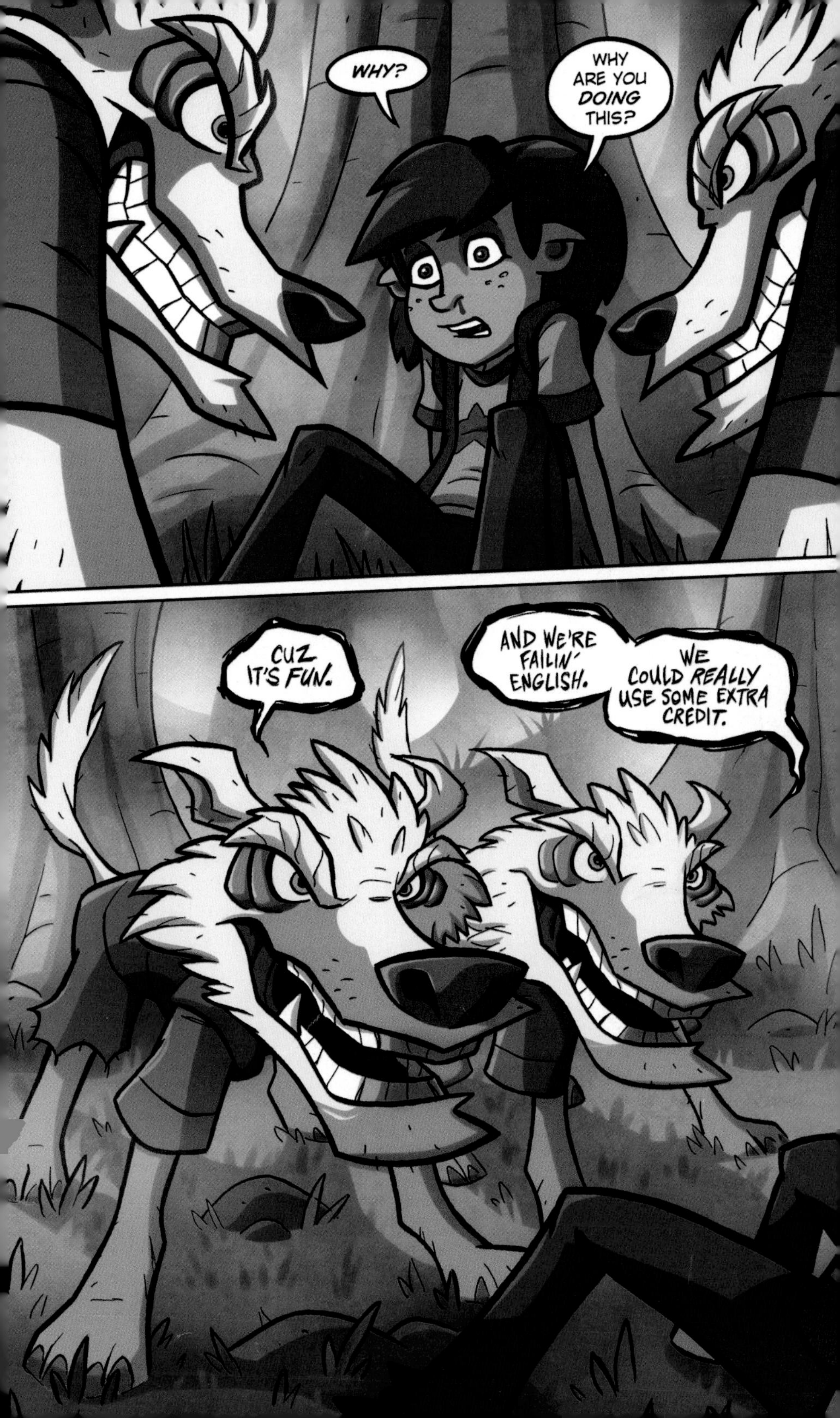
WHY?
WHY ARE YOU DOING THIS?
CUZ IT'S FUN.
AND WE'RE FAILIN' ENGLISH.
WE COULD REALLY USE SOME EXTRA CREDIT.

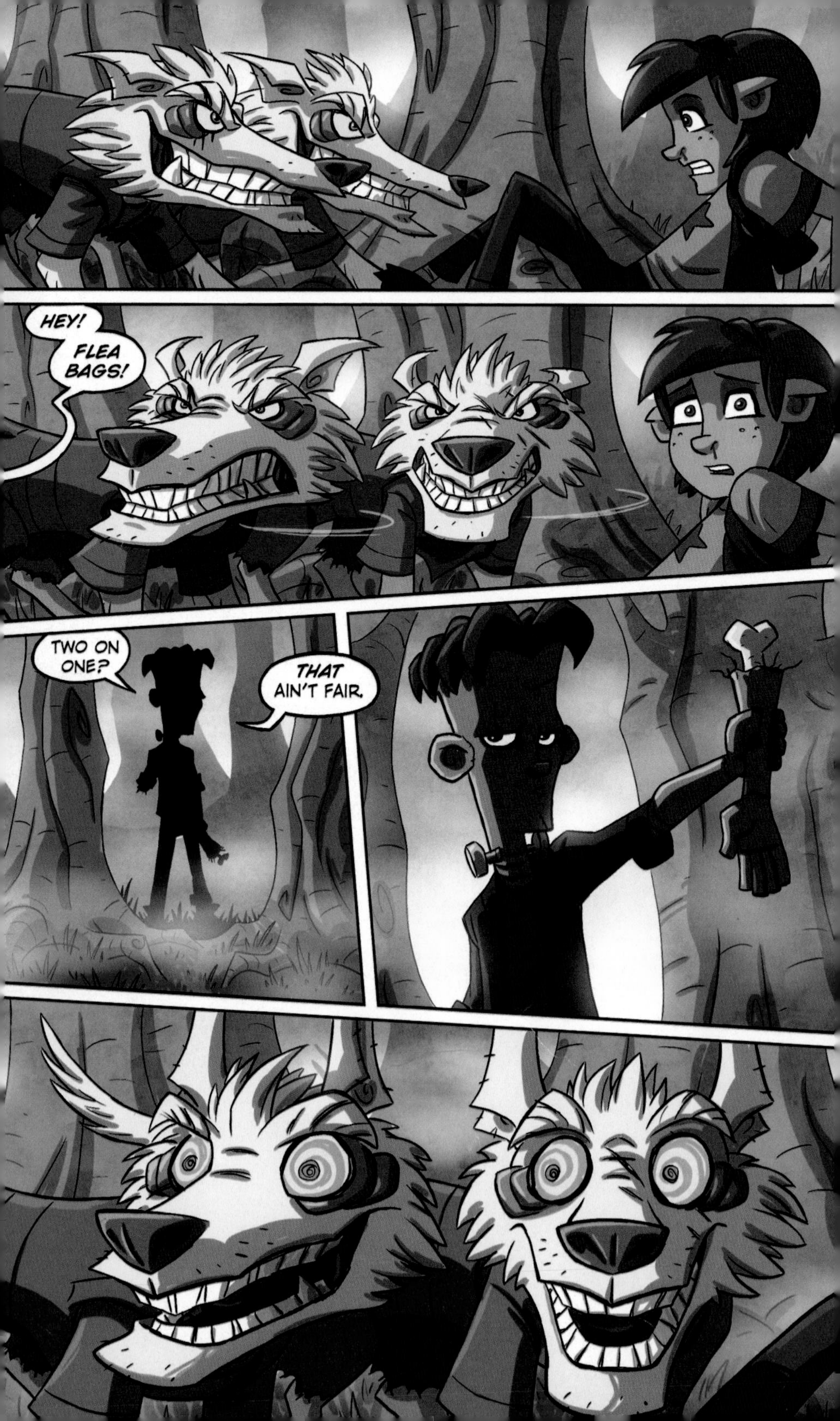
HEY! FLEA BAGS!
TWO ON ONE?
THAT AIN'T FAIR.

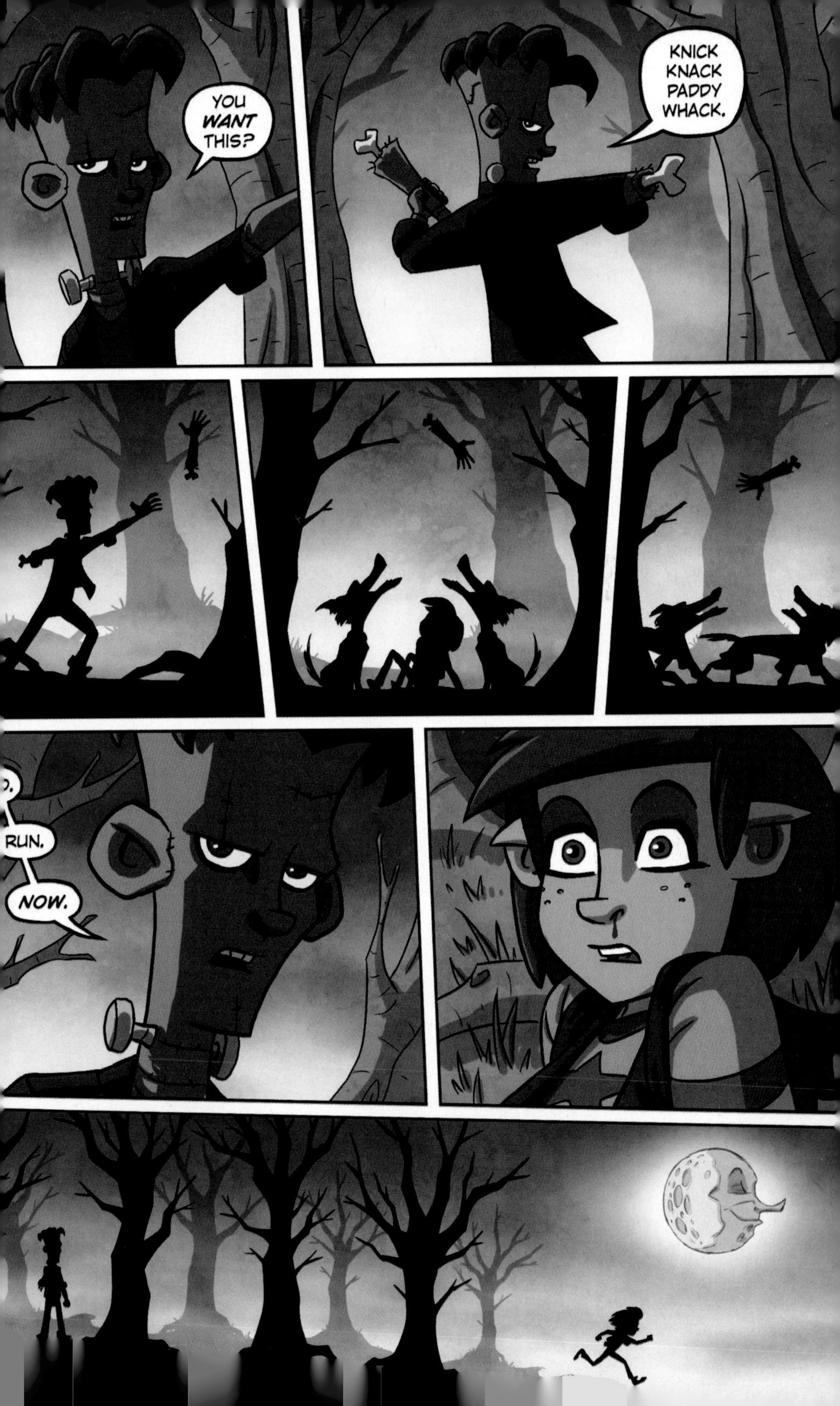
YOU WANT THIS?
KNICK KNACK PADDY WHACK.
RUN.
NOW.

Oddly ★ Normal

BOOK ①

WRITTEN, ILLUSTRATED & LETTERED BY
OTIS FRAMPTON

CHAPTERS 1-4 COLORED BY
OTIS FRAMPTON

CHAPTER 5 COLORED BY
OTIS FRAMPTON & TRACY BAILEY

COLOR FLATS BY
DANIEL MEAD, TRACY BAILEY,
OTIS FRAMPTON AND THOMAS BOATWRIGHT